THE DON

GILLIAN GODDEN

B

Boldwood

First published in Great Britain in 2025 by Boldwood Books Ltd.

Copyright © Gillian Godden, 2025

Cover Design by JD Smith Design Ltd

Cover Images: Colin Thomas and Shutterstock

A CIP catalogue record for this book is available from the British Library.

Paperback ISBN 978-1-83561-489-1

Large Print ISBN 978-1-83561-490-7

Hardback ISBN 978-1-83561-488-4

Trade Paperback ISBN 978-1-80656-125-4

Ebook ISBN 978-1-83561-491-4

Kindle ISBN 978-1-83561-492-1

Audio CD ISBN 978-1-83561-483-9

MP3 CD ISBN 978-1-83561-484-6

Digital audio download ISBN 978-1-83561-486-0

This book is printed on certified sustainable paper. Boldwood Books is dedicated to putting sustainability at the heart of our business. For more information please visit https://www.boldwoodbooks.com/about-us/sustainability/

Boldwood Books Ltd, 23 Bowerdean Street, London, SW6 3TN

www.boldwoodbooks.com

1

A FATAL ENCOUNTER

'Knock, knock; morning, stranger!' Hearing Bruce's familiar voice, Adam Lambrianu cocked his head around the side of his computer screen and grinned. Letting out a slow whistle, he nodded with approval as he took in Bruce's appearance.

'I'd say you're the stranger, mate. You look well dapper in the new get up; very man of the world. I take it Julie and her male household have taken you shopping – suited and booted, Brucey boy! Come on then, give us a twirl.' Adam laughed. He hadn't seen Bruce for a couple of days. Bruce Sinclair was a university professor by occupation, but he was also Adam Lambrianu's best friend. Although Bruce was still a little naive to some of Adam's gangland ways in the underworld, they had a lot in common and Bruce was one of the few friends that Adam had who was similar in age. It was Bruce who had given Adam the knowledge of crypto currency and how it was used today. Unwittingly, Adam's criminal mind had seen a way of making money through illegal crypto and laundering it legitimately.

They had befriended a man called Jamie who had worked for an independent stockbroking company and had been down on his luck. Bruce had told Adam about the woman he was seeing on a casual basis, Kim, who also worked at the stockbrokers and was a friend of Jamie's. During conversations and pillow talk, Kim had told Bruce about Jamie's hard-luck story; how he didn't have any major clients, which made him a key candidate for Adam and his crypto scam.

Befriending Jamie had been easy; offering him a lot of cash to invest in crypto, they'd got him to work on their behalf, making sure every important document signed had his name on it. Adam, Bruce, and Julie Gold, a long-term family friend and the infamous gangland wife of Ralph Gold, had then watched and waited for their shares to go up before cashing in. After a few good deals, Jamie's reputation also grew and once he was acknowledged as a good broker, his boss had given him even better clients, like Arab princes and wealthy celebrities.

Adam, Bruce and Julie had then ripped these clients off, creaming millions of pounds from their accounts. Julie Gold had blackmailed Jamie into helping them, but had also given him thousands of pounds for his part in their plan. Instantly, this poor sofa-surfing broker, who was always sponging off his friends, was now running around buying champagne, Rolex watches and an expensive apartment. Julie had known, if there was any suspicion, that Jamie would be the first name on everyone's lips. His sudden influx of fortune had caused many whispers, and as he hadn't won the lottery, there could only be one conclusion – he was embezzling his clients' funds for himself.

After his reckless ways, Jamie had been arrested and was now facing a long prison sentence. And between Adam, Bruce and Julie, they had made a fortune from their own living rooms. No bank robberies, no guns involved, just laptops and scams. Once Jamie had been arrested, they had all decided to keep a low profile should the police believe any sob stories Jamie might blurt out to reduce his sentence, and by all accounts he was singing like a bird. Mentioning the names Lambrianu and Gold to the police was apparently whetting their appetite, but there was no evidence they had been involved in the scam, and they had definitely made sure there was no paper trail. All alibis were cast iron – they had made damn sure of that.

Bruce had got his fair share of the proceeds too and his fortunes had suddenly changed for the better, but, unlike the luckless Jamie, he had kept his fortune low key. And he had proved to be a loyal and trusted friend. Both Adam and Julie liked him very much.

Julie Gold, the ageing but glamourous and very outspoken widow of the gangland boss Ralph Gold, had been close friends with Adam Lambrianu's mother, Francesca. Since her death years ago, Julie still mourned her friend and kept a close eye on Francesca's children – eldest son Bobby, the twins, Scarlet and Katie and of course, Adam. Their father had been the infamous gangster, racketeer, club owner and Italian-born Tony Lambrianu. Tony and Ralph Gold had been partners in crime and part of the brotherhood with Italian Mafia godfather, Don Carlos, who had treated Tony like his own son.

In the days when they had been friends, Julie, Tony and Ralph had been a happy trio, carrying out diamond heists, gun running and importing drugs. But when Don Carlos recently passed away, he had left trouble for the Lambrianu family that Julie and the others knew they would have to fix sooner rather than later or trouble would come knocking at their own door.

It had been a couple of months since Adam had seen Bruce; they'd all been keeping their distance from each other in case Jamie linked all of their names together. But now, Bruce had turned up to the well-known nightclub, Lambrianu's, which was now run by Adam and his older sister Scarlet.

Opening his jacket to show the silk paisley lining, Bruce did a mock twirl in his new navy-blue, double-breasted suit, while Adam wolf-whistled and laughed. 'Well, at least it's stopped you looking like a model for knitting patterns. You look like you've just stepped off the pages of *Vogue* magazine. And Christ, even your hair looks washed and groomed. Whatever happened to the university lecturer in his old cardigan, baggy trousers and a mop of hair that hasn't seen a comb in years? You look so good, I could fancy you myself. Come here, mate; it's good to see you.' Walking forward, Adam put his arms around Bruce and hugged him.

'Careful, you'll crease my new suit,' laughed Bruce while patting him on the back. 'It's good to see you, Adam, now the heat is off. I've missed my old comrade.'

Blushing slightly, Bruce sat down. 'Julie's butler, Lewis, certainly knows his stuff and when I cleaned my glasses properly, I realised what a scruffy bastard I was. No wonder my students never took any notice of me. But that's teaching for you. Everything else goes out the window.'

Cocking his head to one side, Adam had to agree. 'Well, to be fair to Julie, she wouldn't have Lewis hanging around if he didn't have style.'

Looking slightly worried, Bruce frowned. 'Don't worry, Adam, I'm not spending above my means, not like Jamie buying champagne for everyone and that swanky apartment. He was too obvious, I see that now. I bought my mum her house, but Julie sorted that out and it all looks legitimate.'

Adam nodded, knowing they were all trying to be careful about spending the money they'd got from the crypto currency scam. 'So, what's with the visit, Bruce? Don't lecturers have any work to do these days, or have you just come around to show me the new you?'

'Exams are over and now it's my time to shine. You fancy

something to eat and a catchup, or are you snowed under as usual?'

Adam let out a loud, warm laugh. 'Well, I can't have you all dressed up with nowhere to go, can I?' Adam straightened his own pale-pink tie. 'Let's get out of here. Do you fancy the greasy spoon around the corner?'

Bruce frowned. 'Don't you think we both look a bit over dressed for a greasy spoon in our suits?'

'Well, we will either look like we've been to court, or we don't care what people think. Personally, for me, it's the latter. Let's walk. I need some fresh air.'

Looking around the room, Bruce gave Adam a wry grin. 'Where is dragon lady?'

Raising his eyebrows, Adam laughed at Bruce's description of Adam's sister Scarlet. 'My, we have got brave in that suit. Scarlet's doing her usual morning parade with the staff. I take it breakfast is on you, or I'll tell her you called her that.' Adam grinned, showing a perfect row of white teeth.

'I walked right into that, didn't I?' laughed Bruce. 'Yeah, I'm paying. Come on, let's walk like a couple of swells.' Adam bowed his head and opened the door wide. 'After you,' he mocked playfully.

The greasy spoon café was always busy with black cab drivers dropping in for breakfast before the start of a long day, or for some it was the end of a night shift before going home to rest. This was a usual haunt for Adam; he knew most of the drivers and they were always a hive of gossip and information, which suited him perfectly. He could find out the ins and outs of all his neighbourhood clubs and businesses without having to go too far. He'd often pop in for a bacon sandwich before going into the office to start the daily grind of invoices and staff complaints. Knuckles appreciated it, although Scarlet tried discouraging it and squirmed every time she saw tomato sauce drip on Knuckles's chin or shirt. She would angrily throw a tissue at him to wipe it off, which made Adam laugh every time. Later, Scarlet would miraculously produce a new shirt out of her desk drawer and throw it at him. Knuckles never turned a hair, but would leave the room to change, seemingly totally oblivious to Scarlet's ranting.

Knuckles, as he had been known by everyone for years, had worked for Adam's father Tony. He was a cold-blooded murdering machine. Seven foot in stance, and nearly as wide, but all of it muscle. He had been a henchman and getaway driver in the early days, and he was a trusted member of the Lambrianu team. Somewhere along the way, Knuckles had lost one arm, but no one knew how, and Knuckles, who hardly ever spoke except for one-word sentences, would never tell. He was the strong silent type, who watched everything and said very little. His arm was now a top-of-the-range prosthetic with a grip of iron, which in his line of work came in very useful. Knuckles was excellent at his job; Tony Lambrianu had seen that and used him accordingly, and now Adam and Scarlet continued to put their trust in him.

Meeting Scarlet had changed Knuckles's life. She had begged her father to let her have Knuckles as her bodyguard, and Tony, knowing Knuckles wouldn't abuse his trust and break his daughter's heart, had agreed. Knuckles had done Scarlet's bidding since then and over the years they had unwittingly forged a union. Scarlet's cunning brain and Knuckles's manpower and strength had made them into a fearsome duo. For the first time in his life, he had someone who cared for him. Scarlet, wanting him to look the part, had nurtured him, and his loyalty to her was unwavering.

Scarlet had found solace in Knuckles's arms and a relationship had formed between them. She had given birth to twins. Annette, after her father's mother, and Jake after her father's foster brother and partner in crime. Jake, who had been shot by his wife, Sharon, was still mourned by all.

'Mr Lambrianu.' The café owner smiled. 'How good to see you. I hope you've got your appetite back.' Reaching over the glass counter, Adam spied the unwashed hands of the owner-cum-chef and shook his hand.

'Hungry and ready for you to screw up my digestive system again. Good to see you again. This is Bruce; Bruce, this is the breakfast guru, otherwise known as Alvin.' Likewise, Bruce also shook Alvin's hand. 'Were you named after the singer, Alvin Stardust?' he quipped.

'More like Alvin and the Chipmunks,' Adam laughed. 'Right, Bruce is buying, what have you got for two hungry men?'

Alvin rolled his eyes to the ceiling and stubbed out his rollup cigarette, holding his hand up to stop the protests. 'Don't worry, lads, I know the rules; it's not lit, it just makes me feel better. Reminds me of the good old days when you could smoke in your own establishments – nightclubs too,' he added while winking at Adam.

'Yeah, well, the days of having nicotine cleaned off the ceiling are far behind us, Alvin. And are your fingers supposed to be that brown, yellowy colour while cooking our grub?'

Looking down at his nicotine-stained fingers, Alvin wiped his hands on his already greasy, striped apron then clapped them together. 'Right, two English ball busters, I think. Something to stir the tadpoles in those tight trousers you're wearing.' He laughed, much to the amusement of the other customers overhearing the conversation.

Pulling out a wooden chair at a table, Bruce grimaced and sat down. 'Do these tables ever get wiped down?' he whispered.

'Probably not.' Adam shrugged. 'I've been coming here for so long now, I don't notice any more. Why, you afraid of spoiling your new togs?'

'Well, maybe.' Bruce blushed and moved the stained bottles of sauces to one side with distaste. 'Why does he say your name so loud when you walk in, Adam? Christ, he's got a gob like a foghorn.'

'It's to warn the other customers so that they can stop talking about me or the club. Me being here can make people feel uneasy, worried I've got a gun stashed in my waistband and am planning a shootout. He does the same when the police walk in; it's a warning to everyone.'

Bruce moved in closer, lowering his voice. 'And have you got a gun stashed in your waistband?'

'That's for me to know, Brucey baby. Most of the women I know think I've got something stashed in my trouser pockets...' Adam laughed, and his spirits rose at seeing Bruce again. He enjoyed bantering with him and having a loyal friend he could trust. It wasn't often he mixed with like-minded people nearer his own age, but Bruce was both of those things. He'd worked and studied all of his life and achieved his goal to be a university lecturer. Adam knew Bruce was smart, but that he could also be trusted.

Julie's imminent plans in Italy went through Adam's mind. He'd like to discuss it with Bruce, but it was strictly family business. Although, he did think of Bruce as family and he knew even Julie had taken a liking to him, which was unusual for her – she rarely had a good word for anyone. But Adam didn't want to involve Bruce in this. It was a harebrained plan, thought up by an old woman with vengeance in mind and would be an enormous undertaking. Better to keep Bruce out of it, although he yearned to talk it over with someone other than family. Because Adam was at the heart of Julie's plan, which was part of the problem... Whether he liked it or not, he would be dragged into this mess.

Julie believed that Katie's husband, Christopher, had convinced Don Carlos into writing another will when he had discovered that Adam Lambrianu would be named as his rightful heir and take the place as head of the Italian Mafia family.

Chris had always felt that, being Don Carlo's nephew, he should be the chosen one. He was sick of hearing how highly Don Carlos thought of Adam Lambrianu and how the other Mafia families welcomed Adam into their homes. The Lambrianu legend ran through Italy as much as the wine produced at the Lambrianu vineyard.

But Don Carlos had been left to the mercy of Christopher as his dementia progressed. Once Chris had moved in with his family and taken over, without invitation, no one could oppose it, not even Katie Lambrianu, his wife, who knew that Chris would take her children from her if she ever dared breathe a word against him.

Chris had wanted Julie Gold to witness how ill and confused Don Carlos was becoming, confirming his rightful place as the new heir. He had arranged a call with Julie to put her mind at rest and prove to her that Don Carlos was being adequately cared for. And although Don Carlos's mind was locked firmly in the past, he still had moments of recognition and lucidity, even though these moments only lasted for minutes, until the confusion took over once more.

During this call, Chris had sat beside Don Carlos as he'd had one of his lucid moments and had remembered his old friend, Julie Gold. He had mentioned Ralph's birthday to Julie, but had got the digits in the wrong order until Julie corrected him. Chris had scoffed; the old man got everything wrong nowadays, but rather than brush his mistake off as he normally would, Don

Carlos had screamed down the telephone at Julie, repeating the same six digits. Eventually he had slammed the phone down on Julie, much to Chris's delight, because now, whenever Julie called back, Chris would put her off by saying it upset and agitated Don Carlos.

But Julie was no fool and she had known that something wasn't right. Upset by the way Don Carlos had screamed at her, she had begun to think more about his words and his insistence that Ralph's birthday was on the date he had told her. She knew the old man was confused, but she had known Carlos for years and wondered if he was actually trying to pass on a message without Chris finding out. Carlos had often used coded words in conversations to avoid being overheard or spied on. In the beginning it had meant nothing to her and Ralph, but as time went on, they had learnt to work out these coded words and their meanings, which had made Don Carlos laugh and only brought them closer together as they unravelled his own puzzles.

And although Julie knew he was ill, her gut instinct had made her write down the wrong six digits Don Carlos remembered as Ralph's birthday. 'It may be something, it may be nothing.' she had mused to herself, but either way, she made a note of them.

Within the month, the bells of Italy rang out informing everyone that Don Carlos had died in his sleep. Julie had wept inconsolably, but had gone berserk when the will was read and Christopher was named as the new Don. She knew it was a lie and who was to blame, but she couldn't prove it. Friends of old who had known Ralph Gold and Don Carlos had voiced their suspicions to Julie, giving her inside information of how Christopher had kept Don Carlos isolated from the rest of the household.

The only thing mentioned in the will for Adam was a letter that had been left at Don Carlos's bank. Chris had expected Don

Carlos to have left others money or trinkets, especially his beloved Adam, but there was no mention of any financial amount – for that Adam would have to contact Don Carlos's bank. Chris suspected it was some insignificant bauble from the old days that he felt Adam should inherit. But now he was named and accepted as the rightful heir, that was all he cared about.

He delighted in stealing Adam's thunder and shocking the family, especially Julie. Having them all bow down to him because of his new status clearly made Chris's ego even bigger than it already was. Worming his way into Katie's affections and marrying into the family had given him the golden opportunity to keep his enemies close, and it had finally paid off.

Vowing vengeance, Julie Gold wanted to right the wrong done by Chris and let Don Carlos rest in peace. Adam Lambrianu was the rightful heir to Don Carlos's title and wealth, and she was going to make damn sure he got it. For Don Carlos's sake, for her husband Ralph's sake and for Adam's father, Tony Lambrianu's, sake. She wanted revenge for all of them.

Concocting a plan in her mind, she had realised the only way to do this was by murdering Chris. As far as she was concerned, he deserved nothing less. She knew he wouldn't accept his fate and go quietly; if anything, he would eventually kill them all. The more she thought about it, the angrier she felt.

Now, knowing the whole truth, the Lambrianus and the Golds had made a pact to save their family, avenge their loved ones, and go to Italy to murder Chris. But Adam feared that it wasn't going to be as easy as Julie made out.

Sensing Adam had drifted off into his own thoughts, Bruce spoke and tried to bring him back to the present. 'You're a vain bugger, Adam Lambrianu. Anyway, on a lighter note. What's with all the tents in the West End near Hyde Park? Is it a circus or something?'

'No, you've seen it before. They usually hold the Winter Wonderland there, but this week is the German beer festival; ales from everywhere served in tankards. There are flyers everywhere; do you walk around with your eyes shut, Bruce?'

'It's not often I come into the West End,' Bruce quipped. 'Do you fancy it tonight?'

'Yeah, why not. Sounds good, just don't mention the war!' With that they both burst out laughing, then stopped abruptly as Alvin placed in front of them their large oval plates piled high with sausages, eggs, bacon and black pudding. Both of them looked down at their plates as the baked beans ran over the side, and then back up at each other in awe.

Alvin stood with his hands on his hips looking very pleased with himself. 'There you go, lads; two ball busters. That will set you up for tonight's drinking binge.'

Raising his eyebrows, Adam looked directly at Alvin. 'My grandma, what big ears you have, eh?'

* * *

The crowd at the beer festival was rowdy, but harmless. Hipsters, students and office workers alike rubbed shoulders in the large beer tents bursting with music. No one suspected that behind their designer suits, Adam and Bruce weren't just a couple of regular lads eager to try the real ales on offer from all parts of the world. They were kings of the underworld, especially Adam, being a Lambrianu. Adam's name was spoken in hushed tones across the city. Pushing his way to one of the bars, through the cheering, hot, sweaty crowd, Bruce grinned. 'Do you reckon anyone here knows who you are, Adam? I suspect you're the last person they would expect to be drinking with, let alone in some tent.'

Shaking his head, Adam laughed and adjusted his gold cuff-links. 'Nah, that's the beauty of these places. We are out of our territory, and hopefully out of trouble.' He winked. 'Just two blokes on the lash, even if we do look a bit overdressed.' Scanning the crowd, Adam saw that the office workers who had popped in, wanting to unwind for the weekend, had quickly discarded their ties and were now wearing them around their heads while singing along to Bruce Springsteen songs at the top of their voices. Bruce shouted to the barman, 'What do you recommend?'

The barman took two small plastic cups and poured a sample of two ales into them. 'Either one of these should start the night, lads,' he shouted back and handed them both to Bruce. Taking a sip, Bruce pulled a face and handed the cup to Adam. 'Christ, that's a taste I'll never forget!'

'Give it here, it's a man's drink.' Adam laughed, but before he could take a sip, a familiar face in the crowd caught his eye. Leaning forward, he whispered in Bruce's ear. 'That's Razor Ricky behind you. I wonder what he's doing here? He retired a few years ago and I wouldn't have thought this was his scene. Don't turn around too quickly; he'll notice. Calmly and easy does it, Bruce,' Adam instructed.

Frowning, Bruce scanned the singing crowd, already staggering about as the strongly brewed ale took hold, and eventually his gaze cast upon an elderly man with swept-back greying hair, quietly nursing a pint of ale.

Raising his brows questioningly, Bruce shrugged and absently took a sip of one of the sample ales he'd been given, making him cough as it burned his throat. 'So what about him, Adam? Maybe he's a lover of strong ale; what's the problem?' Rubbing his throat, Bruce coughed again. 'Christ, I wish I hadn't done that. Razor Ricky, what kind of a name is that?' he joked, not noticing Adam's face had grown serious.

'Ricky is a man with a sharp wit and a deadly touch, especially with a razor in his hand. What does he want in a place like this? He's definitely got another agenda; this is not his scene.'

'Well, he's not here looking for you; even you didn't know you were coming until today.'

'True.' Adam nodded, but kept his eyes focused on the direction of Razor Ricky. A sly grin crossed Ricky's face, and as he met Adam's eyes, he nodded. Adam tugged at Bruce's sleeve. 'Come on, he's seen us now. We have to say hello.'

Confused, Bruce shook his head. 'Why? By the sounds of it you're not a fan.'

'That's irrelevant. Keep your enemies close. Come on.' Adam pulled harder on Bruce's arm and steered the way towards Razor Ricky.

'Evening, Adam, what brings you to a place like this?' Ricky's gravelly voice greeted them as they drew nearer.

Tensing his jaw, Adam feigned a smile. 'Same as you. Looking for a good, strong beer.'

Looking towards Bruce with his small plastic sample cup, a sneer crossed Ricky's face. 'Who's your girlfriend?' He nodded sarcastically. 'Haven't you got the bottle for a full pint of the stuff?' Then noticing the lack of a glass in Adam's hand, he grinned again. 'This is men's drinking; why come here if you can't take the heat?'

Adam's blue eyes flashed, and he bit into his bottom lip, enough to hurt, but not to draw blood. 'We're just sampling the goods before making a choice. What are you drinking? Or is that a secret too, like the reason you're checking the place out?' Adam replied, ignoring Ricky's sleight.

Bruce could feel the tension between the two men and felt uneasy. He knew Adam's temper was always near to boiling point and wanted to diffuse the situation. 'The last one I tried had coriander in it. Christ, who puts salad in beer, eh?' he joked, but it fell on deaf ears and Ricky glared at him with disdain. Bruce decided to shut up.

Ricky waved his arm in the air at the crowd around them. 'Look around you, Adam; have you got too high and mighty that you can't see an opportunity when it's staring you in the face? Is this too lowkey for you? I still have friends in the business who might be interested in offering protection for something as big as this.'

'I wasn't aware you had any friends at all, Ricky, let alone in my neck of the woods. Your patch has always been north London. So why come to my neck of the woods? The West End is Lambrianu turf and always has been.'

'Aah, well, I might have retired, as you know, but it doesn't stop me keeping the odd iron in the fire, does it? I'm neutral now, like Switzerland. If I see something worth offering to my friends, I will. I have no boundaries now holding me back.' Frowning, he narrowed his eyes and looked at Adam. 'Where there is an opportunity to be made and no one is making use of it, then it's everyone's free for all. We're taking your leftovers, Adam,' Ricky scoffed.

Annoyed at Ricky's almost cavalier behaviour, Adam spat, 'You don't trade on my patch without offering some kind of commission. Not if you want it to go smoothly.'

'Was that a threat, Adam? It sounded like one.' Emptying the dregs of his glass in one swoop, Ricky dropped his plastic glass on the floor and crushed it with his foot.

'Most definitely, Ricky, and don't forget it. You ask nicely if you wish to trade on my turf. You don't tell me. You're an old man whose friends were glad to see the back of, what with your addictions and brawls... including your wife, if I recall?' Adam replied, knowing full well that would hit a raw nerve. He was irritated, but trying hard not to let this loser wind him up, which he knew was Ricky's intention.

Angry at the rebuff, Ricky turned his back on Adam, and without a word angrily pushed his way through the crowd to leave.

Adam's eyes flashed with anger as Ricky walked away, turning his back on him to prove a point. 'That bastard was sizing me up, Bruce, but the worst thing is he was half right. This is a money spinner and we – Scarlet and me – have overlooked it. Maybe we've got lazy. But the last thing I need is a lowlife like Ricky pointing it out. He'll be selling his information to our rivals and they will be swarming this place, raking in the money and making a stand for turf. *My* turf! The very turf my father made his own. Am I so weak, Bruce, that I didn't see this happening? They are trying to take away everything my father built and I won't have it,' Adam spat. 'Fuck! The last thing I need is a prick like Ricky reminding me of my shortcomings. I'll have this place, and I will sort him out if it's the last thing I do before I leave.'

'Leave to go where?' Bruce looked at him, confused. He couldn't recall Adam saying he was going somewhere.

'Oh, nowhere,' Adam stammered, and regretted shooting his mouth off. He didn't want to mention the Italian plans to Bruce yet.

'But I thought you said he was retired, Adam. He's just winding you up, and let's be honest – you're pretty easy to wind up when you're already stressed. It's all that fiery Italian blood in your veins.'

Casting a glance at Bruce, Adam smiled. 'Well, he's supposed to be retired, sneaky old bastard. If he is on the prowl, that also means he's skint. He's looking for a way in; either that or he's got so much cocaine up his nose he's not thinking straight. If he can sell this information to his old scumbag bosses in north London, they will look into it, and he'll get a payout, and that's what he needs. He was once one of their top henchmen, until the drugs took over. But everyone likes someone with eyes and ears like a ferret who sees good opportunities and passes them on. It's what our industry is built on. Street soldiers, spies, whatever you want to call them. But this is my turf, Bruce, and I won't have him pissing down my back and telling me it's raining.' Adam grimaced.

* * *

Once out of the tent, Ricky took out his mobile and called his old bosses. He wondered if his call would be accepted as they hadn't parted on the best of terms. To his astonishment, they did. He could tell it was on loudspeaker because of the echo, and he could hear sneers from whoever else was listening. 'I've just been to the beer festival in the West End, boss. Thought you might be interested.' Ricky looked around the hugeness of the park and the people milling around. 'It doesn't look like they have any protection, boss; few coppers hanging around for the drunks and some hired security guards; well, blokes in security guard uniforms doing fuck all.' Ricky laughed down the phone, trying to sound braver than he felt. 'I wondered, do you want me to look into it? Find out who's organised this? Believe me, there is a lot of money crossing hands – it's packed to the hilt. I feel it would need "proper security" from someone, say, like yourselves.'

Dutch Hillman, the north London boss, listened to Ricky calmly and frowned at his friends in the room. 'I take it you want something for your tipoff, Ricky? But isn't that Lambrianu territory? Surely he's got his finger in that pie if it's as sweet as you say.'

Lying through gritted teeth, Ricky laughed down the phone.

'Actually, I've just come out of the festival with Adam. He's not interested. A bit lowkey for Mr High and Mighty, apparently.'

Shocked, Dutch repeated what Ricky had said. 'You've just been to the beer festival with Adam Lambrianu, and he's given you the go ahead to tip us off? Are you sure about this, Ricky, cos I am warning you, we want no shit from Lambrianu and his animals. Life's good; they leave us alone. The scrap-dealing business is ours, so are the slot machines on our side of the river... Hang on a minute, Ricky.' Dutch looked at his brother, Ethan, and then at his own soldiers. Muting the call, he turned to Ethan. 'What do you think? Is this on the level?'

'I think if Lambrianu isn't interested, I'd want to know why. But if he isn't, well, it's worth checking it out. It could be a load of shit for all we know.' Looking around the pub table at their henchmen, Ethan pointed at two of them. 'You two go and see if it's worth the bother. Ricky could be bullshitting; everyone knows he hasn't got a penny to his name these days. His wife's disowned him and kept the house, and his savings have gone up his nose. Go!' Doing as they were told, the two men stood up and left the pub. Ethan nodded at his brother to carry on the conversation with Ricky.

'Okay then, Ricky, if that's the case, you see what you can find out, and if it's worth our time there will be something in it for you.'

Ricky grinned with pleasure as he punched the air. He was back in! Tonight, lady fortune had been on his side and God knows, with the debts he had run up at the racetracks lately and his dealers, he needed some luck. Walking up to one of the ticket sellers at the front of the tent, he smiled. Indeed, now he had something to smile about. 'Who's in charge around here? Who runs this thing?' Ricky asked nonchalantly.

'The organiser is Mr Wilkinson. Look,' the ticket seller replied and pointed to the name at the top of the tent. *Wilkinson's World-wide Beer Festival*, it read, alongside flags of all nations.

'Okay, bright spark, don't get lippy. So, where do you find the greatest showman then? I need a word.' The young female ticket seller cast a furtive glance at the security guards stood at either side of her while she took the entrance money. 'He's usually in that large caravan over there.' She pointed in the darkness.

Squinting his eyes to see, Ricky saw lights in the distance. 'That it?' He pointed.

'Yes, maybe one of the security guards could take you over there?' the young girl stammered again.

'I can find my way. You need these two to look after that tin box chained to a wooden table. Just how much is in there, little girl?' Watching her shrug, he smiled at her menacingly. 'Be careful someone doesn't steal it, luvvie.'

'Oh, don't worry about that. It's emptied every half hour. Plus, there are the police swarming around. No one would dare,' she exclaimed.

Ricky burst out laughing, 'I wouldn't be too sure about that.'

Walking deeper into the park, he saw a very large, very expensive-looking campervan. All the lights were on, and he could hear several voices inside. He knocked on the door, and a woman answered. She had obviously been expecting someone else and looked surprisingly at Ricky. 'Can I help you?' she asked, taking in the elderly man's suited appearance and his slicked-back greying hair.

'I'm looking for the organiser of the festival, Mr Wilkinson.'

The woman shut the door in Ricky's face, which annoyed him, and after a few minutes a man opened it. 'I'm Mr Wilkinson, what can I do for you?'

'Well, I'm happy to know that you've got better manners than the woman who answered the door. Can we talk? I have a proposition for you.'

'A proposition for me? I organise events Mr... erm... sorry, I didn't get your name.'

'Smith. Mr Smith,' Ricky lied and held out his hand to shake Mr Wilkinson's.

'Well, Mr Smith, here's my card. I'm busy tonight, but I'll be available first thing in the morning. I'm always interested in organising events to our mutual benefit.'

Mr Wilkinson wasn't what Ricky had expected. Middle aged, although not wearing his suit; he was in his shirt sleeves, and his tie was loosened. The huge campervan, which looked like the size of a house, was obviously the mobile office. Looking over his shoulder, Ricky could see a lot of people inside and so decided not to cause a fuss. 'I'm not organising an event; my friends and I organise security for events such as this.'

Relaxing a little, Mr Wilkinson realised that Ricky was touting for a security contract. 'We have security, Mr Smith, and we have the police to stop the odd drunk who gets out of hand. Everything is alarmed. So we're covered. Okay?'

'Not quite. You're not getting protection from the people who run the streets, make sure your festival has no hiccups.' His smarmy smile and threatening undertones made it hard for Mr Wilkinson to understand for a moment, so Ricky spoke again, trying to get his point across. 'Treading on people's toes, on their turf without offering any kind of commission.'

For a moment, Mr Wilkinson stared at him, trying to take in what he was suggesting. 'Forgive me for sounding stupid, but are you suggesting mobster protection? Racketeering and protection... For fuck's sake, haven't those days of gangsters gone out with the ark? We don't need Al Capone to look after a beer festival, Mr Smith. We're legal; we have council permission and the police to support us. Now, I suggest you leave before I have you arrested for some kind of threatening behaviour. This meeting is over.' With that, Mr Wilkinson shut the door in Ricky's face.

Seething with anger, Ricky stared at the closed door for a moment and felt like kicking it in. He wished he had a gun on him because he would show that clever, cocky bastard about gangster shootouts! Turning on his heel, he lit a cigarette and started to walk away when something caught his eye. Standing still for a moment, he recognised Adam Lambrianu's friend from the tent making his way to the many portable toilets that were on site. Ricky's ire was up; his blood was boiling from the way Mr Wilkinson had shut the door in his face. He knew the man wouldn't have dared do that many years ago. Then there was that Lambrianu, cocky little bastard, Ricky thought to himself. He would gladly slice that pretty boy's face up. Standing near the Portaloo, Ricky saw that no one else was around. As he saw the door open as Bruce was leaving, Ricky's sudden urge was to lash out and take his anger out on somebody, and Lambrianu's stooge would do. Watching him fall to the ground, Ricky pummelled him with his fists and then started kicking him as Bruce curled himself into a ball for protection. Taking out his razor, Ricky slashed Bruce up his leg. Then, kneeling beside him, Ricky was about to slice Bruce's face when he heard a crowd of youths approaching. Ricky made a hasty retreat and ran across the park towards his car. Bruce's cries were mostly drowned out by the music and the groups of men drunkenly singing and dancing in the park. Spirits were high, and people were only interested in enjoying themselves, unaware of Bruce's near-death fate.

* * *

Adam stood shoulder to shoulder with other customers waiting for their turn to be served. His eyes narrowed and his ears became deaf to the loud, raucous laughter and singing around him. All he saw was the bartender holding a card machine out to the many customers and hearing it bleep as their payment was authorised. The vastness of the tent with many makeshift bars meant numerous bartenders were all doing the same thing. Adam tried to calculate how much the beer stalls must all be taking, and not one ounce of profit was going in his pocket. Ricky was right, he mused to himself; this was just like any of the other clubs or businesses on his patch that paid for protection, and yet this one had slipped entirely through the net. If it hadn't been for Bruce, he doubted he would have even noticed it until it had left.

Once he had been served and held out his credit card as payment, he fought his way from the crowded bar and sat on a nearby wooden bench waiting for Bruce. Slowly, Adam concentrated on the crowds and how the customers showed no sign of diminishing. If anything, they got bigger as time went on and more people came in. After a while, Adam looked at his watch. Bruce had been gone for half an hour. His frothy pint had gone flat, and Adam had finished his own. Feeling the sweat beading on his brow and down the back of his shirt, Adam stood up and made for one of the many exits. Almost gasping as he gulped in the fresh air, he saw large crowds stood outside with their drinks. Police walked around the area and Adam noticed a few security guards trying to keep the peace by helping the odd drunk vomit away from the tent. All in all, it seemed like everyone was having a great time. Scanning the crowds, Adam looked for Bruce, then made his way to the Portaloos. On approaching, he heard groaning in the darkness. It was pitch black outside with only the moon and the stars for lighting. Again, he heard moans and groans and followed the sound behind the Portaloo. There, lying on the ground, he saw Bruce. Kneeling down beside him, Adam shouted his name. 'Bruce, Bruce, are you okay? What happened?' Feeling a wetness on his hand, Adam peered into the darkness and realised there was blood. Taking out his mobile phone and turning on the light, he saw Bruce's badly beaten body lying on the floor, blood smeared all over his face.

'Shit, have you been mugged?' Rooted to the spot for a moment, Adam took in the bloodied sight before him. He felt helpless and shocked at the same time. Looking around the park, he saw police and a first aid ambulance parked nearby and was about to shout out for help when it suddenly dawned on him who had done this. Who was the last person he had argued with? Ricky would never have dared to have done this to Adam, but being the coward he was, he had attacked the nearest person with him. He felt helpless and guilty that his temper had caused this to happen to his friend. Composing himself, Adam controlled the anger boiling up inside of him and concentrated on helping Bruce.

'Bruce, mate, can you stand?' Adam asked and tried helping him off the ground.

'My arm, I think it's broken, Adam,' he muttered through bloodied lips.

'Okay, but can you stand? There is a first aid ambulance over there. Let's get you to that and get you cleaned up.'

'I'll try, but don't pull my arm, it bloody hurts.' Almost dragging Bruce to his feet and stumbling backwards himself, Adam heard Bruce give out a loud moan as he put his broken arm around his shoulders. Catching his breath, and barely able to see with the blood running down his face into his eyes, Bruce blinked hard as Adam put his arm around his waist and together, they limped towards the ambulance.

'Help needed,' Adam shouted as he approached the entrance.

Some paramedics were stood outside and, spotting Adam and Bruce, they leapt forward to help. Two of them carried Bruce carefully inside the brightly lit ambulance and placed him on one of the stretchers. Seeing Adam's jacket and shirt covered in blood, they told him to sit down too, but once Adam had reassured them that the blood was Bruce's, not his, they gave him some wet wipes to clean his face and hands while they looked Bruce over.

One of the paramedics turned towards Adam. 'The arm is definitely broken. He will need to go to the hospital and have it seen to. We'll radio ahead so hopefully he won't have to wait too long. Has he been mugged? He doesn't seem drunk.'

Adam looked on as they washed Bruce's bloodied face, and as they handed over his jacket, Adam's suspicions were confirmed. Bruce's wallet was still there in the inside pocket. Surely a mugger wouldn't have gone to so much trouble without taking his wallet, or his watch, which was still on his arm. The paramedics kept questioning Adam about what he knew, but all he could tell them was the truth. Bruce had gone to one of the Portaloos, and when he'd realised he had been missing a while, he had gone to look for him. Two policemen from nearby came in, obviously alerted by one of the paramedics, and they asked all the same questions. Bruce muttered that he had gone to the loo and when he had come out, someone, he couldn't see who in the darkness, had lashed out at him and punched him in the face. Once he had fallen, they had kicked him and searched his body on the floor looking for his wallet. Between the swollen slits of his eyes, Bruce cast a furtive glance at Adam who, slowly, took out Bruce's wallet from his jacket and hid it in his own pocket. The missing wallet would confirm Bruce's story.

Adam knew his good friend was keeping silent about the whole affair, and the police accepted it as one of those things. They could see that neither Bruce nor Adam was drunk and so hadn't got into a fight of sorts. The police took notes, but couldn't promise anything, then another ambulance turned up to take Bruce to hospital to get his arm fixed and to put stitches in his forehead and leg. The paramedics commented to the police that the cut on the leg looked like a knife wound, but it was so thinly cut it could have been done by a Stanley knife, possibly a razor. Adam looked long and hard at his friend in agony, musing to himself as he looked at the long slash down Bruce's leg pouring with blood. Guilt washed over Adam; they both knew who had done this, and if it hadn't been for his own arrogance towards Ricky, poor Bruce wouldn't be in this mess.

After hours of waiting, Bruce finally emerged in a wheelchair. His head was bandaged over the stitches he had received, and his newly plastered arm was in a sling. His trouser leg had been cut so that the long razor cut could be stitched together. The blood stains on his shirt and trousers had dried and made him look even more dishevelled than ever. Adam had called the club and ordered a car to be sent over to the hospital to pick them up. On hearing this, Scarlet had arrived herself. Hearing her heels clacking along the hospital corridors, Adam had a feeling of dread. He knew she would fire questions at him, and be relieved that he hadn't been hurt. Bruce had been the one who had taken the full wrath of Razor Ricky's anger.

'Adam!' Half running down the corridor, Scarlet held her arms wide open. 'What's happened?' Then, angrily, she slapped him across the face, knocking him sideways. 'Why the hell didn't you call me? Why did I have to find out third hand that my brother was at the hospital waiting to be picked up, you selfish bastard!' Then, throwing her arms around him, she hugged him. Adam felt she was squeezing the life out of him and did his best to shrug her off.

'I'm okay, Scarlet; it's Bruce,' he explained. Turning her head, she saw Bruce in the wheelchair and let out a gasp of horror. Giving her a weak smile, Bruce did his best to shrug. He felt tired and drained and although he had been given painkillers, he could now feel his body throbbing with pain and wanted to sleep.

'It's 1 a.m., Scarlet; can't the questions wait?' Adam intervened. 'We're both tired, and I'm sure Bruce needs to rest. He's coming home with me.'

Nodding, Scarlet took the handles of Bruce's wheelchair. 'Come on, you two walking wounded. Knuckles is in the car. Are you okay to walk, Adam?'

'Scarlet, there's nothing wrong with me; Bruce is the injured soldier here. You can frisk me if you like.' He grinned. He knew she had slapped him out of worry and concern, and realised he should have called her first to let her know he was okay. But his first thought had been Bruce and getting him patched up. Now, as they walked out of the hospital and helped Bruce get into the car, his second thought was... revenge!

* * *

Walking into the office the next morning, Scarlet noticed the light was on. Opening the door, she saw Adam sat at his desk working away. 'You're up early, Adam; shit the bed or something? How's the walking wounded? Did he manage to get some sleep?'

'Yes, he fine. I couldn't sleep and I had some things I wanted to catch up on.'

'Such as?' she asked as she sat opposite him. This morning he seemed different; no quip or cheeky remark. And he was suited and booted and working away at his desk before she'd even arrived, which was unheard of.

Taking off his gold-rimmed glasses, Adam looked up at her with a serious look on his face. For an instant, she saw a flash of her father in him. 'Such as how we have taken our eye off the ball. There is a huge beer festival in town and they aren't paying for any kind of protection. Hundreds of thousands of pounds is going into their bank account and not a penny is coming to us. We're supposed to be in charge of this area. Us – the Lambrianus! And yet why do I feel you're content with the way things are? Never chasing new business, just happy with the old ones. All we're doing is riding on the coattails of our family name. We're not hungry any more, Scarlet. Is this what you want?'

Scarlet was taken aback by his outburst. 'Whoa, Adam, where has all this come from? I thought you proved your point with your crypto rip off. Wasn't that meant to bring the Lambrianus up to date?'

Adam let out a huge sigh. 'That's my point, Scarlet. It was up to date and easy to do with a bit of help from our friends.' He smiled. 'But we're missing out on our grass roots. This beer festival is just one oversight and people will notice. The club down the road, for instance,' Adam carried on, almost red faced. 'It pays us for protection, but when it hears we don't have a finger in the pie of that festival organisation, why should they pay us? I would feel like that. It's all or nothing, Scarlet.' Almost out of breath, Adam half smiled. 'So there you have it.'

'Adam, I don't know exactly what's eating you, but to be honest you have a point. We should have looked into that festival, but we didn't. Or I didn't. I didn't feel it was worth the effort for such a short space of time. My oversight, I'm sorry. Are they making a lot of money?'

'They are, but it's not just about the money, Scarlet. It's about who we are. Does our name mean anything out there any more? Does it chill the bones of people any more? Or are we just the fat cats living off our forebearers?'

'Well, I for one, Adam, am not a fat cat,' Scarlet shouted. 'I work bloody hard running this place and the casino, and unless you've forgotten, I still own my hairdressing salons. You sort out the pubs, the slot machines and run the bookies, but what is it you're looking for, Adam? Excitement, is that it?'

'No, Scarlet, you're missing my point. We have a tradition and a legacy to keep up. And I for one intend to do that.'

'So, stop moaning about it and do something. Find whatever it is you're looking for and keep up tradition! Christ, you really have the wind up your arse this morning. Is it since Jenny dumped you?' Scarlet threw in for good measure.

For a moment there was a silence in the room as Adam looked Scarlet squarely in the eyes. 'Low blow, Scat, but it probably does have something to do with Jenny, yes. No one likes to be dumped; it hurts the ego.' Adam recalled his girlfriend Jenny. She'd been good fun and he had enjoyed feeling like a normal bloke dating a normal girl. He had even wondered if this was what love was like, whizzing about on his motorbike without a care in the world. He had never disclosed that he owned the nightclub where he had met her. Instead he'd just told her that he worked there, which wasn't entirely a lie. Their romance had been fleeting and fun, with lots of sex to boot, but when she'd had to leave England on a short work trip, she'd whispered in his ear that she knew who he really was and that he had deceived her. And if he didn't trust her, then he didn't love her.

Without a backward turn, she had walked towards her boarding gate, leaving Adam calling out to her, desperate to explain why he had wanted her to himself, without the media or his family wanting introductions. He would have told her eventually, but the longer it went on, the harder it got. He hadn't heard from her since that day. Adam felt disappointed with himself for not being honest, and woeful at what could have been. That

Scarlet should throw it in his face now reminded him of what an ass he had been.

Softening her tone, Scarlet walked over to him and put her hand on his shoulder. 'Sorry, Adam, I didn't mean that. It's her loss, not yours. I've got other things on my mind, like this trip of Julie's to Italy. It has so many holes in it; anything could go wrong. Chasing festivals isn't the first thing on my agenda. But why don't you put your feelers out about this festival and any other plan you have in mind? But don't get too involved with anything yet. We have a lot to do, and I want you alive at my wedding. Killing Chris off, the self-proclaimed godfather of Italy, isn't going to be as easy as Julie predicts, that's what worries me. Is she a bonkers old woman, or is it maybe us who are old, staid in our ways and bonkers? You could be right, Adam. Maybe it's time to shake up this town a little and remind them who we are. If we're going to die we might as well go out with all guns blazing!' She laughed, almost hysterically.

'Is that what you think will happen? We're all going to die? When you say a lot to do, you mean breaking into Chris's mansion and getting close enough to kill him, all for the sake of avenging Don Carlos. It is a big mountain to climb, Scarlet, and I have my doubts. Julie still hasn't disclosed a lot of her plans to any of us and we've got a lot to lose.'

Sitting down again, Scarlet put her head in her hands. 'I don't know, Adam. But Chris has a lot of bodyguards surrounding him. We would be few against many. It's crossed my mind. Hasn't it crossed yours?'

Rolling his eyes to the ceiling, Adam sat back in his chair. 'I suppose so, but who is all of this for, Scarlet? The trip, I mean? To clear Diana, so she would never be found guilty of murder for helping Katie to murder Sharon? To help Katie escape her controlling, manipulative husband, or for Julie to avenge Don

Carlos's mystery death? I can't make my mind up. And sometimes I feel we jumped the gun agreeing to it all.'

'All of the above, but also to give you your rightful inheritance from Don Carlos. It was never Don Carlos's wishes that Chris takes over his empire. Christ, Don Carlos hated him, and Julie and many others knew that. Julie knows more than we do about the situation and wants to free everyone from the bonds that tie them and let Don Carlos finally rest in peace. She feels guilty for not being there when he needed her, and this has played on her mind. And now Katie has filled in some of the blanks, Julie wants to tidy up her affairs. She's not getting any younger. She knew Don Carlos's wishes. He wanted you to take over from him, but Chris lied and somehow changed Don Carlos's mind. He had dementia, for Christ's sake, so it wouldn't have taken much. But he knew what he wanted and he was duped. Julie wants you to have your rightful inheritance. She also wants you to have the thing our father didn't get the chance to achieve – to become Don Lambrianu. Be it Papa or you, it's Don Lambrianu, the true godfather of Italy, who will serve the people fairly. Okay, we draw in favours and people pay their way, but we do it with respect, not with Chris's threats and fear. He has the charm of a skunk.' As an afterthought, Scarlet felt she had to ask Adam the ultimate question. 'Do you not want the job or responsibility, Adam? And yet, you're the one yearning for excitement and desperate to build on our tradition and legacy.'

'Truly, Scarlet, I'm not sure I'm up to the job. I have doubts, of course I do. Do you think I could do it?'

'Definitely. You've heard yourself that even the vineyard workers have little respect for Chris or the Lambrianu name any more. They think Katie is in with him on his schemes to pay lower wages and work them to death. That's not what our grandparents did and that is why they were respected. But if you're not confident about it, Adam, pull out; it's as easy as that. Julie has other reasons for getting rid of Chris; it's not just about you.'

'Thanks, Scarlet; it just seems like a lot of pressure. And a lot to ask other people to risk their lives for on my behalf. This is my home. I don't know if I would like to live in Italy for the rest of my life.'

'Nobody is asking you to. Carlos lived in England more than he did in Italy. Our father lived here but his heart was in Italy. It's all about good staff and good delegation. Choosing the right people, Adam, but people who respect you. But try to stop worrying; it may never happen.' Reaching forward, Scarlet ruffled his dark locks with her hand, which was her usual greeting, making him smile.

'Why do you do that when I've combed it so precisely?'

'Because when it's wavy and around your shoulders, you look like Mum with Dad's blue eyes. Very handsome indeed.' Scarlet nodded. 'Of course, you could never have been blonde and blue eyed like me and Katie. I hate competition too much!' She laughed, in turn, making them both laugh. And for a moment, thoughts of Italy and what might happen there were forgotten.

2

GOOD PROSPECTS

The sound of the mobile phone ringing stirred Ricky from his slumber. Staring at the screen through half-sleepy eyes, he was going to ignore it, but then he saw that Dutch was calling him. Sitting bolt upright, he cleared his throat and answered.

'You were right, Razor; that place seems like a real money spinner. Two of the lads went and took a look after your phone call and they agreed. If Lambrianu wants no part of it, then we might as well throw our hat in the ring. Come by later to the pub and we'll have a drink.'

Ricky was about to interrupt and tell them he had spoken to the organiser, but the line went dead. Staring blanky at it for a moment, hoping it would burst back into life, he yawned and rubbed his face. The adrenalin surged through him now he was wide awake. Looking at the clock, he saw that it was 10 a.m.

Jumping out of bed, he yawned and scratched at his boxer shorts while switching on the kettle. The cold light of day dawned on him. He had ruthlessly attacked Adam Lambrianu's mate out of anger and frustration. He'd had no reason to, except that he was fed up of being snubbed by people who thought they were better than him. Like Adam Lambrianu, who was nothing more than a kid, but a dangerous one, Ricky had to acknowledge.

Ricky had assured Dutch and Ethan that the Lambrianus wanted no part in his get-rich-quick scheme, but it had been a lie. Adam had never said such a thing, nor indicated it. If he was to put two and two together and realise that Ricky was the one who had beaten up his friend, not only would Adam be after his blood but so would Dutch and Ethan. They were ruthless bastards with a lot of influential people in their pocket, but he knew they wanted no bad blood with the Lambrianus.

Ricky gritted his teeth, and his anger rose; he hated the Lambrianu name. Sitting down at the kitchen table, he stirred his coffee and thought about last night's events. He had been foolish to let his anger get the better of him. Looking around his shitty bedsit also depressed him. He had once lived in a five-bedroom mansion, until he'd lost it all after getting into so much debt with gambling and drugs.

He drank the warm coffee and wondered how much Dutch would hand over for the information. He'd sounded pleased enough on the phone. A wry smile crossed Ricky's face; if Dutch was pleased, he thought to himself, that meant he was back in with the gang again and things would start to look up. Feeling hungry, he thought about making some toast, but saw that the only bread he had left was mouldy, so he decided to get ready early to meet Dutch and get a full English on the way.

Ricky envisaged his meeting. Dutch would be pleased that he had made some headway by learning the organiser's name. Searching through his pockets, he found the card Mr Wilkinson had given him. This was just another brownie point he would earn, by being thorough and learning the facts. Feeling his stomach growl with hunger again, he swallowed what was left of his coffee and made for the shower, singing to himself as he did.

* * *

After a sleepless night, and a lot thinking time, Adam put his head around Bruce's bedroom door. 'How you feeling, Bruce? Just thought I would pop up and see you. I didn't mean to wake you.'

'No fear of that.' Bruce yawned. 'Your cleaner Doreen has been in all morning, hoovering and polishing and making cups of coffee. Oh, and she went and got my prescription for painkillers. Does that woman ever stop?'

Adam laughed. He liked Doreen, and she had been around since as long as he could remember. 'Oh, she's a good old stick and means well, but this is the best bit of gossip she's had in a long time. Did she give you the Spanish Inquisition?'

'I thought she was going to pull out my toenails and put me on the rack to get more information.' Bruce did his best to laugh, but it hurt. In fact, his whole body hurt this morning. He did his best to sit up in bed, and Adam helped.

'Careful, mate, there isn't a lot you can do with your arm in plaster,' Adam said as he plumped up the pillows behind Bruce's head. 'And it could be worse; Doreen might needed to have helped you wipe your arse for you or hold your dick. Now that would really give her something to gossip about!' Adam burst out laughing.

Indignantly, Bruce brushed him off from fussing. 'You say that jokingly, but she has already told me about a friend of hers who has just died. They were being cared for at home and, apparently, their commode and bedpan are still available if I want them.'

Adam didn't want to laugh out loud, but as they caught each other's eye, Bruce held on to his bandaged ribs and laughed. 'For fuck's sake, Adam, I've got a broken arm and a few stitches, and she wants to sit me on a bedpan!' The pair of them burst out into guffaws of laughter.

Adam sat on the edge of the bed and looked closely at his best friend. His bruises were all colours of the rainbow, and his face was hardly recognisable, but he didn't complain.

'On a serious note, Bruce, we both know who did this. You were caught in the crossfire. None of this had anything to do with you. I'm sorry, mate.'

'Shit happens, Adam; usually to me, but it happens. I'll heal. Just promise me that you won't do anything foolish. Revenge is not the answer. Let this be the end of it. That's why I told the police I'd been mugged. Please, Adam, don't go in there all guns blazing.'

Adam's blood boiled. How could Bruce let this go? If Razor hadn't been interrupted, he knew he would have finished the job. He didn't do half measures so something must have stopped him. Keeping that information to himself, Adam shook his head. 'You know I can't let this go, Bruce. You're my mate, my best mate, and through my cockiness you were the one that got the beating. If I say I won't put myself in harm's way, would that suit you? But you can't stop me fighting your corner, okay?'

'People like him aren't worth it. He needed to take it out on somebody, and I was there. I'm here, I'm alive and I have Doreen!' Bruce's attempt at laughter made his ribs hurt, but he squeezed Adam's hand. 'Let it go, Adam.'

'How can you be so bloody benevolent, Bruce? He beat the shit out of you. He's a bitter, twisted old man!'

'Exactly, but your anger is turning you into a bitter, twisted man. The outcome can only be dire. I won't be responsible for you taking a beating – or worse. I'm okay.'

Nodding reassuringly, Adam flashed a wide smile. He felt it was better to appease Bruce at a time like this. Adam felt humbled before him; after what he had been through, his first thought was for Adam's safety. Even so, Adam's blood boiled, but he didn't want to show it. 'Whatever you say, Bruce. Although I must admit, when you suggest having a night out and letting our hair down, you really do make it memorable. I'll go and switch the kettle on, or do you fancy something stronger?'

'Well, I shouldn't because of the painkillers, but I'm drowning in Doreen's tea so a small brandy or whisky would help.'

'Well, you're going to need a stiff drink because Scarlet will be up soon with her bunch of grapes which she'll eat in front of you. Oh, and she's called Julie and told her the bad news, and she thinks you should have a nurse to take care of you. After all, this apartment is above the club, and it has a lot of stairs.'

'For God's sake, my arm's broken, not my legs. I can hobble around. Tell them I have Doreen; tell them I have anyone.'

'It's your turn for the clucking hens, Brucey boy.' Adam shouted from the bar in the lounge, 'I've had it all my life and for once I'm off the hook!' Adam laughed as he returned and handed him his brandy. 'Have this, and then sleep, before they all descend upon you.'

Bruce gulped back his drink, his eyes heavy as he laid his head back on the pillow. Taking the empty glass from his hand, Adam put it on the bedside table and looked on as Bruce's eyes closed as he fell asleep.

Sitting there for a moment, Adam mused to himself. If Scarlet knew who it was who had done this, she would go around his house and shoot the bastard, but Adam had something more strategic planned. Something that kept his name out of it. 'Don't worry, Bruce mate,' he whispered. 'I'll sort this, and there will be no comeback.'

Shutting the door quietly behind him as he left, Adam put his hand in his trouser pocket and pulled out a piece of paper with an address on it. Kissing it, he smiled. Early this morning he had already set his plan in action and made a few calls and found out

Razor Ricky's address. *Time to go for a ride*, Adam thought to himself as he ran down the stairs.

Donning his leathers and helmet, Adam strode towards his motorbike and headed off towards the address he had been given. As Adam rode up the street, he scanned the buildings he passed, looking for the address given. The area was famous for student accommodation and for a grown man of Ricky's age, it showed great demise. Just as he was about to turn into a side street, he saw Ricky as large as life coming out of a café. Adam carefully watched him as he hailed a cab. It seemed like he had made it in the nick of time. Thankful that he was on his motorbike, Adam wheedled in and out of the traffic, while following the black cab. As the cab came to a halt, Ricky got out and handed the cabbie his money. Underneath his helmet, Adam smiled to himself.

As he'd presumed, Ricky was going to his old haunt, Dutch's pub-cum-headquarters. Confirming his suspicions, Adam knew this was the time for Ricky to spill the beans about the festival. God knows what lies he was going to tell to get his old mates back on side, but, for Adam, it was a golden opportunity. Driving off, he made his way back to the festival. It was daylight and didn't open until 5 p.m., and in the cold light of day, the tent looked quite small in the vastness of Hyde Park, surrounded by caravans, which, Adam presumed, was where some of the staff stayed over. A few people were milling around and tidying up the grounds, but other than that, it seemed deserted. Satisfied, Adam rode off.

* * *

Ethan looked up from the corner booth they were sitting in the pub. 'Here he comes, the slimy bastard.'

'Keep that temper under control, Ethan. We both know what

he is, but business is business. He's come with a good tipoff,' Dutch whispered through gritted teeth.

'Maybe so, but I hate the idea of owing that bastard anything. He sickens me.'

'Well, hold it in; we have street soldiers with their ears to the ground all of the time; he's just another one.' Dutch almost smiled at his brother. 'That festival is around for another week or so, and then who knows where it goes and where else it might need protection. This could be a long money spinner if we play our cards right.'

As Ricky walked into the unusually empty pub, he spied both Dutch and Ethan. Seeing Ethan again made his stomach somersault. He knew he would be in for a hard time with him, but at least Dutch would keep his brother in line. Considering they were brothers, the two men had nothing in common. Dutch, known as that because they were both from the Netherlands, and no one could pronounce his first name, was tall, thin and balding with wisps of blonde, gingery hair at the sides. While Ethan had a head full of uncontrollable black hair, making him look almost wild in appearance, and a badly damaged left eye, which he'd received during a prison fight.

Standing up, Dutch held out his hand. 'Ricky, nice to see you again. How's tricks; life treating you well?' Nodding his head to the barman, he indicated a round of drinks were in order.

'Nice to see you, Dutch.' Ricky shook his hand with a little more zeal than he should. Turning towards Ethan, who was still seated, Ricky held out his hand. 'Ethan.' Ricky's face dropped when Ethan didn't hold his hand out to shake. There had always been tension between them, and it seemed like nothing had changed.

Casting a glare at Ethan, Dutch went through the usual preliminary greeting and handed Ricky his drink. 'So, your tipoff was a good one, Ricky. The lads over there checked it out last night.' Glancing over his shoulder, Ricky saw two henchmen sat at the bar behind him. He hadn't seen them when he'd entered and realised that they must have come in behind him, which made his blood run cold. He was obviously under scrutiny from the two brothers. Thankfully, Dutch was the reasonable businessman, but Ethan was the wildcard who hankered for excitement, which usually meant causing a fight and hurting someone. He was the muscle behind Dutch's brains.

Dutch reached into his inside pocket and took out a wad of notes. 'Here's a grand for the information. What else do you have for us?'

Ricky's eyes widened when he saw the money. It had been a long time since he'd had that much cash before him. He reached into his jacket pocket and took out Mr Wilkinson's card. 'This is the organiser. I spoke to him last night and advised him that he should have better security. He seems like an honest man, who relies mainly the police. He has a few security guards, but what power do they have?' Ricky laughed and flashed a glance at both brothers, waiting for some kind of reaction.

For the first time, Ethan spoke. 'There's nothing wrong with an honest man in business, Ricky, relying on the good old English police. So, what did he say when you propositioned him?'

Casting his eyes downwards, Ricky picked up his drink and took a sip to moisten his throat. He didn't have a lot more information to offer, but the next part was even less appealing. 'Well, he didn't take too kindly at first. He laughed at the idea of gangsters and protection, but then he doesn't know the London ways, does he?'

Letting out a sarcastic chuckle, Ethan looked directly at him. 'You mean he fucked you off and sent you packing? Put that money in your pocket. Your eyes are eating into it and everyone knows you haven't got a pot to piss in.' Sarcasm dripped from Ethan's mouth, making Ricky squirm.

Hastily, he picked up the money and stuffed it into his pocket. 'Well, I'd better go. Thanks for seeing me.'

Dutch held his hand up. 'Finish your drink, Ricky, and tell me exactly what this is.' Picking up the card before him, he read the name Wilkinson out loud. 'Mr Wilkinson sounds like a man who runs his business above board and puts his faith in the local constabulary. We all know it doesn't work that way, but it's nice to know some people still have faith. You go back, Ricky, and try to use some charm. You used to be able to pull things like this off with no trouble. Let's hope you haven't lost your touch.'

Ricky knew he was being tested, and given the snub he had received from Mr Wilkinson last night, he didn't hold out much hope. Inwardly sighing, he had hoped Dutch would either go himself or send one of his other men to seal the deal. 'I wonder if he'd like to meet the boss of the operation, rather than the organ grinder or the monkey, eh?' laughed Ricky, although it was hollow and feigned.

Dutch cast a sideways glance at Ethan and pondered for a moment. 'Maybe you're right. You seem to have greased the path. We could always pop in for a drink. What do you say, Ethan?'

'You mean pop in and see if he's telling the truth?' Ethan's dark glare at Ricky spoke volumes. 'Yeah, I'm up for a drink. The lads seemed to think it's worth a look, too.' Then Ethan's eyes darkened, and he pointed his finger in Ricky's face. 'But if you think this is the beginning of a beautiful friendship, you're wrong. We always pay for good tips, but you're not back on the payroll. You're a liability, Ricky. You maim and kill without conscience and drag others down with you. The last time you got pissed and flew off the handle with that razor of yours, slashing away like the big man, you put us all under the spotlight. Go and buy some drugs with your money; you're no fun when you're sober,' Ethan spat.

'Enough!' Dutch shouted. 'We're here to talk business, not settle old scores.' Ricky could feel the beads of sweat on his brow. He knew Ethan wouldn't mince his words, and he was right. He and Ethan had been friends once, and although Dutch and Ethan had their own soldiers, Ricky had been Ethan's man. But he had blown it, Ricky mused to himself. When collecting payments, he had creamed a little off the top, hoping Ethan wouldn't notice, but he had. He'd shouted and forced Ricky to pay the money back and although he had done his best, Ethan's trust was low. There had been a few more incidents, including a pub brawl where he had slashed a man's face with his razor, claiming that it was a message from Ethan. Ethan had known nothing about it and had been arrested and questioned by the police. Ethan had served one month in custody until eventually Ricky had manned up and confessed that Ethan had had nothing to do with it, but his confession had come too late. Someone in prison claiming to be a friend of the man Ricky had slashed had started a fight and cut Ethan badly across the eye, almost blinding him. Ricky had been thrown out of their circle, never to show his face again. It had only been Dutch's intervention that had saved his life; if it had been up to Ethan, he would have been executed.

'Ricky, you piss off for now and go and see that bloke again. We'll pop along later,' Dutch said. Ricky didn't need telling twice; almost jumping out of his seat, he scurried past the two henchmen sat at the bar. His heart was pounding as he stepped onto the pavement and his hands were trembling. He knew it was a sign of the DTs he suffered when he hadn't had a drink. Walking along the high street, he stopped at a pub for a quick pint to calm his nerves before going to see Mr Wilkinson again.

Later that day, back at home, Ricky put down his supermarket carrier bag containing a bottle of whisky. Pouring some into a mug, he gulped it back and smiled as he recalled his second visit with Mr Wilkinson. This time his courtesy had turned to threatening behaviour. Dragging him to one side, out of sight, Ricky had warned him that he would have to pay the protection fee requested, or he would slice him up. Out of fear, Mr Wilkinson had wet himself when Ricky had taken out his razor and waved it in his face, cutting a tiny nick under his eye. The droplet of blood that escaped from the wound looked almost like a tear as it rolled down his face. Ricky had told him that he would be back with his friends later that evening and he expected his commission. Losing all of his bravado from the previous night, Mr Wilkinson had nodded his head in agreement. Already warned that contacting the police would be fatal, Ricky had left Mr Wilkinson roughed up and fearful as he walked away. Ricky smacked his lips as he savoured the whisky taste and laughed to himself when he thought about Mr Wilkinson's face. Surely, he mused to himself, this would make Ethan and Dutch change their minds about him.

* * *

Later that evening, Adam rode his motorbike into a deserted spot in Hyde Park. In the far-off distance, he could see the beer tents lit up in the darkness. Getting off his bike, he opened the glove box at the back and looked at the items he had brought with him to put his plan into action. Years ago, Adam had enrolled in archery classes after attending a stag weekend with some friends and enjoying the activity. Now with his favourite bow attached to the side of his bike, and the arrows hanging in a pouch around his shoulders, Adam truly felt like Robin Hood. Taking out the tiny bags of petrol that he had prepared earlier, he attached one to an arrow, lit the taper he had left out, and pointed his bow into the sky towards the tent. He wasn't sure if he had hit his target and so did the same four more times, shooting his lit arrows into the night sky towards the tent. Pulling down the visor on his helmet, he then held up the rocket fireworks he had brought with him. On the long wooden sticks supporting the firework, he had carved a small niche so that it would fit onto the string of his bow. Lighting it cautiously, Adam fired quickly and watched as the huge bang caused a colourful firework display in the night air. Firing one more time, Adam watched as he saw smoke begin to billow and heard people shouting. Knowing that he had set fire to the tent and caused a commotion, he hung his bow around his neck and rode off as quickly and silently as he'd arrived. His plan had been put into motion, and his thoughts were simple: without a beer festival, Ricky, Dutch and Ethan wouldn't have anything to protect and there would be no money to make. Deed done as far as Adam was concerned, and Ricky would have egg on his face.

At the Lambrianus' club later that evening, everyone who came in was talking about the fire at the beer festival. Adam looked out of the windows and could see billowing black smoke in the air. The sound of fire engines almost drowned out the music inside. People were checking the internet and Facebook to see if there was any talk about it, and Adam scanned the comments and thankfully saw that no one had been hurt. Breathing a sigh of relief, he made a mental note to pass by tomorrow and check out the damage for himself. In the meantime, he had a call to make to the Hillman brothers. In the meantime, after such a busy day, he really needed a distraction. Looking up at the bar, he spotted Ursula; tall, blonde and by all accounts had recently had a great boob job. Now, Adam thought, as he made his way over to her with a stirring in his loins, was the perfect night to find out what they looked like.

* * *

Driving up to Hyde Park the next morning, Adam spied the area. As he had predicted, the police and firemen were still checking the place over and Adam could see that the once huge tent was now just a heap of black, wet ash in the middle of the park. There were only remnants of the bars and pumps that had once hosted a lively atmosphere. Adam stood and watched as the police chatted and took notes from a group of people. Adam presumed one or more of these people must be the organisers. Although the area was cordoned off with police tape for safety's sake, people were still walking through the park for a glimpse of what they had read about on the internet. Some were even taking pictures as they passed by slowly.

'Morning, Mr Lambrianu, what brings you to the park at this time of morning? Fancied a spot of jogging, did you?' Swiftly turning, Adam saw a detective who seemed to be permanently on his tail. They didn't like each other, but they were civil.

Feigning a smile, Adam shook his head. 'No, Inspector Dyson, just being nosey, like everyone else here. This is my part of the world, and I just thought I'd take a look. What happened, do you know?'

'That's what the fire people are looking into now. They say it could have been fireworks, but there is also a strong smell of petrol. Who knows? Arson probably. It didn't make things any better, given the gas bottles used to pump the beer through. Went up like a World War Two bomb it did.'

Adam's face paled. He'd never thought of that, but of course the gas bottles were needed to carbonate the beer. He cursed himself for not realising that earlier. No wonder the sky was full of black smoke. The fire could have been fatal.

The inspector gave a wry grin and took out his cigarette

packet, offering one to Adam. 'I take it, by the look on your face, it's got nothing to do with your antics then?'

Taking the cigarette, Adam looked the inspector squarely in the face. 'What are you implying, Inspector? This has nothing to do with me, I assure you. I was just curious.' Looking at the enormous black circle of burnt grass in the park, Adam shook his head. 'That is going to take a lot of grass seed to make it presentable again.'

'No, the gardeners will dig it all up once we've finished and lay grass squares to take root. That's what they usually do.'

Oozing charm, Adam flashed a smile. 'Goodness, Inspector Dyson, you're quite the Alan Titchmarsh. I wouldn't have known that.'

Smiling cockily at Adam's flattery, the inspector did exactly what Adam wanted him to do. 'See that poor bastard over there.' The inspector cast a furtive glance to a man possibly in his forties. His once white shirt was grey from smoke dust and ash. His sleeves were rolled up beyond his elbows, and his face showed despair and tiredness. Seeing Adam glance over, Inspector Dyson carried on as though talking to himself. 'The bloke with the weight of the world on his shoulders, that's the organiser. He's got insurance, but he's lost everything.' Without another word, Inspector Dyson walked away towards the group of men, including the organiser.

'Mr Wilkinson.' Inspector Dyson made sure his voice was loud enough to carry over to Adam. 'Do you see anyone in the area that might have threatened you, or who could have done this? Does anyone have a grudge against you?'

Adam stood watching, knowing that the inspector wanted the organiser of the festival to point the finger at Adam. He saw the man shake his head, before throwing his head back and raising his hands in the air. 'Oh my God!' Adam heard him shout. 'That bloke who came here threatening me for protection money. That son of a bitch has done this!' He shouted to Inspector Dyson at the top of his voice and pointed to the cut on his face, as realisation dawned on him through his misery. Everyone seemed to stop and stare at the man's outburst.

Shocked by his outburst, Inspector Dyson told him to calm down and asked him to tell him exactly who had threatened him. Everyone listened as Mr Wilkinson recalled his encounter with a man who had offered security and threatened to come back later last night with his friends. Again, Inspector Dyson, hoping to clear up the case quickly, steered Mr Wilkinson towards where Adam stood, hoping for some kind of recognition, but there was none. Mr Wilkinson stared at Adam blankly and then back at the inspector. 'Ricky! That was his name, I remember now.'

Adam smiled to himself when he saw the light of recognition on the inspector's face. The penny had finally dropped. He could hear Inspector Dyson asking Mr Wilkinson to go down to the station and make a full statement of recent events. Clearly, Adam was off the hook.

Now, Adam thought to himself, was his chance to make himself known to Mr Wilkinson. Confidently, he strode over to where the inspector stood beside him. 'I believe you're the organiser of the festival. Adam Lambrianu, at your service.' With ease and charm, Adam held out his hand to shake Mr Wilkinson's. 'I own a club not far from here, and from one publican to another, I offer you my condolences on this tragedy. Why is it we only want to bring a little fun and laughter into people's lives yet get trodden down like this? What will you do now?' Adam asked.

Giving Adam a weak smile, Mr Wilkinson held out his hand and shook Adam's. 'Go home. What else can I do? Without a tent, there is no festival, is there? Your name is familiar; have we met?'

'As I say, I'm a club owner in the West End. People know of the club, rather than me.' Adam smiled modestly.

'Nonsense,' laughed the inspector. 'Every magazine in London has a photo of Adam here. The beloved playboy of Lambrianu's nightclub. You have a finger in every pie, don't you, Adam?' Inspector Dyson sneered.

'Ah, yes, I do recall I've seen photos of you and your club. Very high class. A far cry from this, eh?' said Mr Wilkinson.

Adam could see the annoyance on Inspector Dyson's face, realising that there was no case here. Now looking concerned, Adam leant forward and touched Mr Wilkinson's face.

'That's quite a cut, or razor mark, you have on your face, Mr Wilkinson. Did you get caught in the blast?' Adam knew he had just given the game away to Inspector Dyson and almost solved the case for him. Mr Wilkinson had claimed the man who had threatened him had been called Ricky, and now Adam had added the word razor for good measure. For Inspector Dyson, piecing the two together, the case was cut and dried. He knew who he was looking for now. 'Well, I must be going. Come down to the station, Mr Wilkinson, and make your statement as soon as possible please,' the inspector added and walked off towards his car.

'If there is anything I can help you with, Mr Wilkinson, please feel free to ask. Us publicans have to stick together. Don't be shy now.' Adam smiled and slowly walked away, almost dragging his feet.

'Thanks, but there's nothing anyone can do... unless you know someone with a tent,' Mr Wilkinson shouted towards Adam's back. Clenching his fists together, Adam almost punched the air. This was what he had come for.

Adam turned slowly and met Mr Wilkinson's eyes, before looking to the sky, as though deep in thought. Eventually, he spoke. 'I might, if I make a few calls. Have you tried anywhere yet?' Seeing him shake his head, Adam added, 'It wouldn't be cheap at short notice like this, but I will do my best. If you're successful, let me know. You know where to find me, but just in case.' Adam walked closer. 'Here is my card.' Shaking his hand once more, Adam walked away. For the first time since he had met him, Mr Wilkinson's eyes held hope. Hope of hosting another festival in another tent. And in the meantime, Adam thought to himself, the police would already be knocking at Ricky's door. 'A sprat and a mackerel.' Adam grinned to himself as he drove off laughing. Next, he decided, he would phone every company he knew and inform them that they didn't have a tent for loan, not even a bouncy castle.

Driving up to a pub in the north of London, Adam got out of his car and walked in. Knowing it was the Hillman brothers' headquarters, he breezed in and stopped by the corner booth where they were sat.

'Morning, gentlemen.' The shocked expression on their faces almost made Adam laugh. He liked the shock element. 'Adam? What brings you to this neck of the woods?' Dutch asked, once he had found his voice.

'No, no, no.' Adam smiled, wagging a finger in their faces. 'My friends call me Adam; my enemies, with a knife in my back, call me Mr Lambrianu. Mind if I take a seat?'

Frowning, Ethan cast a furtive glance at Dutch, then back at Adam. 'What's this about, Adam?' he asked, making a point of calling him by his name. 'There's no ill will between us, is there?'

Calmly, Adam adjusted his gold cufflinks and looked up at Ethan under his lashes. 'I don't know, Ethan. That's what I've come to find out. I don't tread on your toes; I always hand a job your way, if I'm too busy. And I never interfere in your businesses. But I'm sorry to say that isn't the case with you, is it? Sending

Ricky the Razor on your behalf, trying to extract money with menaces from the beer festival hosted in my part of London, and not a word to me. Is that what friends do?'

'Ricky!' Ethan spat, and banged his fist on the table. 'What's the sleazy prick been saying?' Ignoring his outburst, Adam looked towards Dutch and raised his eyebrows. 'Am I wrong, Dutch? It also appears that since your involvement, the beer tent has now been burnt to the ground. I guess you weren't paid enough.' Adam's steely blue eyes pierced Dutch, making him almost squirm in his seat.

Nodding, Dutch rubbed the back of his neck and looked down at the table. 'Adam... Mr Lambrianu,' he corrected himself. 'It sounds much worse than it is, I promise you. Ricky called us out of the blue with a tipoff about the beer festival. We haven't heard from him in ages. We asked if you were in on it and he emphatically told us you weren't interested, didn't he, Ethan?'

'Too bloody right he did. I hate that bastard,' Ethan muttered and picked up his mug of coffee he was nursing and took a sip. 'We were supposed to take a look last night, but when we arrived the whole place was on fire. We haven't heard from Ricky since.'

'And you never thought of picking up a phone and asking me yourself if I had any involvement in the festival, Ethan? As for the fire, well, I presumed it was yourselves and Ricky. I know for a fact they know that Ricky is involved with it, but the trail will lead here, to you two, won't it? Ricky won't go down without taking you both down with him...'

Adam could see their minds working overtime as he pointed out the obvious.

Ethan stood, raising his voice. 'We didn't fuck you over, Adam!' Ethan shouted. 'Is this why you've come? You want a fight, revenge, what?' Ethan's face was flushed with anger as he stood towering over Adam as he sat there calmly.

Adam's smooth, chilling voice stopped Ethan's rant. 'Quite the contrary, Ethan! I presumed I must have offended you! After all, why would you want to rip me off and burn my business venture to the ground? Am I missing something?'

Horrified at Adam's accusation, Dutch butted in. 'That wasn't us, Adam. I swear! We were supposed to go later and when we got there, it was already on fire! Ricky doesn't work for us. We paid him for the tipoff, that's the usual. He's set us up, hasn't he?'

Ethan waved the barman over. 'Is there a drought or something? Bring some drinks, you fucking idiot. Adam, I understand we should have called and checked with you first, but stupidly I took Ricky's word for it. But why would we burn the place down? If you didn't want it, then we could have made money out of it. What would be the point of us killing the place?'

'It was my understanding that Ricky had retired, and that you no longer employed him,' Adam drawled, while listening to them both profess their innocence. Of course he knew this, but he needed to make his point.

Carrying a tray, the barman brought three whiskies over and put them in front of the men. With his blood boiling and his face flushed, Ethan picked his up and gulped it back in one. 'That bastard will be wearing his balls for earrings when I get my hands on him. We've been idiots. There it is, Adam. I've appealed to your vanity and said it. What a pair of cunts we are!' Ethan laughed, then picked up Dutch's drink and wolfed that back as well. Smacking his lips together, he adjusted his glasses and squared up to Adam. 'So, what do you propose to do about it? What do you want from us?' he spat.

'Nothing,' Adam answered quietly. 'As I said, I just popped by to see why you had done this and how I could have possibly offended you both.' Adam looked at his watch. 'Now, it's time I was leaving. I'm glad we've cleared up this misunderstanding.'

The brothers looked at each other suspiciously as Adam stood to leave. Ethan looked down at Adam's full glass. 'You haven't had your drink, Adam. Gentlemen drink together; only enemies snub their host's hospitality.'

'Indeed, they do, Ethan; my apologies.' Adam smiled, and picking up his whisky, he downed it in one. 'As a goodwill gesture, I am also here to inform you that the police are already on to Ricky. They've already spoken to me, so I presume you will be next. Especially where your connections with Ricky are concerned. Good day, gentlemen.' Full of ease, Adam shook each of their hands in turn and walked away.

'I'll fucking sort this, Adam. Promise! Give me twenty-four hours. I'll torture that bastard,' Ethan shouted towards Adam's back as he left.

Angry and confused, and almost out of breath from shouting, Ethan turned towards his brother. 'Dutch, why doesn't he shout and have a good rant like the rest of us? It unnerves me that he's so calm and reserved all the time. Everyone knows that behind that charming smile and pretty face he's worse than all of us put together. He's the fucking devil incarnate, and I don't intend being on the wrong side of him. I'm going to send a couple of the boys out to find that ponce Ricky. He has set us up good and proper, but I don't intend being arrested for a fire I didn't start.'

Dutch rubbed the sweat from his brow with his sleeve. 'I know what you mean. It's creepy. He's so polite before putting a gun to your head. But I'm glad he came alone as a social call giving us a chance to explain. My bad, Ethan; you didn't want any of this. I took the call and agreed to see Ricky. I will sort it. Sorry, mate.'

Ethan gave a wry grin and held his hand up. 'High five, bro.'

3

A GOLDEN OPPORTUNITY

'Where the bloody hell have you been!' Scarlet shouted as Adam walked into the office.

'I've been to see Dutch and his brother Ethan. Just a bit of business, why? Have you missed me, Scarlet?' Adam smiled and, leaning over, he gave his sister a kiss on the cheek. 'And now I'm going to pop upstairs and see how Bruce is. I suppose I'd better help him have a shower and then I have a squash court booked in two hours.'

'Not so fast, Adam,' she warned, wagging her finger. 'You have a visitor. Some guy waiting for you in the other room. He's been here about an hour and looks like shit. What's going on?'

Frowning, Adam shut the office door. 'Anyone we know?' he whispered, trying to recall if he had overlooked a meeting.

Scarlet's blank look and shrug told him nothing. 'All he said was that you had met earlier and you had given him your card. When I asked if I could help, he said he would rather wait for you. I tried your mobile but it's switched off.'

'I didn't want any interruptions when I was in my meeting

with the brothers.' Checking himself in the mirror, Adam walked into the opposite room from the office, which was mainly used as a waiting room. Opening the door, he saw Mr Wilkinson sat there on one of the Chesterfield sofas.

On seeing him, Adam's face lit up. Walking forward, he held out his hand to shake Mr Wilkinson's. 'How very good to see you again. How are things? Do you want coffee or shall we have something stronger?'

'I'm fine, Mr Lambrianu, drowning in coffee. It's quite a place you have here, very swish. I'll come straight to the point, Mr Lambrianu, because I have to get back and sort things out. This morning, you said if I couldn't find a tent or something to carry on with the festival, you might be able to help. Is that still the case? Or was it empty words?'

Shocked by his bluntness, Adam realised just how desperate he was. 'Well, I've done some enquiring but nothing solid, because I didn't know your situation. But I think I can help. Is there a problem?'

'People are packing up, ready to move on. Some have just come out of the hospital for inhaling smoke and getting a few cuts and bruises. Nothing major, I add.' A grim smile crossed Mr Wilkinson's face. 'So can you do anything for me? There isn't anything to hire at such short notice in the whole of London.'

'There has been a circus in Essex I believe. Tonight is the last night, and they would let you loan their big tent for two weeks if needs be. The circus acts get a rest, and then time to renew their costumes and sets for the next leg of their tour. Would that suffice?'

'Really?!' Mr Wilkinson's eyes widened, and his jaw dropped. 'Oh my God, I don't believe it. Mr Lambrianu, you have saved my life. Some of the bar staff still haven't been paid, although the insurance will cover that,' he pondered. 'But yes, definitely yes, Mr Lambrianu.' His exuberance was overwhelming, and he hugged Adam tightly. At one point Adam thought he was going to kiss him!

'Wait, Mr Wilkinson, I haven't said how much it will cost yet. It's not cheap and, given the circumstances, they will want proper security on site. I'm sure you understand; this is their living, and they want to make sure they will have a tent to perform in once your two weeks are up, Mr Wilkinson.'

'Please, my name is Daniel. And I didn't expect it to be cheap, Mr Lambrianu. Go on, give me the bad news.'

Adam named an eye-watering price for the hire of the tent and saw Mr Wilkinson pale. 'We will use a reputable security firm that's well known and has been working in London for years to keep an eye on things. The security firm is Sinclair's.' Adam watched Daniel to see if there was any flicker of recognition, but there was none. The security firm in mention was Adam's father's old partner, Jake Sinclair's, mastermind. They hired ex-prisoners who couldn't get a job on the outside and who were grateful for the opportunity to get their lives back on track. It wasn't always above board, Adam mused to himself, but it had acquired a good name over the years and even though some of the DBS checks were dubious, taxes were paid, and the workers were loyal. Now, himself and Scarlet owned it, but Daniel Wilkinson wasn't to know that, Adam thought to himself.

Daniel let out a low whistle and sat down. 'That's a lot of money in one go, Mr Lambrianu. I think I will have that drink after all. Whisky, please.'

Turning, Adam walked over to a drinks cabinet. He hoped he hadn't been too greedy in his figure for hiring the tent. The circus people were taking a break anyway, and they would be grateful for the extra cash to use the tent when it would have just been packed up doing nothing. The security firm, or rather 'protection money', the circus paid Adam to keep everything in order would be halved for a month, if the deal could be struck soon. So Adam would make a handsome profit.

Handing Daniel his drink, Adam smiled broadly. 'Daniel, please call me Adam. I don't want to rush you, but the circus will want to know asap so that they can arrange for it to be sent over to you. I could even ask if some of their men could help put the tent up for you. Well, what's it to be?'

'Well, it's that or nothing, Adam, isn't it? The insurance will come through eventually, but I really need to make some more money, and fast. So, yes, Adam. My answer is yes. I still have the paperwork to say I can host an event in the park and God knows, I've paid to use the site. So my answer is a definite yes!' Daniel bellowed and chinked his glass against Adam's. 'Adam Lambrianu, my new best friend, I am eternally grateful.' Daniel grinned.

'To new friends, partners and new beginnings,' Adam toasted and sipped his whisky, while looking over the rim at Daniel's gleeful expression.

* * *

Adam walked into the office to find a scowling Scarlet. 'What's going on, Adam? You've been shifty these last few days. And who was that man? I've never seen him before.'

'Is that the reason you have a scowl on your face, because you don't know who that man was? Let me put your mind at rest. That was Daniel Wilkinson...'

Adam could see Scarlet was deep in concentration trying to recall the name, but that she had drawn a blank.

Sitting down in a relaxed fashion, Adam grinned. 'No wiser?

Then let me enlighten you. The beer festival in town and the fire?'

Suddenly, Scarlet's face lit up. 'Oh my God, yes!' Closing her laptop, she sat back and took a breath. 'Not the police then?' She smiled. 'No, now I do recall the name. It's been all over the news. Poor bastard; and all of those people out of pocket.' As she watched him, a frown appeared on her face. 'But why is he here talking to you? I thought they would be moving on by now? What's all this got to do with you?'

'Well, I – no, we – are helping him out. He couldn't get a tent to replace the burnt one and under normal circumstances he would have had to move on. That is, if it wasn't for those wonderful Lambrianus who are always on hand for a good cause. And this one will bring us loads of publicity! Daniel will praise us beyond belief!' Adam blew air on his fingernails and pretended to polish them on his sleeve while grinning like a Cheshire cat. 'I have managed to get a circus tent for him, at a very good profit for us.' He winked. 'And he's eternally grateful. I have also managed to install our own security men, whose wages he will pay. Another feather in our cap.' Adam felt very satisfied with himself when he saw Scarlet's jaw drop in surprise. 'My God, Adam, that will save us a fortune!' she exclaimed.

For a moment, Scarlet was silent as she digested what Adam had said. Meeting his eyes, she spied him suspiciously. 'Why do I get the feeling that there is more to this than meets the eye? But well done, unless this venture of yours comes back to bite us on the arse! You visit the Hillman brothers, Bruce is laid up, half beaten to death, and in the midst of all this you suddenly show me your ace hand. Come on, Adam, what's the bottom line?'

'That's the point, Scarlet; there is no bottom line. I've done my bit, the rest is profit margin.' Adam looked at his watch and sighed. 'Well, I've missed my time on the squash court, so I'll pop up and see Bruce.' Leaving Scarlet deep in thought, he left and went upstairs.

Quietly, Adam tiptoed through the apartment, expecting Bruce to be asleep. Slowly, he turned the door handle on his bedroom door, not wanting to disturb him.

'If that's you, Adam, then you can stop tip-toeing around. For God's sake, you might as well come in, God knows everyone else has!'

Shocked at the outburst, Adam opened the door widely and stood there in surprise at Bruce's appearance. 'My God, who got you ready? Surely Doreen hasn't done all of that?'

'Nope, Julie and Lewis, the butler-cum-chauffeur-cum-house-keeper and whatever else he manages for Julie.'

Sitting down on the edge of the bed, Adam threw his head back in laughter. 'Hence your clean-shaven look and red satin pyjamas.' Adam raised his eyebrows and pointed mockingly at Bruce's plaster cast. 'Matches your red satin sling. What the hell has been going on up here?' Adam laughed and slapped his knee. Leaning in closer, Adam breathed in Bruce's aftershave. 'And you smell gorgeous, Bruce!'

Bruce sat in silence, waiting for Adam to compose himself. 'I've already had to deal with Doreen and her friend Maggie, who is a carer in an old people's residential home. Apparently, if I need an incontinence pad changing or anything, she is quite used to it! For fuck's sake, Adam, I'm not incontinent. It's my arm in plaster, not my leg!' Disgruntled, Bruce carried on. 'Then Scarlet came up and, as you predicted, brought grapes and ate them herself! Julie then phoned her for a gossip and your gobby sister told her I was here, laid up and incapacitated.'

With each sentence Adam laughed louder. Tears rolled down his face as he listened to Bruce. 'That woman, Adam, she must have a bloody helicopter. She was round here in a jiffy, with that

Lewis. Don't get me wrong, I like the guy, but not when he is giving me a bed bath and washing my hair with a basin laid under the back of my neck. Julie nearly drowned me with her jugs of water as he held the basin steady. Then came the pièce de résistance, Julie's shopping bag. God knows when she found the time to shop, unless these belong to Lewis.' Bruce looked down at his red satin pyjamas and shook his head. 'What do I look like?'

'Father Christmas?' Adam laughed. 'Without the beard.' Adam cocked his head from side to side. 'Clean shaven suits you. I am so sorry I missed all of this, and you went through it alone. I could have dined out on it for years!'

'Oh, by the way, one more thing.' Bruce struggled to remove his arm from the sling. 'Julie signed it.' A smile crossed his face. 'She lathered on ten layers of red glossy lipstick and then put her lips to my white cast. There is her lip print, and she signed her name.' Bruce laughed. Adam peered more closely at the red cupid bow emblazoned on Bruce's arm and then back up at Bruce, and the pair of them burst out laughing.

* * *

'Ricky, you're a hard man to get hold of. Have you moved?' Ethan had the loudspeaker on his mobile so that Dutch could hear.

'Kind of, Ethan, er, it was time to move on. Why have you been to my old flat?'

'Yes, was passing by, thought I would pop in to see you. You've been rather quiet.'

Ricky paused a moment before answering Ethan, wondering what they knew. 'Well, after our last meeting, Ethan, you're the last person I would expect to make a social call on me.'

Ricky recalled the police banging on his door late last night and their last threat before he quickly packed his bag and left without a backward glance. He had nothing precious to leave behind, so what did it matter? 'We'll be back, Ricky, and next time we'll have a warrant. So don't leave town,' they had shouted through the letter box.

'I saw your wife yesterday, she seems very well. But she didn't speak too well about you. It seems you've fallen on harder times than Dutch and I realised.'

'I don't expect she was too pleasant. Did she tell you she ripped me off over the house – the bitch!' Ricky snarled down the phone, almost forgetting himself.

Dutch pretended to play an air violin while listening to Ricky's hard luck story, while Ethan made a face of disgust. But this was part of Ethan's plan. He wanted Ricky to feel at ease and walk into their trap. Ethan gave a hollow laugh. 'She didn't go into detail, it was just a chance meeting, you know what I mean. Anyway, why don't you pop in for a drink if you're at a loose end?'

Unsure of the niceness in Ethan's voice, Ricky thought maybe this was the olive branch that he had been hoping for. Maybe his tipoff had actually made Ethan think twice about him, and with Dutch's encouragement, he was now ready to trust him again. 'I'd like that, later on this afternoon perhaps, if you're not too busy?' he asked.

'This afternoon would be just fine. I'll see you later.' Ethan ended the call and looked at Dutch. 'I am going to torture that bastard within an inch of his life for bringing Adam Lambrianu to our door. We don't need that kind of visitor or trouble, Dutch.'

Dutch shook his head and sat back in his seat. 'If he's left his digs, it means he probably hasn't paid his rent. It also means people are used to him disappearing into thin air. That's good for us, but bad for him. When you went to visit his wife, she didn't have a good word to say about him. She even handed over his address without a second thought of why we were looking for him. She would never have done that in the old days without tipping him off. I get the feeling she hates him more than we do! Half of me could feel sorry for him; he was a good worker once and earnt a lot of money.'

'You're just soft and reasonable. Sometimes I wonder if we are even related. He might have been a good worker once, but now he's just some saddo, bringing shit to our doorstep.' Adjusting his horn-rimmed glasses, and running his hand through his wild dark hair, Ethan shrugged. 'Once he started sniffing it up his nose, he just got worse and worse. He was a loose cannon, and always as high as a kite, but, well, I did wonder if his wife would let him move in again. They've known each other for years and been through a lot. Wives are funny like that; they have a conscience.'

'Mine doesn't!' Dutch burst out laughing. 'When it comes to wives, I'd rather face that psycho Adam Lambrianu than mine when she is pissed off.'

'Too bloody right, Dutch. Not the forgiving sort, is she? Do you remember when she sold your motorbike when you were at work? You'd only had it two weeks, and she called you menopausal!'

A wry grin passed over Dutch's face. 'Yes, she accused me of knocking off that blonde barmaid with the big tits.'

Ethan gave Dutch a knowing look and grinned. 'Well, you were, weren't you!'

'Well, yes, but to sell my bloody motorbike! Now that's a capital punishment.' He laughed. 'I've got stuff to sort out, I will see you back here at 3 p.m.'

* * *

'Come on, Scarlet, let's show a united front. There has been a massive clean-up of the park and the new tent is being put up today. I sent some of the lads from the security firm to help out and introduce themselves. And some anonymous caller has tipped off the local news about the story – a phoenix rising from the ashes. I like that, don't you?' Adam laughed.

Tutting and rolling her eyes, Scarlet screwed her lips up in dismay. 'Did you think of that all by yourself, Adam?' Scarlet scoffed. 'Anonymous my arse. Why do you need me, Adam? This is your baby.'

'No, Scarlet, this is the bountiful Lambrianus, so we need to show a united front, and that means you. So put on your lippy and a splash of something and let's go and celebrate Daniel Wilkinson's victory.' Standing in front of Scarlet's desk with his arms folded, Adam grinned. 'Well, go on then,' he urged, 'get on with it. Where's Knuckles?'

'Guarding the counting room. It was collection-day-cum-payday while you were out enjoying yourself with circus tents and benevolence. He's sat in the counting room while the machines and cashiers add it all up and check it. I don't know if he can count, but he's such a good thief he would know damn well if one penny was missing. Anyway, the last thing you want after all of this hard work is a photo of Knuckles on the news. They would have to show it after 9 p.m. so it didn't frighten the kids!'

Taking her coat off the hanger, Adam held it up for her and slipped it over her shoulders. 'If you feel like that, why are you marrying him?'

Standing with her back to him, Scarlet slipped her arms through her coat and took her lipstick out of her pocket. Walking over to the mirror on the wall, she saw Adam staring at her in the mirror, behind her. 'Because he knows me, Adam. He knows who

I am and what I am. I never have to explain myself or apologise. He understands me more than I do myself, which is a good basis for a marriage, so take notes.'

Adam opened the door for her. 'Well, he knows me too, but I don't intend sharing a bed with him.'

Prodding him in the chest, she winked at him. 'For your information, Adam, neither do I. That is, unless I want to.' She smiled seductively and led the way to the car.

4

RAZOR'S EDGE

Ricky, like clockwork, stood outside the pub. Usually around 3 p.m. it started to get quieter, and Dutch and Ethan had always turned up around that time to sort out unfinished business. Looking at the familiar peeling red paint on the woodwork and the old sign hanging above the door, hardly recognisable because of age and weather, gave Ricky hope. In the old days he had taken this place for granted, but now it seemed like a haven. If he played his cards right, he would be back on the payroll, and his life would change for the better.

Pushing the brass handle, he walked inside and saw some old faces that he had once worked with sat at the bar having a drink. He greeted them and shook hands, feeling as though he was a member of the gang again. 'How's it going, fellas?' He grinned and worked his way up the bar towards the corner booth, where he spotted Ethan and Dutch.

Dutch was sat at the back of the booth while Ethan sat at the side of it and gave him the nod to sit down. 'Billy, bring a drink over for Ricky, will you?' Feeling very pleased with himself, Ricky rubbed his hands together as the whisky was placed in front of him.

Ethan cast a sideways glance at him before speaking. 'We had a visitor today, Ricky, looking for you. Two, in fact, because the police always come in pairs don't, they?'

Ricky's eyes widened at the mention of the police. 'The police? Here? Why would they come here?' Nervously, he picked up his drink and sipped it.

'Because they know we were once associated, and before you burnt down that tent you implied to the owner that you had friends in the protection racket that he owed money to. People like us. People who could guarantee security of his venue.'

A cold chill ran down Ricky's spine. 'I swear I never torched that place.' Holding his hands up in submission, he shook his head. 'I swear to you Ethan, Dutch, that had nothing to do with me!' His voice rose out of nervousness, but came out almost squeakily, as his throat dried. Reaching for his drink to moisten it, he again repeated his innocence.

'But is it right that you threatened this man who has now made a full statement to the police? You gave this man your name, for fuck's sake! Is your brain so addled, you gave him so much information with so little in return? Then we had another visitor, this time not as nice as the police.'

Ricky felt rooted to the spot. He wanted to run, but his legs felt like lead. Casting a quick glance over his shoulder, he saw the other men that worked for Ethan and felt his stomach somersault. Trapped! He'd been on the other side of this situation in the past and been the onlooker as the brothers had interrogated some poor bastard sitting where he was now. Squirming with fear, Ricky felt a bead of sweat on his brow. He loosened his tie and ran his finger along the collar.

Ethan's eyes narrowed, his face set in a snarl. 'You swore Adam Lambrianu wanted nothing to do with that festival. You set us up, you weasel, and sent that psychotic bastard to our door. We have peace; they leave us alone and that's just fine, but you go upsetting him in our name!' Ethan could control his temper no more, and banged his fist on the table as Dutch looked on calmly. Ethan's face was flushed, and spit squirted out of his mouth as he shouted angrily. 'You bastard, Ricky. Have you no common sense or is your brain so addled with white powder you can't think straight?' With one swoop of his arm, Ethan cleared the table of the drinks, sending the glasses crashing onto the floor.

Out of panic, Ricky stood up and wildly looked towards the door. He decided to make a run for it, but saw that the bolt had been put across the top of the door without him noticing or hearing it. Then someone put a sack over his head while he struggled, kicking and lashing out like a madman fighting for his life. Next he felt someone grab hold of his arms and tie them together. The pain seared through him as the plastic cable tie on his wrists tightened, almost stopping the blood flow.

A bolt of pain shot through him, making him fall to his knees, as he felt the hefty kick in his balls. Writhing on the floor in pain, he could hear laughter, the darkness of the hood disorientated him, and he felt like he was suffocating. He couldn't breathe! He prayed to God that he would pass out and soon it would be over. Feeling himself being dragged to his feet, he felt fresh air through his hood and gulped as much in as possible to fill his lungs. They were obviously now outside, he thought to himself, and tried shouting out and kicking out with legs, until he felt himself being raised and shoved into something. Darkness engulfed him again and he heard the slam of a car boot shut. Gripped with terror, and not knowing what was going to happen to him, he felt his heart pounding so loudly in his ears, he thought his head would burst. Frantically, he tried concentrating on counting, to control his breathing to save oxygen as the car drove off. Cramped in the back, his legs ached, and something sharp was pressing into his back, making him wince in pain. Suddenly, he felt the car stop and the boot being lifted open, letting some form of light into the sacking, which almost blinded him. All he could hear was muffled voices as he was dragged, staggering along into No Man's Land. A cold chill engulfed him, and he shivered slightly. Suddenly, he heard Ethan's loud command. 'Strip him.'

Held fast, Ricky's belt was unbuckled and his trousers were undone, and they dropped down. Shouting out, he felt someone grab hold of his head and grab the hood, pushing a large piece of it in his mouth. 'Shut the fuck up, Ricky.' He heard a voice rasp in his ear, but wasn't sure who it was. Feeling his arms raised in the air above his head, he felt himself being hoisted up high until he dangled in the air, like a puppet on a string. Icy wind gripped him, and he shivered again. Tears rolled down his face. He knew this was serious and wondered about his fate.

Feeling someone grasp his genitals and tie something around them, he kicked his legs in the air to stop them, and then suddenly a bolt of pain ripped through him, making him scream out as his body jolted and bounced in the air uncontrollably. Wracked with pain, he felt another searing jolt, like a hundred knives cut through him, and then it stopped. Weakened and shaking, he thought his head would explode. The hood was ripped off and, blinking, he realised he was in an abattoir, hanging between long sides of beef on meat hooks. Looking down, he saw Ethan and four others with a car battery, and the wires attached to his genitals. 'Do you really think I would let you pass out so quickly! Not a fucking chance, Ricky. Get your breath back and we'll begin again,' Ethan spat out.

Foam almost bubbled from his mouth as he cried and begged for mercy. Ethan nodded at one of his men. 'Again,' he commanded. Once more, Ricky's body bounced in the air as an electric shock shot through him. The scream of terror echoed through the abattoir, making the others laugh. 'Go on, Ricky, dance,' they mocked.

'Make the call, Dutch.' Ethan nodded. 'Let's keep this bastard alive for now and have some fun.'

Adam's phone burst into life while at the park. Looking at the text, he saw it was from Dutch. Opening the message, he saw it was an address and his gut instinct told him it was urgent, and that he needed to leave. 'Scarlet, something's come up. I'll be about an hour. Don't ask, just cover for me, okay?'

'Are you okay, do you need back up?' Scarlet asked with a look of concern on her face.

'No. I just have to go *now*. I'll keep in contact, just keep this lot busy until I get back.' Almost running to the car, he got in and drove off. Looking at the address again, he saw that it was a huge abattoir in the east end of London. The traffic was nose to nose, and so quickly he drove to the club and swapped his car for his motorbike. This way he could dodge his way through this bumper-to-bumper London traffic.

Parking up his bike outside of the building, he looked at the metal shutters pulled down. He took out his mobile and messaged Dutch.

I'm here, where are you?

Adam's ire was rising; had he raced across London on some wild goose chase? A noise stopped him revving up the engine and he saw one of the shutters being raised. Dutch waved him in and Adam decided, possibly foolishly, to follow him in.

'We both wanted you here, Adam. We are men of our words.' Walking deeper into the abattoir, Adam squirmed at the blood on the floor and looked down at his shoes with distaste. He saw a hosepipe running with water, trying to clear the clogged-up drains at the side of the huge, thick wooden chopping blocks, hosting large sides of beef. It made him even more curious as to why he had been brought here. The smell of the dead meat filled his nostrils, and he pinched his nose slightly, but he walked on behind Dutch past huge carcasses. Then, he saw lights and heard laughter. Walking closer, Dutch stood aside. 'We haven't killed him yet; we wanted you to witness it, as a show of goodwill between us.'

Raising his eyes, Adam saw a woeful Ricky hanging in the air on a meat hook. He saw the car battery wires attached to his genitals and, satisfied, he moved closer to sit beside Ethan. Reaching out his hand to shake his, he nodded. 'Is his razor in his trouser pocket as always?' Adam asked calmly. Ethan stared at him and ordered one of his men to search Ricky's pockets. Ethan cast a furtive glance at Dutch and looked away.

Holding the razor in his hand, Adam walked closer to Ricky, who was now screaming loudly. The very sight of Adam chilled his bones with fear. Dutch and Ethan would have got bored sooner or later, but, not Adam Lambrianu. Seeing him, Ricky knew his fate was sealed. His arms were numb and had lost all feeling, and his body felt as though it was on fire, but seeing Adam walking towards him calmly with his own razor in hand silenced him. Urine ran down his leg as he watched, almost hypnotised by the blade flashing in the lights.

'Chair,' Adam ordered. Quickly, someone scrambled to get Adam a chair. The laughter died and an eerie silence took over as Adam stood on the chair. 'You know, gentlemen, in China, treason such as this was rewarded by a death of a thousand cuts,' he announced, making them all frown, not knowing what was coming. 'This is treason and betrayal.' Adam reached out and slashed Ricky across the chest. A huge gash appeared, and blood poured down Ricky's body, dripping down his leg onto his toes. Ricky screamed out, but Adam slashed at him again and again over his body and legs.

'You like using the razor, Ricky? Isn't that what you're known as?' Adam asked calmly. 'Well, this ending seems only fitting, don't you think?' Ricky's blood-soaked body hung aimlessly in the air, making the other men squirm at the sight of him. As horrified as they were, they couldn't take their eyes away, mesmerised by the gory sight. One man walked to a corner and threw up in one of the drains. Hearing him, Adam turned and laughed. 'You, my man' – he pointed with his blood-soaked hand – 'are definitely in the wrong job!' he scoffed.

'Do you have a grave prepared?' Adam asked Ethan. Raising his gaze from the floor, Ethan met Adam's eyes and nodded. 'Well, in that case let's wash him down, or shall we cut his balls off first?' Adam grinned menacingly. Mentally, he knew he was making his point to Ethan and Dutch should they ever cross him again. He felt actions spoke louder than words. 'No, let him die with his jewels in place. Never touch a man's jewels, eh?' Adam laughed.

There seemed to be a sigh of relief in the room as someone passed a hosepipe running with water to Adam, who got down from his chair and pointed it at Ricky, rinsing the blood away from the hanging flesh on his body. They could all see that Ricky was almost dead, and yet, Adam still didn't stop squirting the hose at him until he took his last breath. Rinsing his own hands, and looking down at his blood-stained jacket, Adam tutted. 'Bloody expensive suit this. Never mind.' Letting the hose drop to the ground and kicking it out of the way, Adam wiped his hands on the bottom of his jacket and took it off. There were splashes of blood on his shirt, but not much. Standing before Ricky, Adam looked at Ricky's lacerated corpse hanging in the air like the sides of beef beside him. Satisfied, he walked up to Ethan and held out his damp hand, making Ethan squirm as looked at it. Slowly Ethan held out his own hand. 'Always nice doing business with gentlemen, Ethan. You kept your word. I like that.'

Limply, Ethan shook Adam's hand. 'Are we square now, Adam? No repercussions?' he asked.

'Absolutely not. We're square. Dutch.' Walking forward, Adam shook his hand, too. 'Make sure he's buried in a secure place and clean this place up before you leave, including your car battery, unless you want to charge him up and breathe life back into him. Oh, and show me your mobile.' Dutch's brows crossed, not quite understanding what Adam wanted. Taking out his mobile, he looked at Adam oddly. Adam scrolled through his messages and found the one to himself containing the address of the abattoir and deleted it. 'I was never here.'

Dutch stood, hands in pockets, rubbing Adam's damp handshake off his own, and watched Adam methodically go through things, making sure he couldn't be placed at the scene. Dutch was eager to get rid of him. They had already decided where to bury Ricky and he just wanted to get on with it. This whole business had sickened him.

A broad smile crossed Adam's face. Turning to the onlookers, Adam picked one out. 'You, what's your name?' Adam asked one of the men sat beside Ethan. 'Get him down from these hooks.'

'Billy, sir, erm, Mr Lambrianu.' Standing up, Billy pressed a button on one of the posts and Ricky was lowered to the ground. Spying huge rolls of plastic wrapping, Adam nodded. 'Now, Billy, bring me over one of those big sheets of plastic and let's wrap this poor man up.' He smiled.

Billy unravelled plastic sheeting, almost the size of a carpet, and with help from the others, laid it on the wet concrete floor, all the while glancing up at Adam's face to make sure they were doing as he commanded. They had all seen a taste of his sadistic ways and didn't want to be on the end of it. Between them they lifted Ricky's body on to the plastic and rolled him up in it.

Satisfied, Adam looked around. Ricky was dead and firmly wrapped in plastic like a Swiss roll. He felt his work was done. 'I would help you more, gentlemen, but I'm on my motorbike and there is no room for a body,' he apologised.

Clearing his throat, Ethan spoke up. 'We've got the van outside, Adam. We'll sort it.'

Smiling sweetly, Adam nodded his head and looked at his watch, Scarlet fleetingly crossed his mind. 'I have to go, fellas. Nice doing business with you,' he shouted and heard the sigh of relief as he left.

On the way out, Adam took out any personal possessions from his jacket pocket and put them in his trousers, before rolling up the blood-stained jacket and swapping it for his leather jacket from the box on the back of his motorbike. Riding through London, he spotted a bunch of homeless people gathered around a fire they had made in an old oil drum. It was a regular occurrence in this part of town. Slowing down, he stopped beside the group. Taking out his bloodied jacket, he threw it onto the burning embers, making sure it caught fire. Then he reached for his wallet and took out a handful of notes and handed them over. 'Buy some food for everyone.'

Then he raced towards the West End, stopping by his flat first to change into a suit similar to the one he had worn earlier. Looking into Bruce's bedroom, he saw that Bruce wasn't there and shouted towards the bathroom only to be met with silence. Panicking for a moment, he looked at his watch. Scarlet would have his guts for garters if he was any longer, and he ran to his car through the back entrance and made his way back to Hyde Park.

Ringing the club on the way, he arranged for drinks and champagne to be taken to the park immediately. By the time he arrived, the circus tent was already up and he was shocked to notice how much larger it was than the previous tent. It was drawing quite a crowd of onlookers as they stared at it in awe.

Spotting Scarlet, he quickly ran across the park to stand beside her. 'Where the hell have you been?' she muttered under her breath. 'One hour you said, that was nearly three hours ago!'

'Anyone miss me?' he panted, almost out of breath. Adam clapped his hands to get people's attention, making his presence known. Seeing one of his own vans with the Lambrianu logo splashed across the side, he walked towards it. 'We couldn't let this moment go without a proper toast. Let the champagne flow!' he shouted. 'Including them!' He pointed, laughing and joking with the photographers and journalists standing by. People were holding up their mobile phones and taking photos of the huge crowd surrounding the even bigger circus tent, and Adam made sure he was in most of the photos. It had been a big story, and everyone wanted to see a happy ending. Most of all Adam. Being here was his rock-solid alibi. As he pulled Daniel and Scarlet beside him, they posed for the photographers.

'Any idea where Bruce is? He isn't at the flat,' Adam whispered to Scarlet as everyone drank and ate their way through the food they had brought earlier. The sun was shining, and everyone had found a place to sit in the park and have a picnic.

'Oh yes, he called earlier. Julie has kidnapped him and taken him out for the day. With his face the colour of a rainbow, I'm surprised he wanted to go anywhere,' she snapped. 'I still haven't heard from Katie. I hope she's okay. We can't do anything until we hear from her but it's the waiting around I hate.' Holding her glass in the air and smiling broadly, she sipped her champagne.

Relieved that Bruce was safe, or maybe not, now that he was in Julie's care, Adam breathed a sigh of relief. 'Do you think Bruce really had a choice? Julie just bulldozes her way in and takes over. In my experience over the years, I've found that submission is the easiest way to get her off your back. As for Katie, we'll hear soon.' Raising his eyebrows, he looked her in the eyes. 'Are you so desperate to face the bullet, Scarlet? Let's enjoy ourselves for now and enjoy the sunshine.'

Standing around for a little longer, they both watched as wooden benches and chairs were carried into the tent. Everyone lent a helping hand in payment for their free drink and food, and it had obviously gone viral on the internet as more people seemed to turn up out of the blue. Walking over to Daniel, Adam slapped him playfully on the back. 'Happy, mate?' Seeing the broad grin on his face, Adam nodded. 'Well, once you're sorted, come over to my office and settle the bill, eh? We don't want trapeze artists flying through the air taking their tent back now, do we?'

'I will, Adam. Can we call it a couple more hours? I just want to oversee things and allot spaces to the beer holders. We should be up and running soon enough.'

'That's fine, Daniel, take your time. Just as long as you don't forget.' Adam's warning was friendly, but threatening enough to make his point. 'We're leaving now, but enjoy your day. Bye, everyone! Thanks for all your help and enjoy the champagne!' Adam shouted loudly, and a big cheer rose from the crowd and loud applause followed as Adam steered Scarlet towards the car.

'Fucking champagne for those free loaders,' she moaned. 'Are you bonkers?'

'It's cheap fizzy shit, Scarlet, with a couple of bottles of the real stuff for the reporters. Publicity like this would cost a fortune, and we've got it for a few sandwiches and some fizzy pop.'

'Mmm, well, don't trip over your ego as you get into the car,' she snapped. Looking over at the crowd, she had to agree with him. Everyone was chatting and taking photos, and with each conversation she could hear their name being mentioned. Adam was right, she thought. This publicity was for free, but she would be damned if she'd admit it to him.

5

A CHANGE MEETING

Rushing upstairs, Adam was desperate for a shower; he could still smell the stench of the abattoir on him. As the hot water ran down his hair and body, he noticed diluted blood floating down the drain. Feeling the back of his hair, he realised it was sticky and partially clotted together. Shocked for a moment, he realised some of Ricky's blood must have got onto his hair. He should have worn his motorbike helmet with its visor down, he thought to himself, but no one seemed to notice because no one commented, especially Scarlet, who would have been the first person to do so. Pouring shampoo on his hair and scrubbing at it, he thanked God that he didn't have his father's blonde hair. That would surely have given the game away.

Scrubbing at his body and letting the clear water wash away the day, he began to feel better and relaxed. Walking out of the steamy bathroom, a towel around his waist and rubbing his hair dry, Adam stopped as he heard a noise. 'That you, Bruce?' Walking into the lounge, he was shocked to see a beautiful young woman standing before him. She was wearing a black skirt suit, and her long black hair, parted in the middle, hung in a ponytail down her back, almost touching her waist. Her simple white shirt illuminated her tanned face and simple make-up. For a moment, Adam was stopped in his tracks, almost mesmerised. 'Who are you?' he asked.

'I thought I heard you shout for me to come in,' she answered nervously. 'I'm Poppy, Poppy Nightingale.' The young woman continued. 'Your sister, Miss Lambrianu, said she was busy and told me to follow the backstairs to your apartment and to give you this,' she said, holding out an A4 brown envelope. Nervously, her large brown eyes caught Adam's blue ones as they stood staring at each other. Swallowing hard, she did her best to avert her gaze from his masculine torso, which was still damp from the shower, but couldn't help glancing at this Adonis before her. His muscled, tanned body and slightly hairy chest betrayed the boyish face and showed the alpha male he clearly was. Admiring him and blushing slightly, she waited for him to take the envelope from her. Adam held out his hand to take the envelope, but his towel dropped as he did so. Quickly, he bent to scoop it up and held it in front of him, but it was too late; she had seen all of his nakedness.

Blushing slightly, Poppy couldn't help but admire his bigger-than-average manhood. 'What is it?' Adam asked, trying to sound professional.

'It's my CV. Miss Lambrianu had to go out and she said I should give it to you to look over. She's already read it. Sorry if it's inconvenient. I, I do apologise, Mr Lambrianu.' Looking down at the glass coffee table, she placed the envelope on it and smiled at him shyly. 'I'd better go, so you can... well, you know.' She grinned nervously.

Sensing her embarrassment, Adam ran his hand through his damp hair. 'Look, do you want to give me a minute to make myself look respectable and then you can tell me something about yourself and why you've given me your CV if my sister has already read it?'

Poppy was desperate to leave for fear of betraying herself. Adam was beautiful and even more handsome than she remembered. Seeing no flicker of remembrance in his eyes as he looked at her, Poppy felt slightly embarrassed. Years ago she had worked at the club as a waitress while at college. She had been smitten by Adam, the young darling of the Lambrianu nightclub, surrounded by adoring females, of whom he could take his pick, and he usually did if she remembered rightly. Their close encounter had happened one drunken night on Adam's birthday when he had crept into one of the corner VIP booths at the far end of the club, away from the crowds and well-wishers.

Poppy's mind wandered back to when she had been clearing the tables in the booth and had stumbled across Adam. They had talked and put the world to rights for a while, and then one thing had led to another and they'd had sex right there in the booth! Afterwards, when she'd realised she had just been some drunken one-night stand that Adam didn't remember, she had left the club. Looking at him now, she would never have believed he could have grown even more handsome than he had been over the years.

Gone was the young man permanently surrounding himself with beautiful women in the club. In his stead was the mature man, more confident than ever. Her mouth felt dry, and she ran her tongue over her lips nervously. 'No, I'll just leave it here for you to take the time to read it.' She turned on her heels and walked down the hallway and left.

For a moment, Adam stood there almost rooted to the spot, then he picked up the envelope and ripped it open. It was indeed a CV, but he didn't know what job she was applying for. Sitting down on the leather sofa, with his towel firmly wrapped around his waist, he read the contents with interest. It made good reading; she had qualifications and had spent the last two years working as a travel rep in Spain. She was fluent in a few languages, but again Adam was confused. Mentally, he wondered if she wanted a job as one of the strippers in the club, but dismissed the idea. Whatever she was applying for, Scarlet had failed to mention it to him. Going into his bedroom and drying himself properly, he caught sight of his naked body in the mirrored wardrobes and smiled. Why he had fought so hard to hide his nakedness bemused him. Poppy had seen the very best of him, and his vanity made him flex his muscles even more as he laughed to himself.

Properly dressed in his grey suit, white shirt and tie, he poured a coffee and sat back on the sofa for a moment. It had been a hectic day, and he just wanted five minutes to himself to collect his thoughts. Switching on the news highlights, he saw photos of himself from the event in Hyde Park earlier. Scrutinising the images carefully, Adam looked to see if his hair looked clotted with blood. But luckily nothing was visible. Switching off the television, he let out a huge sigh; his eyelids felt heavy, but he had to show his face to Scarlet. He knew she would be livid because of his disappearing act earlier, but he was curious about the job application and the mysterious woman. Going downstairs towards the office, he could hear chatter and even some laughter coming from Scarlet's office. Popping his head around the door, he saw Julie, Bruce, Scarlet and Knuckles.

'Well, quite a party we have here. Am I welcome?' Adam flashed a smile, showing a perfect set of white teeth and setting off the dimple in his chin. He was secretly thankful for the distraction as otherwise Scarlet would have been sat there waiting for him, like a lion about to pounce on its prey.

'Would it matter if you weren't?' Julie asked and let out her usual cackle. Walking towards her, Adam gave her a peck on the cheek. 'I see you've been keeping an eye on Bruce for me.'

'Well, somebody has to if his friends are anything to go by. Where have you been, apart from posing in front of the cameras? I've seen you, and so has the rest of the world. The worst part is, I'm so bloody old I've seen it all before. Christ, you're your father incarnate.'

Adam smiled and winked at Bruce. 'Well, I knew you would do a better job than me, Julie. Look at him, you've transformed him, even though his face looks like it's been run over by a steam train.'

'Thanks for that, Adam... I'm trying not to look in a mirror,' Bruce muttered.

Standing before Scarlet, Adam tutted. 'Anyway, Scarlet, since when did you become my pimp?' The room went quiet, and everyone turned to Scarlet, who looked at Adam questioningly. 'Since when did you get into the habit of sending women to my apartment? I've no problems in that department, but the very least you could have done was warn me.' He smiled. 'Nice present though. Although she saw more of me than I did of her since I had just stepped out of the shower.'

Making a face that could turn a person to stone, Scarlet nodded. 'Well, if you paid attention when I spoke, you would know why. Didn't you read my text? She's to be your PA, secretary, gopher, that kind of thing. What did you think of her?' she asked, almost too matter-of-fact. 'Oh God, you didn't seduce her or anything, did you? Please tell me you kept it in your pants, because this is strictly professional!' she warned, wagging her finger at him. 'I'd promised her an appointment, but I got held up with you and that circus farce, and then I was late for my next appointment. Was everything okay?'

'Since when did I need a PA? I'm quite capable of sorting

myself out, and you're always on my back reminding me of what I need to do. But, well, I've read the CV she brought, but do we need a holiday rep?' Taking out his mobile, Adam saw there was one unread message from Scarlet he hadn't noticed before.

'Don't be silly, but a bilingual secretary will come in very handy, and you need an assistant. So, what did you think?'

'PAs are nosy, and I like my privacy. And anyway' – Adam grinned – 'I'm more curious to know what she thought of me. I'm a good catch, I'm handsome, and I have an enormous...' Pausing slightly to make an impact, he winked at the others. '...personality that I like to share.'

'Mmm, that's what bothers me. You like to share your person-ality way too much.' Raising her eyebrows to make a point, she peered at him. 'Maybe I should look for someone older. Keep that libido of yours in check. Anyway, you know Poppy; she used to waitress here when she was at college. I am surprised you don't remember her, or were you too busy bedding your starlets to notice!'

Shaking his head, he made a face. 'No bossy old ladies, Scar-let, I've got enough of them in my life already.' He laughed.

Annoyed at his remark, Scarlet looked around, addressing the others, almost holding court. 'Well, the greatest showman here, Mr Barnum, and his circus need taking in hand by someone immune to his charming smile and boyish ways.' She nodded to herself, watching Adam squirm.

'Okay, Scarlet, you win. Let me meet her again, and we'll go through the details. Hands off, I promise.'

'Good, I like to win. Now, while you're here, we're organising the weekend. Sunday lunch, at the house in Southend. It needs opening up and redecorating a little. But I want to carry on Mum and Dad's tradition. All of the family gathered around the table, eating, laughing, and sharing our jokes with each other. No work talk, just family; that includes you, Bruce. I've spoken to Bobby and Jack, and they are up for it. So, keep your diary clear for Sunday.'

'See what I mean, Julie? Why do I need an assistant when Scarlet has just organised my diary? Come on, Bruce, let me get you a drink and then you can tell me all about your day. God knows, I bet it's more interesting than mine.'

Watching them both leave, Julie turned towards Knuckles. 'Would you mind giving me and Scarlet a moment?' she asked seriously, which both Scarlet and Knuckles found unusual. Normally, she would have had some sarcastic remark following her request, but not this time. Nodding to Scarlet, Knuckles left.

'What is it, Julie? Have you heard from Katie? What's the problem?'

Stern-faced, Julie stared at her. 'You're having dinner at the Southend house? Is that what you call the family home now? The warm, loving home that your mother and father brought you up in, invited anyone in with a warm welcome and a meal? That home was held together by love. And you're so high and mighty, you didn't even see the wince on Adam's face when you referred to it as the Southend house. That house, as you call it, has the only real memories he has of his father laughing and teasing him around that very table. He looked on as his mother died there, and part of us all died that day. I decorated that house many years ago for your mother, and now I'm going to go there and see what rack and ruin you have left it in. Please don't refer to it like that again; well, not in front of me. Some of my fondest memories are in that "Southend house" as you call it. It's your childhood home, and a very happy childhood you had too. And as for Katie, stop harping on about it. She's biding her time and will be in touch. I've heard from her; she didn't want to bother you. There! Now you know,' Julie answered triumphantly. 'She will be in touch when the time is right, Scarlet. The world doesn't revolve around you.' Julie shook her head as she gathered her belongings.

Scarlet's face burned to the roots with embarrassment and shame. She was humbled; it had been years since she'd been lectured like that, and Julie's stern voice and stony look made her feel like a child again.

Scarlet's mouth felt dry as she tried to find the words to excuse herself. Finally, she spoke. 'I only called it that because I didn't want people to think they were coming to *my* house, Julie. I'm sorry. And no, I didn't see Adam's face, but I see your point.' Adam had left the office abruptly, which wasn't like him. He'd usually have some sarcastic last word, but he had used Bruce as an excuse and left. Tears brimmed on her lashes, and she sniffed hard to fight them back. 'I'm sorry, Julie, sometimes I can't see what's in front of me because I've got my head stuck up my own arse. Truly, I'm sorry. We'll both do the house... erm, my home together. What do you say?' she asked hopefully. 'When the time is right, eh?'

'No. I will do the house,' Julie snapped. 'Your taste is too bland. Just one more thing. Don't think just because you're organising this that you will sit at the head of the table with Knuckles at the other end. You're not the hosts of that place. If anything, Bobby is older than you and it should be his place; it was his home long before yours. Keep those spaces empty.' Julie shook her head. 'I've said my bit; this conversation is over with no bad feeling.' Julie stood up to leave. 'Make my excuses to the others.'

Nodding, Scarlet's voice was low, almost a whisper. 'I will, and I am sorry, Julie.' Seeing her leave, Scarlet burst into tears and cursed herself for her stupid mistake. She hadn't meant it to sound as bad as it did; she just hadn't wanted people to presume she meant her house, but it had sounded bad, and she hadn't heard it.

After a while, she went into the club, which was still quiet. 'Hello, you two.' She smiled at Adam and Bruce. 'Is this a man talk, or can I join you for a quick drink before I get changed?'

'Where's Julie? Has she gone already?' Adam asked, finding it strange that Julie had just disappeared.

'Yes, she had things to do, and she's finished playing with Bruce for the day.' Scarlet laughed, trying to make light of the situation. Ordering a gin and tonic, she sat on one of the stain-less-steel bar stools with its velvet seating. 'Adam, I'll come straight to the point. I've phoned Poppy and offered her a month's probationary period.' She grinned and sipped her drink. 'Is that okay? I thought we... *you* could give her a chance. She was a good, honest waitress, and now she has had some life experience, she could maybe do the job. But that's up to you – okay?' Nervously, she took another sip of her drink while Adam listened intently and nodded at her suggestion. 'Oh, and please keep your diary free for Sunday for when we have lunch at home.' There, she thought to herself, she'd said it and felt even more ashamed when she saw Adam's face light up.

'Mum and Dad's home – our home? Not your home or mine?' he asked, confused at Scarlet's reasonable nature. 'I'll get my PA to make a note in my diary,' he beamed, letting her know that he agreed to give Poppy a chance.

Her stomach did a flip and she grinned. 'Yes, we're having lunch at the family home with our family, and that includes you!' She laughed, poking Bruce in the chest. 'I will leave you to it, boys. I need a soak before this place gets into full swing.' Finishing the remains of her drink, Scarlet walked away.

'Christ, has she had a lobotomy?' asked Bruce. 'That conversa-tion was almost reasonable – nice even.'

Picking up his own drink, Adam nodded while deep in

thought. 'Mm, I was thinking the same thing. Somehow, I get the feeling Julie was behind that conversation.'

* * *

Once the club was in full throng, Bruce enjoyed celebrity spotting. It felt surreal watching these people he had seen on television and yet, here they were drinking and dancing in the club, seeking out Scarlet and Adam to shake hands, laughing and joking like old friends. 'The celebrities like it here,' Adam explained later, 'because we maintain the security my father and Jake set. Nobody is allowed to take photos of anyone in here unless it's agreed with the person involved. They pay for this privacy, Bruce, which is what makes the club exclusive. They can eat, drink, and dance the night away with their mistresses or whatever, and there will never be a leak to the press.'

'But I've seen photographers and journalists hanging around. Don't people try and sneak cameras into the club? Surely they could earn a fortune from some of the photos taken in here?'

Adam laughed and shook his head at Bruce's naivety. 'You see the bouncers?' He nodded towards the muscular men dressed in their black suits opening the doors at reception. 'Well, they are the front men. They wear their monkey suits and look the part, but if there is a whiff of someone sneaking a photo, then there are the behind-the-scenes bouncers. Now,' explained Adam, 'you see the bouncers wearing radio headsets? We don't want them starting a fight and making the place look untidy, but they will radio the behind-the-scenes bouncers who will rip your head off the minute you click that photo. You will be ushered out discreetly, your mobile or whatever will be taken, and you will be beaten to a pulp in one of the alleys around the back. We have signs up stating no photos and no cameras to be brought in, so what they are doing is illegal anyway. Plus, our CCTV cameras are monitoring everything, and as you have seen yourself, the main office is full of monitors that record everything.'

'So those in the suits are just the front men to make people feel safe? They are ornaments who stop the odd rowdy drunk and gate-crasher? But the ones you don't see are the ones to be afraid of – am I right?'

'You're spot on, Bruce. Scarlet makes a point, even to those high-class celebrities, that if for promotion's sake an actor wants a photo taken in a club drinking with their friends, it's done discreetly or outside of the club as they are leaving. You see, it's like the Oscars. We see everyone arriving and waving for the photographers and walking up the red carpet, but you don't see what happens inside, do you? You get the version on television of people accepting their awards, but you never see or hear about the party afterwards. And that is this place.' Proudly, Adam stood in a far corner of the bar out of sight and waved his arms around the club. 'Somewhere you can come no matter how famous you are and let your hair down without having to read about it in the morning newspapers.'

Bruce slowly nodded his head. 'But there is a pitfall, isn't there?'

Adam grinned broadly and slapped Bruce on the shoulder. 'I do like you, mate. I knew you'd catch on. There is always a but...'

Slowly, Bruce let his thoughts unwind. 'So, the only person, or persons, with this exclusive camera footage are you and Scarlet... which could always be used against someone. So, you're in the blackmail business as well, Adam.' Bruce grinned. 'Just how low can you get?' Bruce laughed and took a swig of his drink.

'Much lower than that, Bruce,' Adam said, tapping his nose in a knowing fashion. 'We have pulled in favours when needed – if you know what I mean. The odd randy police commissioner touching up the strippers can be very grateful when we let them know that these photos have come into our possession and we are doing our best to keep them out of the papers. But here's my favourite part of the evening, and yours too. This will make you forget your bad arm and leg; Christ, you wobble at both ends, Bruce. Look at fairyland.'

Following Adam's gaze, Bruce spotted a group of beautiful women. Each one of them was turned out to perfection with their long flowing hair and golden tans, be they fake or not. Their breast implants were so big it made their waists look even smaller. They sparkled in their very low-cut dresses, displaying their deep cleavages, and the shortness of their dresses made their glossy legs look even longer, along with the height of their heels.

'Models,' Adam whispered, 'on the lookout to be scouted by some fashion designer or movie maker, but mainly some sugar daddy who is going to pay for all of that Botox!' Adam laughed. 'We let them in free because they make the place look good and attract the male customers and encourage them to buy buckets of champagne, just like the strippers do in the week.'

'I do find it strange, though, that for a nightclub and restaurant you still have strippers here.'

'Why? It's theatre, and it's done with taste. It's like showtime in Las Vegas with a little titillation.' Enthusiastically, Adam danced a little twirl. 'Sex sells, Bruce. It always has and always will. Why shouldn't we make money out of it?' Adam linked his arm through Bruce's. 'Now, let me introduce you to Stacey and her friends.' Bruce didn't feel very confident, but after a few more drinks and following Adam's lead, the evening was what men's dreams were made of.

* * *

Separating himself from Holly's arms, Adam heard the noise again. Bleary-eyed, he sat up slightly, then he heard the rapping at the door. Blinking hard and shaking his head, Adam ran his hand through his hair. It had been one hell of a night, and his head was pounding. Hearing Holly's snores next to him, he turned and looked down at her fast asleep, her blonde hair sprayed across the pillow along with last night's make-up. Looking up at the clock, he saw that it was 8 a.m.; he hadn't heard his usual alarm. Flinging back the duvet, he pulled his robe around him and walked, slightly unsteadily, to the front door. Rubbing his face hard to wake himself up, he swung the door open wide. 'Do you have to knock so bloody hard?' he shouted. Adam saw that it was, in fact, his new PA, Poppy.

'Morning, Mr Lambrianu. Your sister said I was to be here at eight sharp, and so here I am.' She smiled with enthusiasm.

Quickly wrapping his robe around him tighter, he tied the belt. 'Tell me, is it your lot in life to see me naked? And presumably when she said eight sharp, she didn't mean at my flat but at the office!'

The enthusiasm drained from Poppy's face, and she looked down at the floor. 'Strike one against me, only another twenty-nine days to go. Sorry, Mr Lambrianu, you weren't downstairs, so I thought I would come up and see if you needed anything. My bad, I'm sorry.'

Through his hangover, Adam recalled Scarlet giving Poppy a month's probation. 'Look, go and find something to type. Preferably your resignation. My mouth feels like the bottom of a birdcage, I need a piss, and you're stood at my door in a black suit and a white shirt, with a briefcase probably holding your pencil case. Go home and change for God's sake, you look like my barrister!'

Looking down at herself, Poppy gave him a weak smile. Inhaling a huge breath, she felt she had to make a stand if she was going to keep this job. She was Adam's PA, and she was determined to act like one. Pushing past Adam, almost knocking him backwards, she looked around the apartment and strode towards the kitchen. 'Well, if your mouth is like a birdcage, let's make some strong coffee. Concerning that other thing, go to the bathroom. I'm okay here. I can find the milk and sugar. Go!' she said, more confidently than she felt.

Standing there, gobsmacked, Adam could hear her clattering and opening cupboards. His head was pounding, and she wasn't helping with her cheerful humming while she made herself at home. But he did need the bathroom, and he felt too weak to put up a fight right now.

Running the tap, he scooped up some cold water and rinsed his face with it. Gargling with mouthwash, he felt more awake to do battle with his new PA.

'Coffee' – Poppy grinned while holding a mug in the air – 'and I've got these in my bag near my pencil case,' she added sarcastically while holding up a box of paracetamol. 'You might need them.' Glaring at her, Adam took the mug off her and held his hands out for the pills. 'Put them on your expense account,' he snapped back while swallowing the paracetamol.

Ignoring his comments, Poppy smiled. 'While you're having your coffee, I'll go and run you a shower, which will make you feel better. Where is your shower?'

'It's en-suite in my bedroom, through there.' He pointed absent-mindedly. Seeing her march ahead, his eyes widened in horror when he remembered Holly still snoring her head off in his bedroom, and he ran behind her. 'I'll sort myself out,' he said, but he was too late. Poppy was already pulling the bedroom curtains back with one swoop. 'Let there be light.' She smiled and turned around, firstly looking at Adam in the doorway and then the bed. 'Oh, I see,' she stammered, seeing Holly sprawled across the pillow. 'I didn't think—'

'No, you didn't. You waltz in here like Mary Poppins taking over. Thanks for the coffee, but as you can see, I am entertaining a lady and don't need your help for that. It's time you left now, like I suggested in the first place.'

Trying to think of something to say, other than sorry, Poppy lowered her eyes to the floor, and then the bed. Something caught her eye, shocking her at first, but then a wry grin crossed her face. 'I will leave you to get showered and dressed now. While I go home and change my clothes and leave you to entertain your lady with three legs!' Barging past him, she almost knocked the coffee mug out of his hand, and he heard the clatter of her heels down the hallway and the slam of the door.

A curious frown crossed Adam's brow, and he walked towards the window where Poppy had stood. Stunned, he saw Holly fast asleep on the pillow, but Poppy was right – hanging out the side and the bottom of the bed were three legs! Carefully, Adam pulled back the duvet and saw another female lying there. Through the fog, he remembered he had brought two of the girls home with him.

Curious, he walked towards Bruce's bedroom, slowly turning the handle to his bedroom door and peering inside. Bruce was fast asleep with a brunette laid on his chest. Standing back, Adam bent low to see if any legs were dangling near the edge of the bed. He lifted the duvet, trying not to disturb Bruce, and was satisfied that Bruce and his mystery woman made up the correct number of people in the bed. Wide awake now and walking back to his bedroom, Adam walked into the shower and burst out laughing! The whole situation was highly amusing, he thought to himself. What a bloody start to the day. He laughed again.

Feeling fully refreshed, he heard the door again. Ready to

apologise for his grumpiness, he walked down the hallway to see Knuckles standing there. 'Fuck, this place is like Piccadilly, either that or people think it's a bloody walkway. What's up, Knuckles?'

Without a word, Knuckles handed him a twenty-pound note. Looking at it closely, Adam wasn't sure what he should be looking at. Then Knuckles took it out of his hand and held it up to the light.

'Counterfeit?' Adam looked at Knuckles for confirmation and saw him nod. 'It's a good one, to be fair, but do we know who from?'

'Tommy the tout.'

'That's the ticket tout whose dad owns a pub on the Walworth Road, isn't it?'

'Nags Head,' Knuckles muttered.

Surprised, Adam held up the note closely to the window again, disbelievingly. 'You do mean Tommy who sells theatre tickets here and around the West End? Our Tommy, who we promote to help him sell more tickets?' Adam wanted to clarify the situation. Tommy had always seemed like an okay guy, and Adam had always been able to get tickets to one thing or another to impress some MP or other VIP. For that, Adam had let him have his own patch to sell his wares without police interference. Of course, there was always a commission to himself and Scarlet to be paid, but Tommy had made a lot of money out of Adam's generosity.

Seeing Knuckles nod again angered him. 'Right, well, it's time we paid that little shit a visit. He's paying his protection money with counterfeit notes and thinks we won't notice.' Adam's face flushed with anger. 'I'll string the bastard up. We protect his dad's pub, don't we? Good,' he said, without waiting for Knuckles's answer. 'Then that's where we will start. Give me an hour.' Knuckles took the note off him and left. 'Right!' Adam shouted.

'Come on, Holly.' He pulled the duvet back. 'And whoever you are. Time to get up. Wakey, wakey!' Adam clapped his hands to the weary groans coming from the bed. Then, walking through, he flung Bruce's bedroom door open. 'Chucking out time, folks. Time to get up!' he bellowed.

Bruce was already stirring. 'Okay, don't shout, there's a man with a hammer inside my head.'

'Good! Well, wake her up, it's time to leave. Speedy now, Doreen will be here soon.' Adam went into the kitchen and made four coffees; three of them he put into vacuum mugs. As the two women in his bed held up their hands to shield their eyes from the sunlight shining in from the windows, Adam handed them a mug each. 'Take that with you, girls. I've got work to do.' Walking into Bruce's room, he handed him a mug, and to the nameless woman beside him, Adam handed another vacuum mug. 'This will stay warm until you get home. Come on, lady, your carriage has turned into a pumpkin – OUT!' he shouted, more rudely than he intended.

He wasn't angry at them, but he was angry at Tommy the tout. His payments were always late, but this was deceit, betrayal, and disrespect. Did he really think they would let him get away with this? As his ire rose, Adam wanted to speak to Tommy to see if this was part of a genuine mistake or if someone had passed it on to him and he hadn't realised. On the other hand, Adam argued with himself, all in all, Tommy paid three grand a week; that was one hell of a mistake to make. But still, he thought to himself, he wanted to face Tommy and let him know that his trick hadn't worked. Knuckles could sniff a counterfeit note at a hundred paces, better than any machine invented.

Popping his head around the bedroom door, Bruce saw Adam adjusting his tie in the mirror. 'That was a bit of a shitty end to a nice encounter, Adam.'

'Sorry, mate, but last night was last night. It was great, but how long do they think they are going to stay for? Surely they must have things to do?' Calming down a little, Adam smiled. 'Sorry, Bruce, I didn't mean to piss on your parade. You get some rest; looking at those bloodshot eyes, you need it. Did you enjoy yourself?'

'God, yeah!' Bruce grinned. 'But how come I only came back with one woman, and you got two?'

Adam shook his head and turned to him in the doorway. 'No idea, mate. Personally, I was so pissed I don't remember coming back with one of them! Let's hope my dick was sober.' Adam burst out laughing. 'I've got to pop out; I will see you later.'

Knowing Adam enough not to ask any questions, Bruce nodded. He knew if Adam wanted to tell him anything, he would volunteer it without any questioning. Shaking his head as he heard Adam running down the stairs, Bruce laughed to himself.

'What a guy!' Bruce said out loud while making his way back to his bedroom.

6

FRENEMIES

Knuckles was already waiting in the car for Adam when he went outside. 'Have you told Scarlet anything about this?' Seeing Knuckles shake his head, he almost felt stupid for asking. Knuckles didn't tell his left arm what his right was doing. 'To the pub; the draymen from the brewery will be delivering at this time of morning. It will be nice and quiet.'

On arrival, the pub was closed and, as predicted, the brewery lorry was parked around the back, taking away empty barrels and delivering new ones.

Seeing Tommy's father in the midst of it, organising things, Adam knocked on the back door and coughed to get his attention. Looking up at the interruption, Phil, Tommy's father, looked stunned for a moment at his visitor. He quickly took in Adam's stance, dressed in his black suit and long black camel overcoat and his face drained of colour.

'Mr Lambrianu, what brings you here?' Taking the clipboard off the delivery men, he signed it absent-mindedly and left them to carry on without him. Adam followed him into the pub.

Stony-faced, Adam looked around the pub as he entered. In

daylight the place was abysmal. It was cold and empty without the lights on and the hub of staff and customers. The stench of beer seemed ingrained in the flock wallpaper. Nervously, Phil walked behind the bar, picking up an already stained tea towel. Adam noticed with distaste that he started polishing clean glasses from the dishwasher with it for want of something better to do. 'I know it's early, Mr Lambrianu, but would you like a drink?'

'No. I want answers.' Adam's stern reply and frosty stare made Phil look up nervously, avoiding Adam's glare. 'Answers, Mr Lambrianu? About what?'

Adam was used to people being slightly nervous around him, but Phil's whole demeanour told him that he already knew why Adam had called today. The game was up, and they had been rumbled. Calmly, Adam smiled. 'It seems you and Tommy are not happy with the protection we provide, so I've come to tell you that our agreement is dissolved. You're on your own, Phil. Please pass that on to Tommy.' Turning his gaze to the ceiling, Adam added, 'I presume Tommy's still in bed. He works late and needs his beauty sleep.' Adam smiled. 'Oh, by the way, put this in your charity box.' Slowly, Adam laid the counterfeit note on the bar and saw Phil's face pale again as he stared at it.

Frowning, Phil shook his head profusely. 'No, no, Mr Lambrianu. We're more than happy. Everything is tickety-boo here.' Staring right through him with his blue steely eyes, Adam was tempted to wring his neck there and then but decided to play the long game as he listened to more of Phil's lies.

Pouring himself a drink to moisten his lips, Phil looked up towards the ceiling where Tommy was sleeping. 'Rough area, this; needs someone keeping an eye on the place. People know we're under the Lambrianu umbrella and leave us alone.' Phil's feigned laughter annoyed Adam even more.

Adam could feel his temper rising as Phil continued to lie to his face, and he did his best to keep his composure, but it was time to drop his bombshell.

'Tell me, Phil, now that we no longer do business with each other.' He smiled. 'Do you launder your counterfeit notes through the pub?' The look on Phil's face wasn't one of confusion or ignorance, but one of fear and shock, which Adam thought showed his guilt.

Adam proffered his hand over the bar to shake hands, and as Phil held out his own, Adam pulled him over the bar towards him. 'I hope whoever you're working with and laundering money for has the muscle to back it up,' Adam growled in Phil's ear. The anger building up inside of him made him want to bite it off, but he thought better of it. He could feel Phil trembling and pushed him backwards. 'Bye, Phil.' He waved and left.

Quickly, Phil poured himself another whisky, gulping it back in one. Then, walking into the back room, he saw Tommy sat on the stairs quietly listening.

'You heard who that was then! Thanks for the backup, you spineless prick. You leave your old dad to face the music with him. I'm lucky I'm still alive!' he shouted. 'He knows, Tommy, he fucking knows,' Phil panicked. 'Easy money, you said!' Spit dribbled down his chin as he spoke. 'You made this deal with those yardies you owe money to, to launder money in my pub. Are you so fucking stupid you handed a note over to Adam Lambrianu? When people find out we're no longer under their protection, this place will be a free-for-all.'

Cockily, Tommy stood up, toe to toe with his father. 'You agreed, Dad, so don't blame me for everything. Maybe he knows I'm in with a new crowd and he's shitting a brick. The yardies are as tough as anyone!' Tommy looked up at his father. 'Why are you moaning? He hasn't done anything, has he? You're still alive. All he's done is just ended our contract. Christ, it's about time. How much have we paid him over the years? I'm the one standing outside of theatres in the pissing rain touting tickets. Why should I pay him extortionate prices?'

'Because nobody touches your patch, Tommy, or your market stall.' Phil looked at his watch and sighed. 'Shouldn't you be there by now?'

'For God's sake, Dad. I've got someone to open up for me. And as for Lambrianu, there are bigger and harder people than him, you know. The yardies are my mates; well, kind of,' Tommy stammered. He knew that statement was a bit farfetched. He'd owed them money, and they wanted his blood. After pleading for a second chance, they had mentioned money laundering and Tommy had agreed to convince his father too quickly, but it meant he had breathing space.

'How much do you owe those yardies, exactly? They won't protect you. They only want you and me to launder money for them. And you're so up to your neck in shit, you daren't say no!'

'I didn't hear you saying no when they offered you a percentage!' Tommy retorted. 'You even laughed at the thought of getting one over on the Lambrianus.' Tommy glared at his father. 'I'm not taking all the blame. You were happy enough to go along with it.'

Tommy was right; Phil had agreed, but now he sorely regretted it. 'Get dressed and go to work. We're on our own now,' Phil spat. The yardies had offered Tommy an easy way to pay off his debt and then once he had done so, any extra cash would be Tommy's and Phil's to keep. Phil had already begun mentally decorating the pub on his share of the earnings and planning an easy retirement abroad. Now, he felt afraid. They were on their own.

* * *

'We'll go back later, Knuckles. Let them stew for now. They are both as guilty as each other. Why couldn't he just hold his hands up and apologise? I'm a reasonable man; I would have only broken one leg.' Adam grinned. 'But no, he stood there lying his head off to me. And I know Tommy was listening. Phil has got so used to his creaky backstairs, he can't hear anyone creeping down them any more, but I did. I have a job for the boys to do later for me, a spot of decorating.' Adam smiled. Knuckles looked at him in the rear-view mirror and frowned. 'Get hold of the rest of that counterfeit money for me, will you?' Knuckles simply nodded, but Adam felt he saw a stirring of curiosity on his face, before it disappeared again.

Walking back into the club, Adam made his way to the office. Hearing a female voice, he froze and looked up at Knuckles. 'Shit, that's Mary Poppins in there with Scarlet. I'm not here, Knuckles,' he whispered.

'Morning, Mr Lambrianu,' someone shouted behind him, and closing his eyes, Adam let out a sigh.

'Adam! Is that you?' Scarlet's voice bellowed out. Knowing that he had been caught out, he shrugged. 'Oh, God, Knuckles. Here we go.'

'Yes, morning.' Flashing a smile, he noticed Poppy sat at his desk. 'You comfortable in my chair?' he asked indignantly.

Scarlet looked at Adam, then Poppy. 'It's only while you weren't here. Poppy needs somewhere to sit for God's sake, and you haven't been very helpful. Anyway, where have you been?'

'Out.' He cast a glance towards Poppy. 'On business. I will explain later, okay.'

Standing up, Poppy turned to leave. 'It's okay if you wish to speak in private. You only have to ask me to leave. Maybe I could have a desk in one of the other rooms, then I won't be in your way.'

'You're not in the way, Poppy,' Scarlet joked. 'Is she, Adam? Or do you wish to speak privately?'

Glancing towards Poppy, who was now stood up, Adam admired her. She had taken his advice and had indeed changed her clothes. The black professional business suit was now replaced with a well-fitted red trouser suit, sporting a black silky vest top. A red headband separated her fringe from her glossy dark hair that hung down her back and shoulders. Feeling a stirring within him as he caught a glimpse of her cleavage, he looked towards Scarlet. 'Later,' he breathed and walked out of the office. Feeling his erection rise, he needed to get out of the office as soon as possible before it was spotted. Phew! he thought to himself. This thing had a mind of its own.

7

LOOSE ENDS

Walking through the club to his apartment, Adam saw two detectives walking towards him. As much as he wondered what they wanted with him, he was also glad of their intervention as his erection seemed to disappear instantly.

'Is there a problem, gentlemen?' Adam asked, wondering if this had anything to do with his visit to the Nag's Head this morning.

'Just making enquiries, Mr Lambrianu. We spoke the other day at the beer festival.'

Adam smiled. 'Of course, I remember. What can I do for you?'

'Well, you've been very helpful to Mr Wilkinson, I believe, and he's very grateful.'

The hackles on Adam's neck pricked, and he wondered what had been said. 'I felt sorry for the man, Inspector, as a fellow publican, if you know what I mean. He's no competition to me.' Adam smiled. 'But I feel we should help each other out. Some of those stalls were from other countries too and I would hate for them to think that hatred and violence were the only hospitality shown to them in London. So, what can I do for you? Let's sit down over here where we won't be disturbed.'

Neither of the detectives smiled, even when Adam offered them a drink. Expectantly, he waited for the worst.

'Indeed, Mr Lambrianu. We've spoken with Mr Wilkinson and seen the photos, of course. He's very grateful for your intervention. But during his statement, he mentioned Ricky.' Knowing full well who they meant, Adam looked at them innocently.

'People in the know, Mr Lambrianu, know him as Ricky the Razor. I am sure you know that name.' The detective watched him closely.

'You know I have, Inspector, so let's not play cat and mouse, eh? What about him?'

'Well, we wondered, as you've been so helpful to everyone else, if you could help us. Ricky's gone missing. We went to his address, but he didn't answer, even though we knew he was inside. When we returned with a warrant, he'd scarpered. There hasn't been a sign of him since. You can see by the state of his flat that he had packed a few things and left in a hurry. We wondered if you knew anything about his whereabouts?'

Frowning at their questioning, Adam's answer was sharp and clear. 'Why would I? We weren't exactly what you would call friends. If you mean have I heard anything on the grapevine, no, I haven't.'

'No need to get defensive, sir. We're just asking around, that's all. Apparently, Ricky had mentioned to Mr Wilkinson that he was going to return with friends of a certain nature and was trying to get money out of him – for protection purposes. Strange that his place got burnt to the ground...'

'So Ricky has done a moonlight flit by the sounds of it, and you're asking if I have a forwarding address. Regarding protection money, that's old gangster stuff. We have a reputable security firm, which I'm sure you're aware of. It's all legal and above board – taxes paid. I've helped Mr Wilkinson, not harmed him. And as for Ricky, there was no love lost, and he didn't work for me. Will that be all?' Adam asked indignantly.

'Yes, yes, no need to get your knickers in a twist, Adam.' The detective dropped the formality, seeing Adam's angry face. He knew Ricky didn't work for Adam, but it was strange that Ricky had disappeared off the face of the earth without a trace and Adam apparently knew nothing about it. 'Maybe if you hear anything, you will let us know. Apparently, the name Dutch Hillman was also mentioned...'

'Oh yes, was Ricky working for them? I thought he had retired. But what has it got to do with me? Why aren't you at Dutch Hillman's place asking him?' Adam stared at the detective, poker-faced.

'We have, and he hasn't said much. But his brother Ethan seems to be shooting his mouth off about how much he hated Ricky.'

'Let's be honest, Inspector, a lot of people hated Ricky, and Ethan isn't what you'd call a reasonable man. They had history; everyone knows that – including you. He'll turn up again, I'm sure of it.' Adam knew they were clutching at straws. Ricky had vanished into thin air. Inwardly, Adam hoped the Hillman brothers had buried him somewhere deep. Very deep.

'Mr Lambrianu, sir.' The detectives and Adam turned as the female voice echoed down the corridor. Seeing Poppy standing at the doorway, Adam's brows creased. 'What is it, Poppy?'

'Your appointment with your accountant, Mr Lambrianu. He's waiting for you.' Straight-faced and matter-of-fact, Poppy looked at the detectives and then down at her clipboard. 'Can I help you, gentlemen? Are you on my appointment list for today?'

Adam smiled and introduced her. 'Sorry, gentlemen, this is

Poppy Nightingale, my PA. Poppy, these are police officers. You might encounter them from time to time.'

Adam noticed the admiring looks she received, especially when she dropped her pen and bent down, giving them a glimpse of her cleavage as she picked it up. 'Nice to meet you,' they said in unison. 'We just wanted a quick word with Mr Lambrianu, Miss Nightingale.'

'And are you done? His next appointment is waiting, or are you arresting him?' Poppy asked in a matter-of-fact way. 'Do we need a lawyer?'

Adam's jaw almost dropped as he stared, wide-eyed, at her. 'Poppy. If you don't mind, I'll be in soon. Now please, do your job and entertain the accountant. And no, we don't need a lawyer!' he snapped.

'Still in training, eh, Adam? Well, we had better let you get on.' The detectives grinned at each other and left.

Watching them leave, Adam took a sharp intake of breath and marched into his office. 'What the fuck was that about? Do we need a lawyer? Why? Have I committed a crime!' he shouted.

Turning around in her chair, Poppy looked up at him. 'Not as far as I know, but I got rid of them faster than you did. And in a light-hearted way, too.'

Surprised, Adam looked at her. 'You knew they were police?'

Her bored expression annoyed him. 'Of course I did. You can spot them a mile away and they always come in twos. Now, is there anything else you need me to do? Mr Wilkinson has made an appointment to speak to you tomorrow. He has also brought a large amount of money in cash. I gave him a receipt for it as he needed it for insurance purposes. I've put the money in your apartment; I didn't know if you wanted it in the office safe. I've not discussed this with Scarlet... Should I have?' Poppy looked at him innocently, batting her eyelashes.

Pausing for a moment, Adam smiled. 'Well, for the record, Scarlet knows about the money. It's not some backhanded bribe or something. It's payment for the tent at the beer festival. More to the point, how do you know so much about the police?'

Looking up into his blue hypnotic eyes, Poppy thought she saw a playful glint in them and smiled. Breathing in the closeness of him, she felt her stomach somersault. She had always liked and fancied him when she'd worked as a waitress at the club, but he had never noticed her. Compared with the women that surrounded him, she had felt dull. Holding his stare, she smiled. 'Like anyone, I've had my dealings, but they were loitering and I thought you might need a helping hand. And it worked, didn't it? They were more interested in my cleavage than your words.'

Adam flashed a perfectly charming smile as he put his finger on her chin and traced it slowly down towards her cleavage before stopping. 'And very good taste they have too,' he whispered.

A sudden interruption from Scarlet as she breezed into the room made Adam stand up straight. 'Right, Adam, are you ready to do any work today or am I on my lonesome?'

Coughing to clear his throat, Adam saw Poppy turn her swivel chair to face the wall, away from him. 'Half an hour and then I'm yours...' Leaving the room, Adam pondered what had just happened, and dismissed it as mere flirtation with a good-looking girl. But he had been glad of Poppy's intervention, and she had used her initiative with the police. Maybe she would fit in here after all...

* * *

Later that night, Knuckles drove the van and parked outside the Nag's Head pub. The street lighting and the pub sign lit up the pub, and Adam laughed. 'This is brilliant, Knuckles. Have they done the inside too as I asked?' Seeing Knuckles nod, Adam looked at the pub again. He had instructed Knuckles to get buckets and wallpaper paste and to stick the counterfeit notes all over the front of the pub and as much of the inside without being detected. As Adam looked up at the living quarters above the pub, he stared in awe at the windows covered in counterfeit notes. 'How did they get up there, Knuckles?'

'Bribed the window cleaner. He was there today. One ladder, one bucket of paste.'

Knuckles did a three-point turn in the road, parking so that the back of the van was pointing towards the pub. Then Adam opened the back doors and sat back behind the tripod holding the machine gun. Putting his finger on the trigger, Adam fired at the pub. Bullet after bullet flew out in quick succession, smashing windows, doors and anything they touched. 'GO!' Adam shouted, reaching forward and pulling the van doors closed, almost falling over as Knuckles put his foot down and burnt rubber as they sped off into the night.

'Fuck me, Knuckles, you can slow down now.' Adam laughed. 'Christ, did you see the state of those bricks? Bob the Builder is going to have to do more than a bit of pointing to repair that!'

'Why paste the notes on if you were going to shoot up the place?' Confused, Knuckles stared at him through the rear-view mirror as he drove.

Adam laughed. 'Because we're not grasses. Someone is giving Tommy and his dad those counterfeit notes to launder. We won't be the only ones he's tried passing them on to. I would think it's already come to the police's attention, but tracing it might be a problem. Well, now they can,' Adam explained. 'It's wallpapered all over the pub. Phil and Tommy will shit a brick because they have no protection any more and I spoke to the Brixton yardies this afternoon.' Adam laughed again. 'Yeah, I know who's laundering it; they've been doing it for weeks. Today I told them Phil was boasting about it and had tried paying his debts to me with it. They were livid. So Phil and Tommy have no protection, their walls are covered in counterfeit notes which the police are looking for, and the yardies are going to get a visit from the coppers, which won't come to much because of my tipoff this afternoon. And now, the pub has been shot to pieces! Whodunnit?' Adam laughed hysterically as he watched Knuckles trying to fathom it all out in his head. As they slowed down, Adam looked around. 'I'm gonna jump out and make my presence known at the club. Can you get this lot out of sight?' Adam knew it was a stupid question; Knuckles would already have it all in hand.

'I'll go back in the morning and collect what is owed,' Knuckles muttered.

Surprised, Adam questioned Knuckles. 'What? You're going back there tomorrow to collect the payments they still owe us – why?'

'They owe Scarlet. Want her money.' Stubbornly, Knuckles stuck out his chin defiantly and Adam knew there was no arguing. He had tunnel vision, and as far as he was concerned, they owed Scarlet, and he wanted it back – end of.

'Look, I'm going to play host in the club; we'll talk about this later. Don't go there, Knuckles, it's not worth a couple of grand. That place will be swarming with coppers tonight and tomorrow.' Standing on the pavement, Adam looked on as Knuckles drove off.

'Shit,' Adam muttered to himself as he walked to the club entrance, 'Scarlet's gonna fucking kill me if he gets arrested!'

Entering the club, Adam was in two minds about telling Scarlet. He knew Knuckles wasn't stupid and could look after himself, but to go back to the scene of the crime and demand money! Christ, what was he thinking?

Making his way over to the bar, Adam spotted Scarlet. Pausing for a moment, he pursed his lips. He could see she was drinking champagne with the new female police superintendent and toasting her promotion. It had slipped his mind, but Scarlet had mentioned she was throwing a party for her to celebrate her new success.

'Adam!' Scarlet shouted over when she saw him. 'Come and have a drink.'

Standing in a circle with a dozen coppers after what he had just done made him swallow hard, and reaching for the champagne Scarlet offered him, he gulped it back. Composing himself and flashing his usual charming smile, he kissed the new superintendent on the cheek and congratulated her. 'I thought you said I wasn't invited. Didn't you say women only and girl power?' Adam shouted above the music. 'Should I have worn a dress?' They all threw their heads back in laughter.

'I think I should leave you girls to party on your own. I'm not the male stripper!' he joked to the onlookers and ever-listening police ears, whether on duty or not.

All the ladies shouted their drunken heckles to him and the superintendent even squeezed his bum cheekily, which made them all whoop with laughter again. As Adam walked away, he felt a sigh of relief and a little worse for wear after being groped that much in a matter of minutes. 'You look like you're in need of a proper drink. Whisky, that's your tipple, isn't it?' Poppy handed Adam a glass and clinked her own against his.

'Thank you.' He smiled. 'I feel like I've been violated. That could be a new term for being frisked by the police.' He grinned, matching her own. 'Shouldn't you have clocked off hours ago?' Adam asked, surprised at her presence at the club.

Casting her eyes down, Poppy nodded. 'I just finished up a few things. I told Scarlet and her party that you were showing me around the casino, considering you spend most of your time there.' Casting a glance over the rim of her glass, she gazed at him. 'Scarlet kept asking where you were, and I felt I should come up with something. After all, I'm your assistant, and I didn't know where you were. So, I told her that you wanted to show me the casino and had said for her to take the night off and enjoy herself.'

Poppy had given him the alibi he needed and had obviously kept Scarlet out of the way until now. His blue eyes pierced her own. 'So, where have you been hiding, because you haven't been with me?'

'This place has lots of dark corners and booths. Fortunately, I was a waitress here, and I know where to keep out of sight when you want to rest your feet for five minutes without the boss noticing.' She grinned.

'I'll keep that in mind for future skivers. I'm sorry, I don't recall you waitressing here.' He smiled, almost embarrassed now that she had been quick and smart enough to give him an alibi.

'Why would you? I was only a waitress; you had bigger fish to fry. But now you're here, I can leave.'

Taken aback, Adam didn't know what to say. 'Well, put the overtime on my bill, and tomorrow I *will* show you the casino. What would you have done if I hadn't come back? What if I was dancing the night away with some young woman?' he teased.

Poppy's face dropped at his snub. 'Well, that would have been my bad, wouldn't it? But if that was the case, then I think Scarlet would have been informed that you had some hot date and would be a no-show. I will put the overtime down; thank you, Adam, and goodnight.' Reaching over to the bar to put her glass down, she breathed in his aftershave. His very presence made her tingle. It always had, but he had never noticed.

Musing to himself as he watched Poppy smile, he wasn't sure if she was flirting with him or trying simply to prove she could do her job. There was chemistry between them; Adam could feel it himself, but suddenly he felt awkward, tongue-tied even. Trying to think of something to say, Adam smiled. 'Maybe I do need a PA after all,' he said, almost biting his tongue the minute the words left his mouth. It sounded much worse out loud than he had meant it to and he saw the disappointed look on her face as she walked away.

Waving at Scarlet to catch her eye, he pointed his thumb towards the ceiling, letting her know he was going upstairs. Seeing her nod and wave, the other ladies here blew him drunken kisses, making him cringe.

'Bruce, I'm home, honey.' Adam laughed as he opened the door. Cocking his head in the lounge, he could see Bruce lounging on the sofa surrounded by treats, watching Netflix. 'Hard day at the office?'

'Oh, definitely. This is the life for me, Adam, being waited on and all kinds of delicacies prepared for me.' Picking up the remote and turning the volume down, Bruce shifted on the sofa to make room for Adam. 'More to the point, where have you been?'

'Out and about.' Adam sighed, picking up some of the grapes on the coffee table. 'I've got to pop out for another hour or so and I need you to cover for me. It's my last trek of the night – promise. And believe me, I'm shattered. Is that okay?'

'Course. Please, Adam, don't put your life on hold for me. It's kind of you to let me stay here, but I'm on the mend. I'll be out from under your feet before you know it. I hear the police have been sniffing around about the Razor bloke we met at the festival. Is everything okay?'

Surprised at his comment, Adam sighed. 'How do you know that? Anyway, yeah, everything is fine. Apparently, he's done a bunk, and they wanted to know if I had any idea where he might have gone.'

Bruce nodded. 'Do you know what happened to him, Adam?'

Bruce's direct question shocked Adam. 'Maybe I do and maybe I don't. I don't want to lie to you, Bruce, but let me tell you this: no one hurts my mate when all he is doing is taking a piss.'

Bruce laughed. 'Anyway, on a lighter note, how are you getting on with Poppy?'

A perplexed look crossed Adam's face. 'Not sure. She pisses me off at times with her Mary Poppins act, but she means well. I'm not sure if she's flirting with me or mocking me.'

'Well, I think you have an admirer. She's got a pulse and she's pretty; I thought that would be enough for you.' Nudging him in the ribs, Bruce laughed again.

'Nah, she's an employee, and Scarlet warned me, "hands off." Anyway, after that Jennifer business, I don't want to get involved with anyone. And if I sleep with Poppy, well, I will still have to work with her, which would be awkward – nice thought though.' Adam winked cheekily.

'You thought you were singing a different song with Jennifer, but you weren't. It was the same song, just a different tune. You were anonymous for a short time, and it felt different. I can understand that; it must have made a nice change for you not being in the spotlight so much. But it wasn't love, Adam, or anything like it. It was just, well, different. A bit like me getting off with that gorgeous bird with the plastic tits. Really, really nice, but I like what I'm used to, and I was punching above my weight. I like Kim. She texted me earlier. She's got normal-sized tits; no Botox, and her eyelashes are her own. She suits me.'

'I didn't realise you and she were that serious. Are you meeting up?'

Bruce blushed. 'We get along and fill each other's gaps. I thought I might ask her to pop round here sometime, or maybe when I go home,' Bruce added slowly.

'Well, who said romance was dead? You fill gaps? Fuck, and I thought I was heartless. Get her over here and fill her gap, Bruce!' Adam burst out laughing. 'I'm going out. Gaps indeed. Well, that's one name for it.' Still laughing, Adam left, while Bruce put his feet back up on the sofa and picked up his mobile phone. Now he had got the thumbs up from Adam to ask her round, he felt better already.

* * *

Leaving his car firmly in sight at the club carpark, Adam got on his motorbike. He needed to see Ethan and Dutch. Driving around the back of their pub, Adam found his way into their cellar from outside, and taking out his mobile, he called Ethan. 'Meet me in your cellar in five minutes,' was all he said. Hearing the hatch open, the light shone in from the bar as Ethan walked down the stairs, closing the hatch behind him.

'What's up, Adam?' Surprised to see him, Ethan stood in the darkness opposite him.

'The police have been to see me regarding Ricky. Why?' Adam spat out. 'I do hope you disposed of him properly.'

Adjusting his eyes to the darkness, Ethan nodded. 'They've been around here too, and to everyone else that knows him by all accounts. But don't worry, he's firmly incarcerated under London Bridge. Christ, we've put so many bodies there it's a wonder we had room.' Ethan sighed. Fumbling for his cigarettes, he lit one, the flicker of his lighter showing the scowl on Adam's face.

'Then move him somewhere different. I'm sure the police know that's your burial ground and will sniff around it for newly laid cement. Move him, Ethan, or chuck him in the Thames. Anything, I don't care. I just don't want the coppers visiting me again,' Adam warned.

'Hey, hold on, Adam. We've said nothing, but they also know me and him weren't mates. I couldn't deny that he had been in touch, because he had more or less described us to that beer festival bloke. But so you really want us to move him? God, he stank the van out after a few hours, Adam.' Ethan squirmed at the idea of moving Ricky's body.

'Yes, sort it, Ethan. After all, it's you he described, not me. It's you I'm looking out for. We're mates, aren't we?' He slapped Ethan on the shoulders, letting his sentence sink into Ethan's brain.

'I will,' Ethan answered slowly, inhaling on his cigarette and letting a ring of nicotine form in the air. 'I see what you mean,' he answered nervously. 'You and that bloke, Mr Wilkinson, were all over the tabloids together.'

'Yes, my alibi and friendship with Daniel Wilkinson are solid. Yours seems a bit rocky, though, so cover your tracks, Ethan,' Adam reminded him. 'Especially if you've been sloppy about it. Tie up the loose ends, Ethan. Now, you'd better go or people will wonder where you are.'

Nodding, Ethan walked back to the staircase, giving one backward glance at Adam as he opened the hatch and disappeared into the bright lights of the pub. Satisfied, Adam left the way he had come in, without being seen.

8

VENGEANCE IS SWEET

Hearing the laugher and giggling coming from Bruce's bedroom when he returned, a wry grin crossed Adam's face. Bruce hadn't wasted much time in inviting Kim around. Feeling like a third wheel, he decided to go back downstairs to the club. After all, he had supposedly given Scarlet the night off and so had better oversee the rest of the evening and play host.

Quickly changing his suit, he went downstairs. Walking over to a group of businessmen he knew, he shook hands and introduced them to some of the regular ladies who frequented the place. They were all young and beautiful, out for a good time at someone else's expense and the men were only too happy to provide the champagne.

After laughing, dancing, and drinking with everyone, Adam sauntered over to the far side of the bar to stand besides Knuckles. 'Have I been social for long enough, Knuckles?' Seeing him nod, Adam followed Knuckles's eyeline towards Scarlet. 'Time to take her home I think; she is starting to sway. Get the limousine to take the other ladies home in style, too. God knows, they've drunk so much I'm surprised they are standing. I'm going to the office to put the takings in the safe.'

Once in the office, Adam sat back in his leather chair, glad of a moment of silence to himself. Looking at his watch, he saw that it was getting late and yawned. A fleeting thought of Poppy banging on his door at 8 a.m. tomorrow morning made him smile. Slowly getting up, he locked everything away. The people in the club had dwindled and the bouncers would soon be seeing them on their merry way. Yawning, he walked back into the club and saw that it had already miraculously emptied, and the staff were clearing away. He clapped his hands to get their attention.

'Go home, all of you. What's left to be done can be sorted tomorrow. Thank you for your hard work, but call it a night – or a morning.' Adam grinned. Instantly everyone looked up and stopped what they were doing. He was tired, and it had been a hell of a day and he just wanted to be alone. Adam stood at the bar as they all emerged with their coats and after a few goodbyes, they made their way out. The bar manager was the last to leave as always, once he had checked everything. 'Night, Robert, thank you.' Adam smiled.

'There is someone waiting for you Adam.' Robert nodded to the far side of the bar before leaving. Turning around, Adam saw there was a woman sitting at the far end, almost in the shadows. There were a few glasses scattered along the bar and, picking them up en-route, he cleared them himself as he made his way towards her. 'Well, well, well, look who's back in town.' Adam smiled, seeing Portia sitting there seductively, in a black satin halter-neck dress, so short it displayed her tanned legs and left nothing to the imagination.

'Flew back in yesterday, Adam. Been on a photo shoot in Italy, thought I'd pop in and say hello. You busy?'

Adam liked Portia. She was a few years older than him and

their easy come easy go relationship suited them both. There were no strings; she had a thriving career as a model and just enjoyed a bit of fun. Feeling his body stir with desire, he decided he was tired, but not that tired. Pouring them both a night cap, he moved closer to her and pinched her protruding nipple playfully, which was almost bursting out of her dress. 'I'm never too busy for a beautiful woman like you.'

Flashing a charming smile, he explained Bruce was staying overnight with his girlfriend, knowing full well that would make no difference to her. They both knew why she had waited and what she wanted. 'I've never known you to be shy, Adam.' She smiled and swept back a lock of his hair from his forehead, letting her hand linger down his face and onto the cleft in his chin. 'You get more handsome each time I see you,' she purred, while looking down at his bulging crotch. 'And I can see that you're pleased to see me.' The pair of them smiled at each other knowingly. As they gulped back their drinks, Adam linked his arm through hers and helped her off the bar stool.

'Shall we go?' Seeing her nod, he slipped his arm around her waist and they walked to his apartment.

* * *

'It's bloody cold in here, Ethan. Why are we at this abattoir again at this time of the morning?' Robbie moaned.

Glaring at Robbie and Billy angrily, Ethan and Dutch stood inside the abattoir, arms folded. 'We're back at the scene of the crime, boys. You see I had a visit from Lambrianu, and he doesn't believe Ricky's body was disposed of properly. So, I am asking you now, what did you do with Ricky's body? Is he encased in cement like we told you?' he demanded.

Robbie and Billy looked at each other nervously, realising it was useless lying. 'Not quite,' he confessed, knowing that lying to Ethan was certain death. 'We put him in the skip where they put all the animal remains. It will get picked up and disposed of. After all, he was just another piece of dead meat, wasn't he?'

'No,' Dutch answered and slapped Robbie hard across the face, knocking him off balance. 'He was a piece of dead meat that could give us thirty years behind bars. We fucking told you what to do with him,' he snarled, and cast a furtive glance towards Ethan. 'Those skips only get picked up when full. That could be another day or so.' Marching towards another part of the abattoir where the waste was kept, Dutch saw two skips. 'Find him!' he ordered.

Shocked, Robbie looked at Billy. 'What? He could be in either one. We can't tip them out over the floor.'

'True, that is why you're going to climb in amongst all that blood and guts to find him. Now get on with it!' he barked at them, his voice echoing around the empty abattoir.

Robbie looked helplessly at Billy; he knew they had no choice and inwardly cursed himself for not doing what they had been told in the first place. Ricky's body had looked no better than the slabs of bloodied meat once Adam had finished with him, and they had both felt it made no difference to dispose of him in the waste skips. Reaching up, Dutch jumped to open the lid of the skip. Instantly, the stench filled the air, making them all cough and baulk.

'Please, Ethan,' he begged, not wanting to face the ordeal before him. 'He will have rotted away in that swill bucket,' he almost cried. 'I can't breathe.' Tears ran down his face as he felt bile rise in his throat, making him spit out vomit. All of them turned their backs on the stench and pinched their noses. 'Find him, now! Or you will be joining him.' Ethan's voice was gravelly from coughing and choking so much.

Dutch and Ethan gave Robbie and Billy a leg up to climb in. Nervously, Billy did as he was told. The last thing he wanted was for Ethan to close the skip lid on him so that he would be trapped, suffocated in the stench, unable to get out. Warily, he took off his jacket and did his best to tie it around his nose and mouth. He felt dizzy from the stench but the sooner this was over with the better it would be. Robbie did likewise. Both of them standing knee deep in blood and guts, they ploughed through the remains with their bare hands. Billy did his best to peak over the top of the skip to make sure Ethan and Dutch were still there. Afraid for his life, he carried on as quickly as he could; he wanted to get out desperately. The deeper he dug, the worse the stench became, making him spew what was left of the contents of his stomach. Dutch and Ethan stood well back, walking away to try and get some decent air into their lungs.

After what seemed a lifetime, Robbie shouted, 'Found him!' and with all of his might, heaved Ricky's rotten body, still wrapped in loose wet plastic, over the side, while Ethan pulled at Ricky's corpse to drag him out, letting him fall to the ground with a thump. Robbie looked down at himself in disgust, his hair, face and body now covered in blood-soaked matter. His trousers were wet, and dyed blood red, and his shoes squelched. The bloodstain on his hands seemed ingrained under his fingernails, and he longed to scrub them clean. Puffing and panting, Robbie struggled to get out of the skip as his footing kept slipping on the cow innards and blood he was standing in. Seeing that Dutch was hoisting Billy's body over the side, he gave one last heave and managed to lift himself up over the side of the skip.

Seeing the mess they were both in, Ethan shook his head. 'Well, you're not getting in the van like that. Strip!' he ordered, while looking down at the mess on his own shoes and trousers splashed with blood. Casting a fleeting look of distaste at Dutch,

Ethan walked to where there was more plastic sheeting and pulled away a length of it.

Shivering with cold, Robbie and Billy waited for the next order as they put their arms around themselves, trying to create some kind of warmth. Dutch scooped up the plastic sheeting that contained their clothes and tied it up into a bundle.

'Now him.' Dutch pointed at Ricky's decaying corpse, still barely covered in the original plastic they had wrapped him in. Hardly able to move because of the cold and wearing only their boxer shorts, they pushed Ricky's body onto another huge piece of plastic and rolled him onto it. Ethan and Dutch gagged at the smell.

Picking up the two bundles of clothing, Dutch made his way to the exit, while Ethan stood behind Billy and Robbie as they carried Ricky's body outside. All of them took big gulps of the fresh air into their lungs. There was no one around at this time in the morning to see them, but Dutch hurried to the van and opened it. Billy and Robbie stood for a moment trying to catch their breaths. Their arms ached, but Dutch beckoned them to hurry up.

Although half frozen to death, Billy felt better. They hadn't been tricked and were still alive, which accounted for something. All they had to do now was bury the body in the grave Ethan had made them dig earlier and go home. They had paid for their sloppiness and folly, and he inwardly vowed never to listen to Robbie again and take shortcuts. He had been all bravado and said the brothers would never find out. Well, somehow, they had. Casting an evil glare at Robbie in the darkness of the back of the van, he looked to the front where Ethan was driving with Dutch beside him. 'Put the heater on, will you please, and any chance of a smoke, just to get that smell out of my nose?' Billy asked. Leaning backwards, Dutch handed him his packet and lighter. Quickly rubbing his damp hands on his boxer shorts, Billy scrambled to light one and inhaled, passing the packet over to Robbie, who did the same.

Ethan turned the lights of the van off as he drove closer to the grave and slowed down. Billy and Robbie were reluctant to leave the warmth of the van. 'Glad we kept our shoes on, Robbie; that forest would rip our feet to pieces. Come on, let's get on with it.' Getting out, they stumbled and carried Ricky's body to the freshly dug grave, following Ethan, who marched ahead, then eventually stood beside the mounds of soil they had dug earlier.

Ethan grinned. 'Lots of my enemies buried around here,' he whispered.

Casting furtive glances at each other, Robbie and Billy rolled Ricky into the hole, knowing the last part was to cover him in soil. Their legs were scratched and torn from the undergrowth, making them wince. Ethan and Dutch stood there watching as Robbie and Billy picked up the shovels they had left there earlier and started to put the earth over Ricky's body.

'Wait!' Ethan snapped. Confused, Billy and Robbie both looked up and saw they were looking into the barrel of Ethan and Dutch's guns. Both brothers fired one shot into their foreheads and watched the two men drop into the grave. 'Those bastards will never disobey me again,' Ethan snapped. 'The last thing I need is Lambrianu sneaking in like a ninja warning me, because of those two.'

'Understood, Ethan, but what makes you so sure that Lambrianu knows they hadn't buried him? How could he know that? Those two were sloppy bastards and didn't follow orders, but he would never have found out, would he? Anyway, the only people who know about Ricky is us, those two, and Lambrianu. Those two loose ends are now silenced.'

The snarl on Ethan's face frightened Dutch. He knew Adam

turning up out of the blue had unnerved him, but this was a different Ethan.

'I told the psycho bastard that Ricky had been buried under London Bridge in cement, and all of the time he is in a skip full of dead leftovers. Now, I don't profess to know what they do with dead animals, but I do know that the last thing the skip man from civvy street wants to see is two human feet sticking out. He would be on the phone to the coppers straight away and we would have been dead meat!' Ethan shouted. 'Lambrianu would know that I had lied to him, and you've seen the psycho in action,' Ethan shouted again, like a man possessed. Spit flew out of his mouth. Dutch discreetly wiped his own chin where some had flown out and landed on him. He had never seen his brother so worked up and frightened for his own life.

'Come on, Ethan, it's sorted now, don't sweat it.'

Ethan poked Dutch in the chest. 'But you didn't stand there and lie to Lambrianu, Dutch; I fucking did! And I don't intend to be the next one on his list of Chinese tortures. I always knew he had a nasty reputation, Christ, I've even laughed when people called him "Damian, son of the devil". Well, that's him. But his alibi in all this is watertight. We're the ones Ricky implicated and if we didn't end up behind bars, we'd be in one of these muddy graves.' Breathing heavy after his outburst, Ethan looked down at the three corpses in the grave.

Knowing he was right, a chill ran down Dutch's spine. 'We're off the hook now, Ethan. We've kept our word and Lambrianu will be okay with that. Let sleeping dogs lie now, eh?' Dutch argued, hoping Ethan would calm down a little. His raised voice unnerved Dutch, and he hoped no one was having a midnight stroll and could hear Ethan's shouting. Dutch nodded and looked down at the three bodies. 'Let's get this over with.'

The pair of them picked up the shovels, sweating as they

covered the bodies with the mounds of earth beside the grave. Then they looked around for bushes and anything else they could find to make the ground look untouched. Covered in mud and sweat, and panting for breath, they looked down at the grave. It was as though they had never been there, although a thought did pop into Dutch's mind. 'Could a dog sniff that out, Ethan?'

Ethan smiled. 'It's going to take any dog a lot of digging to get down there.' He laughed for the first time tonight. 'Nobody comes this far in, Dutch; it's too overgrown. Let's scrap the van in the yard and turn it into a matchbox. It stinks and is full of their DNA.'

'I know I could do with a large brandy and a shower,' Dutch said as he looked up at the sky. 'The sun's rising, but it's eerie. I keep expecting werewolves to appear.' He shivered and grinned at his brother.

'Nah.' Ethan laughed. 'They've all turned human again now it's getting lighter.' Picking up the shovels, he led the way back to the van, satisfied that his job was done and he was off the hook. Both of them laughed at the joke and drove off into the darkness until they hit a main road and turned the headlights on and drove home.

9

OPPOSITES ATTRACT

Waking to the sound of birdsong outside, Adam saw that his blinds were open as he blinked bleary eyed around the bedroom. Turning to his side, he noticed Portia had left. On the pillow was a note:

Borrowed a pair of joggers x

Resting his head on top of his arm, he laid back on his pillow and smiled. He could understand why she felt a pair of jogging pants would be better at this time of morning instead of her skimpy dress. He liked that about Portia; there were no long goodbyes and promises to be in touch. She had just upped and left like a thief in the night.

Hearing a noise coming from the kitchen, Adam got up. Expecting it to be Poppy, he wrapped his robe around him even tighter, but was surprised to see another woman there. Then he remembered Bruce had invited Kim around. Running his hands through his hair, he yawned. 'I hope one of those coffees are for me.' The woman gave a weak smile and reached for another cup. 'I'll be out of your hair soon; I've got to go to work.'

Seeing her shyness, Adam smiled, hoping to put her at her ease. 'No rush, just hand me the coffee and I'm going to take a shower. Is Bruce awake?'

'Yes, I'm just taking his coffee into him. Is it okay if I have a quick shower, too?'

'Mine's en-suite, so we don't have to share.' He laughed. 'Take your time. What time is it anyway?' he queried, looking up at the clock on the wall.

'Seven thirty. Can I call a cab from here, or just get a black one from outside?'

'Neither; you're a guest and my guests always get dropped off. I'll ring for one of my drivers to pick you up. What? In about an hour?' Seeing her nod, he took the coffee mug and walked back to his bedroom while calling one of his drivers who were always on hand.

Once showered, Adam had taken his time dressing in his grey suit and black shirt, especially when he heard his driver knock and Kim and Bruce's long goodbyes in the hallway. Splashing on his aftershave, he walked into the kitchen. 'Is it safe to come in?'

'Yeah, of course. Kim's gone. Thanks for arranging her lift to work.'

'Oh, I thought the plumber was here plunging the blocked sink. Was that you both kissing goodbye?' Adam laughed. 'Christ, do you have any tonsils left?'

Pouring him a coffee, Bruce blushed slightly. 'Well, you're one to talk. Who the hell was that you came home with last night? Christ, I thought the headboard was going to crash through the wall!'

Taking the mug, Adam grinned. 'That was Portia. Lovely woman who never runs out of steam.' Adam rubbed his crotch and winced. 'Christ, my dick is sore. I feel like dipping it in a bucket of ice. She really does like her money's worth, but God she is so good.' Adam grinned.

'You haven't mentioned her before. Is it serious?'

Adam's eyes rolled to the ceiling. 'Christ, Bruce, you sound like a Mills & Boon romance. Why does everything have to be a serious affair? For your information, Portia is an independent woman who likes her sex a little on the rough side. She asks no questions and doesn't expect you too either. Personally, I think there is a rich Mr Portia tucked away somewhere, but that's not my business. She turns up when she's in town and expects one thing and one thing only. And by God, do I give it to her!' Adam boasted and laughed. 'I feel like I've done ten rounds in a wrestling match, and she won!' They both burst out laughing and Adam failed to hear the knock at the door, until he was interrupted by Poppy's voice. 'Morning, Mr Lambrianu...'

Turning on his heels, Adam stood looking at her in the doorway. 'Poppy, how did you get in?'

'The cleaner, I met her as I came up. I came to remind you that you have a meeting with Daniel Wilkinson this morning.'

Adam looked at her admiringly and flashed a smile. 'I know. I hadn't forgotten. I was waiting for Bruce to say goodbye to his lady love.' For a moment they stood in silence, looking at each other, and Bruce watched them both curiously. 'Erm, did you say you wanted to go to the casino today?' she asked.

'Yes, we'll do that later. I need to book my motorbike in for its MOT first and some other stuff.' Adam felt fuddled seeing her standing there, with her large brown eyes gazing at him innocently. He suddenly felt lost for words.

'I've done that already. I saw the note on your cork board in the office as a reminder and rang the garage. I hope you don't mind. After all, that's why I'm here. To take the pressure off your everyday things.' She smiled.

'Really? Do you know everything about me? You're better than a detective. I had better be careful what I write in future.' He had meant it jokingly, but saw the smile disappear from her face.

Poppy's eyes flashed with anger. 'Well, I know you're a size 12 shoe, but that's not half as big as your ego, is it? I'm just doing my job, Mr Lambrianu.'

Shocked at her outburst, Adam flashed a glance at Bruce. 'Crikey, the lady's got a temper. It was a joke, Poppy! Chill out. I'll show you the casino later, that is if my ego can fit through the door!' he snapped, before frowning at her. 'And how do you know my shoe size?' Holding up his hands to stop her answering, he shook his head. 'It's okay, I know, it's your job. Did you know I had a piss at 7 a.m. No point in asking, I presume you do,' he added. He couldn't understand why she made him act like this, but she did.

Stubbornly, she stuck out her chin, and Adam noticed a faint freckle on her nose. 'Is there anything else you need, Mr Lambrianu? I will be in the office if you do.'

Admiring how tall and slim she was in her pale mint skirt suit with matching shoes, Adam smiled. 'Only that you look very nice today, Poppy; that colour matches your eyes when you're angry.' Seeing her blush slightly, he felt he had won her over and made the peace.

'If that's the case, you will be seeing a lot of green then, because you seem to take pleasure in making me angry!' Seeing his scowl, she realised she had gone too far. 'Sorry, Mr Lambrianu. You look nice too,' she added as she made for the door.

Throwing his hands up in the air, Adam looked at Bruce. 'What the hell did I say to deserve that?'

'Chemistry, Adam, definite chemistry. You can feel it in the air between you. She's a fiery sort and unlike you're used to, she answers you back.' Bruce grinned. He knew only too well that, apart from some jealous woman fighting over him in the club, no woman apart from family had ever given him as good as she got.

'She has definitely got to go; she gets on my nerves. Who the hell does she think she's talking to? I'm her boss, paying her fucking wages. Well, I hope she doesn't expect a bonus!'

Bruce smiled to himself as he watched Adam rant on and then slip into Italian and rant to himself even more, pacing up and down as he did.

'She pisses me off, sticking her nose into everything.' Calming down a little, Adam also remembered how Poppy had covered for him, without him asking her to.

'Personally, I think you like her, but, as you said yourself, it's a hands-off situation. Worst of all, I think she likes you too but just seems to wind you up when she's trying to help. It's a strange situation, Adam. I'm curious to see it unfold.'

Bruce smiled and, pouting his lips, Adam shook his head. 'Oh, shut up and drink your coffee.'

On his way out of the room, Adam bumped into Knuckles, who put his hand in his jacket pocket and pulled out a wad of cash. 'Courtesy of the Nag's Head.'

Shocked, Adam looked at the money. 'Is it the real thing?' Seeing Knuckles nod, Adam smiled. 'How did you get that? The place must be swarming with coppers the way the pub was shot to pieces.' Adam laughed.

'Practice,' Knuckles muttered, handing the cash over to Adam. Incredulously, Adam stared at the money and shook his head. 'Practice!' he repeated and laughed. 'Nice one, Knuckles.' He grinned, shoving the cash into his inside pocket.

* * *

Scarlet had been invited to see what changes Julie had made to the family home. Apparently, she had already organised an army of people to freshen it up, which was good, because in a couple of days it was the family lunch that Scarlet had planned. Curious, she felt eager to see the house and left London early to avoid traffic.

As Knuckles turned off the road leading to the house, Scarlet looked up at the wrought iron gates with LAMBRIANU crafted at the top. Peering closely through the car window, she could see the gates had been freshly painted. Knuckles typed in the alarm code and the gates swung open to reveal a newly gravelled driveway with the overgrown hedgerow and trees all cut back. Already Scarlet felt pleased, but pensive. She had loved this home, but always felt sad when she visited it, which was why she had distanced herself from it. Memories flashed through her mind as she drove up to the house of her father holding her first bike as she wobbled trying to ride it.

It felt like stepping into the past seeing it all spick and span, but a feeling of guilt washed over her for neglecting it. Taking out her keys, she heard a voice and noticed the front door was already ajar. Knuckles glanced at her and put his finger to his lips, pushing her aside while he investigated. Opening the door, he turned and looked at Scarlet, bemused; the house was full of workmen painting away. A smile crossed Scarlet's face and, amidst warnings to her that some of the paintwork was still wet, she strode in excitedly. Marvelling at the shining chandeliers newly polished, and the marble flooring in the hallway gleaming, she walked ahead to the kitchen.

The kitchen had always been the heart of the home where everyone had gathered. Looking around, she saw that, although the colour scheme was the same, it had all been freshly painted and cleaned to a very high standard. Scarlet let her hand trail along the worktops, especially the gold bar stool with Julie's name on the back. Fondly, she remembered that was the place where Julie had sat and offered advice and listened to everyone's gossip.

Walking towards the dining area, Scarlet saw a huge round table that looked like something from King Arthur's court. Suddenly, Scarlet wanted to laugh; Julie had been adamant that no one would sit at the head of the table, and this was her way of making sure no one did. The round wooden table had a large multi-coloured mosaic effect on top of it, but looking closer at it brought tears to her eyes. Each odd glass shape had a photo of the family and the whole tabletop was covered in family photos and special memories. The two large glass pieces in the centre were photos of her mum and dad, and Scarlet sniffed hard to hold back the tears. She walked up to Knuckles, who was standing in the doorway, and put her arms around his waist. 'It's beautiful, isn't it? There are even photos of you and the kids on there. I wish Mum could see it.'

'She can. She's here along with your dad. Dynamite wouldn't have got your mum out of this place. She loved it, and everyone in it.'

Shocked that Knuckles had spoken a whole sentence without a grunt, Scarlet realised he had felt the love this house had offered everyone that walked inside it. Impulsively, she reached up and pecked him on the lips. 'Let's go, I've seen enough. I can't wait for the rest of them to see this.' Taking his hand, she walked back through the house to the car. Strangely, she turned back and looked back at the house as something occurred to her. That had been the most loving and intimate she and Knuckles had been for a long time. Musing to herself, she smiled; maybe this house was full of magic fairy love dust. After all, it had just sprinkled some on her and Knuckles.

* * *

'Well, this is the casino. I presume you've seen one before. I'll just say hello to the manager and then I will show you the office where I spend most of my time.' Adam was doing his best to sound professional in front of Poppy. Seeing her shake her head, he looked confused as she looked up at the ceiling and the enormity of the place.

'I've seen small casinos, Mr Lambrianu, but never one on this scale. It's like Las Vegas,' she beamed.

Seeing it through someone else's eyes, Adam looked around. It was an awesome place full of class, and Adam thought that maybe he had taken the place for granted. For him it was his daily workplace, but now he looked at it, he realised she was right; it was awesome. A man came striding towards them wearing a black tuxedo and bow tie. 'Mr Lambrianu, how very good to see you.' Frowning, he cocked his head. 'I hope there isn't a problem?'

Flashing a charming smile, Adam shook his hand. 'Not that I am aware of, Matt. I'm here to show Poppy Nightingale, my new PA, the casino. She will also be working here with me when needed. Join us and you can be our guide.' Adam smiled.

Poppy looked around at all the lights, flashing slot machines and gleaming roulette tables as people, already at this time of day, were playing them. Holding her hand out to shake Matt's, he, in gentlemanly fashion, held the back of her hand to his lips and kissed it, making her blush.

'She's immune to charm, Matt. I know I've tried.' Adam laughed.

Matt linked his arm through Poppy's. 'Let's start with the restaurant, Miss Nightingale. I will introduce the pit bosses and gaming managers in due course. Onwards and upwards.' They stood at the bottom of a red velvet staircase, which started narrow, but got wider and wider as you climbed the stairs, giving you a bird's eye view of everything below. It almost took Poppy's breath away. Flushed with excitement, she looked at Adam, who proffered his arm for her to link her other one through.

'By the way, Poppy.' He grinned. 'Mr Lambrianu was my father. You can call me Adam.' He felt his own excitement rise as he watched her face light up in wonder at the splendour of the casino. Looking even further up, Poppy commented on the wall of glass windows. 'What's up there? It's all glass, but I can't see anything inside.'

'That's the whole point, Poppy; when you're up there you can see through them and all around the casino, but the glass is one way. No one can see myself or the monitors and that's where the main offices are, including mine. That is our bird's eye view,' he boasted, like a child showing off his toys.

Poppy linked her arm tighter through Adam's; breathing in his aftershave, she felt almost heady with joy. His perfect poise in his well-tailored suit made him look distinguished, and his eyes seemed to twinkle like sapphires in this lighting. As she walked around, she thought how relaxed he was here with everyone greeting him and laughing with him, including customers. This was clearly his domain, she thought to herself.

Eventually, they reached Adam's office and Matt left them to it. 'This is absolutely beautiful, Adam.'

'Ah, some would call a casino a den of iniquity.' He laughed. 'There is also my apartment upstairs and Matt has his here too. We need someone on the premises at all times. It has eight bedrooms, so if you ever need to stay over because of lateness, they are at your disposal.'

'Are you expecting me to have late nights here and stay over?' she teased and winked at him.

'Erm, no, that's not what I meant. It's just in case,' he stammered, feeling foolish. Then as he realised she was joking, his face broke into a wide smile, lighting it up. Gazing at him, Poppy looked into his eyes. He had charm, wit, and was beautiful, she thought to herself. Without thinking, the words left her mouth.

'I always thought you were beautiful, Adam. Even when I was a waitress, I would look at you and like the way you brightened everyone's evening.' Blushing to the roots, she sat down suddenly. 'Oh my God. I shouldn't have said that! I don't know why I did.' With her head in her hands, Poppy wanted the ground to swallow her up.

Reaching over the desk, Adam took her hand and squeezed it. 'No harm done, Poppy.' He smiled. 'Flattery like that from a beautiful woman like yourself is enough to boost anyone's ego.'

Horrified at her own words, Poppy stood up to leave. 'Thanks for showing me the casino... Erm, I have to go. Really, I do.' Her face flushed, and grabbing her bag in panic, Adam stopped her.

'Hey, Poppy, it's not as though you have to get back to work, is it?' He smiled. 'I was thinking of having something to eat; why don't you join me and taste the delicacies of the casino restaurant?' Her huge brown eyes, which seemed to take up the whole of her face, had filled up with tears. One blink, Adam thought to himself, and one tear would fall down her cheek. Feeling a stirring within him, he took her hand. 'Boss's orders.' He grinned, flashing a smile he hoped would put her at ease.

Slowly, she followed him and they were seated at his favourite table. 'You know, Poppy, I feel as though you know everything about me and yet I know nothing about you. So let's pretend we're speed dating and only have a few minutes to bare our souls.'

Poppy paused and wondered if he was toying with her after her silly outburst, which she now sorely regretted. But she decided to play along. 'Well,' she began, 'you know my name. My father is a retired navy man. Mum's no longer with us.'

'Stop!' Adam put down his drink and laughed. 'We only have four minutes left. Fast forward, Poppy, time's nearly up.'

Giggling, she threw her head back. 'I suppose that did sound a bit formal. My name's Poppy. I am a PA for Adam Lambrianu. I used to waitress at the club while I was at college and, like my father, I like to travel and trained as an air hostess.' Seeing Adam cock his head and smile, Poppy took a sip of her drink. Inwardly, she felt that even though she had prompted him to remember her days waitressing at the club, he had no recollection of their moment of passion together. Many times, especially tonight as they were talking and laughing together, she'd nearly blurted it out and asked him if he remembered her and what had made him ignore her so cruelly the following day, but why spoil a nice evening?

Although, she had wondered many times since she had left the club if he had ever thought about her and what had happened to change his mind about her so abruptly. It had wounded her deeply, and she had also felt cheap at giving herself so freely. After a time in turmoil, she eventually came to the decision that it was because she had given herself so freely that he had lost interest. She had been just another notch on his bedpost. Why would a man like him want a woman with no morals? Gazing at him as his perfectly formed mouth broke out into a wide smile, making his blue eyes bore into her soul, she smiled.

'Impressive. My very own trolley dolly.' Adam nodded.

'Not quite, it just means I was meant to be a waitress on land and in the air!'

Letting out a throaty, warm laugh, Adam looked at her closely. He liked the sound of her laughter, which was genuine and warm. The lamp on the table seemed to flicker and catch her eyes and illuminate the green flecks shining within them. Letting his mind wander for a moment as she spoke, he couldn't understand how he had missed her when she had worked as a waitress at the club.

Then she carried on, breaking into his thoughts. 'After flying around the world and seeing nothing of it, I applied for a job as a travel rep for the same company as the airline,' she added. 'It was fun and I learnt a lot.' Seeing Adam look at his watch, she playfully smacked his hand. 'I like fish fingers, Batman and Star Wars movies and of course charity shops.'

For a moment, Adam stopped laughing and looked at her, confused. 'Charity shops?'

Taking a sip of her wine, Poppy nodded. As the restaurant started to fill up, Poppy noticed the admiring glances Adam was getting from other women. 'I find the better the area, the better the vintage clothing they donate, like this suit.'

Looking down at her suit that Adam had admired earlier, she blushed and shrugged her shoulders. 'I'm ordinary. Nothing impressive about me, Adam.' She smiled awkwardly and caught his hypnotic eyes full of warmth and attention that seemed to be only for her, for the time being.

Lowering his voice to a whisper, Adam took her hand. 'Well, I can't have my PA searching the charity shops for something to wear to work. I will give you an expense account for your work clothing. The newspapers would have a field day if they thought my right-hand woman went to charity shops.' He laughed.

'I wasn't hinting. I thought we were just baring our souls. Telling the truth...'

'Stop! Time's up, Poppy. Time to move on and accept what I say. Now, tonight, Bruce and his new girlfriend are coming with me to the beer festival. I've got a stall full of Lambrianu wine at their disposal, and I thought I'd check it out. Why don't you come too?' he asked without thinking, then stopped himself short, correcting himself. 'I mean, you might have to take notes or something.' Seeing her nod, he felt more elated than he should have done, but he didn't care. He wanted to see more of Poppy and this was the perfect place to get to know her better.

* * *

Back at the club, Adam hummed to himself as he went into the office to see Scarlet. As he popped his head around the door, he was surprised to see Phil, the landlord of the Nag's Head, sitting in front of Scarlet. The smile dropped from his face as he saw Scarlet's sombre look.

'Sit down, Adam; you remember Phil, don't you? Well, it seems he's had a spot of trouble.'

Nonchalantly, Adam sat down and crossed his legs. 'I hear you had twenty grand of counterfeit notes in your cellar, Phil. So, what do you want?'

Seeing Phil's miserable, unshaven face turn towards him, Adam sat there stoney faced, before flashing a glancing look towards Scarlet.

'My place has been shot to fuck, Mr Lambrianu. Those blokes who give me the money to launder want my guts! The coppers are all over the place asking questions. I don't know what to do, I really don't.' Phil choked and burst into tears of despair. 'Help me, *please!*' he shouted, clasping his hands together, as though in prayer.

'What about Tommy?' Adam asked in a cold, distant manner. 'What does he say about all this?'

'Oh, he's pissed off; packed up and legged it as soon as the shit hit the fan. Probably sofa-surfing on some druggie's floor. He's left me to clear up all this shit, and to be honest I don't know what to do.'

'What about the people that gave you the money to launder?' Scarlet butted in. 'Don't they have any ideas?'

'No, they think I've grassed them up, but I haven't, I swear I haven't! Two big Jamaican fellas came into my bedroom when I was sleeping and held a gun to my head. They warned me if the coppers go banging on their door, the only clothes I'll be wearing is a body bag. For fuck's sake, I wet myself that night, I don't deny it.' Running out of steam, he sat there panting, waiting for Adam to wave his magic wand and make all of his worries go away.

Adam spied Phil closely; he was a miserable-looking man. His creased, unwashed shirt stunk of BO and, looking at his blood-shot eyes, he looked like he hadn't slept in days. Not exactly the way he should have come to his office begging for help, Adam thought. After all, you wouldn't go cap in hand to the bank manager looking like that, so why here?

'What about us? What do we get out of it?' Adam asked. His cold demeanour showed no friendship or compassion.

'Anything! Whatever you say I will do. Just get those fellas off my back, please! They stole legit money from my safe, too. A couple of grand in takings. They won't admit it, but who else would do it?'

Frowning for a moment, Adam thought about Knuckles. It was more than coincidence that he had turned up with the money Phil owed them without a word. Now, the puzzle pieces fit together.

'All that counterfeit money the police are looking into isn't going away, Phil,' said Scarlet. 'We can't do anything about that, and you'd have to hold your hands up to that one. And the police will want to know who gave it to you; I hope you've got a good story, Phil.' Scarlet tutted nonchalantly.

'Tommy! I could tell them Tommy brought it home. He deserves to have a taste of what I've had,' Phil spat. Adam looked at Scarlet and nodded. 'For my services with the gentlemen you mention, we would want your pub. After all, you're going to end up doing a stretch, Phil. Couple of years possibly; money laundering isn't looked upon fondly. Someone will need to keep the place going, and that's my offer – you said you'd do anything...' Adam repeated slowly, taking great satisfaction in Phil's misery.

Crushed, and raising his head from his hands, Phil looked horrified at Adam as the reality of his situation kicked in. He was finished; his life's work was over. All because that stupid son of his had talked him into a get-rich-quick scheme.

'I've fucked up, haven't I?' he asked soberly. 'I might as well be dead. I'm sixty years old with a bit of savings, and I've worked my guts off in that place. Late nights, drunken idiots, early mornings. All for nothing,' Phil said, as though talking to himself.

Adam didn't want to hear his sob story and was already of tired of hearing his pleadings. He had agreed to all of this and had got himself into this mess. Adam was more than willing to take everything away from him. 'What's left on the mortgage of the pub? When the mortgage is paid, the pub is yours, isn't it?'

Phil drummed his fingers on his chin as he tried to recall. 'I reckon I owe about ten, fifteen grand perhaps. The London postcode is probably worth more than the pub. Blood, sweat and tears have gone into that place. Every penny I could muster went as an overpayment to pay off the mortgage for my retirement.' It was the first time Adam and Scarlet had seen a smile cross his face with pride.

'Then sell it to us for ten grand, minus five for getting those fellas off your back. Put the blame firmly on Tommy. It's your word against his, but he's done a runner, hasn't he? And I tell you what.' Adam smiled graciously. 'So that you don't lose your home and everything you've worked for, you can run the pub for us when you get out. That keeps everything neat and tidy.'

Stunned, and knowing he had been beaten, Phil slowly nodded his head. 'Can you save me from prison?'

Adam let out a huge sigh. 'That's a tricky one, but I tell you what I can do.' Pausing for effect, he looked at Phil's eager face. 'We could make sure your time inside wouldn't be a hard one. We could make life comfortable. After all, we're friends of old; we have history. Blame Tommy, take a wrap on the knuckles, and live to fight another day, eh? See a solicitor, complete the sale of your pub and I'll transfer the money we owe into your account.'

'Five grand...' Phil muttered. 'Doesn't seem a lot for a life-time's work, does it?'

Scarlet had been listening intently. 'Well, at least you will have a lifetime, Phil, and a job and home to come back to. It's your choice. You came to us for answers and we've given you them. Have a think about it.'

Phil looked around at them both and nodded. 'I'll be in touch. What about in the meantime – those fellas, I mean?'

'It's sorted.' Adam smiled magnanimously and stood up to shake Phil's hand. 'Get your solicitor to send your bank details and the money is yours.'

Scarlet's eyes narrowed as Adam closed the door behind Phil and put his finger to his lips to stop her outburst. After a few minutes, he nodded for her to speak. 'What have you done?' she asked.

'Simple, the best man won. I've taught that greasy, lying bastard not to lie to my face and think we're so stupid we wouldn't recognise counterfeit notes being handed over in payment for our services. Taking us for mugs and laughing at us, I bet. Disrespect. I won't have it, and for that he's paid the ultimate price. He has lost everything, and we've bought a decent pub.'

'You never told me that he tried palming the fake money off to us? Don't I work here now?'

Giving Scarlet a knowing look, Adam nodded. 'It's sorted, and we haven't lost anything. You remember how Phil blamed those fellas for taking the money out of his safe? That was us. He's so panic stricken and terrified for his life he isn't thinking straight, is he?'

'You got the money?' Seeing Adam nod again, Scarlet smiled. 'My, my, you are a clever boy. So, who are these Jamaican fellas threatening him?'

'The yardies. You remember me telling you they offered us the money to launder, but it was too hot for my taste? So for their twenty thousand worthless bits of paper stashed in Phil's cellar, they get five grand of his money. Legal money is better than nothing, isn't it, and it's a peace offering from us.'

Scarlet's jaw dropped and she threw her head back on the headrest of the chair. 'Fuck, I'd forgotten about that. Yeah, they will take that for their trouble. Five grand in the hand is better than nothing, and the finger isn't pointing at them. Phil will do time, and the coppers will find Tommy. Nice one, Adam.' Scarlet laughed. 'Anyway, how did Poppy like the casino?' she enquired, now that Phil's problem was off her hands and sorted.

'Enlightening, dear sister. Let's just say that, shall we?'

Smugly, Scarlet sat back in her chair. 'Good, I'm glad you're getting on, although I'm not sure what enlightening means. Well, you'd better visit your yardie friends and give them the news, hadn't you? Have you eaten?'

'I had a late lunch with Poppy. Oh, and I need to sort her out an expense account. Everything she comes to work in is from charity shops! She may be working here for a short while, but even the club staff get their uniforms paid for,' he added and left Scarlet in her office.

A wry grin crossed Scarlet's face. A short while, she thought to herself. Me thinks you protest too much, little brother.

10

A FAMILY GATHERING

Sat in the car on her way to Sunday lunch, Julie's phone rang. Answering it, she heard Katie's voice. 'What news, Katie?' She put the call on loudspeaker so Diana could hear, too.

'Bad news, Julie. Chris is still away. I haven't had the chance to tell him about Scarlet or hosting the hen weekend. I was told by his butler that he would be away for a couple of weeks.'

'You sound breathless, Katie – are you okay? You're not in danger, are you?'

'No, I'm just in a hurry, Julie, and Scarlet's mobile keeps going to answerphone. I'll call again as soon as I tell Chris about the hen weekend. I'll keep in touch when I can tell everyone that I love them and will speak soon. Love you too.' Smiling, Julie put her mobile back in her bag. The plan was falling into place.

* * *

Everyone marvelled as they entered the newly refurbished family home. To Scarlet, it resembled a museum with everyone walking around, up and downstairs discussing how Julie had brought the house to life again. The main topic of conversation was the table, with everyone pointing out their own memories as they looked at the photos. Inwardly, Scarlet thought her heart would burst with pride. This was what she'd wanted before their doomed expedition to Italy. All of them gathered around the table, for maybe one last time.

Kissing her on the cheek, her older brother, Bobby, greeted her with his wife Amy. 'What's cooking, Scarlet? I don't see you with an apron on.'

Grandly, Scarlet pointed to a corner of the kitchen. 'I'm no chef, Bobby, but I have a lot working for me.' She grinned. In the corner was an enormous hot trolley filled with huge dishes. Walking over, Bobby shook his head and lifted the lids off each dish. They were full of potatoes, vegetables, and gravy. Two large roast joints, beef and chicken, cooked to perfection, sat there waiting to be sliced, alongside warming plates and a huge apple crumble and custard. 'There's a trifle in the fridge if no one wants the crumble,' she beamed excitedly. 'The chefs were here early this morning preparing and cooking, and I must say, they have done a wonderful job.'

'You didn't think she was actually going to peel potatoes, did you?' Adam laughed and hugged his older brother from his mother's first marriage. 'If I'd have thought she would cook it, I would never have come.' Everyone laughed and greeted each other. Gone was the formality of their professional clothing; instead, this was replaced with jeans, T-shirts and trainers, albeit designer ones. The easy ambience, with everyone chattering away as though they had only seen each other yesterday, when in fact months had passed, pleased Scarlet. Everyone kept in touch, but sometimes life got in the way and they were all busy. Today, Scarlet thought to herself, everyone had cleared their diary and it was time to relax together, as one again.

The last to arrive and making a grand entrance was Julie, with Diana, her daughter, at her side. No way did anyone expect her to turn up in jeans, but they were surprised to see she was wearing an Indian salwar kameez, a long, gold embroidered tunic, with matching trousers. She looked amazing. 'I found her on the doorstep,' she scoffed, pointing to Diana. 'Christ, she looks like some Amazon delivery driver in those jeans and polo shirt. And is that a scrunchie tying your hair back? I thought they had gone out in the 80s.' Used to Julie's criticism of her clothing, Diana made a face. 'Thanks, Mum. I see you came in your casual wear.'

'Well, everyone!' Julie shouted to them all. 'What do you think? Am I brilliant or what?' she cackled. 'Someone open that champagne and let's have a toast.'

Popping the cork, Knuckles, who was still dressed in his black trousers and white shirt, filled a tray of glasses with champagne as Julie and Scarlet handed them around. 'To family!' Julie shouted, raising her glass in the air as they all echoed her sentiments.

Scarlet wanted to make a toast of gratitude. 'To Julie Gold, who never fails to impress us all with her modesty. Or her late arrival while making a dramatic entrance. Thank you!' Everyone gave Julie a huge cheer for her efforts, and she graciously gave a bow.

'I don't do modesty,' she chimed. 'That's for poor people.' Everyone burst out laughing and began getting out the plates and setting the table. 'Anyway, the only reason I am late is because Katie called me.' Julie pulled Scarlet aside on the pretence of pouring more drinks.

'Is she okay, Julie? Why hasn't she called me?' Scarlet asked with concern.

'Because your mobile is going straight to answerphone, possibly because you don't want interrupting during this family get-together.' Lowering her voice, Julie whispered the contents of the call to Scarlet. 'Patience is a virtue, Scarlet; we can wait.' Julie smiled and took a gulp of her champagne.

'At least she is keeping in touch, that's the main thing. I might try and call her later, just to say hello. Do you think that would be okay?' Scarlet asked, sounding unsure of herself.

'It's only natural that you should call your sister and ask her to make notes of famous bridal shops in and around the area, don't you?' Julie gave Scarlet a knowing look, and the smile on Scarlet's face brightened as she nodded her head in agreement.

Awkwardly, Bruce looked at Adam. 'Adam, I'm not really family and I feel as though I'm intruding today...'

'You are if we say you are. Julie and Diana are not my blood relatives, and neither is Jack. Bobby is my half-brother. Look around you, Bruce; hardly any of us are related, but we're family. Biology has nothing to do with it. This house was always like this, and it's good to see it like that again. We are people who want to be with each other, Bruce, not have to be.' Adam looked up and was shocked to see Poppy breeze in.

'Sorry, everyone, the train was delayed,' she panted. Scarlet handed her a glass of champagne welcomingly. 'Well, you're here now. I told you to get one of the drivers to pick you up.'

'I didn't like to; it's a straight enough train, but the trains aren't famed for their reliability, are they?' She smiled and cast a glance towards Adam.

Scarlet slowly introduced Poppy to everyone and, reaching Adam, who stood rooted to the spot, she whispered in his ear, 'I thought it would be a nice gesture.'

Embarrassed, Poppy sidled up to Adam. 'You didn't know I'd been invited, did you?' Seeing him shake his head, she felt awkward. 'I'll make my excuses and leave. I'm sorry.'

'No, no, don't go,' he stammered. 'I was surprised, that's all.

Truly, I'm ashamed I never thought of asking you myself. Please, make yourself at home. Let me show you around; sadly, we have all neglected the place with one thing and another, but Julie has kept the flag flying.' He grinned.

Away from the boisterous laughter and chatter, Adam manoeuvred Poppy around the house. 'It's beautiful, Adam,' she breathed. 'Oh, I don't just mean the splendour of it all; I wouldn't expect anything else.' She blushed, looking at all the family photos. 'But it has a warmth about it, and that little patch of garden leading from the patio doors in the kitchen, with its cherry blossom tree and beautiful border plants, stop it looking less like a country mansion or a hotel. It's Downton Abbey.' She smiled.

Adam watched her closely, and a strange feeling overwhelmed him, like someone had walked over his grave. He found it strange that, of all the things she would comment on, it would be his mother's private little garden. Her space, where she read and potted her own plants. The space where his mum and dad would sit on the garden bench together first thing in a morning and have a coffee before the hectic day ahead. The very place she died. 'That was Mum's garden,' he said sombrely, barely above a whisper, letting his mask fall a little. Composing himself, he grinned. 'I'm sure Julie will tell you that I was conceived under that cherry blossom tree. God knows, she tells everyone else.' He smiled, making her laugh.

Bruce sauntered over to them, breaking the spell between them. 'Dinner's about to be served. I've been sent to get you both.' He smiled. 'Nice to see you again, Poppy. Have you sobered up after trying the delights of the beer festival?' he joked.

'Just about. Kim didn't look too well. How is she now?'

'On the mend, although it will be a long time before she mixes her drinks again. Come on, everyone's sitting down ready to eat. Adam, please sit near me and don't let Julie spoon feed me. My leg's on the mend and my arm may be in plaster, but I can manage a fork on my own!' He laughed.

Bursting out laughing and glad of the interruption, Adam nodded. 'I'll do my best, bro.' Following Bruce and Poppy out of the lounge, Adam remembered how Poppy had insisted on paying her way and buying a round of drinks when they had gone to the beer festival together. It had been a fun night and he felt he had got to know her a little better. She was independent and he liked that, but this was a new breed of woman to him. Normally he was expected to foot the bill, and he was used to that. But he smiled to himself as he thought back to when he had refused to let her pay and she had said, while stubbornly, wagging a finger in his face, 'If I don't buy a round, then I'm not drinking Lambrianu.'

A slight chuckle left his lips. They felt like they were equals, of a sort. And he liked that, but it still puzzled him.

* * *

After dinner was over, everyone agreed it had been a fantastic afternoon. A great success and exactly what Scarlet had planned. This afternoon would be remembered for a very long time, she thought to herself as the brandies were poured and cigars were lit after dinner. She was hoping they could continue to do this on a regular basis, but she didn't want to think about that now. No one knew what the future held.

'What about your stag party, Knuckles? Got anything special planned?' Jack shouted over the table.

'Well, it's not going to be strippers, is it?' Julie scoffed, slightly the worse for wear. 'That would be like a busman's holiday for him after working at the club. Anyway, it will be a small affair. He hasn't got any mates.'

'Yes, he has,' Adam interrupted. 'Who are all these men sat around the table? I'm his best man and I will organise the stag of a lifetime. It's about quality, Julie, not quantity. Strippers or not, he needs a good sendoff if he's marrying Scarlet. That's a brave man sat there, and we need to make his last night of freedom something to ease the pain of wedded bliss.' Everyone nodded their head in agreement, including Knuckles.

Poppy watched Adam playfully bantering with his family. He seemed like a different man amongst them, not the businessman he portrayed daily. If anything, he was the younger brother who took the jibes about his sex life, and their reminiscences about his weird girlfriends from the past, making them all laugh. She couldn't believe the enormity of the table and saw a few empty chairs. 'How come all of those chairs are empty? Has someone not turned up?' she asked innocently, now the champagne had loosened her tongue.

'They're not empty, Poppy, just vacant. There is Adam and Scarlet's sister, Katie, and her kids, and my son, Josh, who is currently in Japan. Ooh, by the way, he is going to do a zoom meeting soon to say hello to everyone.' Julie grinned. 'He's a little older than Bobby.'

'And a bloody good friend,' Bobby piped up. 'We went to visit him last month for a holiday. He looks great,' Bobby told everyone.

Julie listened to him speak about her son, whom she and her late husband Ralph Gold had adopted from her sister when she had died from a drug overdose. She thought her heart would burst with pride hearing Bobby's words, and her eyes welled up. She was pleased they were still close after all of these years. 'Well, you just tell him to get his arse back to

England to see his old mum,' she barked, sniffing back the tears.

'He's coming for the wedding, didn't he tell you?' Bobby looked down at the table. 'Shit, if that was supposed to be a surprise I've put my foot in it, haven't I?'

'Absolutely not. We never heard a thing, did we, girls?' Julie laughed. 'Anyway, Poppy, as I was saying, those chairs are just waiting for the people they belong to to sit on them.'

'That's beautiful,' Poppy muttered. 'What a beautiful sentiment.'

Without thinking, Adam, who was sat beside her, squeezed her hand. 'That's not sentiment, Poppy; it's people who love each other and keep the home fires burning for them until their return. Isn't that so, Scarlet?' Seeing them all nod their heads in agreement, he knew he had said the right thing. And it was true. He was determined his sister, Katie, should be sat there with her family, her real family who loved her and wanted her safe.

Feeling the warmth of his manicured hand in hers, Poppy smiled up at him lovingly. She liked this side of Adam very much, but she felt herself on a slippery slope to nowhere. Looking around at all this grandeur, she knew she was punching far above her weight. But a girl can dream, she mused to herself.

'All we need now is someone to live here, unless we all agree to sell it after all of this time,' Scarlet announced. 'Any takers?'

Bobby almost choked on his drink. 'Sell it? I never thought you would say that,' he said, the smile dropping from his face.

Scarlet's blue eyes flashed at him. 'Do you want it?' Seeing him bow his head, she carried on. 'Well, we have to make a decision sometime. Julie has brought it back to life out of her own pocket. Are we really going to neglect it and use it as a drop-in centre when we're in the area? It makes sense to sell it to someone who will take care of it and use it, but we all have to agree. I know

Katie will go along with whatever we say. So, what's the majority?' she asked matter-of-factly, stunning everyone around the table.

'What about you and Knuckles, now you're going to be married?' Adam asked.

'Not practical. The kids have their schools and their friends, and I need to be near the club with my finger on the pulse. It's not really an option for us.' Everyone sat in silence as they thought over Scarlet's words.

Suddenly, Adam broke the silence. 'I'll take it. I will stay at the flat, especially for late nights and early morning meetings, but this will be somewhere to breathe away from the city. I'll need a housekeeper though, but I'm sure that can be arranged.'

A smile crossed Scarlet and Julie's faces. 'SOLD! To Adam Lambrianu for one penny. Anyone got anything to say?'

'Can we still visit and go to the seaside?' her own children asked.

'I daresay Uncle Adam wouldn't mind you coming here to visit the delights of Southend-on-Sea. Would you, Adam?'

'That goes without saying to any of you. It may be mine, but it's our home and always will be. It's time I laid down roots, and this is as good a place as any. I will pay your asking price, Scarlet.' He laughed. 'Does that include the furniture?' Breaking the tension, somewhat, everyone burst out laughing.

Looking at those gathered around the table, Julie's mind wandered. For a man who was orphaned as a young boy and a single mother scratching a living working as a stripper, Tony and Francesca Lambrianu had left one hell of a legacy. Turning to her own daughter, her heart swelled with pride. Diana was her own woman and always had been, much like herself, Julie mused. She was a much-respected detective of the murder squad and had worked bloody hard proving herself to get there. Ralph would be giddy with pride, Julie thought fondly. All of them had started from nothing with not a penny to their names, and at times the future had looked pretty grim, but all their ducking and diving had paid off so their families didn't have to live hand to mouth the way they had. Thinking back on her own life, Julie remembered her days working as a prostitute. One wrinkly dick had looked the same as any other in those days as long as she could pay the rent. *Now look at me*, Julie thought. Part of one big happy family, and growing bigger every day. It made Julie feel proud of the life she'd made for herself.

Breaking into Julie's thoughts, Poppy suddenly stood up. 'It's time I made a move. I didn't realise it was so late!'

'Come back to London with us,' Adam interrupted. 'I'm going to leave my motorbike here. I've had too much to drink.'

Taking the initiative, Scarlet butted in. 'Why don't you stay over, Adam? It's your house now and there's nothing major going on tomorrow, is there?' She smiled. 'Knuckles will drive me home.'

'I'm okay too,' Julie butted in. 'Lewis will come and collect me and Diana. Anyone else need a lift?' Julie shouted out. Poppy was about to put her hand up when Adam stopped her. 'You could stay too if you wanted to. And, erm, you too, Bruce?'

'Well, I could help you clear up...' Poppy smiled. 'But I don't have anything else to wear for tomorrow.'

'Mmm, and seeing his drooling chops,' Julie whispered in Scarlet's ear, 'she won't need anything to wear in bed either. What have you got up your sleeve, Scarlet?'

'Tying up loose ends, Julie, just like you said. When we have an hour to kill, I'll fill you in on the rest.'

Curiously, Julie looked at her. 'I do love a bit of gossip, Scarlet. Soon, eh?'

Within half an hour everyone was preparing to go. 'Don't bother clearing away, Adam. I've organised the chef and the kitchen assistants to come in the morning and pick all this stuff up. Poppy, if you are staying, there are bits and pieces, pyjamas and stuff, from when myself and the others stay upstairs at times. Up to you, love. If you do want a lift we're ready to go when you are...'

'I wouldn't mind a lift,' Bruce asked. 'I said I'd see Kim tonight...' Bruce didn't like lying, but he didn't want to be a gooseberry between Adam and Poppy, either.

Nervously, Poppy felt they were all looking at her for an answer, and she suddenly wasn't sure what to say. 'I think I'd better go as well,' she said, but her weak smile convinced no one. After lots of drawn-out goodbyes, Adam stood at the door alone waving everyone off. Poppy was about to get into the car when she stopped. 'Actually, I don't like the idea of leaving him all alone here. I think I will stay – sorry.'

As Adam watched his family drive off, he slowly walked up to Poppy, who was still standing on the driveway. 'Are you coming in?'

'Yes, but I still think I should tidy the plates and stack them for the people coming tomorrow. Erm, Adam, I just want to make it quite clear, I'm not staying to sleep with you. I thought you might just like some company?'

Taking her hand, Adam's eyes flashed. 'Don't flatter yourself, Poppy. If that's why you think I asked you to stay here then it might be better if you did get a cab home; I will pay for it, of course,' he snapped.

Silently, Poppy immediately regretted her decision and for letting her mouth run away with her like that. Trying to brighten the mood, she smiled at Adam. 'Well, I think it's time I put the kettle on and helped clear away some of that stuff. We don't want the kitchen assistants thinking we're animals.' Making her way into the kitchen, she promptly started tidying up, while Adam stood in the doorway watching her.

'Leave all that,' Adam said suddenly. 'I've decided to go back to London after all. All this can wait until tomorrow. I've called a taxi for us both and it should be here soon.'

Noticing how the warmth from his voice had disappeared, she knew she'd upset him with her clumsy tongue. 'I've offended you, haven't I, Adam? I'm sorry...'

'You presumed because I wanted you to stay here, I was going to force you into my bed. Poppy, I don't have to force anyone there. That's your fantasy, not mine.' His voice was stern and hollow as he gazed through her. 'And presumably everyone else who was here are thinking the same, so I think I should go home and prove them wrong.'

Poppy felt there was nothing else to say. She had been put firmly in her place and blushed to the roots. She realised how special Adam Lambrianu could make you feel, but also how small and insignificant he could make you feel when he wanted to. Hearing the horn of the taxi outside, she walked ahead and picked up her coat while Adam turned off the lights and locked up. It was going to be a long, silent drive, and she wished she had gone with Scarlet and the others now. Letting out a huge sigh, she got into the taxi.

* * *

'Scarlet, can I have a word?' Poppy stood nervously in front of Scarlet's desk a week after the dinner party. Scarlet raised her blonde head and looked over her computer screen. Seeing Poppy in turmoil, she knew what was coming.

Now that she had her attention, Poppy blurted out her well-rehearsed speech, while handing Scarlet an envelope. 'It's my resignation. I'm still on probation so I only have to give a week. As today is Monday I would like to leave on Friday.'

Taking off her gold-rimmed glasses, Scarlet sat back in her chair and brushed imaginary fluff from her pink cashmere dress. 'Does Adam know about this?'

Poppy shook her head. 'I've hardly slept for the last three nights. Mr Lambrianu insists I stay on at the club every night in case I am needed, when all I am doing is standing around while he sits drinking with one of his girlfriends. I don't see the point, and I have no life of my own. This job was supposed to be nine to five, but he wants me at his apartment early so I can see that his girlfriends get off safely with one of the drivers. Thank you for this opportunity, but I'm shattered and I don't know how long it's going to go on for.'

Inhaling deeply, Scarlet looked at Poppy. She knew full well that Adam had her hanging around like a spare part; she had seen it for herself.

'Well, that's quite a speech, Poppy, and well-rehearsed, I must say.' Calmly, Scarlet reached out to take the envelope. Then Scarlet nodded and she put the letter in her in-tray. 'Well, I will need to discuss this with Adam, but I accept it and you can rely on a reference from me. I'm sorry to see you go, Poppy. You are a good worker.' With that, Scarlet adjusted her glasses and looked down at her keyboard again, indicating Poppy's dismissal.

Expecting a harsher manner from Scarlet, Poppy was surprised at her soft tone. 'Thank you, Scarlet.' With that, she left the office.

Angrily, Scarlet tapped at her keyboard, and as though by magic, Adam walked in the door. Seeing her flushed, angry face, he sat down, perplexed. 'Okay, what have I done?'

'You little shit! You know full well what you've done. Poppy has handed in her resignation, and I don't blame her. You have humiliated her night after night while you've played tonsillectomy with every tart in the place! I'm fucking ashamed of you, Adam. Why do you need her to see your tarts off in the morning? Are you too spineless to do it?' Slamming the desk with her fist, she reverted to Italian, which she often did when she was angry. '*Bastardo vanitoso!*' she screamed.

Shocked by her anger, Adam looked down at the table. 'I'm not a vain bastard, Scarlet. I'm her boss and if I need her to assist me, which is her role, what of it?' Emphasising each word as he spoke, he looked directly into her eyes.

Shaking her head, Scarlet reverted back to English as she continued to admonish her younger brother. 'Did she reject you? Is that it and your pride's hurt? So you've spent the last few nights proving that you don't need her, and showing her what she's missing? Not fallen under your spell, has she? Well, that's your loss and good on her. Who would want a prick like you apart from those wannabe models out there? The only thing they have to boast about on their CV is what a great blow job they give. Get out of my sight, Adam. You're so wrapped up in what people think of you, you can't see daylight. What I am saying is that I know people always compare you to Dad, but he wasn't perfect and you don't have to be either, but you do need to be mature. Humiliating a member of staff is not grown up. Stop being so wrapped up in yourself and see the world from other people's eyes. Now fuck off,' she screamed.

Humbled before her, Adam realised he had gone too far regarding Poppy and that everything Scarlet has said was true. But he wasn't going to admit that easily. 'If she wants to leave, so what?' he snapped. 'Why are you so angry? It's just another employee.'

Scarlet's eyes bored into him, and Adam accepted his lecture with grace. 'Maybe you're right...' Seeing her pout her lips, he attempted a smile. 'Okay, you *are* right. But for the record, Scarlet, Poppy didn't reject me; she presumed because I wanted to spend some time with her that I wanted to sleep with her and told me upfront she had no intention of doing so. Anyway, for what it's worth, I liked having her around, but now is not the time to venture into a new relationship, is it? Christ, we're all walking on eggshells waiting for Katie's call, and none of know what Julie's plans are. So yeah, I'm having a bit of fun; it might be my last chance, after all. And yeah, if you want the truth, I want Miss Clever Clogs to realise she is not the only fish in the sea. I don't have to beg anyone to share my bed, so if she can't stand the heat, she had better stay out of the kitchen!' Adam scoffed. 'Well, I will fuck off and tell her she can go too – immediately. No more early morning visits reading my appointments out. No more picking out my tie to match my suit or ordering me sandwiches because I haven't eaten. I'll be free at last!' he shouted with more bravado than he felt. He *had* felt rejected by Poppy, and childishly, he *had* punished her, which he sorely regretted now. He had gone too far, and he realised it.

After venting his anger, Adam stormed out and a wry grin crossed Scarlet's face. 'Well,' she said aloud to Knuckles as he walked in the door to see what all the shouting was about. 'She really has got under his skin in a short space of time, hasn't she. Watch this space, Knuckles, I think there is another wedding in the offing.' She winked.

* * *

Walking down the corridor, Adam bumped into Poppy. Still angry from Scarlet's outburst, he glared at her. 'You still here?' he growled. 'There's no need to go crying to my sister. I am a grownup.'

Poppy looked up and met his blue eyes, which now seemed darker with anger. 'I didn't go crying to anyone. I just put my resignation in,' she muttered. An awkward silence passed between them, until Poppy felt she should break the ice. 'A solicitor has called. Apparently you're buying a pub and he wishes to go through some details with you. Here's the number.' She handed him a piece of paper, and Adam took it and quickly glanced at it.

As he turned to walk back into his office, he stopped, and as an afterthought, he looked at her. His voice softened as he spoke. 'Poppy... you don't have to leave if you don't want to. From now on it will be strictly nine to five. I've managed all these years on my own, and I can again, but it's up to you.' Having said his piece and slightly embarrassed, Adam walked away to make the call. He had more important business to deal with than Poppy Nightingale.

11

A GOOD DAY'S WORK

Adam listened to Phil's solicitor as he tried desperately to negotiate the price of the pub, possibly hoping to get more commission. Now, the object of what he had deemed revenge was becoming a reality, Adam actually felt excited about ripping out the old pub and breathing new life into it. It hadn't been something he had planned, but the idea was growing on him – his own project. When Phil's solicitor realised that there wasn't going to be another offer, he accepted what Adam had agreed to, and Adam passed on the number of his own solicitor to draw up the necessary paperwork and finalise the deal.

Then Adam ran down the corridor to the office where Scarlet was mid-conversation with Poppy. Both women looked startled as he ran in. 'It's sorted, Scarlet; the pub is ours!' He exhaled.

Stunned for a moment, Scarlet smiled. 'Did you have any doubts? It all seemed cut and dried to me. Why the sudden excitement?'

Adam was grinning from ear to ear, his excitement infectious. 'Why not? I love it when a deal comes together, don't you?' Seeing Scarlet nod and return his smile, Adam turned to Poppy. 'Right, so hopefully, you should hear back from my solicitor today regarding this. If not, give him a call. Oh, and I move to Southend this weekend. Can you sort my packing? I'm only taking half of my suits; did you get the others from the dry cleaners?' Adam looked at Poppy, waiting for her reaction, and then grinned. 'Come on, Poppy, keep up.' He laughed.

Blankly, Poppy turned to Scarlet and could see her almost sniggering as she bowed her head, pretending to read something. 'I have picked up your suits; they are in your closet,' Poppy began slowly, not really knowing how to approach this. Not half an hour ago, he had snapped at her, and now it was as though the past few days had never happened. 'You will need to sort out any personal affects you wish to take with you to the new house.'

'Consider it done.' Adam grinned and ran out of the room.

'Annoying little shit, isn't he?' Scarlet laughed. 'And they call us women mad. He's moved on and expects us all to keep up with him. It's as though he has conversations in his mind and thinks we're all mind readers. You'll get used to it, Poppy... that is, if you are you staying with us?'

Giving Scarlet a big smile, Poppy nodded her head. 'It looks like it, doesn't it? I had better see what else he needs organising for his move.' Hurrying to catch up with Adam, Poppy left the office, and Scarlet shook her head and carried on – business as usual.

Over the next few days, the money for the pub was transferred and it was legally now owned by Adam. The police had caught up with Tommy, who had denied anything about the counterfeit money and was basically leaving his dad to take the wrap for him. Phil was hurt and upset by everything, but especially his son turning his back on him. That seemed to have cut him deeply by all accounts and had made Scarlet go and visit him. On driving up to the pub, her first impression had been the number of bullet holes in the brickwork and the boarded-up windows. The police tape that had zoned off the area while they investigated was now hanging on the pavement, discarded.

Ringing the bell, she waited. Phil opened the door, unshaven and bloodshot eyed, wearing his jeans and a T-shirt; Scarlet could see he had lost weight. 'Get your jacket, Phil, we're going for breakfast. There must be a greasy spoon around here some-where.' Doing as he was told, he made sure the door was locked and walked towards her car.

In the nearest café, they ordered breakfast and Scarlet sat with her mug of coffee. 'How are you, Phil?'

Phil shrugged, helplessly. 'Not good. I'm facing a stretch, which I am prepared to take as my part of the blame. I've lost my livelihood, my home and now my son. I know what I did, even trying to screw you for your money. I'm not pleading my inno-cence, Ms Lambrianu. To be honest, I'm quite looking forward to going to prison. Sooner the better. Three meals a day, no rent, no council tax. No bloody hassle.'

'Are you staying at the pub until you're sentenced?' Scarlet shook her head, trying to think. 'Obviously you're going to stay there, but are you okay? Do you have money?' Scarlet asked as she saw Phil dive into his breakfast and scoop up as much as possible into his mouth at once. It was plain to see that he hadn't eaten for days.

'I've a bit put by. Not much, but I'll be okay.' Scarlet watched him chew, and thought it was like looking into a washing machine, with his food churning around and around until he swilled it back with his mug of tea.

'From what I hear, you will be looking at eighteen months. So, you might serve a year, but you'll be looked after, Phil. As for the pub, when you come back out, I'll see that you have work, rest assured.' She felt sorry for him, although she couldn't deny his own greed had put him in this position. 'What's happening with Tommy?' She knew that boy was the root of all evil.

'Oh, he's been arrested. He's pleading his innocence of course. Apparently, I talked him into it. I was the mastermind.' Phil laughed. 'If that was the case, Miss Lambrianu, I would have masterminded making myself a millionaire years ago! He'll end up doing time as he has a record already. My agony will be standing there giving evidence against my own son.' Phil shook his head sadly. 'Nah, Miss Lambrianu, I can't do that so I will take the wrap. That's what parents do, isn't it? Oh, I know he's tried saving his own skin and blamed me, but he's a scared kid. And he's *my* kid...' Phil took another drink of tea from his mug. 'Adam has been good. He kept his word about keeping those fellas away from me and I haven't heard anything since, thank God.'

Breathing a sigh of relief, Phil drank the rest of his tea, and Scarlet ordered him another one. She felt partly responsible that he had lost everything, but she had never forced his hand into this get-rich-quick scheme. 'I do wish you had come to me earlier, Phil. It was never going to work, laundering money through your pub. It would show a massive increase in customers, which just wouldn't happen out of the blue.'

'I know that now, but Tommy was in debt. You know he likes the horses. Christ, his wages burn a hole in his pocket until he spends it. He borrowed a lot of money from some of your loan sharks, actually...' Phil muttered while spying her over the top of his mug.

Making a face, Scarlet cocked her head to one side. 'We don't have loan sharks, Phil. We have loan companies. And we don't force people to borrow money. That's their choice.' She smiled.

'At 1,000 per cent interest!' he scoffed, and almost choked on his tea.

'Yes, Phil. We tell people to read the document before they

sign the agreement, including the small print. What about our risks? People who don't pay or who leave the country and we never see a penny. It's a risky business but, moving forward, Tommy had a good deal with us. He's a good ticket tout, and we always put work his way. He had his own patch that no one else used. It comes down to greed, Phil. Have you seen Tommy at all?'

Phil shook his head again sadly. 'No, he hasn't shown his face. He's probably at some mates', I reckon. I know we're not supposed to talk, cos of the case, but a text or something wouldn't hurt. Not sure if he's ashamed or hates me. Doesn't really matter now, does it?'

'It always matters when you're a parent, Phil. I'm one and I would take the wrap for my kids, but I would also like to know they are okay and want to keep in touch... even visit me in prison.' She laughed. 'Look, Phil, there isn't a lot more I can do. Adam promised to make life comfortable for you in prison and we can offer you work when you get out. Keep all of that in mind and don't let yourself slide. Tommy will wake up and make contact. He always has before.' Reassuringly, she placed her hand on his, much to the curiosity of the other customers. Inwardly, she had to admit, they must have looked an odd couple. The people in the area would know Phil and probably question him about it later. 'Let me drop you off home; have a bath, watch TV and relax while you can before prison.'

When Scarlet dropped him back at the pub, Phil reached forward and kissed her on the cheek. Blushing, he apologised. 'Thanks for our little chat, Miss Lambrianu. Hope I haven't smudged your makeup.' He smiled.

Blushing slightly at the genuine sentiment, Scarlet wished there was more she could do for him, but she couldn't. Although one thing she could do, she thought to herself as she drove off, was find that shitty son of his and make him go and see his father and make amends before he went to prison. Back in her office, she sat down at her desk. 'Knuckles, are you hanging around in the corridor?'

Within minutes he popped his head around the corner. 'Christ, you're like a fucking stalker. Why do you hang around out there? Why don't you just come in? Anyway, never mind; Tommy, Phil's son...' Now, seeing a spark of recognition in Knuckles's eyes, she prompted again. 'Nag's Head Phil, the publican?'

Once she saw him nod, she felt able to carry on. 'I want you to find his son, Tommy the tout. He's staying at some mates' house I think, but the police will have his address on file. He needs to go and see his dad and do a spot of grovelling, the shitbag. Phil's in a bad way and although he can cope with prison, his son turning against him is the deepest wound. I don't want that playing on his mind. Can I leave it with you?' Nodding, Knuckles walked out of the office.

* * *

As her heel got stuck in the gravel drive again, Poppy pulled it out while carrying yet another box of Adam's into his new Southend home. 'I'd help you more if I could, Poppy,' apologised Bruce.

'Don't worry, it's just for a man who said he was only bringing bits and pieces. There are twelve huge boxes and that one is full of porn DVDs! Oh my God, I shudder to think what I've been carrying in the others, along with the wardrobes full of suits!' She pouted.

'I know, Poppy, he has more clothes than a woman. And as for the DVDs, they are probably home videos, so he can see how good his arse looks on the big screen!' Bruce winked. 'But don't tell him I said that.'

Looking around at the house as she took in another box,

Poppy was overwhelmed again by the size of it. And yet, it felt homely. 'Can you believe he was brought up in a house like this, Bruce? It's enormous! I was brought up in a garden shed in comparison.'

'Me too, Poppy. No doubt you get used to it though.' As an afterthought, Bruce blurted out what was on his mind. 'You like Adam, don't you, Poppy?' Seeing her shocked expression, he held up his good arm. 'Sorry, I didn't mean to make you uncomfortable. I shouldn't have said anything.'

Putting the box on the kitchen worktop and taking a breath, Poppy looked at Bruce. 'Is it that obvious? Yes, after all of these years I'm still punching above my weight, but thankfully you're the only one who seems to have noticed I have a crush on my boss.' Taking a seat for a moment beside Bruce, Poppy brushed her fringe away from her face. 'But he blows hot and cold a lot. I was going to leave and then he needed help with the move, and, well, here I am.' She grinned.

'You've known him before?' Bruce asked questioningly. 'I didn't realise. I thought you had only just met.'

'Yeah, I used to waitress at the club a few years ago. I saw him then...' Looking up at the French windows, it was like she was in a world of her own as she recalled the first time she had met Adam. 'He was a suave and sophisticated nightclub owner, full of enigmatic charm, but surrounded by some of the most beautiful, sexiest women photographed or on the television. In comparison, I felt like a grain of sand on the beach. Although, I did steal a drunken snog once, but he doesn't remember it, whereas it's stayed with me for years...'

Bruce was wide eyed at this revelation. 'Wow, Poppy, that's one hell of a CV!'

'I know. And even though I've travelled the world, he has always been with me, but that's life, isn't it? Now you know my secret; not a word. My probation will be up soon, and I think it's time to move on. I don't know why I took the job in the first place. It was Scarlet who offered it to me when she saw me in the high street. She remembered me' – Poppy laughed – 'and asked what I was doing these days. When I told her I was back in England looking for a job, she came up with this one, although I gather she never discussed it with Adam. Poor sod; I think I'm his worst nightmare.'

Bruce reached out and patted her hand. 'If it's any consolation, I don't think he could do without you now. He's always talking about you, and making mental notes of what to tell you, if that helps.'

A hapless smile crossed Poppy's face. 'You're a good guy, Bruce, and he's lucky to have you.'

Adam came bursting through the doors just then, interrupting their chat. 'I've come on my bike and thought I would pop in to see how you're getting on.'

'Oh, we're just taking a break. Looks like the break is over, Bruce.' Poppy laughed.

'Get the driver to take my suits in upstairs. I don't want them in the kitchen, picking up cooking smells and stuff.' Bruce and Poppy glanced at each other, a frown on each of their brows. 'What cooking smells? What are you talking about?' Bruce asked.

'Well, you know' – Adam shrugged – 'it's a kitchen, with kitchen smells. And I don't want my suits getting damaged.'

Bruce burst out laughing. 'You do make me laugh, Adam. Now we've helped unload that van, it's up to you where to put them. It's your stuff!' Bruce looked around at their handy work. 'Does it feel a bit more like home now?'

'It's always been my home, Bruce. But I think I feel more settled here now, yes,' Adam replied.

'I'm curious,' Poppy said. 'Why have you never spent much

time here? None of your family seem to, and yet it's a beautiful home full of warmth. Sorry if I'm being nosey.' She shrugged. 'I'm just curious.'

'Well...' Adam paused for a moment as he tried to gather his thoughts. 'I was nine when my dad was killed, which I'm sure you're both aware of. And my mother waited another nine years until I was eighteen to join him. Sometimes I felt like I'd held her back in joining him and she was just going through the motions. She died the same night as my father; did you know that? I didn't want to come back here and live. It felt like a private place for just Mum and Dad. I know that sounds silly, but it's like being an intruder. But now it's time to make peace with this place. I'm not an intruder; they want me here, to enjoy their home. *Our* home. Welcome to my home!' Adam held his arms wide open, putting one each around Poppy and Bruce's shoulders.

Bruce looked at Poppy and saw her eyes close as she breathed in Adam's aftershave as they hugged. Knowing what he now knew, he felt sorry for her. Adam was a known heartbreaker, and his gut instinct told him that Poppy was heading for a fall.

'Well,' said Poppy, removing herself from Adam's embrace, 'I have done the usual housewarming present and bought you a terrarium plant, in this beautiful glass bowl. It doesn't need a lot of water and so should survive your neglect.' She laughed.

Adam marvelled at the huge goldfish bowl containing the plant. 'This is awesome, Poppy. Thank you.' Leaning forward, he gave her a kiss on the cheek.

'Well, I had better make tracks.' She smiled, blushing slightly.

Adam looked around the lounge. 'Actually, Poppy, there is one last favour to ask. While I'm sorting this out, would you mind going to the shops and getting me a fifty-two-inch television? That one hasn't been updated in years. I've never really noticed it before, but now I'm here, I'll definitely need a new one. Would you mind? I'll tell the driver to hang on and then he can take you home as well. That way, you won't have to catch the train.'

Deflated, Poppy looked around the huge lounge. The television looked okay to her, but each to his own taste, she decided, and nodded her head. 'Well, I'm here as your assistant.' She laughed. 'Any particular model?'

'You decide. Just as long as it's big and up to date.' He laughed and handed over his credit card.

Watching her leave, Bruce felt sad for her. 'She's not a dog to fetch and carry for you, Adam. Couldn't you have got your own television?' he asked light-heartedly.

Adam run his hands through his hair. 'I wasn't harsh, was I? Christ, Bruce, I can't win. First Scarlet criticises my treatment of her, and now you. If I am too friendly, that must mean I want to sleep with her, and if I'm too professional, I'm cold hearted and treat her like a dog. What did I say wrong?'

Picking up a box and balancing it between both arms, Bruce shook his head. 'Nothing, Adam. Come on, where is this one going?' As they chatted and moved the final few boxes, Bruce mentioned that he had asked Kim if she wanted to pop in and see Adam's new house. 'She's off today, and I thought we could get a takeaway later and have a housewarming, or do you have to get back?'

A large grin spread across Adam's face. 'A housewarming sounds great! Just what the place needs, and the more the merrier, eh?'

'You could ask Poppy to stay,' Bruce chipped in. 'I mean, to thank her for all of her hard work. Just a thought...'

Adam stopped what he was doing as he thought about Bruce's idea. 'No, she has to go. She's already said so, and she can get a lift with the removal van when it returns to London.' Silently, Bruce nodded.

As they were putting the last few things away in his bedroom, Adam sat on the edge of the bed. 'Actually, Bruce, there is something I want to tell you, and I'm glad we're alone. You know you're my best friend – no, closer than that, like a brother to me. Don't ask me any questions, but I feel if I don't say anything to you it would betray our friendship.'

Curiously, Bruce stopped what he was doing and sat beside him. 'This sounds serious. What is it?'

'There is some family business that needs attending to, and to be honest, I'm not 100 per cent I will come out of it unscathed. It's all very hush hush, but I know I can trust you. I just wanted to confide in you, so you wouldn't forever wonder what had happened, or why I didn't say anything to you.'

'Well, you haven't told me anything yet, have you? I presume by unscathed, you mean it could be fatal...' For a moment they both sat in silence. 'Is there anything I can do, Adam, to help I mean?' Bruce knew whatever it was, it had to be serious for Adam to bare his soul like this.

Letting out a deep sigh, Adam rolled his eyes to the ceiling. 'Actually, there is. I need you to spread the word that we're taking Knuckles on a stag weekend or something. No, not that' – Adam seemed confused – 'because that would mean you would be with us, too. And if the worst happened, how would you explain it? No, I need you to just keep the home fires burning, and make sure the staff keep their fingers out of the till.' He smiled.

'Anything you need, Adam. Are all the family involved in this?'

'Not all. Bobby and Jack know nothing. We're going to Italy and it's important, but that's all I can say. There, that's enough.'

'Would it be possible for you to let me know if your safe?' Seeing Adam shrug, Bruce didn't want to press matters any further.

'I'm back! And guess who I found on the doorstep?' Poppy shouted from the hallway. Glad of the interruption, Bruce hugged Adam. 'Bro hug, that doesn't mean I fancy you.' He laughed. 'Come on, let's set up this monstrous television.'

'Kim, glad you could make it.' Slightly embarrassed, Bruce hugged her and kissed her on the cheek.

'Wow, this place is mega!' Kim took in her surroundings and almost did a twirl in the large hallway. 'My God, all of this and right next to the seaside. Blimey, Adam, you did rough it as a kid, didn't you?' Everyone laughed at Kim's teasing. 'This is awesome, and you have your name above the iron gates. I bet the postman never gets mixed up with your mail.' Kim laughed, full of enthusiasm and excitement.

Adam took a bow and grinned. 'Welcome to Chez Lambrianu by the seaside!' He laughed. 'Now, I'm starving. What say we all have a walk up the prom and see what delights there are to offer.'

'Chips and donuts.' Kim laughed. Her enthusiasm was infectious, making the mood lighter and full of fun. Poppy stood in the background, watching the happy scene. 'What about your television?' she asked nervously, looking at the enormous box the driver had brought in and left in the hallway.

'That can wait.' Adam laughed. 'My stomach is grumbling. Do you want to come or are you going to leave with the driver?'

Kim linked her arm through Poppy's before she could answer. 'Of course she's coming! All this hard work deserves some fish and chips. Come on, Poppy, let's go and eat our heads off.' Adam and Bruce looked at each other and laughed.

'Nuff said. Lead on, ladies.' Adam opened the door wide for them as they walked through it.

* * *

Hours later, Adam sat back on the sofa. 'I had actually forgotten what a fun place this was. I can't move I'm so full. What say we open some wine and settle in for the night?'

'Sounds good, mate, I don't think I could move to leave anyway. And you, Kim,' said Bruce, nudging her in the ribs, 'for someone only five feet, I think you've eaten your body weight in donuts.'

'Well, there's plenty of bedrooms so take your pick. I'll get the wine.' Standing up, Adam made his way to the kitchen when Poppy followed him.

'I suppose I should leave you all to it. Thank you for tonight, it was great fun. Can you call me a taxi as it's past eleven and I can't get a train now?'

Opening the fridge door, Adam let out a huge sigh. 'For God's sake, Poppy, I meant everyone could stay, not just those two. But if you want a taxi, I'll call you one. It's up to you. Don't worry, I won't do any creeping along the landing if that's what you're afraid of,' Adam snapped wearily.

Poppy blushed and wrung her hands. 'I'm sorry, Adam. I didn't mean to offend you. I've had a lovely night, but I didn't want to interrupt your evening with your friends...'

Slightly annoyed, Adam picked up the glasses and wine and made his way to the lounge. 'You may not want to offend, Poppy, but by God you do at times. And you're the perfect party pooper,' he said again and left the kitchen without looking back.

For a moment, Poppy stood there stunned, touching her face. She could almost feel it burn with embarrassment and tears brimmed on her lashes. Adam was right; she had spoilt the moment. They had all had such good fun, and she realised now that of course he'd meant her too. Sniffing hard, she glanced at herself in the mirror. Then taking a large breath, she walked back into the lounge. 'I hope one of those wines is for me.' She smiled and sat down beside Kim, who thankfully hadn't stopped talking and was boasting about winning a cuddly toy on the rifle range.

Adam and Bruce started setting up the television, while the girls poured the wine and everyone was laughing and joking. 'Christ, Adam, I'm not used to your late nights.' Bruce yawned. 'Come on, Kim, time for some beauty sleep.' Seeing her glare, and getting hit with a cushion, he laughed. 'I meant me, not you.'

Adam turned off the lights as they all made their way upstairs to the bedrooms. Bruce and Kim shouted their goodnights, while Poppy stood looking at the bedroom doors. 'Is this one okay?' she asked Adam.

'Yeah, any. They are all en-suite so you will be fine. I'll call a driver to pick us up in the morning.'

Putting her hand on the handle, Poppy opened the door. 'Goodnight, Adam.' She paused, looking at his back as he walked into his bedroom.

Lying in the darkness, Adam looked at the ceiling with thoughts of Poppy running through his head. She was inches away, but it might as well have been miles. Tossing and turning, he tried thinking of a legitimate excuse for knocking on her door in the early hours of the morning, but no matter how he tried, he couldn't think of one that wouldn't look like a booty call. Recalling her laughter during the evening, he felt hyped up, and wanted to hold her and kiss her perfectly formed lips so much, he could taste it. Thumping his pillow again, he turned over and let sleep engulf him.

Just across the corridor, Poppy lay awake looking at the door, willing, almost yearning, for Adam to creep along the landing. She could almost hear her heart beating in her chest in the silent darkness of the bedroom. A fleeting thought crossed her mind, and she wondered who had occupied this room before tonight. Scarlet? Julie? She was tempted to take the bit between her teeth and knock on Adam's door, but shuddered at the thought of Kim and Bruce hearing her. It was pathetic, she thought to herself, and she stared at the ceiling again until eventually her eyes began to droop with tiredness as she closed them.

* * *

Once Knuckles had found where Tommy was hiding out, he went to the tower block. Knocking once, his impatience got the better of him as he waited for someone to answer, so he decided to kick the door in. Tommy and his mates were sat in the lounge, and reeling backwards, Tommy's friend shouted to the others, 'Police raid!' They were stunned to see Knuckles's huge frame, dressed in a black suit, white shirt, and black tie. 'Who the hell are you? And look what you've done to the door.'

Knuckles looked at the door almost hanging off its hinges. 'Tommy,' was all he said, and still half asleep, Tommy's friend pointed his thumb towards the lounge. Knuckles looked at Tommy, who was sitting like a rabbit caught in the headlights with no escape. 'You've got to apologise to your dad before he goes to prison.'

'I'm not doing that.' Tommy smiled cockily. 'He won't have anything to do with me. Anyway, he's landing all that shit on my doorstep.' Looking around at his mates, who were rooted to the spot as they looked at Knuckles, Tommy lit a cigarette whilst trying to assure them everything was okay. 'It's alright, I know him. We're old friends, aren't we, Knuckles?'

'You not going?' Knuckles asked, and seeing Tommy shake his head, Knuckles strode forward and opened the French windows that led onto the small concrete balcony. Lifting Tommy up by his T-shirt, Knuckles tutted, 'Scarlet says you are.'

Wide eyed, Tommy braced himself for a punch, but was

surprised when Knuckles lifted him upside down and strode to the open balcony. 'What the fuck are you doing?' Tommy screamed. 'For Christ's sake, man, put me down!'

Tommy's friends laughed at each other, thinking it was a joke, until realisation dawned on them as Knuckles bent Tommy over the balcony, leaving him dangling in the air. Their instinct was to grab hold of Knuckles and pull him back. 'We'll call the police if you don't let him go,' one threatened, picking up his mobile.

'No! No, you prick, don't tell him to let go,' Tommy shouted as he looked down at people going about their daily routines. From this height and upside down, they looked like ants.

'You want me to let go?' Knuckles asked Tommy's friends.

Looking at Knuckles holding both of Tommy's legs in the air with one hand, they felt helpless. 'Fuck, no! Sorry, mate. Tommy, do as the man says. Agree to see your dad. Are you crazy? Cos this bloke definitely is!'

'My arm hurting,' said Knuckles, making the panic rise in Tommy even more.

Tommy, hanging in the air, knew it was pointless arguing, so decided to beg for mercy. 'Knuckles, I can't go and see my dad. Those yardie guys will slit my throat!' screamed Tommy. 'Please pull me back in!' Hanging upside down from the window of the twelfth-floor tower block, Tommy was gripped by fear and, realising Knuckles wasn't listening, he felt his trainer loosening, then watched as it flew past his head and slowly flew through the air before dropping to the ground. 'Knuckles, please!' he shouted again.

'Do you need a lift to your dad's?' Knuckles asked as he held Tommy's legs with one hand and sucked on a lollipop with the other.

'Yes, yes! I need a fucking lift,' Tommy screamed as tears dripped from his face.

Hearing his submission, Knuckles pulled him in and threw him on the floor. 'Get your coat,' he mumbled and waited. Tommy knelt on the floor panting and sobbing, but glad to be on solid ground, he nodded his head. Feeling quite dizzy, he tried getting up, while Knuckles stood there watching, paying no attention to Tommy's anguish. His friends came to his aid and helped him to his feet.

'I'll say this, Tommy, you know some fucking scary people,' one of them commented and glanced at Knuckles, who was totally oblivious to their stares.

'I'll go and see my dad and apologise,' Tommy sobbed. His heart was pounding in his chest and he could barely breathe. Slowly, he stood up and, wobbling as he walked, he followed Knuckles out of the flat. Knuckles drove to the Nag's Head and parked outside.

'Go on. I'll know if you not nice and tell yardies you a grass,' Knuckles said in between sucking on his lolly. His voice was gruff and threatening. Nodding, Tommy opened the car door, while Knuckles watched him enter the side door of the pub. Satisfied his job was done, he drove off to tell Scarlet.

12

JOURNEY'S END

Taking out her mobile, Diana scrolled through the many messages she had received. 'Christ, Mum, I keep getting all of these strange emails and messages from blokes I don't know. I think I've been hacked or something. I need to sort this out before we go away.'

Dressed in her long silk leopard-print dressing gown, Julie Gold lay full length on her chaise longue and frowned. 'Hacked or not, darling, I can't believe you're getting strange messages from men. You don't exactly put yourself out there, do you? Let me see.'

Slightly disgruntled, not only at the sleight, but at the number of messages she was receiving, Diana passed her mobile to Julie. 'Look, Mum, some are disgusting and they are calling me baby. Do you think I should answer and tell them I'm a copper? Maybe that will cool their enthusiasm. I'm going to get the boys on to this.'

As Julie started to read, her eyes widened and she sat up, 'Oh, Di, I really wouldn't do that. Erm, I mean, don't you like any of their photos?' she asked, and handing the mobile to Diana, she grinned. 'Look, he's not bad.'

Instinctively, Diana looked at her mother and then the photo. 'Why do I have a bad feeling that you know something about this, Mum? This smells of one of your pranks. Please tell me I'm wrong.'

Picking up her long cigarette holder, Julie inserted a cigarette and lit it. 'Well, I thought you might need a helping hand, love. You work all the hours God sends and you don't get out much, and, well... if Scarlet can marry Shrek, I can't have my own daughter staying a spinster, can I? Lewis and I thought we'd be your fairy godmothers and find Prince Charming for you, so we put you on a couple of those singles websites.'

'What?! You've put me on a dating website! For God's sake, Mum! Why don't you stop interfering in my life!?' Snatching her mobile back off Julie, Diana sat down and thought about her mum's words for a moment. 'When you say web*sites*, what do you mean? That's more than one?'

'Crikey, I can see why you're a detective, Diana, you picked up on that one quickly. Just nine or ten. I couldn't find one decent photo of you with some makeup on and female clothing. Look at you: black trousers, white shirt, black overcoat. Christ, you look like a funeral director, darling. Blonde hair that looks like it hasn't seen a comb in days. For Christ's sake, Diana, you're my daughter and you dress like a homeless person,' Julie drawled and picked up her china coffee cup, taking a sip.

'Nine or ten!' Diana shouted. 'I can't believe you splashed my photo over dating websites. Take them down now... In fact, let me see the profile you've put up for me. Christ, Mum, what have you said about me online?'

'Oh dear, aren't you detectives supposed to be poker faced and calm? Here, read for yourself, love.' Julie smiled, parting her glossy red lips to take another drag on her cigarette as Diana gasped with horror while reading.

'For God's sake, Mum, I can't believe you've written this about me. "Up for a little casual fun." That means casual sex with strangers. You're making me sound like some bored housewife in the personal ads looking for extra activity behind their husband's back. I'm a professional, Mum. I can't have shit like this posted about me online.' Diana calmed down and sat beside Julie. 'I know you worry about me, but if Mr Right is out there he will find me, okay?' Kissing Julie on the cheek, Diana smiled. 'Anyway, I think what we're about to undertake in Italy puts romance on a back burner for a while, don't you?'

'Personally, Di, I don't think romance should ever be put on the back burner. God only knows when you're going to live to shag another day.' Letting out a loud cackle, Julie laughed at her own joke and hugged Diana. 'If you say so, Diana, let's take them down, but you've had some promising feedback,' Julie urged. Seeing Diana's pouting lips and scowl, she nodded. 'And at least let's do something with your hair. You are going to Scarlet's hen party and I can't have my own daughter looking like a bag lady. You're just like your father. He was work consumed, and it put him in an early grave. Have some fun; have a life. You might be in charge of the murder squad, but live a little sometimes, eh?'

Diana ran her hands through her hair and laughed. 'Dad had Parkinson's, Mum. It wasn't the work that killed him.'

'All the same, Diana, I think all of that stress sped things up a little. Well, that's my opinion anyway.'

Changing the subject, Diana looked down at her flat shoes, which she knew made her mother wince. She was so used to just to being called out to an investigation and throwing something on before leaving the house, she hadn't taken much notice of her appearance. That was until she visited her mother and got it pointed out on a regular basis. 'I suppose I do look a bit shabby. I've been up for the last two nights on a murder investigation that I wanted to wrap up before we go to Italy. I suppose we all need to tie up our loose ends, Mum. None of us know what the outcome will be...' Diana paused, not wanting to say the words.

'Say it, Diana. We could all die. Or at least any one of us. I don't have any loose ends. Chris is my loose end and before I leave this mortal coil, I need to set the record straight.'

Diana's face dropped. 'Don't talk about dying, Mum. You're all I've got. The world wouldn't be the same without Julie Gold, would it? It would be a very sad and dull place. Even if you are a pain in the arse sometimes.' Diana laughed, hugging Julie.

'Murder investigation, you say? Anybody I know? Any juicy titbits for your mum?'

'No and no. If you want crime and gory facts, watch Netflix. And yes, if it makes you happy, I will have my hair done – is that okay? Once this case is wrapped up, I can hand it over and come to Italy with you. I've booked the time off; God knows I'm owed enough.' She grinned. 'I can't remember the last time I actually had time off.'

'And a makeover?' Julie asked hopefully. 'Can I pick your clothes?' she asked excitedly and clapped her hands together. 'We will go clothes shopping. You're as rich as a lord, Diana, although some of the lords I've met are potless. Spend it. Enjoy it. Stop squirreling it away for a rainy day. Cos by the look of you, it's already pissing down!'

'Anything if it stops you moaning, but for God's sake, don't make me look like some drag queen.' She laughed while mentally taking in Julie's leopard-print house coat and high-heeled court shoes at 9 a.m. She couldn't remember the last time she saw her mother without makeup on.

* * *

Katie Lambrianu looked over the breakfast table and sighed inwardly as she took in her husband, Chris. There was no love between them these days. He was a control freak and she hated him. She watched him as he drank his cup of coffee, reading his newspaper and avoiding any conversation with her, but looking like the family man having breakfast with his wife, for the sake of the children and the staff. Clearing her throat, she felt now was the time to drop her bombshell. 'Scarlet's marrying Knuckles at long last,' she said chirpily, knowing this would catch his attention. Slowly, the newspaper lowered from his stern face and through his horn-rimmed glasses, he looked at her questioningly.

'You have got to be joking me,' he scoffed with disgust.

'No, and furthermore, it's going to be sooner rather than later. I've invited her, Julie, and Diana to have her hen party here, in Italy,' she added.

'What? When?' he bellowed over the table. 'For God's sake, those three witches here – not a chance. She can have it in the club, in her own town.'

Katie had expected this outburst. She had waited to tell him until he had returned from his so-called business trip, which she presumed had been another woman. These trips were becoming far too frequent for her liking, and they meant she was stuck at home unable to go anywhere while she was watched by his henchmen. Where had the reasonable man she had once loved gone? 'You forget, Chris. This is Scarlet's town. She is Italian; a Lambrianu like our father and his father before him. And I am her twin sister, so of course I'm supposed to organise her hen night.'

Chris's face flushed. 'You never asked me before inviting them,' he spat. 'Especially that bitch, Julie Gold. It's time she died.

God knows she's past her sell-by date. Her snide remarks are something I can do without right now. Absolutely not, Katie. If Scarlet wants to marry a man who hasn't evolved yet, that's her business, not yours and definitely not mine.'

'She's my sister, Chris.' Doing her best not to start an argument and sound cheerful, Katie smiled. 'And that's just Julie's way. We're all in the firing line when she opens her mouth. But she's family.'

'Well, she's not my bloody family, or yours for that matter. She was your father's business partner's wife, that's all! You're giving me indigestion with all of this talk of happy families. I'm a busy man; you have wife duties. You haven't got time to piss about organising a hen weekend. I let you go and see Scarlet, don't I? Isn't that enough? God knows what you say about me behind my back.'

Katie could feel her anger rising, but tried holding back the things she wanted to say. 'I don't say anything behind your back. How can I when you bug my phone? And you might "let me go" to Italy, but you make damn sure of my return by making sure I leave one of my children behind so that I come back. Sorry, Chris, this is the one time I'm going to oppose you. She is my sister, and she's getting married. I have a duty to her. You can do without your trophy Lambrianu wife for one weekend, can't you?'

'Trophy Lambrianu? I protect you! Your father was a thief, a racketeer and a murderer... although that runs in the blood, doesn't it, Katie? Don't forget you're a murderer too!' His face twisted in anger as he spat the words at her.

Pausing a while to compose herself, Katie squared up to her arrogant husband. 'You are the Don of this Mafia empire, Chris – are your hands so clean? But then again you get others to do your dirty work for you, don't you? At least what my father did, he had the balls to do himself,' she snapped.

'Don't push it, Katie. I am the Don of this empire, because that is what Don Carlos wanted. Your brother was of no age to take on a business like this and so I was the better choice. He was an old man who made the wisest choice. Passing all of this on to Adam was just your father's sentiment... and there is no sentiment in business.'

Katie thought back to the conversation she'd had with Julie Gold. Julie had claimed that Chris had cajoled and wheedled his way into Don Carlos's empire and had snatched Adam's birthright from him. Don Carlos was known throughout Italy and had ruled with a rod of iron, but he had been a fair man and loyal to those who showed loyalty to him. He had initially wanted Adam to take over once he died and had made his feelings known. But Chris had whispered in his ear constantly, about Adam's youth and recklessness. As Don Carlos's nephew, Chris wasn't going to be robbed of what he felt was his right. Once Chris had pointed out all the pitfalls of Adam's inexperience and age, that he was too young to get respect from the people who worked for them, Don Carlos had eventually agreed.

Don Carlos had by then been an old man with the onset of dementia. He'd trusted his family and believed Chris had a valid argument. And then the biggest shock of all, Don Carlos's sudden death. Julie had been certain that Chris had been responsible and to be honest, everyone else suspected it too. Chris had known that Julie could change Don Carlos's mind and assure him that Adam would be a good leader and that he wouldn't have to rule the empire alone. That she, Scarlet, Knuckles and others would all be firmly behind Adam, should he need it. But it was too late.

Chris had it in writing that he was to inherit Don Carlos's legacy and everyone who worked for him should respect and accept Chris as the new Don. The famous ring that Don Carlos had always worn represented his crown, and it was what people kissed to show their loyalty to him. Don Carlos's father had always worn a ruby ring, which Carlos wore on the middle finger on his left hand, out of respect. But it was another ring that mattered more to him. It was the huge gold signet ring with one priceless diamond firmly in the middle on his right hand that Carlos made people kiss to show their loyalty. This ring had been given to him by Tony Lambrianu, who, after a diamond heist, had sent it to Carlos in a box of Cuban cigars to thank him for his help.

Impressed by the gesture and such a huge uncut diamond, Carlos had felt Tony Lambrianu's loyalty was unconditional and had worn the ring from that day on. Once Don Carlos had died, Chris had taken the ring and wore it proudly, like a badge of honour, but a lot of people resented him wearing it, feeling he wasn't worthy. No one particularly liked him, but he was the 'Don' and people accepted it. But Chris had become evil, greedy, and he ruled by fear. People had felt they could go to Don Carlos with their problems, however small, and he would help for a price – a return favour as and when he needed it: loyalty. Chris didn't have time for the small businesses in Italy and the people who owned them. They were beneath him and he put the rates up higher on their protection money with the aim of taking over the businesses they had worked so hard for over the years. People didn't respect him, as they had Carlos. Instead, they feared him, wondering if the next bullet would have their name on it.

It stung Katie when she heard him joke about it. These were families she had known all her life, but now they turned their noses up at her. She wasn't as openly welcome in their homes any more as she once had been and now it felt like they tolerated her simply because of Chris. She was a Lambrianu; her family owned the vineyard and had always been good employers and paid good wages, but now Chris had them working like slaves, for a pittance.

She felt ashamed that this had gone on for so long and she hadn't told anyone – especially Scarlet or Julie. She had wanted to save her own embarrassment and didn't want to admit the hell she lived in. Katie knew that If Scarlet ever found out about his scheming ways, she would fight him tooth and nail. Hearing Chris let out a disgruntled sigh and making a point of folding his newspaper brought her out of thoughts, and back to reality.

'Here's my deal, so don't say I'm an unreasonable man. You can invite them over for this hen party, but it's here, in this house, where I can keep an eye on you. And as for Julie, she had better show me some respect or she's out!'

'Thank you, Chris, I appreciate that. I wanted your blessing on it,' she purred. Inwardly, she felt like punching the air. This had been exactly what Julie had predicted. She had said he would want them under lock and key, and he did! She knew Julie didn't need to be told that she would have to play to his vanity when she arrived; she would know to do that, too. So, everything was now in place and she would make the call. She never said much on the house phone because she knew Chris had them, as well as her mobile phone, bugged and listened in.

'Blessing my arse, Katie! You just want your family to humiliate me in my own home. Always thinking they're better than me. Well, here I am, Katie.' Chris waved his arm in the air at their lavish surroundings, to emphasise his words. 'Master of my own empire and master of *you!*'

Katie looked at his once handsome face and remembered how Scarlet had once called him Clark Kent. In those days he had looked like that with his dark hair and glasses. But now, leaning over the table towards her, his face flushed and angry, he looked like a stranger. He was portlier since he had put on weight and his chin wobbled as he shouted.

'Have your little party, but remember, I can make or break you and your family.' Throwing down his newspaper on the table, Chris stood up, knocking his coffee cup over, making a crashing noise on the floor as he stormed out.

Shaken from his outburst, Katie sighed. The worst was over. She had been nervous about broaching the subject, but the deed was done. Standing up, she looked around the large breakfast room still decorated with Don Carlos's furniture and antique paintings. On the huge mantlepiece, she tenderly picked up the photo frames containing photos of her children. Seeing their happy smiling faces brought a smile to her own face. She loved them dearly, even though Chris had used them as a bargaining blackmail tool. She had vowed she would never let anything happen to them and so had abided by his rules to keep the peace. Trying hard to blink back the tears, Katie thought of all the wasted years she'd spent in this broken marriage.

Only now she felt a glimmer of hope. At last, it was all coming to an end and there was light at the end of the tunnel. Julie wanted revenge; it seemed she had done her own digging and come up with the answers. Now Katie shivered. No one knew what the outcome of Julie's revenge would be. Scarlet's hen weekend was the excuse Julie wanted for them to all get to Italy. Chris would never have allowed it otherwise. But, as it was a hen weekend, this implied none of the men would be going, so Adam and Knuckles would be at home looking after things – or so Chris would think. He didn't know they would be travelling separately on Scarlet's yacht. The plan was for them to slip in and out of Italy without anyone knowing. Chris couldn't be prepared for this, or it would be over before it had even begun.

Nervously, she wondered how this would all pan out. Their lives were now in the hands of Julie Gold and whatever plan she had up her sleeve. Crossing her fingers, Katie just hoped everything would be okay. After a few minutes' contemplation, she heard the front door slam shut, which meant Chris had gone out. Rushing upstairs, she went into her shoe cupboard and took out her walking boots. Inside one of them was her secret mobile phone, one that Chris didn't have a tracker on, nor did he know about it. Running downstairs, and almost out of breath, she glanced around her to see if anyone was watching her as she hid herself near a host of rose bushes.

Dialling Scarlet's number, she felt her eyes brim with tears when she answered. It was so good to hear her voice, and it took some of her loneliness away. 'Sorry it's taken a while, Scarlet. I've had to wait for the right moment. Thankfully, it sounds like his mistress has given him enough sex for him to agree to our hen weekend. We're on, Scarlet!' She almost shouted down the phone. 'Whenever you can organise it, but come soon.'

'Calm down, Katie love. We've all been waiting for your call and we're ready to up and leave as soon as possible. Are you okay? How did it go? I don't suppose he was too pleased when you told him we were visiting. Not long now, Katie, and I will be by your side, where I belong, to protect you.'

'I love you, Scarlet, thank you. Whenever you can get here, I'm ready for you.'

Scarlet let out a huge sigh before continuing. 'While I have you to myself, how do you feel, Katie? I mean really. We're planning to murder your husband, after all. You can tell me; I am the other half of you.'

After a long silent pause, making Scarlet wonder if Katie had ended the call, she eventually spoke. 'Don Christopher of Italy is not the man I married, Scarlet. That man died many years ago. We're all planning to murder my jailer,' Katie added sternly.

Hearing the coldness in her voice, Scarlet felt satisfied. Amongst all of the planning, she had worried about whether Katie really wanted to go this far or if she had just been pushed into it by Julie and her determination for revenge. Whatever else Chris was, he was still Katie's husband and Scarlet felt she deserved to voice her opinions about a man Katie had once loved. 'Fair enough, Katie, I just needed to know that you're sure, that you realise what we're undertaking. I don't want you to feel bullied or resentful towards any of us if we do actually pull this off.'

Katie lowered her voice to a whisper. 'Rest assured, I'm okay with it. My beautiful, supressed children will dance on that bastard's grave, believe me. I welcome my release date. Shit, I've got to go.' With that, Katie ended the call.

Sitting back in her seat, Scarlet felt better that this was what Katie wanted. Now there really was nothing stopping them.

13

PREPARATIONS UNFOLD

It was early morning, and getting out of her car, Scarlet shivered and wrapped her coat closer around her shoulders. Opening the smoked glass doors of the club, she stood in the grand reception and looked around. She liked this time of the morning. There would be no one around but the cleaners, and it gave her time to think. Looking up at the pink neon Lambrianu name blazoned above the club gave her a warm feeling. She had taken this place for granted for a long time and it had simply become a place of work, but she knew it was more than that. It was home and had been her father's most treasured possession – apart from her mother, that was.

Staring up at the large oil painting of her father overlooking things as usual, she smiled, and the words left her lips without her realising it. 'I miss you, Papa. Make me strong. I need your help; we all do.' A tear brimmed on her lashes and she wiped it away as she gazed at the six-foot portrait. He was handsome and immaculately dressed as always, in his grey suit and pink shirt and his blonde hair mirroring her own, she mused to herself. The cheeky grin and glint in his eye seemed to come alive the more she gazed upon it, making her want to smile. The sound of her high-heeled shoes clacked along the marble flooring as she walked into the club. All the lights were on as the cleaners busied themselves hoovering and polishing and nodding to her as she walked by.

Scarlet didn't make a beeline for her office as usual, but instead walked up to the huge horseshoe-shaped bar dominating the room and sat on a silver bar stool with pink velvet cushioning. She had sat at this bar many times, but rarely in the daytime. She wanted to see the place in the cold light of day and drink it in. This was her world, and she had run this place for years, but had she ever really appreciated it? Today she felt much like she imagined her father had once felt when he had first breathed life into it. This place was the centre of the Lambrianu enterprise; the jewel in her father's crown. He and his foster brother Jake had worked night and day to make the club work and neither of them had been well known or wealthy in the beginning, so it had been an uphill struggle at times. To own it outright and to have his name above the door meant everything to her father. This had been his humble beginnings and, sadly enough, Scarlet mused to herself, his ending.

'Can I get anything for you, Miss Scarlet?' one of the cleaners asked.

Smiling, Scarlet shook her head. 'No, Doreen, but thank you.' As an afterthought, Scarlet stopped her walking away. 'How many years have you worked here, Doreen?'

The old cleaner stood before her, mop in hand, and rolled her eyes at the ceiling while pursing her lips. 'Must be thirty years or so now, Miss Scarlet.' Looking at her as she spoke, Scarlet found it hard to remember ever being at the club without Doreen being there.

'You knew my father, didn't you?' Scarlet asked.

'Oh, I did,' Doreen cooed, while resting her hands on the top of her mop. 'He was a real card; an absolute charmer like Mr Adam. Chip off the old block there.' She nodded and grinned.

'How are things, Doreen? I always feel the cleaners are the invisible rocks of the place. No one ever sees you, but without you where would we be? Nothing but dirty floors and unpolished tables, eh?' Scarlet smiled.

A frown crossed Doreen's brow. 'You're not giving me my cards, are you, Miss Scarlet? I know I'm no spring chicken, but my work is up to scratch and I keep these young 'uns on the ball, believe me.'

Scarlet held up her hands to stop her. 'Oh no, Doreen, nothing like that. I was just thinking, that's all. Time passes so quickly and we've never really had time to chat, have we? And it's good to talk to someone that remembers my father. My apologies, I didn't mean to worry you.' Scarlet glanced at the odd look that Doreen was giving her.

'Well, thank goodness for that. I need every penny at the moment. Got three jobs, I have. Here and two schools. This one pays the best though.' Doreen winked, feeling more at ease.

'At the moment? Why do you need every penny at the moment, Doreen? Are you saving for your villa in the sun when you retire?'

'Nothing like that – I wish!' Doreen grinned. 'That and a nice young man on my arm, eh? No, it's for my granddaughter's operation. She's on the waiting list but that could take ages. She has a hole in her heart, Miss Scarlet, and we've decided to try and go private. Gonna cost a few quid mind you, but we're doing our best and we'll take out a loan for the rest. So, you see,' Doreen stressed, 'I really need to keep my job here.'

Scarlet suddenly felt ashamed. She knew nothing about her staff and didn't take an interest as long as they did their work. Her father and Jake would have known about this, she felt certain. 'Doreen, your job is safe. It's just me going down memory lane. Absolutely your job is safe. And I am sorry to hear about your granddaughter. How is her mother coping with all of this?'

'She's dead, Miss Scarlet. Car accident a few years ago and so it's been up to me and my husband to bring her up, poor little mite. Two old biddies like me and Len bringing her up. That's why Mr Adam let me put those collection pots on either side of the bar to help with her operation.'

Scarlet's head spun around the bar looking for the collection pots. 'Adam knows about it?'

Doreen paled before her. 'Oh, Miss Scarlet, have I spoken out of turn? I can take the pots away... I thought you knew about them.'

Scarlet could have kicked herself. She had stood at the bar night after night and never even noticed the little charity pots. Her face burned with shame. Adam always made time to talk to the staff and joke with them, and he had obviously let Doreen get it all off her chest and suggested the charity boxes. 'I did... erm, I mean, I do,' Scarlet stammered. 'Sorry, like I say, it's just one of those days.' Picking up her handbag, she smiled. 'Well, nice talking to you, Doreen, and see you get that young lady over there to give that mirror another shine, will you?'

Walking into her office, Scarlet hung up her coat and bag and flicked imaginary dust from her pale blue cashmere skirt suit. Walking towards the huge desk with its two large leather chairs, she fondly touched the headrest of one and thought again of her father. What would he have done if he'd heard about Doreen's granddaughter's operation? Taking out her cheque book, she wrote a cheque for Doreen for fifty thousand pounds. She wasn't sure how much the operation would cost, but she would find out and pay the rest. In the meantime, she felt she could do some good with her money that she had worked so hard for, forever in meetings at the club and missing out on the things that mattered. Mentally, she felt it was like absolution. Absolution for being an absent mother. Her mobile buzzed, interrupting her thoughts. Looking down, she saw it was a text from Katie.

> All good to go. Chris is allowing me to host your
> hen party at the house xx

'Good girl,' Scarlet said to her mobile, now Chris could read this text and everything would seem normal. In a day or so, Scarlet would text Katie her flight times. Smiling, she dialled Julie's number. Looking at the clock on the wall, she could see that it was still early and these days Julie didn't rear her head until noon, but this was something worth disturbing her for.

'Hello, Scarlet, hoping to raise the dead are you? It's still nighttime.'

Ignoring her comments, Scarlet carried on. 'I've just heard from Katie. Chris has given his permission, so we are good to go.'

'Permission? Who the fuck does he think he is? Permission for his wife to host her sister's hen party? Fuck, he really does have his head up his arse, doesn't he?'

Sighing, Scarlet carried on. 'You know we needed his blessing, Julie. You expected it; now everything is up front and normal. But you're right, he does have his head up his arse. Prick! When can you be ready and packed?'

'I'm already packed, Scarlet. Suitcases in the hallway. Diana has had a makeover so she looks more human and less like a bag lady. Mind you' – Julie broke out in howls of laughter, making Scarlet grimace and hold her mobile away from her ear – 'once I got her into that beautician chair, you could have heard the screams on Mars when they waxed her eyebrows. Christ, I didn't scream that loud when I gave birth to her! Sometimes I wonder if she's mine. So we need to book the flights to Italy and Adam needs to get going today, because going by yacht will take longer than our flights. Is everything else okay with you?'

'I'll sort that when he comes in.' Scarlet paused before saying her next words. 'I've spent a few days with the kids, but to be honest they don't really need me, Julie. All they talk about is Knuckles. I've been looking around the club and thinking about Dad quite a lot this morning.'

'Oh my God, are you menopausal? You seem a bit maudlin, love. I tell you what, get some HRT patches and you'll feel well again.' A wry grin crossed Scarlet's face as she heard Julie's cackle down the phone, almost deafening her.

'Don't you ever have a moment to reminisce, Julie?'

'Nope, it's bad for my health. Looking backwards stops you walking forwards, and all that reminiscing sounds like it has made you miserable. As for your kids, they are happy and that's the main thing. A million husbands who are the breadwinners miss out on their children's lives, but no one bats an eyelid. Stop beating yourself up about it; they are two happy kids, with parents that love them. That's all any kid wants. Knuckles might be a bit weird, but he's a good dad and he loves those kids. So stop moping around, you sad cow, you're making me depressed now. The past is behind you; the future hasn't happened yet and today is today. Live for today, Scarlet.'

'Did you make that up or have you read it somewhere?' Scarlet snapped.

'I can tell you're feeling better because your sarcasm is coming back.'

'Well, you know what buttons to press, Julie. I will sort out flights and let you know. The managers can cope here. Adam is supposedly staying at the casino and Knuckles has taken the yacht for repair so that's them covered.'

'Okay, me and Diana will meet you at the airport; now bugger off and buy tickets, I need a wee!'

Scarlet couldn't stop herself from laughing out loud. Julie would never change, and Scarlet wasn't sure she wanted her to.

Looking up, she saw Adam entering the office. 'Shut the door, Adam. Is Poppy with you?'

'Erm... no, she's gone home to freshen up. She stayed over with Bruce and Kim last night.' Giving her a warning look, he wagged his finger. 'And it's not how you think. She had her room and I had mine. It was late, that's all.'

'Katie's called and we're good to go. Julie wants you to start travelling on the yacht today because it will take longer than our flight. Can you be ready to leave today?'

Taking a sharp intake of breath, Adam nodded his head. 'I'll get Poppy to clear my diary.' They had all been waiting for this day but now it was here, the anxiety was beginning to creep in.

Scarlet smiled; both of them could feel the nervous tension between them. Impulsively, she put her arms around Adam. 'I love you, kiddo. Now go pack a bag and I will see you in a few days.' Almost pushing him out the door, she let out a huge sigh. Would she see him again? Hearing a knock on the door, Scarlet presumed it was Adam having forgotten to say something, but opening it, she saw Knuckles standing there. 'What are you looking so pleased about?' she asked.

'Tommy gone to see his dad.'

Scarlet's face broke into a smile. 'That is good news. Phil was at such a low ebb about the rift between him and Tommy. After everything else he's lost, that would finish him off.' The smile dropped from her face as she cast a sly look. 'How did you convince him?'

'Just said he would be heading for a fall and regret it if he didn't.'

'Did you beat him up? Is he covered in bruises?' Scarlet snapped.

'Nope and nope,' was all he said. Scarlet knew she wouldn't get to the bottom of it, but at least the job had been done. 'Right, well. I've heard from Katie; you and Adam are leaving today. Well, as soon as possible. Get your stuff together.'

'Three hours.'

Frowning, Scarlet looked at him. 'That's not as soon as possible, Knuckles. What do you need three hours for?'

'Passport, see kids, Harry Potter,' was all he said, much to Scarlet's confusion. 'Harry Potter? Is he going as well? What the fuck has that got to do with it?'

'Five pages left. They going to finish it before I leave, Annette promised. Gotta see them before I go.' With that he turned his back and left the office. Standing there for a moment, Scarlet took stock of this huge man with no conscience she was going to marry. But his love for their kids, Annette and Jake, had no boundaries. Annette, who ruled him with a rod of iron, had told him that now she was a teenager, he couldn't call her Teddy in public, even though everyone knew her as that, so Knuckles had complied. Apparently, she had also given her word that she would finish Harry Potter with him tonight.

So be it, Scarlet thought to herself. It wasn't much to ask for a man laying his life on the line for herself and her family. 'Harry Potter,' she said aloud and laughed.

* * *

Breezing back into the office with his bag a few hours later, Adam looked at Scarlet's empty chair. Seeing Poppy, he asked if she knew where she was. 'Business; she told me to say goodbye to you.'

Disappointed, Adam nodded his head, 'Business comes first.' Although, he knew Scarlet had already said goodbye earlier and hated long drawn-out confrontations. 'Actually, I'm disappearing for a couple of days with Knuckles, too. He likes fishing,' Adam lied, 'so that's what we're doing for his stag weekend. I've made a list of things I need you to sort for me while I'm gone, if that's okay?'

Shocked, Poppy took the piece of paper from him. For a moment, their hands touched and, looking up, she gazed into his piercing blue eyes and felt a shiver run down her spine. 'You never said last night you were going away.'

'Must have slipped my mind,' Adam said softly, while still touching her hand. Feeling the strong chemistry between them, Adam was unsure of what to do. He knew this might be the only time he would get to kiss her, and impulsively, he swept her up into his arms and did just that. For a moment, her response was shock, but as his lips sought hers, she melted in his arms and returned his kiss as ardently as his own. She ran her hands through his hair as she held him tight and felt the hard, male nearness of him pressed against her body, while their lips remained locked in a passionate embrace.

Poppy felt her own excitement rising, and as she clung to him, she wrapped her leg around him as she explored his mouth again, searching for his tongue. Fireworks seemed to explode inside of her body as she felt his manhood pressing against her, and she knew he felt the same.

'Well, don't mind me. I just left my purse behind, but I'll be out of your way in a minute.' Hearing Scarlet's voice, Adam and Poppy leapt back in surprise, faces flushed and panting as they stood before her.

'Sorry,' she apologised sincerely, 'but if you're going to do that, you shouldn't leave the door ajar.' Neither of them spoke as

Scarlet reached forward to her desk and picked up her purse. 'Carry on.' She grinned and left.

The pair of them stood staring at each other, then burst out laughing. 'What just happened?' Poppy asked.

Straightening himself up and running his hand through his hair, Adam's first instinct was to carry on where they had left off, but looking at the clock on the wall, he knew he had to leave. 'I'm not sure,' he answered with a hint of sadness in his voice.

Suddenly, the door flew open again and hit Adam in the back, making him stumble forward. 'Ready now,' said Knuckles, oblivious to the situation he had interrupted.

'For fuck's sake!' Adam snapped. 'Doesn't anyone knock any more?' Feeling his erection slowly diminish, he felt the moment had gone. Seeing Poppy's disappointed face, he knew she felt the same. 'I have to go, Poppy. But that was either the last time, or the first... Your choice.' Leaning forward, he pecked her quickly on the lips.

'Come on, Knuckles, let's go.'

14

GIRLS JUST WANNA HAVE FUN

'Four suitcases, Julie? Christ, I presume three of them are for your makeup, or your Botox. It's supposed to be a long weekend!' Scarlet snapped. 'I've only got one case!'

'You're not paying the extra for the luggage, Scarlet darling, so shut up. Anyway, one is Diana's.'

'Where is Diana? I thought she was coming with you?'

Julie turned towards a crowd of people, looking for Diana. 'Cooee! Diana, over here!' Julie shouted loudly and waved her arms in the air towards the crowd.

Flushing with embarrassment, Scarlet tutted. 'For God's sake, Julie, you look like air traffic control waving your arms about like that. And who are you waving at? I can't see Diana anywhere.'

Just then, Scarlet's jaw almost dropped as a newly made-over Diana walked towards her. She hardly recognised her, with her blonde highlights, short bob, and red skirt suit.

'Dear God, Diana, you look amazing!' Scarlet let out a low whistle. 'Where have you been hiding yourself all of these years, under a bushel?'

Julie beamed with pride and linked her arm through Diana's.

'Scarlet, meet my daughter; the ugly duckling has transformed into a swan.'

Making a face and rolling her eyes, Diana smiled. 'Thanks for that, Mum; nice to know you thought of me as an ugly duckling. You don't get much chance to dress up in the murder squad! I'm a copper, and sometimes we're in a hurry!' Diana stressed.

'Not any more you're not, Di. This weekend you're just my daughter. You look beautiful, although the pale pink lipstick is a bit dull. You need something brighter like mine.' Julie laughed. 'My God, Scarlet, pick your jaw up from the floor and push the trolley. I hope you've booked first class and not business. I'm not having someone sitting on my knee all the way to Italy.'

Mesmerised by Diana's makeover, Scarlet held up the tickets, waving them under Julie's nose. 'I wouldn't dare book anything else.' Scarlet took in Diana's tall stance and slim waist. She really did look like Julie when she had been younger, although she had Ralph Gold's Irish green eyes, which were highlighted by the new blonde colour of her hair.

Scarlet shook her head. 'Di you look lovely, even if she had to drag you kicking and screaming into the beautician's chair.' Scarlet laughed. 'It's lovely to see you looking so well.' Leaning forward, she kissed Diana on the cheek. Scarlet, Katie, and Diana had been like sisters when they'd been small children, but Diana had chosen her own path in life much to the shock of the family. She had wanted to join the police force and had worked hard having to prove herself to her superiors. She was a millionaire's daughter whose name had been linked with scandal and racketeering in his early days. But this was the path she had chosen and Julie more than anyone supported her daughter's decision to follow her own chosen career. Julie liked Diana's fierce independence and ambitious nature. It reminded her of herself. Diana was her own person, but she never forgot she was a Gold, or that she was linked with the Lambrianus.

'Kicking and screaming? I was bloody howling, Scarlet! Every part of me has been tortured and waxed, and I mean everything!'

Scarlet burst out laughing when she realised what Diana meant. 'Don't worry, Di, it doesn't itch too badly when it starts to grow back.' She burst out laughing again.

Diana took hold of the trolley handle. 'I'll push this, Scarlet. My heels are lower than yours and this floor is like a skating rink.'

Julie clapped her hands together with glee. 'No need, girls, the troops are here.' Julie nodded and pointed as Scarlet and Diana followed her gaze. 'I've got Lewis and his boyfriend to tag along. No need for introductions, you all know each other. Do you really think I'm going to carry my own bags, Scarlet?'

'Julie, we're supposed to be being discreet!' Scarlet almost screamed. 'What the hell are you thinking?'

'I don't do discreet, darling, surely you know me by now, and if I did, people would think something was wrong. Anyway, Lewis is like a priest. For goodness' sake, Scarlet, chill out. I feel like having champagne on ice.'

'Is anyone else going to pop out of the woodwork, Julie? Anyone else I should know about?' snapped Scarlet.

'You sound just like your father. He loved a good moan. Now, do you remember my old villa in Italy? Well, I haven't been there for years, so it's time it was looked over. Lewis and the others will make their way there, out of sight from anyone else. Do you really think I'm that stupid that I would make it obvious they were with us?'

Blushing slightly, Scarlet lowered her head and muttered an apology under her breath.

Julie grinned and linked her arms through Scarlet's and Diana's. 'Lead on, ladies; sun, sand, and sex – my idea of fun.' As an afterthought, she cast a sideways glance at Scarlet, not being able to resist one last dig. 'And you can dream of marrying Shrek!'

* * *

As the sun cast a shadow over the yacht, Adam turned his head to the stern end and heard the familiar sound that had been going on for hours. Sighing deeply, he stood up and rubbed his hand on his jeans, trying the find the words he wanted to say without causing offence. Walking towards Knuckles, who had his head firmly over the side of the yacht, emptying the contents of his stomach – again – Adam tapped him on the shoulder.

'For God's sake, Knuckles, why didn't you say you got seasick? More to the point, why did you agree to come on the yacht?' Exasperated, Adam threw his hands in the air as he spoke to Knuckles's back. 'Are you listening to me? You've been on Scarlet's yacht a million times, so why are you seasick now? The weather isn't rough; in fact, it's blue skies and plain sailing.' Adam felt like grabbing hold of the huge bulk of a man before him and shaking him.

Raising his head from over the rail, Knuckles turned around, wiping his mouth with the back of his hand. Staring at him, Adam held the palms of his hands open before him. 'Well?' he asked again, while noting Knuckles's ashen face as he looked at him.

Since they had been cooped up on the yacht together, all Adam had seen of Knuckles was his back as he bent over the ship's rail vomiting. He couldn't understand it. Scarlet had had her prize yacht for years. She had hosted some of her infamous celebrity parties on it and Knuckles had been there constantly at her side, looking out for her, keeping her safe from harm.

'Not been moving,' Knuckles muttered before turning towards the ship's rail and spitting bile into the sea.

Frowning, Adam stood rooted to the spot as realisation dawned. 'Are you telling me that you have never been on this yacht when it's been moving? Only when it's been moored in the marina?' he half shouted, disbelievingly.

Seeing Knuckles weakly nod his head, Adam paced in a circle. Taking out his cigarettes and lighting one, Adam waited until Knuckles had just about composed himself. Exhaling deeply into the air, he couldn't help but feel angry and confused. 'Then why the fuck did you agree to come on the yacht with me? You knew it was going to be sailing to Italy. For Christ's sake, Knuckles, we have a deadly feat before us and you're going to be laid up sick. Why did you agree to come on board?' Adam looked up at the huge bulk towering over him and paused, waiting for an answer.

'For you,' Knuckles answered, almost shyly, whilst shifting from one foot to the other, like a child standing before the head-teacher.

The anger Adam felt drained from him as he listened to Knuckles's feeble words. Taking another drag on his cigarette, he looked out to sea as guilt washed over him. Even though Knuckles obviously didn't like boats, he had come along on this trip with him to keep Adam safe. Casting aside all thoughts of his own safety, he had chosen to accompany Adam on this journey purely out of loyalty.

Using a softer tone, Adam walked towards him and stood beside him. 'You could have flown, Knuckles; I wouldn't have minded. One of the others could have come on the yacht with me. Or I could have come alone. We could have sorted something out... You don't always have to be my guardian angel. I am a grownup.' Adam half smiled, while linking his arm through Knuckles's and leading him below deck. 'Come on, big man, let's go and see the captain. I'm sure he has come across this before and has some magic potion to cure it.'

'He better not laugh at me,' Knuckles muttered.

'He wouldn't dare, mate. Nobody is that brave. We'll sort this out.' Adam laughed.

Later, sitting on deck as the yacht headed towards Italy, Adam looked up from his sun lounger as Knuckles walked towards him. 'Are you feeling better now, Knuckles? I notice you haven't been sick for a while.' Noticing that the colour had returned to Knuckles's drained, ashen face, Adam patted the lounger beside him. 'Well, did the captain have a cure? What was it?'

'Pills and ginger. Mainly ginger drinks.'

Cocking his head to one side, Adam smiled. 'Well, as long as you're feeling better. Let's sit back and enjoy the sunshine. It's not often we have time on our own without the women... and talking of women, I had a postcard from Jennifer just before we left. Do you remember Jennifer, the marine biologist? It's strange really, as all she's written on it is "Sorry, Adam." I had hoped we would find a middle ground, but I fucked up, didn't I, Knuckles?'

Sighing deeply, Adam ran his hands through his thick auburn hair, damp from lying on his lounger. He turned his head, waiting for an answer from Knuckles; instead, he heard deep snoring sounds and smiled. 'Nice to have you back in the land of the living, mate.' Adam grinned. Adjusting his sunglasses, he laid back on his own lounger and soaked up the sun, although his mind wandered back to Jennifer. He had liked Jennifer, and she had liked him. She had been different to the other women he had met. She had worked in a supermarket to supplement her university education, but she felt he had lied to her by not disclosing who he really was.

How the hell he had ever thought he could keep his true identity a secret was a mystery to him now. It had been an idiotic idea.

Their tearful departure at the airport as she had left him standing there had never been resolved, and they had never seen each other again.

All he had received after all of this time was this postcard out of the blue saying sorry. Adam's mind spun as he remembered their affair. He had enjoyed the easiness of their time together. Talking about normal day-to-day things, eating and making love together. He would pick her up from work on his motorbike and they would ride off into the sunset, but all of the time she had been brooding. Because although Adam had thought he was keeping his identity from her, she had known the truth all along and had been waiting for him to tell her. She had known who he was but had never broached the subject. If she felt so strongly about it, why hadn't she just asked him? She was a woman with her own mind and usually said what she thought, so why had she held back on something so important?

And what had she done that now required her to apologise? He'd been used by women before, and it was hard being in his situation wanting a woman to get to know the real him, the man behind the Lambrianu empire. He was flesh and blood, and he had hopes and dreams like anyone else. But none of the women he slept with had ever asked normal questions like, what was his favourite colour, meal, or even who he voted for. Christ, they hadn't even asked him what movies he liked.

The only person who knew those things, apart from Scarlet, was Poppy. A smile crossed his face when he thought of her. She could be annoying at times, but she was honest and incredibly sexy, and she had got to know more about him in such a short space of time than anyone he'd met before – including his shoe size! But now was not the time to enter into any relationship. Who knew what the future held. The warmth of the sun was making him feel drowsy and, closing his eyes, he drifted off to sleep with thoughts of Poppy running through his head.

* * *

Picking up one of the magazines Julie had bought for the journey, Scarlet flicked through the pages hoping to drown out Julie's constant chatter. 'Dear God, Julie, have you seen this magazine?' Scarlet exclaimed again without being able stop flicking through the pages. 'The absolute bitch.'

Shocked by Scarlet's outburst, both Diana and Julie stared at her. Diana had worn her eye mask feigning sleep, but the sound of Scarlet's voice made her sit upright. 'What the hell is it that's got you so excited, Scarlet? What am I looking for?' Julie snapped. Without a word, Scarlet opened the glossy magazine and held it out towards them. 'It's about Adam.'

Snatching the magazine out of her hands, Julie scoured the pages carefully, before looking back at Diana and Scarlet.

'It's a bloody kiss and tell! That woman Adam was dating has sold her story to the magazine. Her nights of lust with Adam Lambrianu! For fuck's sake, is she that skint?' Scarlet scoffed.

'Really shown her true colours, hasn't she?' Julie waved her hand in the air dismissively. 'But what has she said that's all that damning? He's a good lover, how he adored her, blah, blah.' Julie shrugged, 'Well, there's no such thing as bad publicity.'

'But he liked her, Julie; when she first left, he was walking around like a bear with a sore head, just hoping to hear from her. Was this really necessary?' Scarlet queried.

'No, and I know he felt he was to blame, but your father went through it daily, Scarlet. People riding on his tailcoats. Read me some of it, Diana. You're calmer than Scarlet is.'

Pensively, Diana looked at Scarlet, who looked like she was

about to internally combust. Frowning, Diana read the first couple of lines, then took a deep sigh. 'It reads more like a juicy porn novel or a Mills & Boon. Listen to this. *"Night after night, Adam would pick me up on his motorbike and whisk me home, and we ripped off each other's clothes off and made love in my flat I shared with my friends. Desire ran through our veins, but I knew he was more in love with me than I was with him. I didn't want a future with him at his club being an upmarket barmaid, like his sister. And after heady nights of passion and being plied with champagne at his club, I got bored..."* Do you really want me to read on, ladies?' Diana asked as she stopped reading.

Julie burst out laughing. 'Upmarket barmaid like his sister. That's you, Scarlet!' Julie laughed again. 'Oh God, I need another drink.'

'Shut up, Julie! This isn't funny, it's slanderous. How the fuck dare she?'

'Actually, Scarlet, it's libelous, because its written down. And it's not so very far from the truth depending how you look at it. You do have a club, and that's her impression of you. Who cares? It will be tomorrow's chip paper, Scarlet. Let it go.'

'Let it go? I bet Adam hasn't seen this. He'll be mortified when he reads this. What a bitch, Julie.'

Diana sat between them both and felt like she was at Wimbledon as she turned her head from left to right listening to them argue it out. 'If I may butt in. If I didn't know better I'd say she'd planned this when she found out the truth about who he was. Look at those photos of him; they are old ones and there's not one of them both together. So, he ripped off her clothes in her bedsit... Isn't that what most young men do with their girlfriends? And, Scarlet, she might think you're a barmaid, but you work in the poshest club in town. I think she has just dug herself a hole. Everyone she works with will be talking about her and whispering behind her back. They also know that she can't keep a secret and that she's a backstabber. Adam will get over it; it's not the first scandal about him in the papers, is it?'

Sipping her champagne, Julie patted Diana's hand. 'The voice of reason, Di, and nicely put. You almost sound like your father.' She smiled. 'He was always calm in a crisis, unlike me.'

Exhausted, Scarlet laid her head back on the seat. 'I know what you're saying, but it's a shitty thing to do and I don't like it. And I know I'm going to be the one to have to tell him.'

'Why?' Diana asked. 'You only need to tell him if he mentions her. What's the point of raking over old coals? We have bigger fish to fry than some kiss-and-tell woman trying to earn a few quid.'

Making a pained expression, Scarlet looked at Diana. 'But you don't understand, Di...'

Diana's tone softened. 'Oh, I do, Scarlet, much more than you think. You've been Adam's mother figure for so long, you've forgotten how to be his sister. It hurts you more than it will hurt him. We all know how much you love him and guard him like a rottweiler.' Seeing Scarlet blush slightly, Diana waved over the air stewardess to fill Scarlet's glass with champagne. 'Let's sit back and enjoy the flight. Then maybe, just maybe' – Diana winked at her – 'this crazy old woman who I call my mother will let us in on her plans.'

Scarlet burst out laughing, breaking the tension. 'Fair point. Has she thought that far ahead, though?'

Nudging Diana in the ribs, making her wince, Julie piped up. 'You're not too big for a clip around the ear you know, Diana. And as for your uppity barmaid friend, I have thought that far ahead, so there! And don't you even think of sulking for the rest of this trip, Scarlet, you're souring my champagne!'

Diana patted each of their hands, changing the subject. 'How is Adam getting on with his new PA? She seems nice from what I saw of her at the lunch – Poppy, isn't it?'

Hearing Poppy's name, Julie jumped up in her seat and, leaning forward, spilled some of her drink on Diana. 'Ooh, you said you had some juicy gossip about her,' she said as she looked at Scarlet.

Wiping away the splash of Julie's champagne, Diana looked at them both. 'Look, why don't you just sit together? It would be simpler and I can still hear without getting wet.'

'Okay then,' Julie said excitedly, 'but keep your ears open in case I miss a bit. Come on, Scarlet, tell me.' Standing up, she exchanged seats with Diana and held up her hand to make Scarlet pause until she had got settled in. Then she gave her the nod.

'Well, do you remember Poppy being a waitress at the club a few years ago?' Julie looked in the air, trying to recall her, and shook her head. 'She used to wear braces on her teeth,' Scarlet prompted. 'You said she couldn't give a blow job in case she circumcised them.' Scarlet laughed and waited for the penny to drop.

Suddenly, as though someone had flicked the switch, Julie's eyes widened, and her jaw dropped. 'Metal Mickey!' she shouted. 'That's not her, surely? She had badly dyed blonde hair with pink bits in and those bloody braces. Oh my God, I do remember her.' Julie sat back in astonishment.

'That's our Poppy. And do you remember the scandal she left behind her when she vanished without trace, not even giving her notice in?'

Julie sat back in silence. 'Does Adam know?'

'Well, you didn't recognise her, or the name. Thankfully, I have a sharper eye. I couldn't believe it when I saw her in the high street. She's grown up and got some life experience, and by God, I have to admit, she's pretty. I've checked her out of course, and there are no skeletons, apart from the odd useless boyfriend, and we've all been there,' Scarlet scoffed.

Curiously, Diana frowned and nudged Julie in the ribs. 'Hey, you two, rewind. What scandal? Or is this a secret coded conversation for the in crowd?'

Both Scarlet and Julie bent forward in their seats and turned towards Diana sitting near the aisle. 'God, Diana, you're a shit detective. You walk around with your eyes and ears closed.'

Once their glasses were refilled again, Scarlet began. 'So, Poppy worked for us while she was at college, and she was a brilliant, efficient waitress. I couldn't fault her work.'

Still confused, Diana stared blankly at them. 'And what happened?'

Using her usual discretion amongst an aeroplane full of people, Julie couldn't hold it in any longer. 'She shagged Adam in one of the VIP booths used for the strippers when they do private stag parties.'

Diana grimaced as she looked around at the aisle full of people stopping what they were doing to listen to this juicy titbit.

'No!' Scarlet butted in excitedly. 'We *think* they did. There was gossip, but we couldn't be sure. Adam was so pissed he would have put his prick in the ring of a donut that night.' Diana could hear sniggering amongst the passengers, and she wanted the ground to swallow her up. The more the pair of them drank, the louder they got.

'It was his birthday.' Julie grinned. 'And Poppy had always hung around him starry eyed, like a lovesick dog. But Adam was too busy bonking the models and anything else he could find with a pulse. Poppy in her uniform and braces just didn't meet the criteria. He used to shag that opera singer, until she found out he hated opera,' Julie added for good measure.

Diana couldn't recall which opera singer her mother referred to, but let that detail pale into significance, not wanting to spoil everyone else's amusement.

'Well,' Scarlet butted in again, not wanting to be left out, 'when she came in the next morning, all starry eyed from her quickie, Adam completely blanked her. Oh God, Di, my heart went out to her, and that's when I realised what must have happened. She kept looking at him to make some indication about what had happened, but he just barked his usual orders and was totally oblivious to Poppy's feelings. And to make matters worse, he had a date the following evening with some half-dressed woman, who fawned all over him.'

'Men are like that,' Julie chipped in. Diana cast a furtive glance to other passengers on the aeroplane, and she could have sworn blind that she saw some of them nod in agreement. 'I would have spit in her drink,' Julie scoffed indignantly.

'Poor Poppy was in tears in the staff room when I went in. She never said why, but I guessed. She left the club that night and never returned.' Scarlet shrugged. 'The worst thing is, when I saw her recently, the first person she asked about was Adam. That torch is still shining brightly, believe me. That's when the idea of Adam needing a PA struck me. It was impulsive I know, but once we got talking and she told me what she had been doing, it occurred to me that Adam needed someone to sort out his diary and his life. And she has crept under his skin without him notic-ing.' Scarlet grinned, knowing that she had the upper hand on Julie. 'I walked in on them in the office snogging the face off each other. A minute later and she would have been spread over my desk with her knickers down. What do you think of that!'

Annoyed at Scarlet's revelation, Julie stopped her. 'You never told me that.'

'Well, I'm telling you now, aren't I?' snapped Scarlet. 'I just picked up my purse and left. They were both breathless and red faced. Not sure if they continued, but Adam's trousers couldn't have stuck out any further; he looked fit to bursting.' Scarlet laughed, encouraging Julie to join her.

Diana felt like the innocent in all of this. 'So you're throwing them together... why?'

'Oh, for God's sake, Diana, keep up. Poppy's right for him, I know it. She fights her own corner and answers him back. She's independent and efficient and she's not one of those bloody kiss-and-tell girlfriends!' Scarlet shouted, waving the magazine in the air. 'Otherwise, she would have done that a long time ago. He needs someone to watch his back; I can't do it forever. And a drunken shag with a waitress; well, there must have been something to attract him.'

'What?' asked Julie. 'Apart from the fact that she was gagging for it, and he was pissed. But I see what you mean; there must have been something he saw that night. Sometimes when you're pissed, the truth comes out. Maybe he had been watching her for a while; she was quirky and funny I suppose. Personally, I thought she looked like that bloke Jaws in the James Bond movies.' Julie's cackle at her own joke exploded around the aeroplane, making Diana feel even more uncomfortable than she already did.

As she listened to them giggling, she thought about what they had said. It seemed sad to her, and yet Poppy had agreed to work for Adam. Maybe she wanted to prove to herself she was finally free of him – closure, Diana thought to herself. She thought back to the family lunch at Southend. Adam had purposely sat beside Poppy and had seemed relaxed in her company. Maybe Scarlet had a point, and we all need a helping hand when it comes to love and fate.

Hearing a noise, Diana shook her head, and she saw Scarlet

and Julie with their heads rested on each other's shoulders snoring their heads off. Sharing their gossip had worn them out. Diana smiled to herself and pulled her mother towards her own shoulder to make her more comfortable.

Brushing Julie's hair from her face, Diana smiled. She loved her mother very much. It was hard not to; she truly had a heart of gold, even though her ways of showing it were a bit wayward at times. Smiling, she slowly pulled the magazine from Scarlet's droopy hand and flicked through the pages. Seeing the air hostess, she looked up. 'Coffee please. And take these glasses away before they spill them.'

15

A WARM WELCOME

'Where's all your luggage?' Diana asked once they had landed. 'All your cases are leopard-print, Mum, you can't miss them.' Julie had arrived at the airport with four cases, but now only had one. Diana let out a huge sigh. 'Christ, let me go and sort this out.'

Julie stopped her. 'Lewis took the rest to the villa. As you said, I don't need to turn up with that much, and look, the largest one is the only one I'm taking. Hold fire, Diana.' Taking the hint, Diana nodded. 'No surprises now, Diana; the enemy will be watching us.'

Katie was waiting at the barriers as they walked into arrivals and couldn't contain her happiness. Running towards them, she hugged and kissed them all in turn. 'The car's outside,' she said, giving each of them a knowing look.

Julie beamed a smile, her red lips lighting up her face. 'Then let's not keep it waiting.' They all walked to the black limousine waiting outside of the doors, where a chauffeur waited holding open the door for them. Glancing at each other, they knew to keep the conversation to a minimum and to discuss weddings and the usual preliminaries of how they all were – including Chris.

They eventually arrived at the house and, getting out of the car, Julie looked up at the mansion. It was still beautiful; even Chris couldn't take that away, Julie thought to herself as fleeting memories of her happy times there with Ralph and Carlos flashed through her mind. She hadn't been inside for years and part of her was curious to see what Chris had changed. The other part of her didn't want to see how he had spoilt it.

Scarlet felt they had already received a snub when Chris hadn't been there to greet them. Even if he was busy, he could have excused himself to say hello to his family, she thought, but said nothing. Chris was clearly already making the point that he was the one to decide when he would meet them and on his terms. Arrogant bastard, she thought to herself.

Katie shouted to her children that Aunty Scarlet had arrived, and she heard bedroom doors slamming and the sound of feet running downstairs, which lifted their hearts. Genuinely pleased to see Katie's brood, Scarlet hugged them.

Diana felt the children seemed more reserved than they should. They looked uniformed, like the Von Trapp family when they first met Maria in *The Sound of Music*. There was an underlying uneasiness about it all that she didn't like. It was plain to see that the children had been warned to be friendly but not over the top.

Julie looked around the large house, taking it all in. 'Well, this place hasn't changed a bit. Crikey, I would still think Don Carlos was alive and well looking at all of this.'

Katie caught Julie's eye and smiled tightly. 'Why don't we have afternoon tea in my parlour. It's my own sitting room and we won't be disturbed there.' Immediately sensing something was wrong, they all cast glances towards each other and followed Katie along the huge corridor at the far side of the house. Once inside Katie's parlour, she took a breath. 'Don't worry, this room isn't bugged. Nothing ever goes on inside it that's interesting for Chris and I make sure to move the furniture around a lot, which annoys him, because he knows I'll find a microphone or camera.'

'You live in the east wing?' Julie asked, astonished. 'Christ, this is worse than I thought. You don't even live together?'

Slightly embarrassed, Katie hung her head, 'No, we haven't for a while now. We breakfast together, for the sake of the children and servants, and we host dinners together like a happy family, but we hate each other really. God knows what they think about us in private.'

'The same as we do probably,' Julie snapped. 'What the fuck is going on here, Katie? This house is like a funeral parlour.' There was a knock at the door and Katie opened it. A maid was stood there grim-faced holding a tray of tea and cakes. Opening the door wider, Katie showed her where to put the tray, and silently they all sat there as she arranged the small triangular sandwiches and cakes on a stand before them. '*É tutto, signoria?*' she asked.

'Yes, that will be all thank you. I'll pour.' Waiting until the maid had left, Katie poured the tea.

'Aren't the kids joining us in here, Katie?' Scarlet asked. It all seemed very formal to her; she couldn't understand it.

'Not until they finish their studies. Chris makes them study for two hours extra every day, no matter what.'

Julie yawned, 'My, what a fun place this is. Christ, I remember when this place was full of fun and laughter. It was always full of people eating, drinking, or just sitting by the pool soaking up the sun. Christ, Katie, this place is the land of the living dead and I bet the whole place is bugged. He's probably watching us on his monitors now, masturbating. Do you think I should show him my tits?' Julie laughed.

Handing Julie a cup, Katie nodded and forced a sad smile.

'Well, he hasn't seen my tits in a very long time, only his mistresses'. And as for parties, well, Chris isn't exactly popular with the locals, or his staff. Don Carlos had genuine friends who admired and respected him. They enjoyed spending time with him. This is a parallel universe from what you remember, Julie.'

Seeing Katie weakened by her own humiliation, Diana knelt down beside her and opened her arms wide. 'You've been brave for far too long. I know for a fact your father would have strangled him a long time ago, let alone what mine would have done to him. We have to be strong, Katie. From today, there is light at the end of the tunnel,' Diana whispered.

'Thanks, Di. Look, come on, this is supposed to be a fun weekend. Let me show you your rooms and you can freshen up or have a nap. So come on, eat this triangular sandwich. Yuck. Chris's idea, not mine. He thinks it looks classy like Fortnum and Mason.'

Julie shook her head in dismay. 'Come on, Katie, show me my coffin for the weekend, I need to unpack.'

As they unpacked, word spread that Chris would be joining them for dinner. Later, they sat in the main dining room, normally reserved for formal dinners, and Julie saw how the table was laid, in all of its grandeur with the best cutlery laid on the grand oak table with the butler organising everything. A wry smiled crossed her face. For all of Chris's bravado, he was still insecure. Why did he need to show off in front of family like this? What did he feel he needed to prove? More to the point, who cared?

During dinner, Julie decided to set the wheels in motion for her plan. 'Chris, I was wondering,' she asked in a very subdued voice, almost dewy eyed. 'Would you mind if I took a look around the west wing?'

'Why?' he snapped. 'There is nothing up there and we don't

use that part of the house. It's more a storage place now than anything else,' he barked defensively.

'Oh, it's just that when Ralph and I used to stay here, that's where we used to stay.'

Frowning, Scarlet looked at Diana. Who was this weak, feeble woman sitting beside her? It certainly wasn't Julie Gold, that's for sure, Scarlet thought to herself.

Chris chewed harshly on his lobster like he hadn't eaten for years, then burped loudly. Everyone looked down at the table, disgusted. 'Well, Ralph isn't buried up there, is he?' Chris added sarcastically.

Wincing at the remark, Julie continued. 'I'm an old lady, Chris, with happy memories of this place. But memories are all I have these days,' she purred. 'You don't see it through my eyes...' Julie sniffed for good measure and wiped the back of her hand across her eye.

For a moment, Chris stopped chewing and glared at her. They could all see him pondering her words. 'Okay, knock yourself out with your memories, but you will be sorely disappointed. Do it as my parting gift before you die.'

Diana's blood boiled at Chris's remark, and she couldn't bite her tongue any longer. 'Was that really necessary, Chris? Is that how a host speaks to his guests? What kind of a person are you?'

Julie held up her hand to stop Diana's outburst. 'It's his house, Diana; his rules.' She winked surreptitiously at her daughter without Chris seeing.

Enjoying her subdued state, Chris's vanity was satisfied. 'Go to the west wing, Julie. Spend as long as you like up there. And as for you, Detective Diana,' he snarled and continued chewing, almost spitting out his food as he spoke between mouthfuls, 'you're not *my* guests, you're Katie's, and I am the Don of Italy.

The very godfather of this whole country,' he boasted, and spread out his arms for good measure.

'Indeed you are, Chris. Thank you,' Julie muttered through gritted teeth, lowering her eyes as she spoke.

After a very uncomfortable dinner, where Chris hadn't allowed the children to join them, he stood up. 'I'll take my brandy in my study and let you talk weddings.'

It was the first time he had mentioned the wedding, so Julie piped up once more, this time with a gleeful smile on her face. 'So, what do you think about our Scarlet marrying Knuckles, Chris?'

'Each to their own, Julie. It's about time her children were legal!' Chris spat as he threw his napkin down onto the table and left without another word. Everyone let out a sigh of relief and picked up their drinks.

'I'm sorry about that, Julie,' Katie apologised.

'Why?' Julie grinned. 'Did you expect anything else from that fat, arrogant pig who speaks with his mouth full? Because I didn't. Have you been so brainwashed you can't see the woods for the trees?' she snapped as she threw down her own serviette. 'Come on, let's go to the west wing!' Excitedly, she almost jumped out of her seat, startling them all.

Scarlet was the first to laugh. 'My Julie Gold.' She giggled. 'You should have won the Oscar for that performance.'

'Good, eh?' She winked. 'Come on, let's go and see where he has Miss Havisham hidden in the west wing.' The three women glanced at each other, shaking their heads, and smiled.

Marching their way across many landings and staircases, Julie stopped at the top of the stairs that used to be the west wing. It was dilapidated and her heart sank. She had stayed there many times with Ralph and had a lot of happy memories, but now cobwebs hung from the ceiling and across the walls. The dust was so thick, you could write your name in it. Julie couldn't believe it. 'Does nobody ever come up here?' she asked Katie, astonished at the sight that greeted them.

'To be honest, I never have. This place is so big, I didn't even know there was a west wing,' she admitted.

Julie frantically brushed the cobwebs from the walls. Diana looked at Scarlet and shrugged. If they were looking to her for answers for Julie's strange behaviour, she had none, although it was clear her mother was looking for something.

'Oh my God!' Julie stood back, dusty, with cobwebs in her hair. 'Look!' Pointing at a wall, she stood back and wiped a cobweb from her shoulder. Julie stared at the wall in awe.

'Mum, it's a wall, what of it?' Putting an arm around her shoulder to comfort her, Diana stared at the blank wall and wondered if this had some distant memory of her father attached to it.

Julie burst out laughing. 'Look at the fucking wall! You know, Di, Don Carlos wasn't as stupid as that prick downstairs thought he was.' Tears of laughter ran down Julie's face, until she sat down cross-legged on the floor.

Annoyed, but bemused, Scarlet put her hands on her hips. 'So what's the joke? Do we get to share it?'

'Look at this house, Scarlet, are you blind? This place drips with antiques and Louis XVI chandeliers, so why the fuck would that wall have pine cladding on it?'

In turn, everyone turned to the wall and stared. It was true; the wall was clad with cheap pine panels. Dumbstruck, but curious, they all turned back to Julie. 'We need to take those panels off... from the left.' Looking around, she found a long brass poker, discarded in a heap. 'Use this as a crowbar.'

Scarlet looked down at her newly polished nails and sighed. 'Give it here.' Pushing the long iron bar in between two panels,

Scarlet pushed and pulled until eventually the small pins holding the cladding were released and a panel popped off. 'Now we've got a starting block, the rest should be easier.' Looking up at Diana and Katie, she made a face. 'Well, come on!' Shaking themselves from their stunned state, they started tugging and pulling until all the panels were off.

Julie stood there triumphantly. 'Now look at the bloody wall...'

Scarlet peered past the cladding, frowning. Taking out her mobile phone, she pressed the torch on it, lighting up the inside of the gaps. 'There's another wall, but it looks like...' Perplexed at what she thought she'd seen, she looked at Julie. 'Is that a door, Julie?'

'You're damned right it is. Let me show you and then I will explain all.' The wall was wallpapered, although dated and faded, but behind the cladding stood an oak door. Julie tried hard to turn the handle, but age and rust had sealed it shut. Between them, they heaved it, almost falling backwards as the door flung open. A gasp of surprise escaped them. 'It's a bathroom. Why would anyone board up a bathroom, Julie?'

'Because Don Carlos was a genius. And only anyone who knew this house would know that this place ever existed. Pine cladding! Carlos was a bloody joker, I'll give him that. This, ladies, is our friends' way in from the outside.' Huddling them closer together, Julie whispered, 'Carlos had the FBI, MI5 and whoever else in his pocket. But he knew, should the shit ever hit the fan, he'd need an escape tunnel. It's a bathroom – not suspicious at all. I can't believe that prat Chris has never sussed this. Did he really think Don Carlos would never have an escape room built into his own house? As far as I'm aware, there are only five people who knew about this. Carlos, of course' – she grinned – 'myself and Ralph, your father,' she said, pointing at Scarlet, 'and of course, Denny. Three of those people are dead and so they aren't telling anyone.'

'Okay, now I'm intrigued, Julie,' Scarlet butted in. 'But who is Denny? I've never heard of him. What if he has said something?'

Laughing again, Julie turned towards Katie. 'You know Dennis, that old, grey-haired butler of yours, well past his sell-by date? Well, that's Denny.'

Shaking her head, Scarlet grinned. 'The butler did it in the bathroom with pine cladding!'

'Something like that.' Julie nodded. 'He's been here for years; Christ, he's half bent over with a hump on his back, but he's the best hitman I've ever known and as sharp as a razor.'

While the others spoke, Katie stood there rooted to the spot. 'Are you telling me,' she said slowly, 'that Dennis, the loyal household butler, is your inside man?'

'Give that girl a coconut. Spot on, Katie.' Julie laughed. 'Come and join me in the bathroom. Damn! There's no light. The bulb isn't working,' she exclaimed.

'What! After all of these years, are you surprised? For fuck's sake, Julie, nothing lasts that long.' Scarlet laughed and, still holding the torch on her mobile, they all shuffled into the bathroom while Julie looked around the dark, thickly cobwebbed room.

'Point your torch to the floor, Scarlet.' Doing as she was told, they all watched as Julie pulled back a rug; dust flew into the air as she did so.

'Is that a manhole?' Diana asked.

Nodding, Julie explained, 'Yes, that's where he would either leave or come in, whatever the situation required. It also meant Don Carlos could leave the house with a rock-solid alibi from the staff that he was home for the evening, when he wasn't. This is where the boys come in,' Julie added. 'There are quite a few stairs down into the tunnel, and to be honest no one has been down there for years by the looks of it. It leads out about a mile from the house on the other side of the gates. It's possible there are rats down there as it's near the water pipes, but Carlos had the walls filled and plastered properly so there shouldn't be too many to deal with.'

'Fuck! You want us to go down a dark tunnel with rats and water. Have you ever considered that it could be *full* of water?' Scarlet exclaimed. 'Are you fucking crazy? This is your master plan, Julie Gold?' Scarlet kept her voice low, but she was fuming, and the thought of what was down there filled her with horror.

'Yes, big mouth, I have; and that's why, in my luggage, I've brought us all wetsuits. We will be dry and safe. Carlos had wooden torches hanging in brackets on the walls to light it up, but they could be damp now...' She faltered. 'On the other hand, they might light if we poured a bit of petrol or something on them. We can't just walk through the front door and blow that sarcastic bastard's head off, as much as I'd like to after the insults he threw out tonight. We need rock-solid alibis, especially the men.'

Scarlet listened to her words and nodded. 'I suppose it's worth a shot. We all have an axe to grind with that bastard. Hell, we all knew there was a possibility we could die, but I didn't think it would be drowning in a pool full of rats or through lack of oxygen. What if the men are claustrophobic? More to the point, how is Knuckles going to fit through that hole, for Christ's sake?'

'That's a minor detail.' Julie pouted. 'We'll cross that bridge when we come to it. Show some Lambrianu balls, Scarlet; we will work it out, okay?'

'Well,' said Diana, 'no plan is foolproof and what have we got to lose... apart from our lives? We already knew that was an option. Has Chirs been up here, Katie? I mean, is any of this upstairs bugged, do you know?'

'As far as I'm aware, he's never been up here. He always said this part of the house was cold and draughty and used it more as a storage space. Look' – she pointed – 'it's stacked high with furniture. He's not likely to come up here with his expensive suit on, is he?'

'No, but Denny would. He would gather the servants to bring stuff up here, preventing Chris having to do so. There is none so blind as those who can't see.' Julie grinned. 'And of course it's cold up here. There's a great big hole in the bathroom with nothing underneath it but a tunnel! My Ralph liked it here. The cold made you snuggle up closer together,' Julie said, pointing to the opposite side of the landing. 'That was our bedroom there, and there used to be a big fireplace in it. Very romantic.' She grinned.

'Oh God,' Scarlet moaned, 'that's too much information about you snuggling up near a log fire with Ralph. Don't give me nightmares.'

'Nightmares? Believe me, Scarlet Lambrianu, those were nights that dreams are made of.' She winked saucily. Julie walked to the bedroom she had once shared with Ralph and, turning the handle, she pushed the door open with her shoulders.

Diana nodded to the others to follow, and Scarlet held up her torch to light the room up, saying nothing. They were all aware that Julie was having a flashback moment and left her to it. In the dim torch light, Julie could see the huge four-poster bed, and recalled the nights she had shared it with her husband. Sadly, the once lush red velvet pelmets hung dusty and cobwebbed, unloved. Mentally, she could hear the laughter she had shared with Ralph, and suddenly it was as though he was there beside her. Walking ahead, Julie went further into the room. It was as though she didn't need light; she had her memories to guide her.

Looking down at the quilt on the bed, she stopped and gazed at it lovingly, but running her hand over it, she found the cloth rotten, and it almost crumbled under her touch. She was about to leave when something caught her eye on the bedside table. Tearing away at the cobwebs, she saw frames of happy photos of herself and Ralph in their younger days. Her stomach somersaulted as she picked one up and held it to her breast. It was a wedding photo of them both that she remembered Ralph had placed beside the bed. For a moment, her eyes brimmed with tears, and she felt her throat tighten. 'Soon, Ralph love. Soon,' she whispered in the dimness of the light.

16

A GOOD ALIBI

'Morning, Bruce; can I have a word when you have time?' Poppy was sat at her desk going through the mail and paperwork, while making a mental note of what Adam and Scarlet had asked her to do.

'Well, Poppy, I definitely have time on my hands now. Adam asked me to keep an eye on things for him, but the managers already have everything in hand. And it's not like they are going to rip anyone off, especially after all these years. Personally, I think he just wanted to give me something to do while I'm on holiday.' Letting out a deep sigh, Bruce looked down at himself. 'My leg's healed well, but I need the stitches out and another dressing on. And my arm is healing well too...' he rambled on, much to Poppy's annoyance.

'For God's sake,' she snapped, 'I asked if *I* could have a word, not for you to talk my ear off! Although, it's obvious that you're missing Adam.' Poppy wanted to bring up the subject without causing suspicion, so she knew she needed to tread carefully. 'Sit down, Bruce; I've had a call this morning from the owner of house in the Lake District, you know, where Adam is staying with Knuckles fishing?' she prompted.

Silent for a moment, Bruce shrugged. 'Why are they contacting you?' Bruce asked cagily.

'They contacted me because Adam hasn't turned up to collect the keys. Have you heard from him? Is he okay – has he had an accident or something?'

Averting his eyes, Bruce shook his head. 'Not that I'm aware of, Poppy. Maybe they've stopped somewhere along the way. Tell me again what the property owner said.'

For God's sake Bruce, she thought to herself, *for a clever mean you are slow*. It's just as well he didn't need an alibi if he was having some dirty weekend he didn't want Scarlet to find out about. 'No one has picked up the keys; Adam hasn't turned up,' Poppy pressed, waiting for Bruce to catch on.

Suddenly, much to Poppy's relief, Bruce's eyes lit up. 'Right, I'm with you now. He hasn't picked up the keys and no one has seen or heard from him to say he's been delayed.' Trying to think of a solution, Bruce looked at her hopefully. All he could think of was to call the key holder and tell them he had been held up.

Losing patience, Poppy threw her hands up in the air and stood up. 'For God's sake, Bruce; we both know this last-minute holiday is a ruse for something. So, let's be frank, because you can't see beyond your nose. A man, claiming to be Adam, needs to visit the key holder and pick up those keys. It doesn't matter if they stay at the property or not. I don't know anything about what's really going on, but I get the feeling you do. Are you following me?'

Bruce burst out laughing. 'Well, to start with, Inspector Clouseau, I do get what you're saying. I don't know anything about why Adam has gone away with Knuckles, but I grant you, it's probably business he doesn't want spread around. So maybe I should go and pick up those keys and make the place look lived in. Maybe Kim could throw a sickie or something and we could have our own romantic holiday cottage.'

Clapping her hands together, Poppy let out a huge sigh. 'Bruce, you do make hard work of it, don't you? Especially for a clever bloke,' she added.

'Well, why didn't you just spit it out, Poppy?'

'Because I was trying to be tactful and hoped you would take the hint. But I'll know better next time, wont I?'

Apologetically, he looked at her. 'I'm sorry, Poppy. I'll go and pack and make that call. Christ, Kim will be over the moon if she thinks I've booked a holiday cottage for us both.'

'Well, it does have a hot tub.' Poppy smiled enthusiastically. 'And maybe a log fire. Us girls like that kind of thing,' she encouraged.

Bruce smiled. 'Yeah, and I could catch up with my reading. Okay, I'm off.' Standing up, he left. Poppy looked at her desk and, leaning forward, banged her head on it, exhaustedly. A weekend cottage and he was going to catch up on his bloody reading, she groaned to herself. Poppy thought that if she ever got the chance to go away with Adam to somewhere like that, she definitely wouldn't take any bloody books!

* * *

Chris, dressed formally in his black suit and tie, walked into the breakfast room to join them. The way he stood at the head of the table made Scarlet wonder if he wanted them all to stand in his presence until he gave them permission to sit down again. She couldn't believe his arrogance. He was so bloody rude. Power and authority had definitely taken over his personality. Looking at him closely for a moment, she remembered their younger days when he had been handsome and she'd nicknamed him Clark Kent. But there was no sign of the handsome Superman now; he was obese, red faced and balding. He had let himself go, Scarlet thought to herself, and he didn't care. He had his kids, the heirs and spares and the trophy wife. Now, he also had his 'godfather presence', in Italy.

'Well, Julie, did you find anything interesting in the west wing?' he probed. They all knew he was probing, with a touch of sarcasm to boot.

'Actually, I did, Chris. In the room I used to share with Ralph, I found an old wedding photo of us both that I'd forgotten about. I'm glad you let me go there.'

Chris, narrowing his eyes, looked at her with distaste. He had always disliked her sharp tongue and sarcasm and, eyeing her up and down, he thought how old and cheap she looked. It was early morning and she was already dressed to the nines as if she was going to a nightclub. Her makeup was cemented on to try to hide the wrinkles, and he wondered just how much plastic surgery held it all together. Still, he thought to himself, age seemed to have mellowed her if last night's performance was anything to go by. He decided to keep his sharp retort about it being a very old photo and as derelict as her to himself.

'Well, I'm glad you found something worthwhile in that part of the house. I've found it draughty and musty when I've been up there. Like an old perfume bottle had been spilt. What Carlos was thinking of, leaving that place to rot, I can't imagine. But then he was an old man verging on dementia; he probably saw the same old memories that you did.'

Julie knew he was having a dig at her, but didn't rise to it. She saw Diana was about to speak in her defence, but gave her a knowing look to ignore him. Pouring herself more tea, she caught his eye. 'You don't go up there often then?' she enquired.

'Good God, no.' He laughed. 'Personally, I think that part of the house should be demolished. Maybe I will give that some thought. Out with the old, eh?' His smarmy smile and manner gave Julie hope. She needed to know if he intended going up there, and he definitely didn't. His slight digs about being old annoyed her. She knew how old she was, but had satisfaction in knowing he would never reach her great age.

'Well, I brought the photo down with me.' Bending down, she took it out of her bag to show him the evidence of what she had said. 'I'd like to take it with me, Chris, if you don't mind? But I don't want you thinking I'm stealing out of your home.' She grinned.

Letting out a large guffaw, everyone turned to look at him – this was the first laughter they had heard from him since they had arrived. His face had turned the colour of a beetroot. 'What the hell would I want with that?' He laughed again. 'You knock yourself out, Julie, and take whatever relics up there you want to remind you of your younger days.'

Smiling at him, Julie thanked him cordially for his kindness.

'So,' he barked, 'what have you lot got planned for today?'

'We're going into town to look at Italian lace for my wedding dress. Make a girl's day of it. Lunch, shopping and the like.'

'Don't tell me you're going to wear white, Scarlet,' Chris scoffed. 'That's an insult in itself.'

Scarlet's eyes flashed at him, but like Julie, she bit her tongue. 'Well, Chris, you tell me how many virgin brides there are these days. Most women have had boyfriends before they tie the knot, and yet they all wear the traditional white wedding dress.'

'These days most women are tarts. Well, I will tell one of the drivers to take you anywhere you wish. After all, you're our guests and should be treated as such.' Turning to his left, he spied his uniformed children sitting there quietly eating breakfast. 'Eat up, the car will be outside in a few minutes to take you to school.'

Seeing the children's subdued nods as they left the room, Diana felt sick. This was abuse at its finest. She had investigated cases like this, where the wife had snapped and murdered her husband after years of mental torture.

Chris wandered over to Katie and kissed her on the cheek. 'Don't spend too much, Katie. I'm not made of money for you to squander. Excuse me, ladies; I have things to do.' Everyone took a sigh of relief as he left the room. Julie put her finger to her lips to stop them all blurting out insults about him.

'Katie, love, the gardens look lovely. Shall we have a walk around them to let our breakfast digest? There used to be some beautiful roses in those gardens.' They all followed Julie outside. The morning breeze of the outdoors greeted them, taking away the sour tastes in their mouths.

'I hate this word, but it's the only one I can think of,' exclaimed Diana. 'He's a cunt! There, I've said it. A lowlife nobody, pretending to be somebody. He doesn't need us to kill him; that obese bastard with his red face, gobbling up fried breakfasts, will end up having a bloody heart attack!' All of her anger and venom came pouring out of her mouth. Looking at Katie, she apologised. 'Sorry, love, it's your husband, but if he insults my mother once more, I will strangle him with my bare hands. Mum, how the hell can you keep so cool?'

'Oh, I've sucked up to worse, love. He's an amateur.' Julie laughed. 'Remember the fable about the hare and the tortoise? Well, let him have his fun while he can. The condemned man deserves a hearty breakfast, doesn't he? And you hold your tongue, Diana. Give him no reason to suspect anything. After all, he is the Don of Italy, and he deserves respect!' Julie burst out laughing. 'My arse, he does! Anyway, I know how old I am, and I am comfortable with it. I'm at peace with myself, which is more than I can say about him. Come, I need to look around.'

'At what?' Scarlet asked curiously. She hated gardens and mud; they were bad for her heels.

'I want to see how many guards patrol the balconies and house with guns. Christ, he is certainly scared of something. Look at them all, dressed in their black trousers and shirts. What the fuck is that all about? Your kids can't breathe in that house, Katie. He's a blackmailing bastard who has you by the short and curlies. He knows you and Diana killed Sharon that night and he would use it if you ever threatened to leave him. Well, my daughter's not going to prison, no way. And you, Katie, you would be swapping one prison for another, but you would be leaving your kids with a manipulating control freak. Anyway, why are the kids going to school today?' she asked, puzzled.

'They have extra tuition at a weekend school and Chris insists they go to get out from under his feet. He says he wants educated children, not idiots.' Katie sighed. She felt humiliated with her family seeing her home life like this. It made her look weak and submissive. But she felt she had been strong inside for putting up with it for so long for the sake of her and Diana's freedom.

'I liked the part where he told her not to spend too much money! Considering he got this house for free and is squeezing the blood out of the people around here for every last penny, he's got a bloody cheek. Anyway, we don't need his money. Fuck him! I wouldn't take a penny from that greasy bastard.' Scarlet scoffed as, each in turn, they let out their pent-up feelings for Chris in the quiet gardens with no bugs for Chris to listen in to.

Wagging a long, polished finger in each of their faces, Julie beamed a smile. 'Now, now, my little bad-tempered girls, we now know he wouldn't go to the west wing if they pulled his teeth. Strike one to us. Secondly, we know how many guards there are, which tells me we aren't the only people who want to see the back of him. He's scared shitless; and bullies are always cowards.' Drumming her fingers on her chin and deep in thought, Julie raised her eyebrows. 'Katie, we need to find Don Carlos's original will and testament. The one where he named Adam as his heir, not the one Chris dragged out of an old feeble man.'

'Well, if he hasn't already disposed of it, which I daresay he has, it would be in his office, I presume. I've no idea, Julie. Personally, I would have burnt it.'

Julie pouted and nodded. 'So would I, love, but my gut instincts tell me he hasn't. Apart from mentioning Adam, that will would also contain what Carlos would have left to Chris, wouldn't it? His fortune was vast and he would have left something to Chris, possibly even this house. After all, he was his nephew and although Carlos hated him, he believed in family values. You girls and Adam have the vineyard. Maybe Carlos thought Adam could be the new Don from there. Maybe this house does belong to Chris. The bottom line here is that we don't know what was in the original will.'

'So all this could be for nothing, Julie?' Katie asked. 'Maybe Don Carlos lied and did intend making Chris the new Don. Have you ever thought about that?'

Julie threw her hands up in the air. 'Don Carlos had dementia, girls; he wasn't fucking stupid. Nobody in their right mind would give that much power to a narcissist. But that original will has to be somewhere in this house. About that I'm bloody positive.'

'What about copies? Wouldn't his solicitor have a copy of the original?'

'Oh yeah, and he's really going to hand that over to us, isn't he? The guy must be in fear of his own life. He doesn't give a fuck about yours,' Julie snapped. 'Anyway, we'll cross that bridge when we come to it.'

'Well, apart from anything else we have to do today, I want to go to the vineyard,' Scarlet said. 'I appreciate Dad left me and Adam the club and the vineyard to you, Katie, but it was still Nonna's home and I would like to see it.'

Katie shook her head. 'I don't care what Dad left to whom; we're all the same blood and we don't rip each other off. Moving to Italy and running the vineyard was Chris's idea, not mine. Of course we'll go today.' Katie soothed and hugged her sister.

Having organised a car, they drove up to the vineyard. Even Scarlet had to admit the factory was in top condition and working like clockwork. The one thing Scarlet did notice, which she found odd, was all the workers were beavering away, but not one of them stopped what they were doing to say hello, which was unusual for Italians and even more unusual considering she was a Lambrianu and they worked at the Lambrianu vineyard. A lot of the workers she noticed were new faces, and that bothered her. Some of the people who had worked there had been there forever, but things had clearly changed. Stopping a couple along her route, she smiled and introduced herself, and was met by a shy nod and a smile. 'This place has no warmth, Julie,' Scarlet muttered under her breath. 'There is just something missing in the air. I don't know what it is...'

Watching everyone around her wearing their white overalls and white hats and following hygiene procedures, Julie nodded. 'A lot of these people aren't even Italian, Scarlet. Look around you. Your name means nothing to them apart from being the name on their wage slip or the label on the wine bottle. He's sacked or got rid of a lot of the people who gave this place heart.'

Catching up with them, Katie bowed her head humbly. 'Some of them are here on five-year visas with a condition that they can't leave. It's cheap labour. And like I told you, when I venture into town, some of the original workers' families snub me because Chris has robbed them of their livelihood.'

'Are you telling me he's got those poor bastards tied to this factory for five years?' Julie asked. The very thought horrified Julie, and a fleeting memory of her younger days with her sister came to mind when they had been trafficked into slave labour. It had been a nightmare and one she had tried to forget, but some things never left you, she thought to herself.

'I think so,' Katie stammered. 'He doesn't let me have any say in the running of this place any more. He says they have chosen a better life, job, and an opportunity to look after their families. Ask them,' Katie urged, trying to absolve herself.

Julie tapped a man on the shoulder, and he turned towards her. 'Where are you from?'

'Gambia, miss.'

'And do you like working here? How much do you earn?' Julie pressed. The others could see the man was nervous as he shuffled from foot to foot. He wasn't sure what to say in case he caused any offence. Julie asked again and glared at him, and once the man muttered his wage under his breath, Julie paled. 'That's half the minimum wage in England!' Julie's blood boiled, and her face flushed. 'And on top of that they have to pay the rent for wherever they are living, send money home and keep themselves. For fuck's sake, I can't believe this.'

Clapping her hands loudly, Julie shouted, 'Oy, you lot, take a break. Go and have a coffee in the sunshine, for fuck's sake.' Everyone stopped what they were doing and stared at her. 'Well? Go on, fuck off out of here. You've got an extra hour. GO!' she shouted. Without another word, the workers headed for the exit.

'And if Chris finds out?' Katie asked. 'He will be boiling mad, Julie.'

'Fuck him, and to be honest, fuck you for letting things get this bad and not saying a word. I appreciate you've been in a tricky situation, Katie, but open your fucking eyes. No wonder Italians snub you. This isn't the Lambrianu vineyard. It's Chris's sweat shop!'

'Mum.' Diana tried pacifying Julie. 'Isn't that why we're here, to make things right? It's not all Katie's fault; none of us have been here for a while. Chris has had it sewn up nicely. Nobody coming in or out to keep an eye on him. What could she do? He's a control freak; just look at his uniformed kids. They act like zombies in his presence. Katie's protected me for years and given up her own freedom in the process. And what would happen to the kids if Katie left him? Do you really think she would be able to take them away from Italy? Not a chance! Her hands have been tied either way.'

Calming down a little, Julie nodded. 'It's just a hard pill to swallow, Di, seeing this place like this. I remember the good old days. Maybe I'm just an old woman, after all, living with her memories. All the staff who worked here seemed happy, and the party that was thrown when all the grapes had been picked was amazing. Food and wine flowed and dancing and laughter filled this place. And now, it's cold and sterile. It saddens me, Di.'

She put her arms around her daughter, and Diana hugged her back. 'Don't worry, Mum, when all this is done, we will have a party to blow your socks off.' Diana laughed. 'You won't be sober for days.'

As Julie drew back from Diana's arms, she looked her directly in the face and her eyes filled with tears. 'Do you promise me that, Diana? Whatever happens, will you throw a party for everyone and make this place a family business again? And if I don't survive this, will you promise to get me back to England and bury me with your father?'

For a moment they all stood staring at each other, and Diana could feel herself welling up. 'I promise, but you're scaring me a little, Mum. You will be home in your own bed soon enough once you've drunk this vineyard dry.' Attempting a smile, Diana felt her stomach churn, and she hugged Julie again.

'Come on, Scarlet, do you want to look around the house, or shall we go into town and look for wedding dresses? After all, isn't that why we're here?'

Glancing at Julie's sad face, Scarlet nodded. 'Yes, I've seen enough here. Let's go shopping.' Pasting a smile on her face, Scarlet linked her arm through Julie's. 'Julie Gold surrounded by designer shops and she hasn't spent a penny. Come on, show us how it's done. Although I warn you, I don't want a big flared-out thing like those crocheted toilet-roll holders from the seventies.' Scarlet laughed.

Seeing the glint of humour back in Julie's eyes, they all walked out of the factory, smiling and waving goodbye to the workers enjoying the sunshine and eating their sandwiches.

17

TIME TO ACT

As they made their way back to the house, their spirits were lifted in more ways than one. The champagne had been poured as Scarlet had disappeared into changing rooms trying on numerous wedding dresses, while the rest of them lounged on the sofa, sipping from their glasses and watching the entertainment. With each dress Scarlet tried, they either gave the thumbs up or made a grimace and definitely put their thumbs down.

'I prefer the A-line satin one,' Diana commented. 'Scarlet's got a nice figure, and it shows her shape off nicely.'

'Nah, it's got to be big!' Julie announced. 'You know, lacy and satin. She's the bride and she needs to make an entrance.'

'I wouldn't get through the bloody door in something like that! Simple and elegant, that's me.' Scarlet nodded and took a drink.

'Then, if Armani isn't doing it for you, let's go to the house of Dolce and Gabbana,' Julie shouted, turning to the poor assistant waiting on Scarlet. 'Sorry, love, I get the feeling we won't be back. Take this for your trouble.' Julie handed her a wad of cash, and they were all laughing and joking as they got into the back of the car. The waiting chauffeur had dozed off but, with a poke in the shoulder from Julie, he sat bolt upright.

'Does Chris let you sleep on the job, my good man?' Scarlet laughed and quickly, the driver took them to their next stop.

* * *

Sitting below deck on the moored yacht, Adam ran his hands through his hair. 'Oh God, Knuckles, I really need to stretch my legs. I've heard from Lewis, and they are staying at Julie's old villa about four hours from here. Do you fancy going there? Apparently he's our contact man. Julie has told him everything, and we're not to contact her. Seems a bit strange to me. He knows everything and we're still waiting to find out.'

Slowly, Knuckles nodded his head. 'He lives with her, bound to know the facts. We haven't heard anything from them. Hope they okay.'

'Well, no news is good news I suppose, and Lewis never said anything else. I get the feeling he wants to talk privately.' They were both going stir crazy. Even though the yacht was luxurious, they both felt the need for dry land, even if just for an hour. 'I'll get the captain to hire us a car.'

An hour later, dressed in the crew's white uniform and caps, Knuckles and Adam got into their waiting car and headed for the open road. 'Feel that breeze, Knuckles. Go on, open the window. The roads are empty. We will stay off the main route and travel the back roads, then no one will see us.'

For a few days now they had kept below deck in the stifling heat without a word from the girls. They were on tenterhooks, waiting for the go-ahead from Julie, and clock watching was draining whatever energy they had left. The pair of them yearned for fresh air.

'What about the captain? Will he talk, Adam?'

'No, he's sound as a pound. And let's be honest, he's got a cushy job riding around in a yacht and getting paid for it.'

An hour into their moment of freedom, they heard a bang. Knuckles grabbed the steering wheel and braced himself as the car swerved and veered off the road. 'Shit, we've had a blowout. The tyre's knackered,' Adam puffed. 'Are you okay, Knuckles?'

Nodding, Knuckles pointed at Adam. 'You've banged your head. It's bleeding.'

Touching his forehead, Adam saw the blood on his fingers and the red stain on his shirt. 'I'll be okay. Let's see what's in the boot tyre wise. We'll need to change it.' The sunny dusty roads were empty as Knuckles got out of the car and looked into the boot for the spare tyre and jack. Adam looked into the mirror at his head. It was only a minor cut and there was more blood than wound. Getting out of the car, he knelt beside Knuckles as they both changed the tyre.

'We're lucky, Knuckles; some cars don't have spares these days.'

Two cars passed them; one hooted its horn, but neither of them paid attention to it. 'Fine lot they are. Never even stopped and asked if we needed help. Just blowing his horn for us to get out of the way,' Adam moaned. 'Well, that's all done so let's go. And remind me to get the captain to tell the car hire firm we want our money back!'

Once back into the car, they headed off for the villa. Hearing the car approaching, Lewis came out and greeted them. 'It's good to see you, Adam. I haven't heard a word from Julie and the others. They said a long weekend. Well, the weekend is nearly over. What's holding them up?'

Both Knuckles and Adam shrugged, but they both agreed it was worrying not to have heard from anyone. Lewis had prepared a banquet for them all, and to sit around having a few beers being able to speak freely was a welcome relief. Adam was fed up of being couped up with Knuckles. They couldn't particularly talk to the crew. They had their orders and their job to do, and as much as Adam liked Knuckles, the conversation was a bit limited. What on earth was keeping Julie from making contact?

* * *

Back at Don Chris's manor, an old man with finely swept-back grey hair, a silk suit, and a heavy accent stared at Chris. 'It's been a very interesting meeting, Don Christopher.' Don Lorenzo looked at Chris's outstretched hand to shake his. After pausing for a moment, he shook Chris's hand, but Chris watched as the old man then rubbed the hand down his jacket, as though rubbing off something dirty. Chris hated the way this old Argentinian Don looked him up and down all of the time. Chris looked at this sharp-suited old man in his seventies who turned up each quarter wanting his suitcase full of money for the business Chris did in Argentina and the surrounding areas. Bloodsucker, Chris thought to himself.

Neither of them liked each other, but business was business. 'I will see you next quarter, Chris. Oh, by the way, say hello to Adam for me. I did get the chauffeur to hoot his horn, but he paid no attention. Probably had women on his mind.' Lorenzo laughed. 'I remember being that age. He's a good boy, although I doubt he would thank me for calling him a boy.' He laughed again and it was the first time Chris had seen him smile, let alone laugh all day. And then it occurred to him what he'd just said.

'Adam? When did you see Adam?' He'd taken him by surprise, and Chris's eyes narrowed and bored into Don Lorenzo.

'Early this morning, here in Italy of course. He was changing his tyre. Send him my best.' Dumbstruck, Chris watched Lorenzo as he got into his car, and painted a smile on his face. He hated this old man; as well as ripping him off, he had never wished Chris well. Only Adam. *Adam,* he thought to himself, the annoying fly in the ointment. Chris hated him more.

Pouring himself a drink, Chris felt his hand shaking as he drank his whisky. Adam was in Italy? Nobody had mentioned Adam was coming to Italy. This was supposed to be a girls' shopping spree for a wedding and a hen party, or so he had been led to believe. Chris's mind was in turmoil. So what was Adam doing here? And why had nobody mentioned it?

All day long, Chris paced the house. He couldn't concentrate. All kinds of scenarios went through his mind. Maybe the ladies didn't know that Adam was in Italy. Why hadn't he come to the house? None of it made sense. After he ordered his car, he drove up to the vineyard. If anywhere, Adam would be staying there. Asking questions at the factory, Chris came to a halt. The staff mentioned that the women had been, but no males.

His blood boiled. He knew Scarlet would know if Adam was in town. Christ, he told her everything. Slamming his fist down on his desk, and throwing his paperwork into the air, Chris shouted into the emptiness of his office. 'I will bloody well find out!' he vowed to himself. His henchmen who permanently walked around the corridors glanced furtively at him. 'What the hell are you lot looking at? Do your fucking job!' he bellowed.

After a long, stressful day, Chris finally heard a car turn into the driveway. Looking out of the window, he saw that it was Katie and the others. His temper rose, but after taking a few breaths, he composed himself. Walking outside to meet them, he was disgusted to see the women almost fall out of the car. It was clear they had been drinking, and their loud laughter as they carried their designer bags into the house made him want to vomit.

'Katie!' he barked. 'You're a disgrace. Look at you, acting like some drunken lush. I expect it from them, but not from my wife.' He had tried stifling his outburst, but his nerves were raw.

'Hey, calm down, Chris. You knew we were shopping and having a ladies' lunch. And less of the insults, brother-in-law,' Scarlet snapped. 'So we've had a few drinks; what of it?'

'I have a reputation to uphold, Scarlet. I cannot have them thinking my wife and her family are drunks.'

'The only person thinking that, Chris, is you. I'm speaking to you coherently, aren't I? We've had a few laughs and jokes. Done some shopping, and we were having a good time, until you opened your mouth.'

'I've told you before about drinking, Katie. You will get one of your headaches, and we don't want that now, do we? Dinner will be in an hour. Make yourself presentable. I will see you then.' As he sneered at them as he walked away, they all cast questioning glances at each other.

'What's his problem?' Scarlet asked as she flopped down on to the sofa. 'I think at my age I am allowed to have a few drinks on my hen weekend, don't you?' While talking, she put her fingers to her lips to warn the others. She wanted to remind them all that the lounge was wired and that Chris would most likely be listening. Taking the hint, they all nodded.

'Well, yeah, what did he expect?' Diana moaned. 'We're grownups. It could be worse considering what some men's stag nights are like.' She laughed, even though it was hollow and for Chris's ears only. They were all aware that, even though he had left them, he would be listening through his monitors in his study.

Picking up her shopping bags, Katie nodded her head towards the door. 'We'd better freshen up. As Chris said, it will soon be time for dinner. I'll go and check up on the kids first.'

Julie rolled her eyes to the ceiling. 'Well, your husband certainly knows how to pour cold water on a fun afternoon, I'll give him that. And what are these headaches he mentioned? I didn't know you had a headache problems... apart from him,' she slurred.

'Oh, I get these headaches occasionally, like a migraine. But once I've had a nap, I feel much better. I don't know, it must be stress or something.'

Concerned, Scarlet held Katie's hand. 'Have you been to see a doctor, Katie? They have medication for migraines; you should have it checked out if it's a regular occurrence.'

Shaking her head, Katie gave a weak smile. 'Chris said there was no need, that it was probably the menopause or something. Like I say, once I've gone to bed for an hour or so I feel much better.'

'Chris won't let you see a doctor? If it's menopausal then you can get something for that, too. What do you think, Julie?'

Listening to the sisters, Julie sat up, seemingly a little more sober. 'Presumably these migraines happen like today, when you've gone against his will or disobeyed him?' Julie asked. 'Cos I've never seen you have one in England when you visit.' Julie didn't want to say what had crossed her mind out loud, but the answer made sense in some ways.

Scarlet could see Julie was deep in thought, and it frightened her. Did she think Katie had a tumour or something? 'Julie, whatever prognosis you think you have, spit it out and we can get it sorted,' she snapped, more out of panic than anything else.

Knowing that Chris would be listening, Julie took a pen out of her bag and scribbled something on a piece of paper. Standing up, she put her finger to her lips and held up the note. They all sat there stunned and trying hard not to blurt anything out. Scarlet looked at Julie and then the note again:

I think he's drugging her to keep her in control

Calmly, Julie spoke. 'Chris is right; it could be menopausal and maybe patches or something would help. Don't you think so, Diana?' Julie could already see Scarlet's cheeks flushing, and she had an angry glint in her eye. Looking at her, and praying that she wouldn't blurt anything out, Julie could see that she was fit to burst. Diana was her only hope.

Taking her lead, as the voice of reason, Diana nodded. 'Are there any other symptoms, Katie?' she asked, knowing it would sound as though she was asking out of concern, and not probing.

Reading the note, Katie sat down and put her head in her hands. She wanted to cry and felt the tears brim on her lashes. Chris had spread the word that she was fragile and a bit crazy at times. Of course, it all made sense now. Of course he wouldn't let her see a doctor. A doctor would say that she was sane and investigate these non-existent headaches. He was slowly trying to kill her and then he would inherit everything she owned. She didn't want to believe it. She knew her marriage was a sham, but would Chris really go to these levels to get rid of her? Yes, he would, she thought to herself.

Whenever they had argued, she had a headache afterwards. Whenever she wanted to go out alone, she had a headache and didn't go. And whenever Chris possibly went to see his mistress, she would sleep through those headaches, none the wiser. Christ, what a fool she had been, she inwardly cursed herself.

'No more symptoms, no,' she croaked eventually, 'and Chris is always there and makes sure I have a lie down.' Standing up, she hugged Scarlet tightly and let her silent tears fall.

Julie scrunched up the note and put it in her bag. 'Let's go and have a nap before dinner and freshen up.' Leading the way, she opened the door and, seeing that the coast was clear, beckoned to the others to follow her upstairs.

Once in her bedroom, Katie collapsed on the bed. 'Why didn't I see it? What is wrong with me?'

Going to her aid as she cried, Diana sat beside her on the bed. 'In my job, Katie, I've seen this a million times. It's manipulation and control – grooming, if you like. You can't always see what's under your nose.'

'He's going to get one hell of a headache when I get hold of him. I'm going to confront that bastard now!' Scarlet shouted and headed for the door, but Julie barred her way.

Staring her squarely in the face and seeing the burning rage in Scarlet's eyes, Julie shook her head. 'On what evidence, Scarlet? On some old mad woman's say so? No. I have seen this kind of thing before when I was a young woman. Keeping you drugged so you keep in line. It was many years before I met Ralph, and these people used drugs in the food, water, anything to keep their slave workers in line. In the end it made my younger sister an addict, eventually killing her. Keep a lid on it, Scarlet. Don't blow our cover. Vengeance is best served cold.'

* * *

During dinner, Chris sat at his usual head of the table, lording it over them. Eventually he asked the question he had been dying to ask all day. 'By the way, how is Adam?'

Frowning, Scarlet looked up from her plate. 'He's okay, thanks for asking.' Something deep inside her told her something was wrong. Chris never asked about Adam, so why now?

'When will he be visiting Italy? He hasn't been for a while, has he? Doesn't he miss the old place?'

'He's a young man and I believe there is a new lady love on the scene,' Scarlet replied.

Picking up his glass of wine, Chris guzzled it back, looking at each of them in turn. 'Strange, because I had a visitor today who could have sworn he'd seen Adam, here in Italy. How about that?' Chris's probing unnerved them all, and their eyes darted around the table at each other, looking for answers.

'Well, as far as I'm aware, he's back in England, or he better be while I'm enjoying myself here. The club won't run itself, will it?'

'If you say so, Scarlet, but it is one hell of a coincidence, don't you think? Tell me, is Adam in Italy?' Chris demanded. The twisted look on his face chilled Scarlet.

'Not as far as I'm aware, Chris. Have you called him? Have you called the club?' she bluffed.

'You're right.' Chris grinned and took out his mobile. 'I won't call his mobile though, because mobiles ring all over the world and he could be anywhere, including Italy.' His menacing voice made the hairs on Scarlet's neck rise. 'I will call the landline of the club. Then we will know where he is, won't we?'

The room went silent as Chris dialled the number. Scarlet's heart was in her mouth. 'To whom am I speaking?' Chris snapped, putting the phone on loudspeaker for all to hear.

'Hello, this is Poppy Nightingale, Mr Lambrianu's personal assistant. How can I help you?' Hearing Poppy's voice, Scarlet looked down at the table. Julie stayed poker faced.

'I am Adam's brother-in-law, married to his sister, Katie, and I wish to speak to him. Is Mr Lambrianu there, Miss Nightingale?' Chris asked politely.

'Not at the moment, sir, but I could get him to call you back. He's entertaining the commissioner of the police as it's his birthday. Scarlet is in Italy at the moment though, isn't she? Is there a problem, as I was made to understand that Scarlet was visiting your wife. Has she arrived safely?' Poppy asked matter-of-factly.

Chris almost blushed and took a drink of his wine. 'There is no problem, I just wished to speak with Adam.' Chris ended the call, without a goodbye.

Scarlet breathed a sigh of relief. Poppy had lied her head off, and she was grateful for that. Obviously Poppy had sensed something was wrong, considering that Scarlet was supposed to be with Katie.

'She shouldn't have said that about the commissioner, but she's new. She shouldn't disclose who is drinking at the club. I must have a word with her.' Scarlet tutted, feeling more at ease now.

Ignoring her comments, Chris carried on. 'On another note, I popped into the factory today. It seems Julie here is now the new appointed supervisor giving my workers extra time off.' Turning to Julie, he looked her squarely in the eyes, a smarmy grin crossing his face. 'Don't worry, Julie, I will deduct the long lunch break from their wages, because of you.'

'If you're that hard up, Chris, I will pay whatever loss you think you've had. It's not their fault, it's mine. Just let me know what the damage is, and I will pay it. What's the big deal?'

'Indeed you will, Julie, but they will still pay for their bone-idleness. I won't have it. And I won't have you undermining me in my own company.'

Julie's ire rose, and her eyes widened. 'Your company? I wasn't aware it was your name on the wine label. It's a Lambrianu vineyard, with Lambrianu wine. Where does your name pop up in all of that?' she snapped. She couldn't hold back any longer. All this walking on eggshells around a controlling manipulative fool angered her.

'It's my wife's dowry to myself,' he exclaimed. 'It was given to

Katie, but used as a dowry for our marriage. I have left the name because it is a known trademark. Why would I change it?'

'Dowry?' Scarlet laughed. 'What the hell is that? No dowry was given to you by our dad. He never paid you to marry Katie, that's for sure. Come on, Chris, what's eating you up? The fact that Katie's having a good time? We will be out of your hair soon enough and then you can carry on being a pompous prat.'

Chris slapped the table with his hand, spilling his red wine, and laughed. 'Well, it didn't take you long to drop the mask and show your true colours, did it? Have some manners in my home or get out of my house, you surly bitch,' he snarled.

Scarlet threw her serviette on the table. 'Manners? If we're talking about manners, let me tell you something; you will get good manners when you treat people with some of your own. Respect earns respect and, believe me, no one around here has any for you. Eating with your mouth wide open and dribbling down your fat, obese chin. Yeah, I will go, that's not a problem. But look at yourself, Chris. You're a walking heart attack, you fat bastard! You would have to drug any woman to sleep with you,' she snapped. She couldn't stop herself from mentioning 'drug'; it had played on her mind all afternoon.

'Scarlet!' Julie butted in. 'There's no need for insults. Sit down.' Calmly, Julie turned towards Chris. 'All families have their arguments. Just another day or so and we will be out of your hair. But if you want us to leave now, then of course we will.'

'Why are you being so nice, you witch! What is it you want?' Chris asked, while wiping red wine that had dribbled from his mouth to his shirt. 'I may be a fat bastard, but I am Don here and people do as I say, and that means you lot!' he shouted, while pointing at each of them in turn. 'I am sick of your self-righteous ways. Stay, go, I don't care. Just keep out of my way and your noise to a minimum. Katie, you've had your fun and let your family insult me. Tomorrow, you will stay home and be a mother to your children and a wife to me. I have to go out tonight, but tomorrow, I expect you to fulfil your wifely duties and be in my bedroom at 10 p.m. Enjoy the rest of your dinner, ladies.'

'Why, can't your girlfriend make tomorrow night, Chris?' Katie shouted.

Shocked by her outburst, Chris looked up at his wife. 'My, has the mouse found a tongue? A couple of days with the Witches of Eastwick and you feel brave again. I can crush you, Katie, and don't forget it. Tomorrow night.' With that, they all watched him as he slammed the door behind him.

Julie sipped her drink and looked around the table. This outburst had brought things to a head, and now was the time to act, she thought to herself. 'Tomorrow,' she whispered and raised her glass in a toast.

Each in turn looked at her and raised their glasses. 'Tomorrow.'

The food had turned cold, and they had all lost their appetites. 'Anyone fancy a late-night walk in the gardens before bed? Let's clear our heads, eh?' Julie winked. It was dark, but the house was surrounded by floodlights which lit up the grounds. Lighting a cigarette, Julie strolled well away from the house and leaned against a tree. Taking out her mobile, she called Lewis. 'Tomorrow, Lewis. It has to be tomorrow. Things have taken a nasty turn.' As an afterthought, she thought about what Chris had said. 'Have you heard from Adam? Because Chris knows he's in Italy,' she whispered.

'Adam's here. Apparently they had a blowout on the road and had to stop and change the tyre... Wait.' There was a silence and as Julie waited, she heard Adam answer the phone. 'I've fucked up, haven't I, Julie? Sorry, I – we – just needed to get off the yacht. The roads were empty, but... oh, Christ, one car did blow his horn, but didn't stop. We were wearing crew uniforms. How the hell did anyone recognise me?'

'Don't beat yourself up about it, Adam. Lewis knows where to meet, but it has to be tomorrow. Chris is turning nasty and now he knows you're here. Whatever we're going to do, we need to do it now.' Julie ended the call before Adam could apologise any more. The only thing to do now was continue with their plan as soon as possible. It didn't matter what they had in store for Chris, but what he had in store for them, Julie mused. Taking a long drag on her cigarette, she looked up at Diana. She could barely see her face under the trees. 'You're a copper, Di. Why is Chris suddenly so unbothered about whether we stay here or not? He was going to throw Scarlet out but changed his mind... Why?'

'If you stay, he's got you under his watch. If you live at the vineyard, he can keep an eye, but not as close as he would like. What is it they say, Mum? Keep your enemies close.' Seeing Julie's cigarette, Di smiled in the darkness. 'Have you got a spare one of those?'

'I thought you had given up?' Julie chuckled and handed her packet over.

'What doesn't kill you makes you stronger, eh, Mum? But I definitely need one of those.'

'You two okay?' Scarlet asked. Seeing them nod, she pursed her lips together. 'Is it true? Have his spies seen Adam?'

Julie exhaled smoke into the air. 'Yes, he went on a jolly and his car broke down and he was spotted by someone. Even Adam doesn't know who, though.' Throwing her hands up in the air, Julie shrugged. 'What does it matter? All this has done is speed up our plans. Lewis knows what to do and maybe it's just as well he's with Lewis; he'd have had to make his way here sooner or later anyway. Act as normal tomorrow at breakfast. Chris is seeing his mistress tonight by all accounts so that should put him in a better frame of mind. I'm going to bed; it's been a long day.'

Julie walked back towards the house. 'Has Adam pissed her off, Di? I'm sorry,' Scarlet apologised.

'I don't think so. I think it's just everything. She wants to put everyone's lives to rights, like some kind of fairy godmother, but most of all she wants to avenge Don Carlos. He's been robbed of everything, and he and Dad were like brothers. Adam has been robbed; Katie has been robbed of her freedom, and let's not forget Chris sent people to England to murder Adam. And they would have if he didn't know how to fight and Knuckles hadn't jumped in to save him. Put all of that in a melting pot, and that's what's eating Mum up.'

Slipping an arm around Katie and Diana's waists, Scarlet yawned. 'I think we should all get some sleep. Tomorrow is going to be a big day for all of us.'

18

THE DARKEST HOURS

Julie couldn't sleep. The past, present and future had flown through her mind while tossing and turning and she'd finally given up trying at dawn. Getting out of bed, she showered and dressed then made her way to the west wing. The house was quiet, but there were one or two of Chris's men sitting on chairs, resting their heads while dozing off. Looking at them, she thought about Chris and how angry he would be if he knew they were sleeping on the job.

As she got closer, one of the men opened his eyes and muttered, 'Miss Julie...'

Putting her finger to her lips, she smiled. 'Go back to sleep; everything is okay,' she whispered. Still drowsy, he nodded and closed his eyes again while Julie crept past him.

Opening the bedroom door she had once shared with Ralph, she looked around. Suddenly the room wasn't dusty or full of cobwebs any more; it was as it had once been. The bedside lamps were on, and she could hear laughter. Her own and Ralph's, who had been so easy to wind up. Her memories seemed so full of life, she felt a tear run down her face. She had to admit it to herself;

she was lonely. No matter how many people she surrounded herself with, they weren't Ralph. Sitting down on the dust-encrusted eiderdown, she could almost smell Ralph's aftershave and recalled how they had made love on this bed, and how afterwards they had lain in each other's arms whispering in the darkness. How she missed him.

'Come on, Julie, get a bloody grip! You have stuff to do,' she whispered to herself in the darkness. Walking out onto the landing and looking up at the pine cladding that had been carefully replaced by Scarlet and Diana, she pulled at a panel gently. After removing four, she slid sideways into the bathroom behind and looked down at the square hole in the floor. She had prepared for this with Lewis. For all her bravado, Julie knew she wasn't as young as she used to be, but kneeling down, she pulled with all of her might to try and open the trap door in the floor. It was as heavy as it was large, like some kind of drawbridge in this icy-cold bathroom, and she saw her own breath in the darkness. Puffing a little, she managed to raise the door, and the stench from below wafted under her nostrils, making her gag a little. Looking down into the darkness, she could see nothing of the tunnel, only the dirt and years of neglect forming rust and mould on the side openings. Opening the door wider still, Julie stood up, satisfied. This end of the house was now prepared.

Methodically, she replaced the pine cladding as best as she could, leaving it loose and easy to remove again, this time from the other side. Standing back, she made a face; it wasn't right, she knew that. It looked a little odd after being pulled away a few times and had even cracked at the sides. But no one else would be coming up here to see it, she thought to herself. After all, it was known as the derelict part of the house. Creeping back down the winding staircase, she crossed the landing back to her own room.

Smelling herself and seeing the state of her clothing, she showered and had a nap before going down to breakfast.

* * *

Waking up without hearing the lapping of water against the yacht, and feeling the constant swaying, felt like a holiday to Adam. Looking at the bedside clock, he saw it was 8 a.m. It was the best night's sleep he'd had in days. Reaching for his mobile to check his messages, he recognised Poppy's number, but was shocked and confused to read the text she'd sent. Blinking hard, he read it again.

> You creep, how dare you stand me up! Fuck you.

For a moment, still bleary eyed, Adam couldn't understand why he'd get this text from her. Angrily, he dialled the number. 'Just what the hell is that text all about, Poppy? Are you sure it was meant for me?'

'I take it you're alone and no one else has seen my message on your mobile?'

'No, why would they? What the hell are you on about?'

'Well,' she began slowly, 'I had a call from your Chris in Italy. He seemed angry and wanted to speak with you. I told him you were busy at the club. Surely if he wanted to speak with you, he would have just rung your mobile? But he called the office landline. Did I do right, Adam?'

Sitting upright in bed, Adam thought about her words. 'Yes, you did right, Poppy. If he calls again just fob him off. What else did he want to know?'

'I can't be sure, but it was as though he was checking you were here. That's why I sent that awful text. Sorry. I wanted to tip you off, but didn't want anyone to know that's what I was doing...'

A smile crossed Adam's face. 'Well, thank you for intervening and covering with Chris, and before you ask, I'm not going to fill in the blank spots.'

'I didn't expect you to, Adam. I'm just doing my job. I'm your PA and I'm supposed to have your back, aren't I? Talking of that, there is something else you should know about...'

Adam could hear the nervousness in her voice. He was pleased to hear from her, and hadn't realised just how much he had missed her. 'Go on, Poppy, I'm listening.' He laughed.

'The holiday cottage you booked for yourself and Knuckles... The owner called and wondered why you hadn't picked up the keys.'

Stunned by her words, Adam felt the pit of his stomach somersault. Christ, he hadn't thought about that. He inwardly cursed himself. He had thought that just paying the money would be enough to keep the owner off his back. What did they care if he turned up or not? He'd paid them and it was booked for the duration. 'What of it?'

'Well... I hope you don't mind, but I've sent Bruce there along with Kim. I had to confide this information with him because I needed his help,' she panicked. 'I thought if he went it would satisfy the owners... Oh God, Adam, I didn't know what to do, or if you were alive, but I had to do something. I'm sorry.'

'Whoa, slow down, Poppy. I'm not angry – you thought ahead of me and did the right thing. You must think this whole mystery is a bit strange and I'm sorry you've had to put up with the back-lash. But I am pleased you are on my side. I trust Bruce with my life and I'm sure he is enjoying his time away with Kim. And I am alive and well and that is all you need to know for now, isn't it? I'm sorry you've been dragged into this.' Adam's heart sank when he realised everything she'd had to put up with in his absence. More to the point, it concerned him just how much she knew... or thought she knew. 'On a serious note, Poppy, you do realise that you're bound by data protection to not discuss any of my business with anyone else, don't you?' He felt bad about reminding her about it, but also felt he needed to. He could sense the disappointment down the line; she felt she had done well, and he had just poured cold water on her achievements. She had done her best, and he sounded like he didn't trust her. He could have kicked himself. After all, she had saved him twice.

'Yes, of course I know that,' she snapped. 'I signed the confidentiality contract with Scarlet. I'm just filling you in on the details. That's my job, isn't it?'

'No. Poppy, that's not just a job, it's friendship. Friends have your back. I'm an ungrateful paranoid prat and I don't deserve you. My bad. I'm just a bit stressed.'

'Well, I'm just trying to keep the home fires burning.' Her voice had softened to a whisper.

'You're doing a great job. How did I ever manage without you? I miss your bossing,' Adam blurted out. He hadn't meant to say that, but he had missed her and hearing her voice gave him a warm feeling inside.

'I miss you too, Adam.' The awkward silence on the other end of the phone made Poppy feel she should wind up the call. 'Well, I'd better get on, I have a very demanding boss.' She chuckled, trying to make light of it.

'I hope he appreciates you, because I know I do, Poppy.' Adam's warm, soothing tones down the phone made Poppy's heart skip a beat.

'Have a good day.' Adam wasn't sure how to prolong the call, because he wanted to continue talking to her, but couldn't think of anything else to say. Hearing her say goodbye and ending the call, he stared blankly at his mobile. He had wanted to say much more, but was worried he might have sounded like an idiot. Lying back on his pillow, he put his arm under the back of his head and thought about Poppy. He recalled their passionate embrace, and how she filled his thoughts lately. He had never felt that way before about a woman. They had come and gone; some he had been sorry to see the back of, others he couldn't get rid of soon enough. But Poppy was different. Not only was she beautiful, she was also intelligent, sincere and had his best interests at heart. And when she kissed him, he felt his whole body tremble.

'Come on, sleepy head.' His bedroom door was flung open and Lewis walked in with a cup of coffee. 'We're in Italy and the sun is shining. The pool is warm, so get up, have a swim, relax those tense muscles. Did you know that Knuckles doesn't swim?' Lewis announced in a surprised voice.

'Well, he wouldn't with one arm, would he? Unless he wants to go around in circles. His arm is prosthetic, Lewis.' Adam laughed. 'Anyway, I've gathered over the last few days that Knuckles is not a water baby at all.' Adam recalled Knuckles's seasickness and shuddered. 'And he's so big, he'd probably sink.'

Standing there with his hand on his hips, Lewis laughed. 'How tall is he, seven foot? Christ, he makes King Kong look tiny! Anyway, get out of bed, get some sun and relax. Danny is making a good breakfast for you.'

'Okay, I get the message. Let me drink this and I will be up and about in a few minutes.'

After his swim, Adam walked back inside and picked up an orange juice, gulping it down. Frowning, he watched as Lewis closed the French windows. Five other member of Julie's household were sat around the breakfast table along with Knuckles. 'What's going on?'

'Time to talk, Adam. Get some breakfast while we do.' Lewis

pointed to the table full of fruit, crusty bread, cereal and coffee, and sat down. 'Right, we all know why we are here, but this is the plan.' Adam was slightly shocked hearing Lewis's serious voice. It wasn't camp or joking like normal; instead, he was deadly serious.

'There is an old water system on Don Chris's side of town. Access to the tunnels that run underneath the town are via an old iron drain, which is thick and heavy. It's also very rusty. God knows when the last time anyone went down there. From what I've heard from Julie, Carlos created a tunnel from this old water mains hole to his house. I've no idea what you're facing. All I know is that Julie's friend Denny is Don Chris's butler. Apparently he went down the tunnel a year ago and said that everything Don Carlos put in place is still there.'

Frowning, Adam thought it was odd that Denny had been down there a year ago. 'Why did he go down there, Lewis? Do we know?'

Tapping his fingers on the table, Lewis shrugged. 'Julie and Denny have both been planning Chris's demise for a while. As far as we know, this manhole hasn't been used by anyone else for a long time. Presumably it would have cost too much money to take away the old pipes, so they just disconnected them and laid new ones.' Lewis gulped back a large glass of orange juice, while everyone waited patiently for him to carry on. 'All Denny said was that the tunnel was waterlogged in places. So given that, Julie has bought everyone diving suits, which is what I have in the cases. Since being here I've also acquired one small tank of oxygen with masks. It's all I could get my hands on without causing suspicion,' Lewis apologised.

Twirling his finger around the table at his friends, he continued. 'We will take you both and the bags to the manhole, help you inside, and then close it behind you.' He sighed. 'We'll make sure that it looks undisturbed should it ever be investigated. Then it's up to you guys to walk the full length of the tunnel, which is long, and pop up at the other end. It all sounds a bit cloak and dagger, I know. But the main thing is, you're not seen going into the house. Afterwards, Scarlet and Diana will go "shopping" so they will be away from the house. Katie is to stay at the house with the kids, in full view of the bodyguards, and eventually sound the alarm.'

Turning towards Adam, Lewis looked directly at him. 'You cannot be seen in Italy, Adam. You would become the prime suspect for Chris's death and he would have the last laugh. You wouldn't be the next Don and all of this would be for nothing.'

'Wait a minute, Lewis, you've mentioned everyone apart from Julie. Where is she in all of this?' Adam asked.

'Fair point. I don't think she has the strength as a woman of her years to make it through the tunnel with all of that climbing. She must be planning to stay at the house with Katie, but she hasn't told me that. I'm sorry, Adam, this is all a bit vague, but it's all I have.' Lewis seemed exhausted by his explanation.

Stunned, Adam looked at Knuckles. 'Are you okay with this?' A chill ran down Adam's spine as he thought about what they were going to find in that black tunnel. Panic rose within him, and for the first time since all of this, Adam felt truly afraid.

Listening intently, Knuckles nodded. 'Need to rub my wetsuit with oil or lard so I can squeeze through properly. Went through a tunnel once during a bank robbery. Lard helps you slide through better.' Knuckles seemed relaxed about it all, which humbled Adam.

Lewis continued talking. 'You've also got belts for your suits, but each one is different because there is only so much you can carry. There's a bottle of water, a knife, a crowbar, small of course, and a torch. I've also got headbands with LED lights, which will help you see in the dark. One mobile, but I don't know about getting a signal in that tunnel that far down. You've got two hours and then we will come down and find you. You have to be swift and brave to do this as you're going to be on the clock. Any questions?'

Adam felt his throat go dry. He didn't have any spit, but tried to find his voice. 'Julie,' he croaked. 'Where is she?'

'All she has told me, Adam, is that she will be in the house when you arrive and that everything will be ready for you at the other end. I believe the tunnel emerges into an old bathroom in Don Chris's house, but that's not a lot of help, is it?' Throwing his hands into the air, Lewis sat back, exhausted.

'It's a bit hit and miss, Lewis, even you have to admit.' Adam sighed as he tried to process the plan.

Lewis stood up. 'We leave at noon. Until then, don't eat too much, keep hydrated, and get some rest if you can.'

Lewis left Adam alone with Knuckles, and Adam swallowed hard. 'It's one hell of a risk, Knuckles. I don't know about you, but I'm breaking out in a sweat just thinking about it.'

Knuckles nodded. 'Lewis be there after two hours to drag us out if needed. Have some juice.'

Dumbfounded, Adam stared blankly at Knuckles, who didn't seem to be shaken by this plan one bit, unlike himself. It was the not knowing that bothered Adam. Shaking himself, Adam thought he would feel better once they were doing it, as opposed to thinking about it... which currently felt like torture.

* * *

Chris sat at his usual place during breakfast. Scarlet decided to ignore him and talk to the others, but his face looked like thunder. They all watched as he gorged himself on another cooked breakfast, firing out orders to Katie and the staff. 'You're spending time with your children today, Katie. Remember?'

'You don't have to force me to spend time with my kids, Chris. I love them, I gave birth to them, I want to spend time with them. I presume you've got them marching around the courtyard for their morning exercise.'

'Children need exercise, Katie. If I left it up to you, you would let them sit on the sofa all day playing video games.'

'Maybe you should take your own advice,' Julie butted in. 'When was the last time you exercised apart from lifting your fork to your mouth?'

'Shut the fuck up, Julie, I'm talking to my wife. Do not disrespect me in my own home.'

'How can I disrespect you, Chris, when I didn't respect you in the first place?' Julie snapped.

'How dare you speak to me like that!' he screamed. 'I don't want you in my house any longer. Go home, and I hope your plane crashes!'

Calmly, Julie sat and poured herself more coffee. 'I take it your evening didn't go so well. What? Didn't you get your weekly blow job, Chris?' Julie cackled.

Horrified, Scarlet looked at her. She couldn't understand why Julie was causing an argument when she had been the one to tell everyone else to keep a lid on it.

'Get out, you slut!' he yelled, sweeping his arm across the table, sending all the crockery and food flying to the floor. Katie and the others stood up to avoid being hit by a flying coffee pot or anything else on the table. The din brought Chris's men running through the doors. Red faced and angry, Chris held his hand up to stop them. 'It's okay,' he snapped, 'but make sure this bitch leaves the premises today,' he fired, pointing at Julie.

Standing up, Julie looked around at the smashed plates and

food on the floor. 'Seems like breakfast is over. I will go and pack,' she purred, kicking a cup out of the way as she walked towards Chris. 'And you, you jumped-up arsehole, can fuck off yourself. You don't frighten me, Chris. You're so afraid of your own ghosts, you're pathetic.' Gliding to the door, she opened it and left. Scarlet, Katie and Diana stood there shocked. Breaking the silence, Diana spoke up. 'I'll go and help Mum pack.'

'I'll come too. I need to change,' Scarlet added, and quickly walked beside her to leave. Giving a backward glance, Scarlet looked at Katie and nodded her head, indicating for her to follow them, too.

Chris glared at Katie. 'Well, aren't you going to follow them like the sheep they all are, dearest?'

'There has been no need for all of this, Chris. You've hated the idea of them coming from the beginning. They could have stayed at the vineyard if you were so opposed to it.'

'Just see that they all leave, and get the servants to sort this bloody mess out; I have calls to make.'

Waiting until he had left, Katie quickly ran out of the room and up the stairs to Julie's room.

'Are you okay, Julie? I'm so sorry.'

'Why? I wanted him to throw me out. All part of my plan.' She grinned. 'Now, you two.' She pointed at Scarlet and Diana. 'You need to go and have that dress fitting and take a walk around the shops. Katie is going to play house, and I've been evicted.' She cackled. 'Diana, I need a word alone with you before I leave.'

'Where are you going to, Mum? Are we aborting everything and going home?'

Frowning, Julie pouted. 'Don't be so ridiculous. Apart from a mansion house in the middle of a vineyard with all of that lovely wine, there are a million hotels and my own villa to go to. Does he really think he will chase me out of Italy? Nope!'

Katie opened the en-suite door and beckoned them all into the bathroom while running the taps. 'Late last night when Chris had gone out, I went through his study to look for the will. I couldn't find anything, but he has a safe in there. I don't know the combination; I tried the kids' birthdays and his own, but nothing happened. I searched everywhere and found a lot of paperwork about investments I didn't know about. I'm an accountant and even I couldn't work some of that stuff out. He seems to be paying a lot of money into accounts I've never heard of. Huge sums.'

Raising one eyebrow, Julie lit a cigarette. 'People only pay out huge sums of money if they are being blackmailed. He's a trained accountant too and so it can't be money laundering. He knows how to get around that without leaving a paper trail. No wonder he's cutting corners and wages. Have you heard of these companies before? What do they sell or provide? Could he be supplying drugs? Even so, that would be cash, and he wouldn't be so stupid as to leave a paper trail...'

Suddenly, the penny dropped for Julie. 'Oh my God, Katie, could they be offshore accounts? He's stashing money away. Maybe he wants to run off with his mistress and leave you penniless. You can't sell the vineyard without Scarlet and Adam's signatures, but in the event of your death...' She trailed off. 'That really must annoy him, knowing he can't take it off you without these two saying so. No wonder he wants you all dead. I bet he's creaming half the profits away...'

'If that's the price of my freedom, he can have it, but I want my kids,' Katie muttered.

'Don't be silly, Katie. That was a good clause in your father's will which means the vineyard will always stay in Lambrianu hands. I suppose he thought if you were ever divorced, Chris wouldn't be able to claim half. That was your father's roots and your families' roots. Never give it away!' Julie snapped. Humbled,

Katie realised what she had said. Of course her father would never part with his roots, especially after it had taken him years to find his roots in the first place.

Julie gave a wry grin. 'I stashed some money offshore in Jersey and Monte Carlo when I sold the haulage business. I got out just in time and sold it cheaper than it was worth, but better than nothing.'

Surprised, Diana looked at her. 'You sold the haulage business? You never said.'

'Why wouldn't I? Keeping it would affect your inheritance more than me selling it. Don't worry, Di, you're not broke.' Julie smiled and kissed her cheek.

Diana cocked her head to one side and made a face. 'It would be nice to be kept in the loop, and for your information, I wasn't wondering about the money. Bloody cheek.'

'Good God, Diana.' Scarlet laughed. 'You're Gold by name and affluence. Good business though, Julie. Selling just in time. If I didn't know better, I'd swear you'd had a tipoff.'

Fluttering her long, black false eyelashes, Julie looked horrified. 'Are you accusing a nice old lady like me of corruption, Scarlet?' She winked. 'Perish the thought. Anyway, off you go. I want a word with Diana.'

'You okay, Mum? What's the matter?'

Julie walked towards Diana, looking her up and down. 'Nice makeover you had, Diana. You could be my doppelganger from the back. Granted, you're a bit taller, but no one really looks at a lady's heels. Nevertheless, you look just like me from behind.' Quickly packing her case, she gave it to Diana. 'My luggage sticks out like a sore thumb and would be recognised anywhere. Every time I've gone in the garden, which has been quite a lot, I've worn this wide-brimmed white hat and sunglasses. You are going to leave the house as me, Diana, and Denny will drive you. Go and put a change of clothing of your own in the case and change in a public toilet or something. Then meet Scarlet at the shops in town.'

Diana stood rooted to the spot, shocked. 'My God, you planned all of this. That's why you had the blonde put in my hair and had it bobbed like yours. But won't they expect me to leave with Scarlet? We're using their chauffeur, Mum.'

'Mmm, not necessarily. He won't care what you two get up to as long as he's thinks I've gone. Now go and fill Scarlet in and get Katie to organise a ride. The main thing is, Chris will want to know I've been escorted off the premises. That's all he cares about.'

'You're staying here?' Diana asked. Panic rose inside of her. 'Where? What if he checks? Surely one of the maids will come to clean the room or something.'

'Bloody hell, Diana, yes, I'm staying here.' Impulsively, Julie put her arms around her daughter. 'Later, Diana. Lewis will call you. Not Scarlet; you. Just follow my instructions and all will be revealed.'

Unsure of what to do, Diana was in two minds about leaving Julie alone hiding in the house. It seemed foolish to her, but even she wasn't brave enough to challenge her mother's plans. 'Okay, but stay safe and don't do anything stupid.'

Nodding, Julie pushed her hat into Diana's hands and opened the door. 'Don't forget the sunglasses, and don't look anyone in the face.'

'I have worked undercover before, Mum. Okay, but that's a bloody big hat though. I won't be able to see where I'm treading. I'm surprised you got it through customs.' She smiled.

Standing with her back against the closed door for a moment, Julie let out an enormous sigh. Her brain seemed to be firing in all directions. Hopefully, Lewis would have filled in Adam and

Knuckles and then he'd meet up with Diana and Scarlet later. Mentally, she wished them luck. She knew more about Chris than Katie did. He had spread the word that Katie had mental health problems, indicating she had been suicidal, and he didn't like to leave her alone with the children for too long. If he did get rid of Katie and run off with his mistress, he would get custody of the children, whether he wanted them or not. It was just another piece of power he held over her. If there was the slightest hint that she had hatched a plan to kill Chris, she would also lose the children, because it would confirm she was crazy.

Poor Katie must never find out, Julie thought to herself. She'd suffered enough and that would break her heart even more. Then Julie waited out of sight in the bedroom until she heard Scarlet and Diana, dressed as herself, leave the house.

19

THE PLAN UNFOLDS

Sitting in his study, still seething at Julie's outburst, Chris suddenly heard the front door slam. Jumping out of his seat and almost tipping his chair over, he ran out into the main hallway. Seeing one of his henchmen stood in the hallway, Chris pushed him in the chest. 'Where is Katie? Has my wife left this house?' he demanded.

Startled and staring, with his rifle hanging around his neck, the henchman looked up at Chris. 'No, *signor*,' he stammered and pointed.

Just then, Katie walked out of her parlour. 'Are you looking for me, Chris?' she asked without emotion.

Shocked at hearing her voice, Chris swiftly turned and looked at her. 'Good, you're here. I heard the door slam and wondered if you had sneaked out with them,' he barked. 'Don't think I don't know what you're up to, you scheming bitch!'

Katie stared at him with a confused expression on her face. 'What am I up to, Chris?'

'You think you're going to leave me? You! Leave me? That's a fucking joke.'

'If it is such a joke, why are you bothered if I stay or go? You clearly don't love me any more, so why would you care either way?'

'Because no one leaves me, Katie. I do the leaving. Do you really think I'm prepared to have everyone around here laughing at me because you've left me, after everything I've done for you?'

Her mouth felt dry. Chris screaming at her like this always unnerved her. 'What have you done for me, Chris? What have you ever done?' For once, Katie felt angry. The truth was out with her family now, and somehow, she didn't care what happened to her marriage any more. Without seeing it coming, Katie fell backwards and felt a burning sensation on her face where Chris had slapped her.

'I expect respect off my wife!' he shouted.

On her knees trying to stand, Katie brushed her hair away from her face. Slowly, she found her voice again. 'Why do you need to justify yourself all of the time? What is this constant need for respect? Surely that comes with this job. You sound almost insecure.' She smiled as she stood up. For the first time in a long time, Katie felt strong again.

'I don't need to justify myself to anyone, especially you. Now, where have the others gone?'

'Scarlet and Diana have gone wedding shopping. And Julie has left the house at your request.'

As he stared at her for a moment, Katie felt a chill go down her spine as she waited for what his next move might be. This wasn't the first time he had lashed out at her out of frustration and anger.

Chris turned to his bodyguard, who had stood in silence watching Chris's outburst and had winced when he saw Chris lash out at Katie. 'Where the fuck has Julie Gold gone? You know, the older of the bunch, red lipstick, loud laugh. Do you know where she is?' Chris shouted, his face flushed with anger.

'She has left, *signor* Don. The two ladies said they would take a taxi, because they didn't know how long they would be and didn't want the chauffeur having to hang around. The butler, Dennis, took the older one. He said he wanted to make sure she was off the premises.'

'Dennis the butler took Julie Gold for a ride? He's a fucking butler, not a chauffeur. Why would he drive her?' Confused, Chris stood there for a moment in silence. Casting a glance at Katie, he said nothing and simply walked away, back to his study.

Sitting at his desk, Chris put his head in his hands and rubbed his face. 'This wasn't how it was supposed to be,' he said to himself. He had admired Don Carlos and the way people held him in high esteem, but he had never had that same level of respect. It didn't matter what charities he gave to, or whose arse he licked, none of the other Dons felt he was good enough. He had expected marrying a Lambrianu would seal the deal. The family were highly thought of, and it was a good match. But no, it hadn't turned out as he had hoped. Sitting back in his chair deep in thought, he stared at the wall before him. Suddenly, his eyes caught sight of his bookcase. Everyone knew he had OCD and liked everything in alphabetical order. But it seemed that wasn't the case today. Slowly standing up, he stared at the books and, with his finger, went along them quoting the alphabet. One was out of place. Dickens, as in Charles Dickens, was before Lewis Caroll. Rooted to the spot, Chris couldn't believe he would make such a mistake. That could only mean someone had been in his study snooping around and, in their haste, they had put the books back in the wrong order. Searching again, he saw a couple more discrepancies. Inwardly seething, he wanted to shout and scream.

Instead, he looked up at the security monitor in the far corner of the ceiling.

Rewinding the recording, he stared blankly at the screen as he watched Katie rifling her way through his study. Pulling out books and trying different combinations on his safe. Christ, he thought to himself, she was like a frantic burglar, taking the backs off photo frames and looking inside. Beneath his anger, he was in turmoil wondering what she was looking for. Then suddenly, it dawned on him. Switching off the monitor, he left his study and made his way to the west wing of the house, remembering how eager Julie had been to go to that part of the house. Now, he wanted to see for himself what the attraction was.

* * *

Clapping his hands to get everyone's attention, Lewis shouted, 'Time to get ready, everyone!'

The adrenaline building up inside Adam hadn't let him rest and he was feeling twitchy and agitated. Walking into the air-conditioned lounge, he could see Lewis and his friends beavering away at their jobs. 'Where's Knuckles? Is he awake?' Adam asked.

'Yes, he's in the bathroom. Did you get any sleep?'

'Not really. Just dozing, I think. What about you?'

Lewis grinned and poured Adam a coffee. 'Drink this, it will wake you up.' Then Lewis threw a wetsuit at him. 'Then go and put this on under this tracksuit. Shoe wise, I can't really help you. You have to wear what you're comfortable in as you have a long walk ahead and they'll need decent soles in case it's slippery in that tunnel.'

Looking at the wetsuit, Adam nodded and went back into his room to change. Cursing himself, he hadn't really thought about footwear. He only had what he had come in, which was a pair of leather loafers. Picking them up, he looked at the soles; they seemed sturdy enough, he thought to himself. Besides, he mused, if the water was deeper than his ankle, he would get wet feet anyway.

Pulling on the black tracksuit over the wetsuit, he felt hot already, and the warm Italian sun wasn't helping. As he walked back into the lounge, he saw Knuckles had done likewise but then noticed his feet.

'You're wearing Dr Martens boots?' he queried. 'Why didn't you get me any?'

Shrugging, Knuckles answered, 'Dunno.' The air was sombre as everyone went about their tasks.

Lewis handed them both belts. 'These are yours with the equipment I told you about. Knuckles has the one with the knife. I figured he would be the first to use it.' Lewis grinned. 'Now we must go and pick up Diana and Scarlet – they will be coming with you in the tunnel so you won't be completely alone. It will take about an hour or so depending on traffic. Get in the back of the Land Rover and cover yourselves. We can't risk either of you being spotted.'

Both doing as they were told, Adam and Knuckles waited for Lewis and his friends to drive off. Sweat was pouring down their faces underneath the tarpaulin Lewis had covered them with and Adam's heart was pounding in his chest. Each time the Land Rover stopped, he looked at Knuckles thinking they had reached their destination.

'Traffic lights,' Knuckles muttered, as though reading his mind. Eventually after what seemed an endless journey, the car halted. Adam could hear voices but couldn't make out what was being said. A streak of sunlight shone through the Land Rover and then he heard Scarlet's voice. Poking the tarpaulin, Scarlet spoke as the Land Rover started. 'Are you two okay under there?'

'No, we're sweating to death. But, yeah, we're okay. How about you and Diana?' Peeking from underneath the tarpaulin, he saw that Scarlet had raised hers slightly to get a glimpse of him. Seeing Scarlet and Diana's weak smiles made him feel better. 'Are you wearing a wetsuit, Scarlet?' he whispered.

'Yes, we've got them on, and they are bloody tight!' she moaned. 'Lewis made us go into one of the shops and get changed in the toilets so the CCTV cameras of the shop saw us. That's our alibi I suppose.' She smiled. Slowly, she reached her hand out from under the tarpaulin, and finding Adam's, she squeezed it. He squeezed back, silently communicating with his big sister.

Once the Land Rover stopped again, Knuckles nodded to Adam in the darkness. Sweat poured down both their faces and Adam wanted to stretch his legs. The four of them had been couped up in the back of the Land Rover for what seemed hours, and he ached all over. Eventually, they felt the sheet being pulled off them and, blinking hard, they saw Lewis wearing a boilersuit along with the others. Frowning, he couldn't remember Lewis putting that on back at the villa.

'We're road workers, Adam. It would look suspicious us all sitting out here in our white shirts and black trousers. We'd look like a bunch of waiters who have lost our way.' He laughed, trying to lighten the mood. Lewis could feel the tension between them and wanted to ease it somewhat. 'We're going to drive around the front of the main road and park in a shaded bushy area. Now, come on; we're parked right beside the manhole. Put your belts on, all of you. Knuckles, I might need your strength for this bit.'

Nodding, Knuckles got out first. Seeing the manhole, he made a face. It was covered in rust, and weeds and bushes had grown around it, almost covering it.

'Is this the right one?' Knuckles muttered as he stared down at it.

'Yes.' Lewis looked at Knuckles. 'Do you see that yellow spray paint? Well, as they say. X marks the spot. Here, I've got a crowbar to help.' Taking the crowbar off him, Knuckles knelt down and with all of his strength, managed to prise the lid of the manhole cover upwards, giving him a chance to get his other hand underneath the edge. Lewis knelt down beside him and between them they heaved it up. 'Christ, this is rusted. I should have brought some WD40 or something.'

As Knuckles raised it up and slid it along the roadside, Adam looked up at Lewis. 'Don't put it back fully. Just lay half of it across and cover it with those weeds. People driving past won't pay attention to it. And it will give us daylight to follow when we need to get out.'

Nodding his head, Lewis agreed. 'Belts on, shoes tight, let's go.' Lewis handed a square bar of something to Knuckles and they all glanced at each other curiously. Knuckles thanked Lewis and, opening the wrapper from the thick bar, they saw that it was old-fashioned lard, which was already beginning to melt. Quickly, Knuckles rubbed it all over his wetsuit, making it slippery.

'I go first,' he muttered once there was nothing left of the lard. 'Adam, you go last behind the girls in case they need you.' Knuckles seemed in full charge of the situation, and sitting on the roadside, he swung his legs down into the gaping hole of the tunnel. Taking a deep inward breath, with his arms in the air, he slid down into the darkness. Scarlet peered over the edge. 'Are you okay, Knuckles? What can you see?'

Knuckles blinked hard in the darkness. 'You next, behind me. There's a ledge leading to a ladder.' Doing the same as he had, Scarlet followed suit and felt herself being caught by Knuckles. Looking up at the manhole, and the only glimmer of light they had, they both helped Diana down and then Adam. A cold feeling ran over all of them as they saw Lewis slowly closing the manhole cover above them. Following Knuckles's instructions, they saw the daylight disappear as Lewis covered it with moss and weeds. It felt like being buried alive.

They tried adjusting their eyes to the darkness. 'What's that noise? Is it coming from above?' Scarlet asked. Adam took out the torch from his belt and shone it into the darkness. All of them stared in horror as they climbed off the ledge on to the ladder to make their way down. Hundreds of glassy beady eyes stared at them as they moved, and Scarlet felt rooted to the spot. Her legs wouldn't move and her body was trembling. Panic rose within her and she wanted to get out. She *needed* to get out. A feeling of claustrophobia and fear engulfed her.

Knuckles got hold of her. 'Panic attack. Give me some of that oxygen and put the mask on her face. You can do this, Scarlet. Breathe gently. I'm here.'

Diana gripped Adam's hand and squeezed it tightly. He could feel her trembling with fear, too. 'It's a sewer, Diana; there were bound to be rats.'

'This many?' she croaked, barely able to speak her throat was so dry. 'The water is deeper than I thought it would be and its moving.' Diana looked at the dark muddy water and the slow motioning of the waves.

Adam felt sick but knew he had to hold his nerve. Inspecting the water closely, he could see the water wasn't moving, or waving. The movement covering the floor was rats. Hundreds of them. On the walls, in the water, everywhere. They were surrounded. For a moment, fear gripped him, and he too felt they should abandon this crazy plan. Nothing was worth this, he thought to himself. Knowing that Diana was still waiting for an answer, he had to tell her the truth. 'It's rats that are moving, Di, not waves. The place is full of them.'

Scarlet was now breathing more regularly with the oxygen mask on. She felt lightheaded and woozy as Knuckles held her. Switching off the oxygen, he waited for her response. 'We need to save it. All we have. You be okay now. Just stay with me.'

Adam butted in. 'Come on, sis, we need to leave this place. Nothing is worth this. It's a horror movie. Knuckles, help her back on the ledge,' Adam instructed.

Finding her voice, Diana shouted, 'NO!' There was a screeching noise and a scurrying of feet as her voice echoed around the darkness. Her anger had taken over her fear. 'Somewhere at the end of this shithole tunnel, my mother is waiting for us. And if this way is the only way to find her, then I'm staying, you spineless bastards. I don't like it any more than you. Go if you want but I'm carrying on with the plan. And if you are with me then decide fast, because we're on the clock, remember? The quicker we start walking, the sooner we're out of here,' she snapped.

Diana's outburst brought everyone to their senses. Standing without support, Scarlet nodded. 'You're right, Diana. Let's do this.'

Humbled by her strength, Adam took Di's hand, too. 'We are with you, Di. It's just a bit overwhelming, isn't it?'

Scarlet's eyes widened with horror as she saw the long-tailed rats wandering around and swimming in the water. 'Will they attack us, Knuckles?' she asked meekly.

'Only if they feel threatened, or are suffering from starvation.' He looked around at them all. 'But they all look fat enough to me,' he observed. 'Probably eating each other. Keep your voices low so not to disturb them. They will squeal or bite if you stand on one but we are going to... Can't see a thing in this water.'

Startled by his revelation, Scarlet burst into tears. 'Oh God, Knuckles. I've just pissed myself – sorry.'

'Hold on to my back and step where I step. Think of Julie. She is waiting. Focus.'

Taking a large breath, they slowly moved forward. They waded through water that was up to their calves, while rats jumped and scurried around them. Half bent over, to avoid hitting the ceiling, Diana swallowed hard, barely able to speak, and she turned to Adam. 'One is on my back, isn't it? Its tail has just come over my shoulder.'

'Yes. I'm not gonna brush it off; it might bite you.' He whispered, 'I've got one on mine too. I think they are high above us on the ceiling and dropping down. Keep walking, Di. Just put one foot in front of the other and walk.' Adam didn't feel as brave as he sounded; inwardly, he was finding it hard to hold it together. The walls were piled high with rats laid on top of rats. Some sleeping, some watching them; some looked ready to pounce. Trying to control his breathing, he knew he had to be calm and not let them sense fear, but it was bloody hard, he thought to himself.

Scarlet let out a yelp of pain and screamed. Turning, Knuckles saw a rat on her. It had bitten her through her suit. Taking out the knife from the belt, he stabbed it, making it squeal loudly in the process. Picking it up, he threw it towards the others on the wall, making them all scuffle. They all squirmed as they saw the other rats run towards it to eat it. 'Am I going to die? I'm bleeding.'

'You've had tetanus. Just be careful of that blood. We get it cleaned later. I've been scratched a lot, but they can't sit on me with all of that lard on me. They keep slipping off.'

For a moment, Scarlet wanted to laugh at his comment, but

didn't. *I wish I'd put lard on myself*, she thought. She envied him the pleasure of not having them jump on to his back.

In slow crocodile fashion, they walked in silence, trying to ignore their surroundings. They were coming to terms with it and didn't cry out in horror when one jumped on their backs. As they trudged along and almost slipped on the waterlogged floor, their feet squelched their way through the dirty water. They all had the same mental goal. To reach the end of this hell-hole tunnel in one piece and alive.

20

THE END IS NIGH

Puffing and panting, they carried on for what felt like hours until Knuckles stopped, making them all grind to a halt. 'Light, Adam.' Shining the torch towards Knuckles, Adam could barely breathe in this foul smell. Bile had risen in his throat a few times and he had spat it out.

'Up there,' Knuckles instructed. Doing as he was told, Adam shone the light in the direction Knuckles pointed to and they all took a sigh of relief and almost burst out laughing when they saw a large neon yellow 'x' on the ceiling. That was their exit and it was only a few feet away from them. Impulsively, they all sped up, almost running and disturbing the rats, making them run just as fast in all directions. Diana slipped and fell face down into the water. Grabbing her, Adam lifted her up and shouted, 'Spit. Spit any of that water out that got into your mouth.' Coughing and spluttering, she did as she was told. Her hair was soaking while Adam slapped her back.

'I'd like to ask if I look like a drowned rat, Adam, but I don't want to tempt fate.' She half grinned.

'You know, Di, I've never noticed before, but you're more like

Julie than I thought. Only she, in these death-defying circumstances, would come up with something like that!' Whether it be
relief or just insanity, they both burst out laughing.

Knuckles stood aside and guided Scarlet's hand to the wall
ladder. 'Up you go on to the ledge.' Her foot slipped on the first
step; her trainers were covered in mud and slime, and she nearly
fell. Bracing herself, she tried again. They were all exhausted, but
this one last dose of adrenaline urged them on.

'The hatch is open. I can see light,' she whispered down as
they all climbed onto the ledge. Reaching up, while half standing
on the ladder, Knuckles pushed Scarlet from the ledge and
through the open hatch. Next it was Diana's turn. It was made
easier having Scarlet to pull her up, and then Adam. Knuckles
followed. Getting closer, he raised his arms and took an inward
breath. They all hung on to him and pulled with all of their might
and finally managed to get his large bulk through the hatch in the
bathroom.

Exhausted and dripping wet, they all stood in the bathroom
panting. Scarlet nearly collapsed into Knuckles's arms, and she
gathered them all together for a group hug. 'What now?'

Diana saw the missing cladding panels. 'Looks like Mum's
been busy. Through here to the staircase.'

Walking through the false wall, each of them in turn stood
rooted to the spot. Sat in a big armchair waiting for them was
Chris. Diana's heart sank when she saw his emotionless face
staring at them, and she wondered where her mother was. Her
mind was in turmoil as she stood, dripping water on the carpet.

Wearing his black suit, white shirt and black tie, Chris looked
at them all. 'Well, if it isn't the fantastic four. And in wetsuits!
What do you look like.' Reaching into his inside pocket, he took
out a carefully folded piece of paper and opened it. 'I take it this is
what Katie was looking for in my office?' he sneered.

Each of them cast furtive glances at each other. They had well and truly been caught in the act. All that suffering in the tunnel had been for nothing. Helplessly, they looked towards the letter as Chris unfolded it. Scarlet saw it first and looked at Diana. In Chris's hand was Don Carlos's original will. The very one that Julie had wanted to find.

Chris's rasping voice was full of victory. 'With something as precious as this, do you really think I would leave it out of my sight? No!' he bellowed. 'Do you lot take me for a bloody fool? Katie rummaged through all of my things to find this, and in her haste she didn't put things back the way she found them. My CCTV caught her like a burglar in the night. So, what is your plan? What have you come here to do?'

Finding her voice, Diana spoke first. 'Whatever our plan is you've beaten us, haven't you? Where's my mother?'

Pointing his finger at her, he grinned. 'Now that is a very good question. Firstly, don't try that police psychology on me, Diana; it won't work. And secondly, you can come out now!' Chris shouted behind him.

Diana's heart was in her mouth as she saw a figure slowly being brought forward from the shadows. Feeling it was Julie, she stepped forward, but then she saw it was a man. Faltering, she turned to look at the others and then back at Chris, confused. The man's wrists were bound by rope and he was gagged. One of Chris's henchmen stood behind him forcing him to walk forward.

'As they say in all the best movies,' Chris sneered, 'the butler did it.'

Scarlet recognised Denny the butler. Her heart was pounding in her chest. She knew Chris wouldn't let them go after this. They were all doomed. 'What's he got to do with anything?' Scarlet asked, trying to brazen it out.

'Wasn't he the one who drove your mother away from this

house, Diana? With all of these chauffeurs hanging around, why would the butler drive your mother anywhere? He says he took her to the vineyard, but my men have been there and there is no sign of her. Can you fill in the blank spaces?'

Slowly, Diana shook her head. 'No. I haven't seen her since this morning. That's why I asked you where she was. I thought that's who you were bringing out just now.'

'Down!' Chris ordered. His henchman pushed Denny to the floor on his knees. 'You've been planning my demise for quite some time, haven't you, Denny? Eating and sleeping in my home and yet the very viper in my bosom. You're a traitor, and traitors die!' Chris nodded his head, and his henchman fired his gun into the back of Denny's head. As he fell forward before them, they stepped back in shock as the blood poured from the back of his head, turning the staircase carpet crimson. The bullet hole from the back had gone directly through his head, leaving a hole in his forehead.

Moistening her dry lips, Scarlet found her voice. 'Where's Katie?' she asked. She needed to know if her sister was alive.

'She is in the garden with the children, totally oblivious to your betrayal. Believe me, her turn will come, but first I must decide about you lot. Maybe I should send for her, and she can watch you all die. After all, you like to keep it in the family, don't you? She's in on it, I know that. Sneaking around through my personal belongings out of loyalty to you!'

Realising she had nothing more to lose, Scarlet felt suddenly braver. They had all known it could end like this, and they had prepared themselves for it. 'So you haven't drugged her today then?' Scarlet snapped. 'Do what you have to, Chris, but what are you going to do with our dead bodies, or his for that matter?' She glared.

'You know, Scarlet, I always hated your smart mouth, thinking you were better than everyone else. There had been stories that Don Carlos had an escape route built into the house, but now I discover that during his last years on this mortal coil he instructed Denny there to cover the wall so it would never be found.' Chris nodded. 'And he did a very good job, didn't he, because I never noticed! Loyal to the cause, our spying butler. Presumably he relayed all of this to Julie, wherever she is. I thought she would pop out of there with you lot. As for what I intend to do with you, that's easy... The tunnel you have just walked through... it's full of rats, isn't it? I can see they've nibbled away at you here and there, by the scratches on your faces. And Scarlet, has one bitten you and let its saliva leak into your bloodstream? Maybe I'm wasting my time killing you. A good slow death is your fate.' Chris's voice dripped with sarcasm. 'You're all going back down there, dead of course, encased in a tunnel of rats. They will eat your dead bodies until you are only a carcass. You will never be found, and sooner or later, Katie will join you.' Chris was enjoying seeing them squirm before him. He had outsmarted them and was enjoying every minute of it.

Scarlet's face dropped and she felt her blood run cold. Reaching her hand up, she felt the tear in her suit and saw the bite mark. Inwardly, she was shaking, but she wouldn't let him see her cry or beg for mercy.

Hearing that he didn't know where Julie was, Diana let out a huge sigh. 'So you really don't know where my mother is?'

'No, Diana. She has abandoned you all. Left you to die while she lives another day. Not very maternal, is it?'

Adam felt it was time he spoke up. 'Before we do die, Chris, what is in that will that you would want to hide from the world? Why keep it so close to you? Don't let us die in ignorance, will you?'

Letting out a huge guffaw, Chris's face turned red. 'Fuck me,

Boy Wonder speaks. I thought you just stood there while your sister pulled your strings!'

Mentally, Adam was trying to calculate the time. Lewis had said that they had two hours and then he would come and get them. Surely that time was nearly up now. Where the fuck was Lewis? More to the point, where was Julie? This had been her idea and yet she was nowhere to be seen. His mind was in turmoil as he tried to bide time until Lewis turned up, if he ever would. For all they knew, Julie could be sitting on an aeroplane by now sipping champagne with him. No, dismissing that idea from his mind, Adam knew she would never desert Diana like that. The truth of the matter was that she was probably already dead, and Chris wasn't saying. He was dangling Diana in the air, giving her hope, when the truth was he'd probably already killed her...

Clearing his throat, Chris smiled sarcastically and waved the will in the air like a flag. 'So, you want to know the contents, Adam? Well, firstly, you are all correct – Carlos never wanted me to be Don. Even though I am his fucking nephew, he didn't think I was good enough. And yet he was willing to hand it over to you – a spoilt young boy!' he shouted. 'Well, let me read it to you. If that is your last wish.

"'I, Don Carlos, fear for my life from my twisted nephew. I don't know how much longer I will remember one day from another and so I write this now while I am in sound mind. Antonias Lambrianu was the son I never had. He was loyal and carried the Italian flag of honour for his people. In his absence, I pronounce that Adam Lambrianu, his son, will be my heir. He may be young, but he is fair and surrounded by guidance and support. I have already transferred all of my monies to a bank account solely for Adam's use. Once this will is read, lawyers will activate the account in Adam's name. As for my nephew, I leave him my home and contents. None of the antiques are real and the ones that are have been stolen and can never be sold. I always said I liked collecting antiques. I never said I paid for them."

'A bastard, even at the end,' Chris spat out. Looking around the grandeur of this house, Chris waved his arms in the air. 'None of this is worth a jot!' He laughed, manically. 'I'm glad I killed the old bastard!' Chris sneered. 'Yes, that witch Julie had her suspicions. She had seen Carlos and although he might have lived with the fairies, he was still physically healthy. As soon as he copied what I had written, it was easy. He was so drugged up, he didn't know what he was doing, so I just sat there and let him help himself to the bottles of pills. He ate them like sweets, and then I put the pillow over his head. Everyone, including the doctor, said he had overdosed himself accidentally. Fucking easy!' Chris boasted, making them all wince at his sordid confession.

Listening intently, Scarlet let his words sink into her brain. 'You're broke,' she whispered disbelievingly. 'You can't access Don Carlos's fortune and it's all in Adam's name. You must not have known this when you made Don Carlos write a new will, and then there was nothing you could do about it. You had sealed your own fate by being greedy for power. You wanted to be the godfather of Italy to salve your massive ego, but you are penniless... truly worthless.' Scarlet started to laugh. 'That is why you're cutting corners and stealing money from the vineyard. Presumably, you've emptied Katie's bank accounts too. We know you're squirreling money away, Chris...' Scarlet was now intrigued about these offshore accounts. How could Chris be broke? To her it didn't make sense.

'Shut up, you bitch! A few bad investments, and the fact that Don Carlos had let his wishes known to the other godfathers, have ruined everything. Between them, the other godfathers have agreed to do business with me, but they want their fair share and have increased their commission. Together they are bleeding me dry, because they do not believe I am the rightful Don. Wherever I can, I cream money off the top, but without Don Carlos's wealth I have nothing. And I planned to make damn sure that Adam would never get his hands on the cash either.' He nodded his head, as though talking to himself, and the others watched him helplessly.

His henchmen had guns pointing towards them, and Chris held his own in his shaking hand. They had nothing to defend themselves with and one wrong move and they would all be shot. As he carried on with his strange confessions, a wry grin crossed Chris's face. 'Yes, I drug Katie, Scarlet. When she is half asleep and not knowing what she's doing, she signs cheques from her personal Lambrianu account, which I cannot have access to unless agreed by you and Adam. For fuck's sake, I'm her husband! But your father tied up her money so tightly, anyone would think he didn't trust me. Why should I have to go cap in hand to your family to gain access to my wife's money? Anyway, enough talk. I'm tired of you all.'

By now, they were all shivering with cold. Silently, Adam was urging Lewis to come to their rescue, but time seemed to have stood still. Adam wanted to keep Chris talking, although the way he was reminiscing, he seemed to have totally lost all sense of morality with his boastings. Looking at the knife Knuckles held, Adam was tempted to snatch it and stab Chris, but looking at the guns pointed at them, he knew it would be futile. It would be a gesture which would get some or all of them killed.

Taking them all by surprise, one of the doors across the landing suddenly opened. Everyone's jaws dropped as they saw Julie emerge from the bedroom she had once shared with Ralph. Now Julie stood there glaring at Chris. 'You have a lot to say for yourself, don't you? I heard you torturing Denny and I've sat here and listened to you whine about your lack of funds.'

In an instant, Chris pointed his gun and fired two shots at Julie, making her fall to her knees. Diana screamed out and ran towards where her body lay on the floor. Tears fell down her face as she sobbed. 'You bastard!' Walking towards him, she had a murderous look in her eye, and she gave him one hefty slap, almost knocking him off balance.

Chris fired his gun again, but the bullet hit her in her thigh. Diana howled with pain and couldn't move off the floor. 'You will pay for that, you bitch!' he screamed and pointed his gun at Diana's head.

Adam moved forward but stopped suddenly as Julie stood up, a little shaken, but nonetheless alive and well. Chris paled as she opened her coat concealing her bullet-proof vest. 'I knew you would go for the body because you can't shoot straight, unlike me.' Holding up her gun, Julie fired a bullet directly through Chris's head. It was swift and clean and Chris fell to the floor – dead. Everyone stood rooted to the spot as Julie fired again at Chris's henchmen, killing them all too.

'Mum, you're alive!' Diana screamed and gripped her leg as the blood poured out of it. Knuckles grabbed Chris and took his tie off, tying it tightly around Diana's leg to stop the blood loss. Managing to speak, Diana asked, 'How did you know he would shoot you?'

'Because he hates me and he had an inkling all along that I knew the truth. Your father always had guns stashed in a trunk underneath the bed in that room, and no one has ever been in it to find them, which surprised me. They're a little old, but they still work after a bit of cleaning... A bit like me.' Julie scoffed. 'You must go now, back where you came from. But first, we're in this together.' Julie handed the gun to Scarlet. 'You first.'

Knowing what she meant, Scarlet took the gun and fired a shot into Chris's already dead body, then handed the gun to

Adam, who fired another bullet into him. Diana was laid on the floor still holding her leg. 'Give it to me,' she shouted. 'I want to make sure that pig is dead!'

Adam held the gun in her hand, and she fired two bullets. 'One for me and another for Katie,' she spat.

Kneeling beside her, Julie took the gun off her once more. 'And this one is for Don Carlos. He loved Ralph like a brother and this is Ralph's revenge.' Firing directly into his face, Julie smirked. 'All Italian funerals like an open casket. Well, Chris can't have one with a face like that. Adam, pick up Carlos's will and keep it safe. His other stooges will have heard the shots up here but will presume it's Chris killing you. But they will come and investigate soon. Get Diana out of here. Sorry, but you all have to leave the way you came in. GO!'

Incredulously, Scarlet looked at Julie. 'Aren't you coming? What about you?'

Running across the landing, Julie brought out an automatic rifle. 'I can ward them off for a few minutes only, so you can get through the hatch safely. Please go.' Stopping for a moment, she put her fingers to her lips. 'I can hear them coming up the staircase.' Pleadingly, she looked at Knuckles. 'Get them out of here, Knuckles, please,' she begged.

Doing as he was told, Knuckles picked up Diana and put her over his shoulder, taking her through the cladding into the bathroom. Looking up, her eyes full of tears, she knew her mother was going to sacrifice herself to let them get away safely. 'Mum!' she cried. 'Come with us!'

Watching her, Julie's heart broke seeing her daughter so distressed. 'Look after her, Adam. Do as I say... Now go!'

The thunderous footsteps got louder and closer. Knuckles threw Diana down onto the ledge and then came back and dragged Scarlet away, kicking and screaming. 'We will all die,' Knuckles stressed. Slowly, she relaxed and did as she was told.

'Knuckles!' Adam cried. 'We can't leave her here!'

Knuckles punched him hard in the face, almost knocking him out, and whilst he was dazed, he picked him up and threw him down the tunnel, too. Hearing a thud and a scream, he knew Adam had fallen on top of one of the girls, but Knuckles didn't care. 'I will leave the hatch open, Julie. Let the rats come up here. Give them somewhere to run.' Seeing Julie nod, he disappeared down the hatch.

Alone, Julie stared at the main staircase as the men got closer. Bracing herself, she started firing her rifle as they ran to the top of the staircase. Instantaneously, they fired their powerful machine guns towards her. The force of them knocked her off her feet and sent her flying into the air. Full of bullet holes, Julie slid down the wall on to the floor. She was dead.

Pandemonium broke out as the bodyguards ran around with their guns looking for more intruders, but there were none. Seeing the hole in the cladding wall, they pulled it away and looked through it and paled as an army of rats scurried towards them. The rats had been incarcerated long enough, and this was their escape. The bodyguards fired their guns at them, but seeing the number multiply, they turned and ran down the staircase, afraid for their own lives.

From the garden, Katie heard the gunshots and the bodyguards running around shouting to each other. She knew it was time to make the fatal call. Calmly, she rang the police and screamed for help, just as Julie had instructed her to do. Pulling her children towards her, she couldn't imagine what horrors were behind the walls. She even wondered if Chris had killed her family and he was still alive. She just had to hope and pray that Julie Gold had once more saved them all.

* * *

Knuckles put Diana over his shoulder and they trudged back through the tunnel. Adam had blood running down his nose and felt a bit woozy after his punch from Knuckles. They all felt desperate and afraid. A loud bang echoed through the tunnel and, seeing a flash of light, they shielded their faces. Hundreds of rats ran past them, up and over their bodies, scratching them all in blind panic to escape through the hatch. Again, another thunderous bang rang out and the tunnel lit up.

Looking up, Knuckles saw a figure in the distance. 'Lewis!' he shouted.

All of them took their hands from their faces and saw the silhouettes of men approaching. Seeing them, Lewis and his friends ran forward. 'Are you all okay?'

'What the banging?' Knuckles asked, handing Diana over to Lewis's care.

'Hand grenades. We will blast this shithole to pieces to get you out. Come on,' Lewis urged. 'Sorry for the delay. Some of Chris's bodyguards were patrolling the main entrance gates as though they expected something.'

'Chris knew we were coming.' Knuckles panted.

'Diana's hurt. Bullet in leg,' Adam explained, now coming fully to his senses.

'Julie?' Lewis mouthed to Knuckles. Seeing him shake his head, Lewis knew she was dead. Momentarily, he faltered. She had been good to him, and he was sorry it had ended this way.

Quickly, everyone seemed to be carrying each other as they waded through the muddy water back to freedom. Only this time, the rats were running past them, almost tripping them up in their haste.

Scarlet felt their exit seemed much nearer than it had before, and as she looked up, she saw another one of Lewis's friends and Julie's household kneeling down waiting for them.

'Quick!' he shouted. 'I can hear police sirens. We need to run, for fuck's sake!'

Clambering their way up the ladder, they were pushed into the back of the waiting Land Rover. Lewis threw another hand grenade into the tunnel as they left and sealed the manhole again. Then he took the wheel and drove as everyone fought to catch their breath. 'Diana!' Scarlet shouted. 'Stay awake, Diana. Don't close your eyes.'

Half turning in his seat, Lewis shouted to Scarlet, 'We're taking her to the vineyard; it's closer than the villa. But you have one last thing to do, Scarlet. You need to get changed. Don't forget you were meant to be shopping today. You have to go back to the house later to support Katie. Diana left you and got on a flight home with her mother. I have Julie's passport. Where is Diana's? The police cannot be allowed to find it,' he yelled.

'I dunno... it could be in her bag from before. I look shocking. I don't look like I've been on a shopping trip, Lewis.'

'Comb your hair, put some clothes on and search Diana's bag,' he shouted.

'You want me to change in the back of here, now?' she asked, looking at Adam and Knuckles.

'Oh, for Christ's sake, Scarlet, just strip! And you two, look the other way. This is not the time for modesty,' Lewis shouted. 'I'm dropping you off at a taxi rank here. Then you need to go back to the house.' Frantically, Scarlet peeled off her wetsuit, and she could see she was covered in scratches. As though on autopilot, she struggled to put on the trouser suit she had left the house in earlier that day and her shoes wouldn't fit properly, her feet were so wet and swollen. She felt and looked grubby, and worst of all she stank. Looking through Diana's handbag, she found her passport. 'Got it!' she shouted, waving it in the air.

Lewis snatched it off her and stopped the Land Rover. 'Use my brush and put some lipstick on in the taxi. Go on, Scarlet, go.'

About to leave, unexpectedly Scarlet halted and reached for Knuckles. Throwing her arms around his neck, she kissed him ardently. Adam blushed; he had never seen Scarlet show Knuckles this kind of affection before. But Scarlet held on to him as though she never wanted to let him go. Knuckles held her tightly as they kissed again.

'I love you, Knuckles. Remember that whatever happens.'

'I love you too, Scarlet. Always have,' Knuckles answered huskily. Stroking his face lovingly, Scarlet heard Lewis shout again for her to leave. Reluctantly, she did as she was told with a heavy heart, while Lewis waited until Scarlet got into the back of a taxi and drove off to the vineyard.

21

THE AFTERMATH

Scarlet turned up at the house and got out of the taxi. She'd combed her hair and wiped her face with some makeup wipes in her handbag. Fortunately, her perfume was in there too and she'd sprayed that everywhere to cover the smell that seemed stuck in her nose. Inwardly, she was shaking after everything that had happened, but she knew she had to appear calm. The roadside was full of police cars. As she walked up to the gates, she was stopped and questioned. As she told them who she was, they said she couldn't enter the house and instead led her to a police van around the corner. Stumbling on her shoes, she looked inside the van and saw Katie and the children waiting inside. Frantically, she bent forward and hugged Katie.

'Chris is dead!' Katie cried. 'Oh my God, Scarlet. Someone has broken in and killed him. We can't go in the house; it's infested with rats,' she cried, playing the woeful widow brilliantly. Scarlet listened as Katie told her what had happened while she had been playing in the garden with the children, just as her husband had asked her to do. She had even got a couple of the bodyguards involved in a football game. Everyone could swear that Katie was innocent.

The police asked if there was somewhere the family could stay. Katie was about to say the vineyard when Scarlet stopped her. 'We will stay in a nearby hotel in case we're needed here.' The last thing Scarlet wanted was the police snooping around the vineyard with Adam, Knuckles and Diana there with a bullet wound in her leg.

Driving them to a hotel, the police said they would be in touch. They had no luggage as everything was back in the house. 'We will buy something,' Scarlet explained to the police officers. 'Thank you.'

No sooner had they got into their room than Scarlet collapsed on the bed. 'I'm so fucking tired,' she groaned.

Katie led the children into their adjoining rooms and told them to play video games. They were upset and confused. Soothing them, Katie said she would order room service, lots of pizza and cola, and this seemed to take their mind off their missing father. Once they were settled, she walked back into her room with Scarlet. 'I'll run you a bath. Are you okay?'

'No. Julie... our Julie is dead, Katie. She sacrificed herself so that we could get away. It was such a mess. He knew that you had been in his study and was waiting for us when we got out of the hatch in the bathroom.'

'Julie's dead?' For a moment, Katie couldn't comprehend the words. 'She can't be, surely.' In disbelief and denial, she looked at Scarlet questioningly.

'She's dead, Katie. The police will confirm it. They will say it was Julie who killed Chris. She shot Chris and saved our lives. For fuck's sake, what are we going to do without her? Diana is distraught. She'll never forgive us for letting her sacrifice herself like that. She shouted to Knuckles to get us out and he did. Oh,

Katie.' Scarlet fell into her sister's arms and wept a million tears until there were no more left.

Katie felt cold and empty but went and ran a bath for Scarlet and then checked on her children. Room service would be along soon, and they would eat themselves silly and fall asleep, she thought to herself. But inwardly, she cursed herself. Her family, all of them including Julie and Diana, had been to hell and back today, and she hadn't even touched the surface. She would never be able to understand Scarlet's pain at seeing Julie being a hero. Or Diana's despair at being left without her mother. Katie knew that she would spend the rest of her life trying to make it up to them all.

* * *

'Bring her upstairs into this bedroom,' Adam shouted as they carried Diana into the vineyard.

Laying her on the bed, Knuckles loosened the tie he had strapped her leg up with. 'Seems like a neat hole. Bullet gone straight through, look.' Knuckles half turned Diana's leg for them all to see.

Suddenly, one of Julie's men who lived alongside Lewis and the others taking care of her household pushed them out of the way. 'I'm Graham, I usually do the cleaning, but I was a para-medic. Let me take a look and see what the damage is. It's a flesh wound, no bones chipped, and yes,' he said after feeling his way around, 'there's no bullet in there, so that's a bonus. It will need packing. Let's get her washed up, and there must be a first aid box or definitely something in the factory we can use, surely?'

Knuckles was about to stand up, but Adam stopped him. 'I want you to go and lie down. You've been brave all day and not given a thought to yourself. Everyone is safe. Let the paramedic do his stuff and I'll get what he needs. Please, Knuckles. You've been amazing and so fearless. I'm ashamed I wasn't as brave as you,' Adam confessed.

'Lived in a care home with rats like that. Got used to it. You brave, Adam. Like Julie. She the bravest person I ever known.'

Remembering Julie brought a tear to Adam's eyes. 'I can't believe she wouldn't come with us, Knuckles.'

'She knew what she was doing, Adam. Had it all worked out, believe me.' Yawning, Knuckles looked at the doors on the landing.

'Choose any room, Knuckles. Just get some sleep. Graham, I'll get you some water and find something for you to fix the wound. Anything else while you're asking?'

'Vodka. Do you have any vodka, Adam?'

Half smiling and so weary he was near to collapse, Adam smiled. 'I could do with a drink myself.'

'Well, you can have one. But I meant to clean this wound, you prat.' Graham smiled.

Adam wanted to laugh but didn't have the strength. Going over to the drinks cabinet, he held out a bottle of vodka then disappeared to find a medicine box. Returning shortly afterwards, he handed Graham a box with bandages and scissors, then sat down on the sofa as Graham meticulously cleaned the wound and packed it. It felt hypnotic to Adam, and he felt his heavy eyes drooping. He was exhausted and needed to rest. But they weren't out of danger yet. There was still a long way to go until they were home free.

* * *

Katie had the television on, and Chris's death was being reported all over the news. Details were sketchy: it was believed a woman had broken in, but some of Chris's guards had confirmed she had once been a guest there. But she had died with a gun in her hand, and it had been fired many times. The butler had also been murdered. A lot of the evidence, the police stated, had been ruined by an infestation of rats, which had escaped from a nearby bathroom leading down into a tunnel that had been bomb blasted. Katie listened as all kinds of stories poured out. It was supposedly a 'hit job' from Mafia members. Others claimed it was a love affair gone wrong. The stories went on and on. But all Katie could think about was Julie. No one mentioned her name on the news, and that was the saddest part of all.

Seeing Scarlet emerge from the bathroom, Katie asked her what she wanted to eat. Scarlet shook her head. 'I can't eat. I'll have a whisky though to calm my nerves.'

Pouring her drink, Katie handed it to her. 'Have this and then get some sleep. I will be in there with the kids if you need me.'

'I'm afraid to sleep, Katie. All I can see is rats before my eyes. Look at me.' Scarlet opened her dressing gown. 'I'm scratched to pieces,' she cried.

Katie observed the scratches and the bite mark in horror. What had they been through to save her? 'Right, I'm going to pop to the shop and get some antiseptic ointment. It needs cleaning. Your physical wounds will heal, Scarlet, but the mental ones you have suffered today could last a lifetime.'

Seeing how badly shaken her sister was upset Katie further. Finding a pharmacy near the hotel, she asked their advice about bites and scratches. They gave ointment and antihistamine. Satisfied, she took them back to Scarlet. The creams would ease her discomfort now, but the deeper scars would be harder to fix.

* * *

Adam woke up to darkness. Jumping up, he realised he was on the sofa at the vineyard and not still down that tunnel. It had given him nightmares, but he doubted he would be the only one. The house was quiet, so he crept upstairs. Opening a bedroom door, he saw that Knuckles was sound asleep and snoring. Then across the landing he saw a light from under another door. Opening it, he found Graham and Lewis both sat there with Diana. 'She's been cleaned up and has had antibiotics. The paracetamol will take away the pain and fever. The next twenty-four hours we need to keep her temperature down. I don't know when she will be able to fly home.'

'She doesn't need to. She can come on the yacht with me and Knuckles. What does it matter now?'

'Hey, Adam. It matters a lot that we stick to our story. Julie didn't die in vain today,' Lewis snapped. 'Diana will be boarding a flight with me tomorrow. It's quicker than the yacht.'

'Lewis, why do you always make me feel like shit?' Adam yelled and turned to leave. Quickly, Lewis stood up and stopped him. 'Sorry, Adam; I didn't mean to. I'm just trying to hold things together. I just want to follow the plan, okay?'

'Sorry, Lewis, my nerves are raw. You were great today, although I wish you'd arrived sooner. Maybe then Julie...'

Lewis grabbed Adam's shoulder and looked at him carefully. 'You've all been traumatised today. I wish I had got there sooner too, but let's not dwell, eh? Get some rest, and – phew! – a shower!' Lewis laughed. 'Are you hungry?' Seeing him shake his head, Lewis gently pushed Adam out of the room and went and sat beside Diana with Graham again.

Adam quietly closed the door and went to get a hot shower. He needed to keep his wits about him now. And Lewis was right; they needed to make sure that Julie hadn't died in vain. Adam was suddenly determined that they were all going to get out of this alive and free.

* * *

Katie was interviewed by the police about the woman found on the landing. She identified her as Julie Gold, who the police already seemed aware of. Calmly, Katie stuck to the story about them visiting for Scarlet's hen weekend but that she'd believed Julie had left early and returned home to England.

The police had informed her that the house would need fumigating, and that pest control were already on site. After having the all-clear from Lewis, Katie had informed them that she would be staying at the vineyard with her children for the present time. Adam and Knuckles had been safely deposited back to the yacht and were already making their way home. And Lewis had somehow managed to get Diana onto a flight home. Lewis had been Julie's wingman for a long time and wanted to do her justice by following her plans to the last detail.

Scarlet, although staying with Katie a little longer, would soon make her way home too. But first, she had things to organise. Her main one was to have Julie's body brought back to England. The police didn't need it, and they weren't 100 per cent sure Julie had been the murderer. There had been so many bullets fired from all different angles, it could have been any number of people responsible. Everyone knew Chris was hated in the local community, and the police believed that Julie, an old woman, had merely been caught in the crossfire. It was all substantial. Every piece of evidence was contaminated.

Chris's body, full of bullet holes, was in the morgue. Scarlet almost laughed when she had heard that the rats had nearly taken the rest of his arrogant face off. On hearing this, she asked about Julie, but had been told that the rats had stayed away from her. Scarlet had been thankful for this and when she had been to see Julie in the morgue to identify her, her face had looked peaceful as though she was fast asleep. The police had told her that she had received twenty gunshot wounds to her body. And although it sounded harsh, it made Scarlet smile. Even in death, she thought to herself, Julie had protected her face and it was as immaculate as always. What a woman.

* * *

Unwinding on the journey home, Knuckles drank his ginger ale for his seasickness and he and Adam both recuperated underneath the warm sun. The last few days weren't mentioned by either of them during the whole trip, especially as the crew of the yacht circulated regularly, with their ears wide open. Adam had played up the idea of a stag weekend to top them all and, seeing their weary state, the captain had no reason to assume otherwise. Adam had acted shocked and disbelieving when the captain informed him that Chris had been killed, but nothing more was said about the matter.

But inwardly, Adam felt angry about everything. Especially Julie's death. As soon as they landed, Adam turned the last will and testament of Don Carlos over to his lawyers, then headed for home. Poppy was the first to greet him as he popped his head through the door to say hello.

'You look tired. Are you okay?' she asked, concerned. She could see that something was troubling him and, standing up, she instinctively put her arms around him.

'Julie's dead,' he blurted out and clung on to her for dear life. Adam couldn't stop sobbing on her shoulders.

'I know, Adam. It was on the news. Also, about Chris.'

Soothing him, she told him to go upstairs and rest. This was a different Adam Lambrianu than the one who had left for Italy a few days ago. And Poppy wondered what was about to happen to the whole Lambrianu empire without Julie to guide them all...

* * *

A few days after their ordeal, Adam arranged for a family meeting at the Southend house. Everyone was there except Scarlet and Katie, who were still in Italy dealing with the fallout of Chris's death. Diana seemed to be on the mend, but still grieved for her mother heavily. Lewis had been a constant support for her and hadn't left her side.

Bobby and Jack arrived, and Bobby demanded to know the truth from Adam. When Adam told him, he went berserk at them for risking their lives and not trusting him enough to tell him. He felt betrayed. 'Why didn't you trust me, Adam? We're brothers. What if you had all been killed and I was oblivious to it all?'

'Julie didn't want you involved, Bobby. Your reputation is squeaky clean and she didn't want you dragged into this. You didn't need that.'

Although angry, Bobby calmed down. 'What you're really saying is that you didn't think I'd be up to it.'

'That's not it at all, Bobby. Julie didn't want you involved, and we all went along with it. End of,' Adam snapped. He was tired of answering questions. He thought his brain was going to explode.

After a few drinks, they sat around the table and spoke about their ordeal. Pouring out their story and fears made them all feel better. Lewis sat there listening before making his own announcement. 'There is something I have to tell you. Julie has written all of you a letter; she wanted her affairs in order and to be able to rest in peace. I'll let you read your own letters privately, but I will just share this with you all. She, she…' Lewis croaked, and his eyes welled up. 'She had cancer.' Pausing, Lewis let his words sink into the stunned faces around him. 'She was dying, Diana. Lung cancer. Don't you recall the coughing fits she had now and again?' he asked.

'What? Why didn't she tell me? I'm her daughter.' Diana wailed as tears once more filled her eyes.

'She refused to accept treatment. She didn't like the idea of chemo in case she lost her hair and she didn't want to feel even more ill than she actually did. But what spurred her on, and possibly kept her alive, was the thought of killing Chris.' Throwing his hands in the air, he smiled. 'Her main goal was to kill Chris and free you all from his reign of terror. She didn't want to leave unfinished business. She also felt she owed Ralph and Don Carlos. Anyway, you have the letters, but what I am trying to say is that Julie knew she was on borrowed time. This way, she went out in a blaze of glory, like the superwoman she was. No one could imagine Julie Gold dying in her sleep peacefully. There was nothing quiet or peaceful about her. She lived her life, Diana. And she wanted you to live yours. All of you, without Chris and his poisonous ways. She is happy now. She is back with Ralph, and they both know that you're all safe from harm.'

Stunned at Lewis's words, they all agreed. Julie was never going to die a boring death. She was a fighter and would go out fighting. Inwardly, Diana felt comforted by the fact that Julie had chosen to die, before fate had made that choice for her. She'd chosen the time and place and, as always, Julie had been the one in charge until her final breath.

* * *

After two weeks, word came regarding Chris's funeral, which for appearance's sake, they would all have to attend. Scarlet had also informed them that after this, she would be bringing Julie home, too.

They all dreaded catching the flight to Italy and returning to the scene of the crime. Don Lorenzo was the first to stop Adam when they met. 'I believe your lawyers have been in touch with the late Don Carlos's lawyers. It seems you were appointed as his true heir, Adam, to his title and also his fortune.'

For now, Adam decided to play it safe. 'I just handed the will over Don Lorenzo. Don Carlos's final wishes needed to be heard after being kept silent for so long. I have no agenda here.'

Don Lorenzo smiled at his choice of words and, putting his arm around Adam's shoulder, introduced him to the other Dons in the church. Scarlet smiled. She could see Adam was getting their approval already. Julie would be looking down on them smiling. This was what she had wanted. Adam Lambrianu was finally the true heir. Don Carlos could now rest in peace and so could she.

22

A HAPPY ENDING

Julie's golden casket made its way through the streets of London carried on the back of a white horse-drawn carriage with gold plumes on the heads of the horses. David Bowie's 'Golden Years' played loudly as the procession moved slowly, so people could pay their respects. People lined the streets, throwing flowers and crying. Shops closed for the day, and London seemed to come to a standstill as it wept. At one point there were so many flowers, you could barely see the coffin at all.

Diana broke down in tears, not just for the loss of her mother, but for the way other people were saddened by the loss of Julie and mourned her deeply. She had touched so many lives in her time, and they all thought highly of her. Julie hadn't wanted anyone to know she was ill. In her letters, she explained that she didn't want pitiful looks if someone mentioned the cancer word. She didn't want to appear feeble and weak. Well, she hadn't, Diana thought to herself. She had died a legend who would be remembered for her quick wit and mischievous ways. Diana couldn't thank Scarlet enough for bringing her home so that she could be laid to rest with her beloved Ralph.

'Look at that. I thought it was a coincidence, but they are all wearing them,' Scarlet whispered in Diana's ear.

Looking up through her dark glasses, Diana saw people were wearing gold ribbon bows on the front of their clothing. 'Oh my God, Scarlet, she would have loved this.' All Diana could hear was praise about how wonderful and great her mother was, which lifted her spirits high. People stopped her as she walked behind the horses and told her of the charitable acts Julie had done, to make their lives better.

Diana hadn't known about most of their stories and realised her mother had given them a legacy to remember. Julie Gold would never die, Diana thought to herself, but there would never be another like her.

After the service, Adam and Scarlet opened the club for Julie's wake to everyone who wished to pay their respects. Champagne flowed freely, while they all enjoyed some of the comical stories people remembered Julie for. They all agreed Julie had been an incredible woman, strong, vibrant and fun. But also, a very kind one. They would all miss her deeply.

* * *

Having a coffee with Katie, and going over things, Scarlet felt it was time to drop the bombshell that had been on her mind. 'I've decided I'm going to marry Knuckles in Italy. In the same little chapel on the ground where Mum and Dad said their vows. And I already have the perfect dress – the one Mum wore. Julie kept it all of these years and it's in perfect condition. In her letter, Julie told me where it was and said it was her wish that I wear it. Sentimental old sod.' Scarlet laughed. 'And then I am going to have my wedding celebration at the vineyard. Workers, locals and everyone will be welcome to sing and dance our good health and new beginnings.'

'That's a beautiful idea, Scarlet. I wondered where that dress had disappeared to. Julie had it all of this time and never said a word.' Seeing Scarlet nod, Katie beamed. 'A beautiful family wedding, in a family chapel, in a beautiful dress. It's deep rooted in our family, Scarlet.'

'What about you, Katie? What are your plans now? Money isn't a problem for you, and you have us, you know that.'

'If possible, and if you and Adam agree, I'd like to live at the vineyard and take over the running of it. I'm going to bring back some of the old workers, but keep the new ones too, but pay them proper wages. The police investigation seems to have gone cold, and I think the other Dons have paid the police to have it all swept under the carpet. No one liked Chris; they put up with him, didn't they? No one is going to miss him – except maybe the kids, but they have been happier lately than I have ever seen them without him bullying them all day. The house has been fumigated to kill the rats. I pity the poor bastards who had to go in there and pick them all up. No one would ever want to live there; I certainly don't. I want it knocked down to the ground...' Katie reached out her hand to Scarlet. 'We've never really spoken about it, Scarlet, but I can't even begin to imagine the horror you all faced down there. I can't thank you enough. You have given me my life back.' Her eyes glazed over with tears.

'Well, it was no picnic.' Scarlet blushed, trying to play down their ordeal, but even now it gave her nightmares. The slightest noise when she was alone in her bedroom took her back to that dark hole with the manhole cover being closed above them, and the rats. For all her bravado, she couldn't get them out of her mind. Their long tails, and the stench. She had scrubbed her skin raw trying to get the smell off her, but there was no point in telling Katie that; it would only make her feel worse. Sighing, she patted Katie's hand. 'To be honest, if it hadn't had been for Knuckles, I don't think any of us would have survived that day. He was amazing, and truly, Katie, I couldn't be marrying a better man. There was no thought for himself, just us. What more can I ask for?' Scarlet smiled as she thought about the man she was going to marry.

She smiled, changing the subject. 'I think it's time you lived your life as you want to, Katie. What is it you really want to do?'

'I intend to, Scarlet. I'm going to look after my children like Mum and Grandma and die at the vineyard in peace surrounded by my grandchildren... if I have any!' Katie laughed. 'What about Adam? I believe the solicitors are dealing with the will, and Don Carlos left his entire fortune to him! That cryptic line in the will that Don Carlos had left a gift for Adam at the bank, that was a big oversight on Chris's behalf and an amazing idea from Don Carlos. And making it Ralph's birthday, too!' Katie enthused. 'When Julie had last spoken to Don Carlos, he had screamed Ralph's birthdate at her, remember? She had been upset because he had got it wrong, but the combination to the strong box in the bank vault was the date he had shouted at Julie! He was giving Julie the combination, because he didn't want it written down for Chris to find, and he had put it in the letter that he left for Adam at his solicitors. If it hadn't been for Julie's plan, that letter would never have seen the light of day and Don Carlos's fortune would be left unclaimed. Thank goodness she wrote that down and put it in all of her letters to us all. I've heard word in Italy that he is already accepted as Don Lambrianu. Dad would be so bloody proud, Scarlet. It's unbelievable. They already speak of Adam as the Don – Don Lambrianu, even though he hasn't been sworn in properly yet or got the ring that all of the Dons wear. Chris wore it for ego's sake; Adam will wear it with pride.' Katie threw her arms around her sister, feeling her pain and hugging her tightly.

* * *

'I haven't seen much of you lately, Adam. Are you okay?' Bruce asked. He'd seen the news and read the papers and although his gut told him there was more to this story, it wasn't his business to pry.

'Just been catching up, Bruce. Did you have a good time with Kim at the holiday cottage?'

Beaming, Bruce nodded. 'The best, mate, absolutely.' Catching sight of Poppy as she came into the office, Bruce winked. 'I'll go into more details later. Although Kim wants us to have tattoos with each other's names. Do you think that's the same as an engagement ring in the twenty-first century?' Bruce laughed.

'I'd say that's a downward slope, Bruce. What happens if you split up? Are you going to roam the country for another woman called Kim?' Adam laughed. It felt good to laugh again, he mused to himself as he bantered with his friend. 'Actually, I once slept with a woman – God, I can't remember who – but inside her thigh she had a tattoo. On the left it said "enter the dragon" and on the right was a tattoo of a dragon breathing fire. Can you imagine what her carers will think of that when she's old and in residential care?' Adam laughed again.

Sitting there, Poppy's face burned with embarrassment as she heard them laughing. The tattoo he mentioned was on her thigh, the result of a drunken joke with her friends when she had been seventeen and at college. Ever since, she sorely regretted it, but she thought to herself, Adam did remember her, sort of. Even if it wasn't the most flattering thing to be remembered for.

Waving Bruce off, Adam was about to speak to Poppy when he noticed how flushed she looked. 'Are you okay, Poppy? You look quite feverish.'

'I'm fine, Adam.' She sighed. 'Just a bit warm, that's all. It's good to hear you laugh again. I know losing Julie has hurt you deeply. And Bruce sobbed his heart out when he heard the news.'

'He hasn't said much, but she looked after him a lot, and he enjoyed having her as a mother figure. Even if she did make him wear those red pyjamas.' Adam laughed. Lowering his voice to a softer velvety tone, Adam got up and sat on the edge of Poppy's desk. 'I haven't really had the chance to thank you for covering for me, Poppy. Things have been a bit manic.' Taking her hand, he kissed the back of it.

For a moment, their eyes met, and a deep longing for each other emerged. Their lips met and became more ardent as their passion rose. 'Not here,' Adam whispered lovingly in her ear. Taking her by the hand, he led Poppy upstairs to his flat. Once inside, they kissed again passionately, locked in an embrace, and tore at each other's clothing as they made their way to the bedroom.

Adam's hands roamed all over her silky body, flicking her nipple with his tongue as murmurs of ecstasy escaped her lips. Wrapping her legs tightly around him, she threw her head back as he thrust into her, time and time again. Adam's head spun with a passion he had never felt before. His body trembled as their lips met and she clung to him, urging him on.

With each thrust, Poppy felt her body tense as it reached its peak. Suddenly, it was as though fireworks had gone off inside her body and, tingling from head to toe, she cried out. Gasping for breath, Adam threw his head back with one last thrust and felt an explosion inside of him go off, making his head spin.

Hot and sweaty, they clung to each other, feeling the sweet release of their passion for each other. Panting, Poppy laid her head on his chest, running her hands through the auburn hairs and down towards his manhood, which felt full of life again.

As they lay in each other's arms, contented, Adam spoke first. 'Nice tattoos you have.'

Blushing, Poppy stroked his muscly arm lovingly and kissed him.

'Why have you never said we've met before?' His voice croaked with passion. 'I remember you now...' He tailed off as his mind wandered off to the night of his birthday, when he had drunk too much and hidden away in a private booth away from all of the pomp and ceremony of the party. The waitress, shocked at seeing him, had wished him a happy birthday.

Patting the seat beside him, he had poured out his sorrows to her. One thing had led to another, but he had felt guilty about abandoning her so abruptly. He had done it for her sake, not for his. He didn't want the other staff whispering and sniggering about her. Not knowing what to say to make amends to her the next morning, he had felt foolish, and had hid behind his employer's mask and carried on as normal. He had vowed that he would catch up with her later to apologise, but he had never seen her again. She had vanished into thin air, without trace. He had enjoyed being able to speak freely to the girl about his dreams and ambitions without being judged or laughed at. And he now realised that girl had been Poppy. And now they had come full circle. She had protected him, lied for him and, at times, he mused to himself, he had treated her badly. Like a spoilt kid.

'Is it a good memory or a bad one?' she asked nervously. Her heart sank as she waited for an answer.

His voice full of desire, Adam smiled. 'It's a very, very good one, and I hope to make many more good memories with you.' His body ached and throbbed for her as he pulled her on top of him, moaning sweet nothings as they explored each other's body once more.

* * *

Turning the key in the door of Julie's house, Diana was surprised to see suitcases in the hallway. Curiously, she walked into the lounge where Lewis was sitting. 'What's with all the suitcases, Lewis?'

Surprised by her presence, he stood up. 'I wasn't just going to leave without saying goodbye, Diana. But this is your home now, not mine.'

'Don't be foolish, Lewis. This will always be your home. You and the others looked after Mum, were her confidants when she needed them. You entertained her and kept her mind active while I was busy with my police work. You cared for her and kept her cancer a secret as she requested. She would never forgive me if I booted you out. I know Mum left you a lot of money in her will, and if you wish to leave, that's your prerogative. But I also know she would like you to carry on looking after this place and me... and so would I.' She smiled.

Sitting down, she held out her hand and proffered him a seat. 'I've had a lot of thinking time, Lewis. I want to leave the police force, preferably before they retire me.' She laughed. 'I want to travel, see something of the world. I realise how short life is; and I would like you to keep the home fires burning for when I return. I'm an orphan now.' She smiled. 'But it would be nice to have someone who knew Mum so well and had her best interests at heart, be there for me too. I could do with someone like that, Lewis. What do you say?'

Touched by her frankness, Lewis didn't know what to say. Jokingly, he looked her up and down. 'Well, someone has to keep that makeover in good order, don't they? You look just like her, Diana, especially now you've upped your game, as your mum would have said.' He laughed. 'If I left it to you, you would go to Scarlet's wedding in joggers and a jumper. But, if I stay, I will want to pay rent or something. I won't live off you, Diana,' he stressed.

'I think a bottle of gin a month would suffice, and you do all the cooking and cleaning. Cos I can't cook to save my life, as you well know.' She laughed.

'True, if it doesn't come out of a tin, or isn't microwaved, you have no idea.' He laughed. 'Sounds like a done deal then, Diana Gold. Gin it is.' He laughed in his camp way. 'Just one last thing though. Somewhere out there is a Ralph Gold for you. Just not in the police force. Find a Spanish waiter and get laid.' He chuckled, making her blush.

Laughing out loud, Diana rolled her eyes to the ceiling. 'Why is it that I see you, Lewis, but hear my mother?' She laughed. 'Only she would say something like that... and now you!' She laughed again. 'What would I do without you?'

Standing up, Diana hugged him. She couldn't thank him enough for the friendship he had shown her mother. And his loyalty, saving her life the way he had. 'I'm going to put in my resignation and put my flat up for sale. Empty your cases, Lewis, the house wouldn't be the same without you.' Kissing him on the cheek, she left. Satisfied that her mother would want this.

Julie had been very generous in her will to all of them, and she had given Lewis the opportunity to buy whatever he needed, but, deep down, Diana felt she needed the same friendship he had shown her mother. He was one of the few people she could openly talk about her mother with, and that meant more than money to her. Now was the time to spread her wings and fly away knowing that Lewis would always have her back.

* * *

'Well, Don Lambrianu, show me your ring,' Scarlet asked excitedly.

Adam held out the gold signet ring with his father's pure uncut diamond in the middle. 'All the Dons had a meeting, and they have all sworn me in and pledged their allegiance to me, as I have to them.' Adam blushed. 'I am now the Don, Scarlet.' He smiled. 'And you look beautiful in Mum's wedding dress, might I say.' Leaning forward, he kissed her on the cheek.

'You may.' She beamed. 'Do you think Knuckles will approve?' Scarlet scoffed. Holding his hand, she looked in awe at the priceless ring. 'God, that's beautiful. Apparently, Dad sent him that diamond. Don Carlos still has the original Don ring, but he always wore the one Dad gave him.'

Adam grinned, waving his hand around so that the diamond caught the light. 'I've heard about Dad's diamond heist many times.' Adam laughed. 'On another note, Knuckles looks as nervous as hell, but he's all washed up and in his grey morning suit waiting for his bride. Lewis has done an amazing job on him; I've never seen him look so good! I could even fancy him myself. And the amount of aftershave he's wearing could knock you out from a distance. He's got the kids behind him for good luck too, and Annette has warned him not to fluff his lines.' Adam laughed and hugged her.

Raising one eyebrow, she gazed at him. 'And what are your plans? I hear you've been spending a lot of time with Poppy. I even hear she has moved a lot of her things to Southend?'

Adam burst out laughing. 'Well, that just goes to show what big ears you have, Scarlet. But yes, Poppy has moved in with me, which you already knew. I'm also planning to build a house, here in Italy. Nothing over the top. I want to be approachable, not aloof. I want the people around here to be able to speak to me, if you know what I mean...' Adam stammered.

'I do, Adam. And that is why Don Carlos saw you as his rightful heir. He knew you would keep in touch with the people. You will do well and, with Poppy at your side, you will do even better. You look happy, and that pleases me.' She put her arms around him and hugged him.

'Well, the whole of Italy is standing in and around that chapel to see you married and drink the vineyard dry.' Adam laughed. 'I had better take my place beside Knuckles before he faints.' As an afterthought, Adam turned to Scarlet. 'By the way, what will your surname be? I don't even know what Knuckles's real name is, but you can't be Mrs Knuckles!'

Pouting, Scarlet folded her arms in a defensive manner. 'Lambrianu, what else? Knuckles is taking my name. Knuckles has never used his own name, and I'm sure he has his reasons, which I am not going to probe. And for your information, little brother, this crowd may want to see me married and drink us dry, but they also want to see the new Don Lambrianu and celebrate you.'

'Then let's give the people what they want, sis.' Adam grinned.

Outside the chapel, Katie proudly linked her arm with Scarlet and walked her slowly down the aisle for all to see. In their mother's wedding dress, with its soft satin A-line, lace sweetheart neck and sleeves, she looked beautiful. Faltering slightly, Katie noticed the front row of the seating area was empty. Nervously, she cast a glance towards Scarlet, who grinned broadly under her short veil and winked at Katie. Surprised, Katie looked again at the seats before grinning back at her sister.

On each empty seat, Scarlet had placed a framed picture of her missing family members. One for Tony Lambrianu, Francesca Lambrianu, Ralph Gold, Jake and, of course, Julie Gold. Each had their own seat.

'Did you really think I would get married without my family here?' Scarlet whispered.

'No, absolutely not.' Katie grinned and squeezed her arm tightly.

They had lost many loved ones along the way, but the Lambrianus were now stronger than ever. And their empire would live on.

Standing beside Knuckles as his best man, Adam handed over the wedding rings before returning to his seat next to Poppy. He searched for her hand and squeezed it. He felt content and alive with her by his side.

Once the ceremony was over and Scarlet and Knuckles walked out into the sunshine, Adam turned back and looked at the little chapel, as though seeing it for the first time. He had been there a million times, but never really looked at it, or felt the strange presence it represented in his life.

The many well-wishers who had gathered there shouted their congratulations and threw confetti towards Scarlet as she blushed girlishly beside her new husband as they made their way to the open venue at the vineyard that was lined with makeshift tables and bursting with music and laughter.

Taking hold of Poppy's hand, Adam kissed it. 'I do hope you would like to be married in that chapel, Poppy, if you know what I mean?' He blushed, getting carried away with the moment.

A grin crossed her face as she looked at him lovingly. 'I couldn't think of anywhere else I would like to be married. I love you, Adam; always have, always will,' she purred happily.

Scarlet stood up for her first dance, but Adam stopped Knuckles. 'Would you permit me as Don Lambrianu to open the ceremony with a first waltz with the bride?' he asked.

Beaming, Scarlet felt her jaw would break, she was smiling so much. For the wedding to be opened by the Don was an honour indeed, even if it was her brother. As they both started to waltz, the shouts from the locals grew louder. 'Are you happy, Scarlet?' Adam whispered in her ear.

'Absolutely. It's always been me and Knuckles; I don't know why I didn't see it sooner. He's my rock.'

'Well, I think I have a rock of my own, and she has agreed to follow Lambrianu tradition and marry me in our chapel. What do you think?' he asked tentatively.

Beaming with pride, Scarlet nodded. 'I had a good feeling about Poppy. She reminds me of Mum. I couldn't give you up to just any woman. It had to be the right one. And Poppy is exactly what I was hoping for. Congratulations.'

'All hail Don Lambrianu!' people in their hundreds shouted in unison and raised their glasses, cheering as Adam waltzed Scarlet around. Don Lorenzo, and the other Dons of the Mafia families, happily stood up and raised their glasses in a toast, too, silencing everyone for a moment out of respect.

'To Adam Lambrianu, now known all over the world as the Don, Godfather of Italy!'

As he danced with Scarlet, Adam suddenly felt cold, even though it was blazing sunshine. An image of his father smiling suddenly popped into his mind. It dawned on him as the crowds cheered that he was now the Don. His and Poppy's sons would reign after him. Feeling that he had his father's blessing in this new adventure, Adam was determined to do his family and the people around him proud. He felt content. Today was the start of a new era for the Lambrianu family. He was Adam Lambrianu, now known as the Don.

An uproar of clapping and cheering echoed throughout Italy, 'DON LAMBRIANU!' everyone shouted and raised their glasses. Happy that their country was in safe hands again.

* * *

MORE FROM GILLIAN GODDEN

The next explosive gangland thriller from Gillian Godden is available to order now here:
https://mybook.to/NewGoddenBackAd

ABOUT THE AUTHOR

Gillian Godden is a brilliantly reviewed writer of gangland fiction as well as a full-time NHS Key Worker in Hull. She lived in London for over thirty years, where she sets her thrillers, and during this time worked in various stripper pubs and venues which have inspired her stories.

Download your exclusive bonus content from Gillian Godden here:

Follow Gillian on social media:

 x.com/GGodden
 instagram.com/goddengillian
 facebook.com/gilliangoddenauthor

ALSO BY GILLIAN GODDEN

Boldwood

Boldwood Books is an award-winning fiction publishing company seeking out the best stories from around the world.

Find out more at www.boldwoodbooks.com

Join our reader community for brilliant books, competitions and offers!

Follow us
@BoldwoodBooks
@TheBoldBookClub

Sign up to our weekly deals newsletter

https://bit.ly/BoldwoodBNewsletter

www.ingramcontent.com/pod-product-compliance
Lightning Source LLC
Chambersburg PA
CBHW011642010726
47495CB00011B/2877